EYAL KLESS

THE LOST PUZZLER

THE TARAKAN CHRONICLES

HARPER
Voyager

Harper*Voyager*
An imprint of HarperCollins*Publishers* Ltd
1 London Bridge Street
London SE1 9GF

www.harpercollins.co.uk

First published by HarperCollins*Publishers* 2019
This paperback original edition 2019
1

Map by Eric Gunther / Springer Cartographic LLC

Eyal Kless asserts the moral right to
be identified as the author of this work

A catalogue record for this book is available from the British Library

ISBN: 978-0-00-827230-2

This novel is entirely a work of fiction.
The names, characters and incidents portrayed in it are
the work of the author's imagination. Any resemblance to
actual persons, living or dead, events or localities is
entirely coincidental.

Printed and bound in the UK by
CPI Group (UK) Ltd, Croydon CR0 4YY

MIX
Paper from
responsible sources
FSC™ C007454

This book is produced from independently certified FSC™ paper
to ensure responsible forest management.

For more information visit: www.harpercollins.co.uk/green

To my loving parents,
Anat and Yair

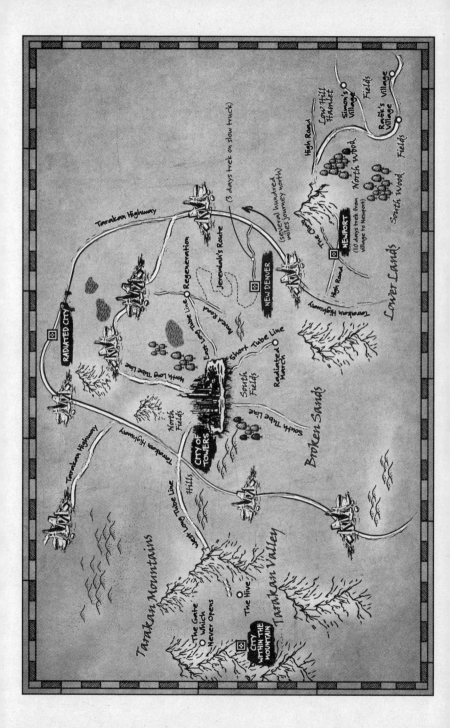

1

Officially, the City of Towers was not divided. Modernity and progress, law and order reigned supreme. That is, if you believed the Council's manifesto. Yet my cart driver didn't seem to believe the official line and stopped his horses at the gate leading to the lower spires that most of the city dwellers called the Pit.

The cart's driver bent down until his face was showing at the door's open window.

"That's as far as I go," he grumbled.

"But this is not—" I began to protest.

"It's as far as I go," he repeated, as if this was the only explanation needed before his face disappeared. He did not even bother to jump down and open the cart's door. That's city cart drivers for you . . .

I should have argued with him—I'd paid hard metal in advance for the ride down all the way to the Pit—but I decided not to bother. I told myself that I was too tired to waste time and energy on a few coins, but in my heart, I knew that after months of traveling, it was a blessed change to have found anyone willing to take me, even for the shortest of distances. Only a few days' travel from the city, most cart drivers took one look at my face and sped away. Some spat on the ground as they passed, while others, more often than I care to recall, aimed their spittle at me.

I climbed out of the filthy cart, holding the hem of my black coat in my free hand. The driver drove off without uttering a word, rightly assuming that no tip would be coming his way.

I carefully adjusted my cowl as I surveyed the enormous square of the city's Central Plateau, happy to be breathing fresh air. Almost everywhere else in the world, the darkness of night meant the halt of all outdoor activities. If you were a villager, you barricaded yourself and your family inside your walls, made sure your weapon of choice was within reach, and prayed to whatever god you believed in for the safety of daylight. Not in the City of Towers. Even at this late hour it was bustling with activity, from the shouts of sellers in food stalls to the miserable lowing and stench of livestock.

The Plateau was lit from above by several dozen, evenly spaced, gigantic Tarakan lamps, their collective effect closely matching daylight. Like all of the city's artifacts, the Tarakan lamps were secured by the ever-vigilant ShieldGuards. Though their faces were hidden behind black helmets, the movements of their heads indicated that they were scrutinizing the crowd. One of them spotted me, and I could almost feel his stare as he turned in my direction.

The area was too well lit, there were no shadowy corners to retreat to, so I chose a direction at random and began moving with the crowd. When I risked a glance back, the ShieldGuard was looking elsewhere. I eased my steps and circled around the area.

The cowl hid my tattoos from passersby, but it would not conceal my face completely. Eventually I would have to make eye contact, which would mean I might be remembered. I couldn't take that chance. Not tonight.

I considered my options: my original plan was to descend to

the Pit via Cart's Way, but the road, albeit scenic, was too long to travel on foot, and I was pressed for time.

My next option, perhaps the most obvious one, was to 'take the disc,' meaning to board one of the Tarakan lifts from the centre of the square. Despite the fact that no one knew exactly how they worked—and several unexplained, deadly accidents— the huge oblong discs remained a popular way of connecting the Central Plateau to the rest of the city. I guess they appealed to humans' unhealthy attraction towards danger, novelty, technology, and death. This kind of illogical behavior led me long ago to the conclusion that we are, essentially, a stupid race. Perhaps the Catastrophe was meant to clean the slate and start humanity over, but we managed to screw up even our own destruction.

One thing was sure; I possessed more than enough hard coin to pay for the lift. My LoreMaster was uncharacteristically generous with his purse when he sent me out on this venture—so generous, in fact, that I would be surprised if the Guild of Historians would be able to fund any other expedition in the foreseeable future. But I knew I should avoid taking the Tarakan lifts if I wanted to stay anonymous. Instinct told me there were too many eyes looking at me ever since I had come back to the city— and not without good reason. The woman I was looking for had amassed an impressive group of powerful enemies, but she still had a few friends in this city who could warn her. My lead was too solid to waste on amateurish behavior.

Look on the bright side, I told myself. *After almost two years of travelling, chasing shadows, and following leads, you ended up back home, in the City of Towers, exactly where you started.*

Sighing, I turned around and moved cautiously back through the mass of sweating humanity, away from the Plateau's central square and into the side streets of the middle spires. It was not long before I was enveloped by the night, which for some irrational reason made me feel momentarily safer.

2

I still remember when the streets of the entire Central Plateau were lit by Tarakan lamps. Now, only a few blocks away from the ever-lit square, the back streets were almost pitch-black, and the inhabitants were of a more sinister type. I passed several groups of people huddling on street corners, standing around heating stones and open bonfires. The people were idle, drinking and talking among themselves, but I knew they were just waiting, like beasts of prey, for someone like me to come along and be dinner.

Quite early in my mission, I reached the conclusion that weapons were of no use to me. I owe many of my victories, as well as several *near*-death experiences, to my quick thinking and fast talking. Yet for all my self-reliance, I became painfully aware that I was walking in a dangerous part of the city with a heavy purse that jingled with every step I took. Heads turned and calculating stares followed my pace. A few of the more enterprising young men began following me, jostling for position and waiting for an opportunity to pounce.

There are not many times when my glowing red eyes are a blessing, but this was one of those occasions. I turned my head so my followers could see the fiery pupils from the depths of my cowl. Had I possessed a scythe, I could have achieved a better effect, but my glare was enough, and the shadowy entourage dispersed quickly.

I WAS BORN AFTER THE HORRORS OF THE PURGES, WHEN TATtooed people like me were hunted and killed. The markings appeared on my face shortly after my thirteenth birthday. Although I was devastated, I was spared the suffering that most of my kind endured thanks to parents who were kind, loving, and—more important—wealthy. My father knew the man who is now my LoreMaster. Master Harim saw my potential, took me as an underling, and made a fine profit from my father's coin. Notwithstanding the morning I discovered the tattoos that had appeared on my eyelids, my life until this assignment had actually been quite secure and relatively trouble free. I can honestly say I was content with my post as a secondary scribe at the Guild of Historians and looking forward to copying data and deciphering old books and salvaged Tarakan pads for the rest of my days.

Then one day, my LoreMaster sent me on this little errand. I remembered the moment I stepped out of the tower and into the real world, still believing in humanity. *Well, that feeling's definitely out of my system now.* "Reading scripture can be satisfying," my LoreMaster would tell me often, "but there is no greater adventure than going out there and finding knowledge by yourself."

"Sounds dangerously close to Salvo-speak, LoreMaster," I half-teased him.

There was not much about the Salvationist's era, despite being recent, post-Catastrophe history, that my LoreMaster had not mentioned to me countless times. I could almost silently mouth the words of his next sentence.

"Very colourful cussing, I have to admit," he chuckled. "It's been a while since I rubbed shoulders with a Salvationist crew, but I suspect their speech is still as imaginative today. The Salvationists were right at least about one thing: there is no greater thrill, I tell you, than to salvage technology and dig information out from the ruins with your own hands."

"Or pry it from a dead man's hand," I added without thinking.

LoreMaster Harim frowned, took his pipe out of his mouth and pointed it at me. "You, my dear boy, have been reading far too many Salvo-novels, and don't even try to deny it. I know where you stash them."

I blushed. "Purely for research," I mumbled, "about social cohesion in times of struggle."

The old man muttered something almost inaudible, which nevertheless sounded like Salvo-speak to me, before declaring, "Well, son, you can pack your saucy novels away. I am sending you on a research mission. Something terribly important may have just happened, and I need you to investigate it. Fully. There is a woman, an ex-Salvationist. Her name is Vincha."

I felt my heartbeat accelerate as my LoreMaster mentioned the Salvationists.

"I need you to find this woman and find out what this Vincha knows. She is an elusive one, but I already have a few leads regarding her possible whereabouts." Master Harim leaned over and handed me a sealed scroll. His stare was nothing short of intense. "Spare no costs. Nothing we have ever done is more important than finding out what she knows."

The odd way he phrased it should have alerted me, but I was too surprised to be chosen for a mission by my LoreMaster to dwell on his carefully chosen words. Instead, I tried to persuade him that I was the wrong guy for the job.

"I just copy books, LoreMaster, I wouldn't know where to begin looking for this Vincha, or how to persuade an ex-salvationist to talk to me even if I found her."

"Nonsense." He shoved two fat leather coin bags towards me. "You are perfect for the job. I'm sure of it."

The first thing I did when I left the towers was to rent a room in the Green Meadow, a fancy tavern in the Central Plateau. The second thing I spent my coin on were two redheaded prostitutes. One fucked me senseless and the other stole all my coin, stabbed her coworker to death, and ran for it. It took me two weeks to track her down and three more days to get most of the coin back, but at least my LoreMaster was right about one thing: I never went back to reading those Salvo-novels again.

Many times during my search for Vincha, I had wondered about my LoreMaster's reasons for choosing me, of all people. One would logically want to send a military expert, perhaps a Salvationist veteran or at least someone with expertise in combat, someone who, unlike myself, did not instinctively recoil from violence. Was my nomination an act of desperation? Lack of another suitable candidate? A punishment for my idling ways? Or did he already see something I never knew I had in me—a lust for adventure and a knack for quick, creative thinking when my life was in danger? At the time, I did not know the answer, but I certainly learned much in the course of my two-year-long wanderings, most of which I would pay hard metal to be able to forget.

I found myself standing suspiciously still in a dark alley of the Middle Spires. Sighing softly, I forced the memories away and concentrated on my immediate problem: finding a way down to the Pit.

And then, if I managed to stay alive, locating Vincha.

3

Even with my special sight, it was easy enough to get lost in the twisting streets of the Middle Spires. I kept walking, navigating on a hunch, looking for the signs described by a contact so inebriated she could barely stand up. Just when I was about to give up, I spotted the first of the local gang graffiti I was told to look for. I followed the graffiti signs through a series of short, narrowing lanes that were half blocked by piles of human rubbish the Council had stopped bothering to collect. I walked under two archways, one so low I had to crawl underneath it to pass. Shortly after passing through the second archway, I found myself in a cul-de-sac with a closed courtyard.

There, a group of five men clustered around a crackling bonfire, next to a poorly built wooden cabin. Behind them stood a high wall built to block people from accidentally falling down the vast drop into the lower levels of the city. The wall had a human-sized hole in it. These were the smugglers I was looking for. Now I only had to find out how fast they would drop me.

Four of the men were large; two were visibly enhanced by Tarakan augmentations on their arms, torsos, and shoulders.

People called them Trolls. When augmented with the right Tarakan gear and by a skilled Gadgetier, a Troll was a formidable creature, a deadly warrior capable of inhuman feats. But by the look of their deformed bodies, these guys attached the cheap stuff, overused, unmaintained, or pieced together by an amateur Tinker.

The group turned to watch me approach, standing looselimbed and relaxed since, after all, they outnumbered me five to one. Even so, given I had flaming red dots for eyes, their expressions naturally demonstrated caution. I pulled back my cowl.

"I'm looking for a way down," I said.

"No problem." The shortest guy thrust his thumb at the hole behind him. "And since you probably have wings to go with those eyes, it'll only cost you a fiver."

His companions chuckled and exchanged a glance.

"Assuming I don't want to spread my wings tonight," I asked, "how much?"

He surveyed me again, taking his time, perhaps to see how I handled the pressure. "You carrying anything?"

"Just me," I replied, opening my cloak to show I was unarmed—which was a mistake, of course. The man—whom I judged to be the group's leader—smiled to himself.

"Eighty in coin or kind," he said.

It was absolute robbery and I knew it.

"Thirty," I countered without thinking, which was my second and nearly fatal mistake. My offer was too low. I was behaving like an amateur, and they sensed it.

One of the other men took a few casual steps to the side, preparing to flank me. "I wonder if you actually could fly," their leader said, flapping his arms for emphasis. "Perhaps the wings materialize when you're already in the air? Maybe we should test the theory. What do you think?"

I let my eyes see through them. Their skin faded to transparency, revealing bones and muscle and, more important, knives, knuckle-dusters, power daggers, and stun grenades.

They were already closing in on me, about to pounce, when I opened my own fist to let the one closest to me see the ShieldGuard-issue marked power clip nestled there. The man actually recoiled, and before the others could react further I fished the second one from my pocket and held it between thumb and forefinger, for all to see. The power clips were obviously Tarakan original, two perfect round balls emanating a blue hue that indicated they were fully charged. The clips were the sort that powered many of the artifacts in the city and beyond, even the SuperTrucks traveling on the Tarakan highways, and could only be found deep within the mysterious nodes of the City of Towers. Long ago, when Salvationist crews roamed Tarakan Valley, power clips like these were in abundance, but nowadays things are different.

The easy brutality faded from the leader's face, replaced by something between calculation and anxiety.

"All I want is to get down to the Pit quickly and quietly," I said, tossing the clips over to him. He grimaced even as he plucked them from the air. As valuable as they were, being in possession of such items these days was a capital offence.

He eyed me with considerably more respect than before, then nodded and pocketed the items. The clips marked me either as a dangerous and resourceful man or the lackey of such an individual—but either way, a worthy client.

The man nearest the cabin door opened it, darted inside, and returned holding a large, alarmingly rusty metal cage, a man-sized version of a singing bird's cage I once saw in a village's market fair. He held it with both hands, his face already red with exertion, and handed it to one of the wannabe Trolls, who picked it up with only one hand. As his shoulder brace whined in protest, the Troll tilted the cage sideways, grinning proudly at the show of strength, while his equally large colleague attached a rusty hook to the top and a very long, much-too-thin metal cable. The cage was then slammed down in front of me with a loud bang and more than a few dust clouds.

"Ever done this before?" the leader asked, and chuckled nastily when I shook my head. "Just crawl in—the hatch is quite small, but without your wings you'll fit in nicely, and hold tight." He indicated the wooden handlebars inside. "It's not a long ride, but it's bumpy."

"Who's waiting at the bottom?" I asked as I entered the cage.

"Three to six guys, tops." He hesitated only briefly before deciding to share a tip. "I'd go with the bearded one. He's an old-timer, a little wired but a tough Troll, and his metal's still sharp."

I nodded and grasped the unpleasantly slimy handlebars, but any thought of letting them go vanished as the cage was picked up and I was shoved unceremoniously through the hole in the wall, feet first.

"Nice doing business with ya," I heard the leader call as I plunged into darkness.

4

It was a short but nasty free fall before the cage suddenly stopped, probably just a practical joke, but enough to make me heave the contents of my stomach. On the bright side, throwing up stopped me from crying out loud at the agonising pain the abrupt stop caused my shoulders. After what must have been a short pause—swinging in a cage high above ground tends to distort any sense of time—descent resumed at a fast but bearable pace. I still held the handles tight, as if this could somehow save me if I was suddenly dropped to my death. I decided it was better to look around instead of down. It was easy to spot two of the Tarakan lifts to my far left. They were floating majestically in full artificial light, each carrying dozens of people, propelled by mysterious Tarakan technology. I, on the other hand, was swinging in the darkness inside a rusty cage, my life hanging, literally, in the hands of an oversized and most likely overdosed Troll.

Another notable difference was that the people on the discs were sheltered by an invisible barrier from the smoke and the heat that rose from below, while I was coughing up what was left of my guts and feeling as if I were being lowered into an oven. I turned my head away from the ascending smoke and looked up. From where I was looking, the tops of the towers above me seemed as unreachable as the stars.

The low, rumbling noise, a constant feature of the Pit, signalled my descent was coming to an end.

The cage landed on the ground with a bone-crushing thud. I still managed to retain my grip on the handlebars despite my body's painful protests. Thankfully, the cage remained upright. Fearing that the cage would ascend before I managed to clear it, I forwent dignity and let my backside lead my body out of the cage.

Even with my back to the yard I could sense there were people watching me with professional interest. From the edge of my vision I saw a slender figure, perhaps a woman, stepping to a large bonfire, the only source of light in the area. As soon as I was out of the cage she picked up a burning log and waved it several times in the air. The cage jolted and disappeared into the darkness above.

I took a step and barely managed to stay upright. It was not just the rocking motion of the cage that had made me unstable; the ground was shaking. This was yet another phenomenon peculiar to the Pit. It was called the Downtown Swing or the Newcomers Half-Step—a slight rattle that was enough to make some visitors walk unsteadily or even seasick, and mark them as easy prey for the locals. It was just one of the many reasons why visitor protection was such a big business in the Pit. Walking without it meant you were either competent or a fool, and locals knew exactly how to differentiate.

The Pit was always a wild place. Years ago the ShieldGuards had full control of most of it, but things have changed. Nowadays it was the part of the city where you had to fend for yourself, or pay for someone to protect your back. Whether coming through Cart's Way or dismounting from one of the discs, buying visitor's protection was as close to an orderly affair as you could get in the Pit. Mixed groups of men and women were spread around the perimeter like a welcoming committee. Officially they called themselves Guides, but everyone referred to them as the Companies. All were armed to the teeth, of course, and consisted of ex-Salvationists, now unemployed augmented Trolls who needed to pay for their Skint addiction, a drug that was becoming dangerously sparse in the city. The different company groups had names such as Metal Fists or the Bloody Blades, wore colourful matching uniforms, and stood next to signs indicating prices, which were, unsurprisingly, pretty much the same. You could, of course, walk away without hiring anyone, but your chances of keeping your belongings, or your life, were nothing one would wager on.

I, however, was not walking off a disc or climbing out of a cart, I had just climbed, arse first, out of a rusty metal cage. If the Companies were generally made up of thugs who would rob you if they weren't paid to protect you, the people who surrounded me were the kind Companies thought of as too unstable to employ. There was no etiquette here, so when I heard heavy footsteps behind me, accompanied by the unmistakable metallic whine of unoiled hinges, I had a pretty good idea what I was about to face. Still, the mountain of flesh and rust I confronted when I turned around left me speechless and gaping.

When Tarakan artifacts were found and reintroduced to society, there were plenty of men and more than a few women who were tempted by the idea of inhuman strength, stamina, and speed, and thus Trolls came to be. It was only natural that some people would take their lust for physical superiority to an obscene level, collecting and attaching augmentations to their bodies with no sense of what they were doing to their appearance or their mental stability.

The Troll facing me had only one healthy eye; the other was a messy, stitched-up job, most likely the remains of a botched attempt at attaching an aiming mechanism. His right arm and shoulder were completely covered in metal, as well as both legs from the knees up. Where the right arm should have been was an enormous power cannon, braced to his rib cage with metal rods and poorly attached wires that ran up the right side of his head. That was the prettiest part, the rest was too much to take in.

I didn't need my enhanced sight to notice the distinct green markings around his nose, a clear sign that the monster was a hard Skint user. Skint considerably dulled the pain when the body tried to repel the attached augs, but too much of it made Trolls even more unstable and susceptible to violent episodes.

This Troll—I couldn't decide whether to call it a "him" or an "it"—prodded me with his free left hand and said, "You need protection." There was no question in his tone whatsoever. He had a squeaky, unnaturally high voice, which would have been absolutely hilarious if I were telling this story over scented wine to a bunch of drunken friends in a tavern up in the Upper Spires, but it was just scary and odd from where I was standing.

I glanced nervously to my right; the slender figure kept her distance.

"Hey, don't be looking over there," barked the mountain of metal. He prodded me again. "I'm your Troll. Look at this cannon, eh?" He waved the massive cannon in front of my face as if it were a children's toy instead of a weapon that normally needed the strength of three men just to be picked up. "This baby can blast through stone walls, eh? Clean a whole street in two shots. Mister, you want me"—he pointed the cannon at himself—"protecting you"—and aimed it at my face. There was a very distinct suggestion of threat in the Troll's voice, but the high pitch made it dangerously unconvincing.

I peeked to my left and spotted a man who was watching us from a short distance with what I instinctively felt was quiet disdain. He had a white beard, cropped short in a fashion long out of style. It was probably the individual whom the gang leader so helpfully recommended just before throwing me off the ledge. I caught his eye. He nodded once and began walking slowly towards us. This time the prodding from the huge Troll was strong enough to make me take a step back.

"Hey, don't be looking over there. I'm the escort you want, man, twenty in coin or kind. We have a deal?"

The man approaching us was a Troll as well, but the old-fashioned kind, not an oversized, crazed junkyard who pumped himself up with Tarakan toys. He looked like the Trolls who used to do Salvation runs, back when that wasn't just a suicide mission. He certainly showed more flesh than his bigger version, and there was no trace of Skint on his face. Metal gauntlets covered his arms from the elbows down, the back of each hand marked by three dart ducts. Short tubes were protruding from the side of his neck, in the classic fashion of a Salvationist crew tactical Lieutenant, but no wirings were attached to them. The rest of his body was covered in flex armour so worn that it was grey rather than black. From the way he walked I guessed he was also wearing a torso brace and a spine protector.

"Hey, look at me, fleshy. Twenty, yes?" insisted the giant, but the man was now close enough to intervene. He eyed my face just for a heartbeat, taking in my facial tattoos, and nodded at me.

"I believe I can counteroffer this . . . man." His tone of voice was mild, but the word *man* was overpronounced and probably meant as an insult.

The metal monster sure seemed to take it that way. "Lift up, sucker," he warned, but the man ignored him and fixed me with a calm stare.

"Where are you heading?" he asked.

"Atrass District, but perhaps other places as well," I answered, trying to ignore the cannon swinging angrily above my head.

"I said take a lift, Galinak," the large Troll squeaked again.

"Twenty-five in coin, no kind," the man said, not taking his eyes off me.

The bigger Troll grinned in triumph. "Don't listen to the old man—his metal is rusty. I tell you what." He leaned close enough for me to smell the stench emanating from his metal-tipped teeth. "I'll sweeten the deal. Fifteen in coin or kind, special price for you, deal?"

I looked back at Galinak, who shrugged and said, "Thirty in coin, no kind."

That didn't make sense. He was supposed to be haggling the price down, not up. Even the big Troll managed to work out the rudimentary economics and laughed out loud.

"See? The flesh brain is at the top tower. What you want? Flesh hookers? Dope? I know everyone here. I'll take you around the block for some good time, no problems. Now give me fifteen." The last phrase was said with desperate urgency.

Galinak raised an eyebrow and said, "I am about to raise the price to thirty-five."

"Thirty," I said quickly, knowing I was paying Company price for an old, burned-out Salvationist with no visible weaponry while making a very unstable giant of a Troll who was holding—I read the letters as he repeatedly swung the cannon by my face—a "GY blaster 2015-d special edition" extremely angry.

"Agreed," Galinak said, and we shook hands.

It took the giant a few heartbeats to realise what had happened, and when he finally did I was sure he was going to shoot us both. The colourful obscenities that came out of his mouth were impressive, but he turned out to be all bluster and no blaster. Galinak shot the Troll a threatening glare, and we walked away without incident.

A few streets away Galinak stopped me with a touch to my shoulder. "Where exactly you need to go to in Atrass?" he asked.

"Margat's Den," I said.

He grimaced. "Look, if you want hookers, I know some real nice, clean ladies with interesting augmentations that could touch you in places you never thought . . ."

"I don't want hookers," I said hastily. For some reason I was anxious to convince the old Troll I was not another sleazy merchant looking for a cheap lay.

He nodded and tried a different tack.

"If you need suppliers, or have anything to sell, I know one guy with even scales. He'll give you a fair trade, and yes, before you ask, I get a cut."

I shook my head again. "I need to meet someone."

"At Margat's?"

"Is there a problem? Because I just hired you for Company price."

"Not for Margat's Den you didn't," he answered drily. "You're looking at fifty starting price and two escorts plus extra if something exciting happens. And something exciting always happens."

I swallowed. "So, you're out?" I asked. "Should I have hired the big boy with the big gun?"

"No, I'm in," he responded a bit too quickly. Clearly, he needed the coin. "But on two conditions." He waited for my full attention before continuing. "I get fully paid two streets before the Den—" he saw my expression and raised a metal-wrapped, claw-shaped hand to stop any protest "—no negotiations. That place is dangerous and I'm only going in there with hard coin in my pocket."

I had no choice.

"Fine," I capitulated. "And what's your second condition?"

"I'm hired to protect you. I watch your back and peel off trouble, but I am not finishing off a fight you start." His tone suggested previous experience. "If you're one of those mad tower-heads, wanting to bleed your knuckles in the Den just so you can boast about it to your friends, you'd better learn to fight for yourself."

"I assure you I have no intention of initiating a fight," I promised. "Just take me to the place as quickly as possible."

He didn't look convinced, but he nodded and we resumed walking, me at the front, him at my side but slightly behind me, covering my back while ordering me to turn left or right. Before I knew it, I was completely lost. I could hear the noise of the ever busy main street ahead of us, but Galinak directed me to walk down small, half-deserted streets, where there were no shops or taverns, just a never-ending series of hovels containing the poorest and weakest. The only source of light was the occasional reflection of the lamps high above us in the Central Plateau as the Tarakan lifts crisscrossed the skyline, creating a disorienting display of light and darkness. The stench was close to unbearable. I began to suspect he was leading me somewhere quiet to rob me, but just as I was about to get really nervous we emerged into Downtown Alley, the Pit's most notorious street.

Hundreds, perhaps thousands, of people were walking up and down the narrow street, moving between street vendors and food stalls, passing scantily clad prostitutes, drinking houses, and gambling dens. "Walk casually and avoid eye contact," instructed Galinak from behind me, "especially the women."

I nodded, feeling Galinak tense and move closer to me. With every step we took, all around us, a dozen things were happening at once. Throwing my instinctive caution to the wind I enhanced my vision, and every movement, every gesture, became achingly sharp. A nude hooker haggled over a price with two customers. Three heavy Trolls accepted a sweet-smelling pipe from a young boy, their own hands too clumsy and weapon-loaded to fill the pipe themselves. A robed soothsayer argued over turf with a mental-witch. A smiling, half-naked fat man gestured for visitors to enter his gambling den. A juggler threw apples in the air, cutting them with a machete and catching them as they fell. There was a part of me that wanted to stop and take it all in. Bukra's balls, when was the last time I touched a woman? I was a newcomer, a first-timer, and what was wrong with slowing down and sampling a little of Downtown's famous pleasures?

Whether he was aware of my inner turmoil or just wanted to get on with the job, Galinak pushed me forward relentlessly, and soon we turned away to a side street and were enveloped again in relative darkness. I used my sight without fear of reprisal. In Downtown Alley you were a freak if you didn't have tattoos or augs. If Galinak had or was using enhancements I couldn't tell, but he kept pace even in near darkness.

"Can I ask you a question?" I asked, suddenly curious and trying not to think of the red-haired hookers that we passed.

"Ask, but I might not answer."

"How old are you?" I felt foolish the moment I said the words.

"Old," he chuckled.

"So were you—" I hesitated, but decided to complete the question "—a Salvationist?"

"What are you, one of those religious quacks?" His voice rose in annoyance. "Going to lecture me how I brought this on us, eh?"

"No, not at all, I'm just curious." I turned my head but could only see his shoulder.

"Well, you're not paying me to satisfy your curiosity, so keep walking."

"It just seems to me that you are a bit—" I hesitated again, feeling I might be pushing my luck too far, but to my surprise he laughed again, softly, as if to himself.

"—too old for this rust?"

"I was going to say 'too professional for an escort job,' but 'old' will do."

He was still behind me, but I had a feeling he shrugged to himself.

"I am old," he admitted, "too old, but with all my age and wisdom, I never learned to play my cards right and when to call it quits. So I need to pay my debts."

"But you were a Salvationist," I said. "Those must have been glorious days—"

"Pha," he cut me off dismissively, and stopped. "If any Salvationist tells you the old days were one long, glorious adventure, know that he's on a Skint trip or serving you liquid metal for a drink."

I turned back to face him, "But the stories? The books—"

"Guild-dictated crap. They were running out of troops so

fast they were shipping fresh recruits every day in crews of five to eight, sometimes thirty crews a week. We used to call them 'spare parts,' if you know what I mean."

He looked straight at me, but his eyes were seeing something else entirely. "Most of them survived till the fifth or sixth outing, then they would get cocky. 'This isn't too hard,' they would say to each other at the bar, 'just popping lizards and collecting heads for rewards.' With the metal they earned from Lizard popping they would upgrade their weapons and Tarakan augs or use the coin on purer Skint and other drugs, which would make them even more arrogant. Then they would chase a Lizard down the wrong rusting shaft or get too close to the City within the Mountain, and suddenly they would be surrounded by a hundred of those fucking buggers. A solid crew can probably walk away from that with only two or three casualties. But a new crew that barely knows each other and carries weapons and augs they haven't learned to use properly? One would bolt and try to run away, he's a goner; one or two would try to save the runner, they're goners, too. The rest would be overwhelmed so fast you wouldn't have time to pinpoint their screams."

I felt an involuntary shudder running up my spine as the veteran Salvationist added, "And that was just Lizard popping, easy clean-up stuff to make way for the experienced crews who went into the actual City within the Mountain. When you entered that place, there was no telling how you might die. Those traps reset themselves or somehow appeared in places where they previously weren't, and if you stumbled upon a nest, well, even if you survived the encounter you never wanted to go back there again. Oh, and I must apologize." There was the sudden sound of a power buildup.

"For wha—" I began to say, but then he hit me hard in the chest with open palms. It felt as if I'd been slammed by a power hammer. As I flew backwards I was blinded by a flash of searing light that passed through the space I'd occupied only a heartbeat beforehand, followed by a deafening explosion to my right. I was grasping at empty air in panic, knowing I was about to hit the ground and hurt myself. Galinak somehow managed to jump back while pushing me out of the way of the energy blast. His right hand was raised, already aiming at whoever shot at us from the dark street on our left. Something thin and silvery shot from his gauntlet.

I hit the ground hard as pieces of stone, burning wood, and hot, bent, metal debris rained down on me. My only piece of luck, under these circumstances, was the fact that most of the ground in the Pit was soft muck, so I wasn't knocked out. For a while all I could do was shield my head and roll from side to side, praying I wouldn't get squashed by a large slab of stone. I was already on my knees when a strong arm gripped me, and I was hauled to my feet. When I could take in my surroundings I saw a gaping hole to my right where a makeshift house used to be. The edges of the hole were still smoking, and a small fire burned in the exposed room. I could hear shouts but couldn't discern which direction they were coming from.

Galinak looked at me calmly and simply said, "You are unharmed."

I could only nod as I checked my head with my hands, they came back filled with muck but no blood.

"Can I let go of you?" he asked.

I nodded again, though it took a lot of willpower and pride not to collapse once Galinak released his grip.

"I'm fine," I brushed away the dirt from my shoulders and lower back, thankfully I was wearing black, "but what in Bukra's balls was that?"

Galinak strolled to the left. I followed him and saw the large and still-twitching body of the huge Troll who had aggressively invited me to employ him.

"I heard him a while ago," he said, kneeling down to check the Troll's pupils. "He was making so much noise trying to shadow us, I'm surprised you didn't hear him."

"Is he dead?"

"No. I used a shock dart, and an expensive one at that." He plucked the dart from the Troll's shoulder and looked at me as if this was entirely my fault.

"Now what? Are you going to kill him?"

Galinak shook his head. "You're quite bloodthirsty, even for a newcomer."

"Well . . . he did try to kill us."

"No. He tried to kill *me*. You he just wanted to rob and maybe throw around a bit for good sport. But his brain is so full of rusting metal he used his cannon, which would have fried us both with nothing for him to pick up afterwards, unless he was planning some odd kind of a barbecue."

"And you saw him coming?" I was hoping Galinak didn't spot the shudder which coursed through my body, but I suspected he did.

"Of course I saw him coming," he said calmly.

"And you let him pull the trigger?" I was suddenly very angry. "Is this a kind of a game for you?"

"No," he said patiently. "I simply knew exactly when to move. Once he powers up the cannon there's a brief delay during which the weapon locks up and is immovable. If you know what you're doing, you just need to move away when you hear the sound. It's very distinct."

He gestured toward the cannon. "I remember finding a stack of these little honeys on our fourth deep run into the City within the Mountain. We were a happy bunch coming back. Originally, I think they were meant to be some kind of mining equipment, self-mounting and probably automated, without the need to use a Gnome or a cheap body-fixer like this." He gestured at the bracers holding the GY blaster 2015-d special edition. "But some Trolls fell in love with the idea of having one of these babies as a personal weapon, and who wouldn't, I ask you? We sold them like fresh bread and made a fortune, then we celebrated in style."

He shook his head. "If there was a time I could have walked

away from it all and lived a quiet life, that was the time. I had the coin to do it, but those were good times. We had a strong crew, good people, we were even hoping to get enough between us to buy a Puzzler, you know, go solo—" He stopped abruptly and shook his head slowly, as if pulling himself away from the memories. "No need to stay here," he said, and even I spotted the approaching silhouettes.

"What about him?" I pointed down.

"He'll come around soon enough, and anyone trying to detach his augs will find that the knockout effect wears off really fast, so let's move."

He began walking away and I trailed after him, still shaking. "Won't he come after us when he wakes up?"

"I doubt he'll remember a thing. Anyway, he's tried to kill me before."

"Really? How many times?"

Galinak's expression indicated mental calculation. "I think six, perhaps seven if you count trying to kill me during a Skint rage, although it wasn't personal that time."

"And you don't mind?"

He shrugged and tweaked his short white beard. "Not really. Every man needs a hobby."

5

For many years, Margat's Den was nothing more than a lo-cale for the toughest inhabitants of the Pit, who only wanted a quiet, nonwatered drink after a long hard day. It was one of those places where you were polite to the people around you and avoided eye contact. You drank inside and brawled outside, like civilised men.

It all changed a decade ago, when a tower-head walked in on a dare and started a fight. Miraculously, the boy lived to tell the tale, with only a few broken bones and several missing teeth. This minor incident inspired other brash youth living in the up-per regions, and very soon it became a rite of passage for the privileged and foolhardy. They descended on the establishment in droves, looking for fights. The owner of the Den, in a mo-ment of epiphany, saw the potential for profit; the tower-heads brought plenty of the Council's steel coin with them and spent to impress. The Den was now the largest, most profitable *legal* establishment in the Pit. There were fighting tournaments and duels, along with good, old-fashioned bar brawls, some planned, some authentically spontaneous. Margat's Den was not the sort of place you went into for a quiet drink anymore, although if you kept to yourself and had good protection, you could probably get in and out without a major confrontation. Basically, you had to pay your coin and take your chances, which was what I was going to do.

The clearing in front of the Den was lit by more than a dozen sources of flame, and there were people lying about, most of them nursing wounds. A few bodies I was only guessing were unconscious were sprawled on the ground, prize possessions taken either by the victors of whatever confrontations they'd had or by one of the many local opportunists prowling the area.

Four guards stood at the main entrance to the place, armed to the hilt with every weapon known to Trolls and looking alert and ready. I made a point of not looking around with too much interest, but sensed a few more guards lurking in the shadows.

Considering its reputation, it was surprisingly calm outside; the Den's proprietor wanted to keep any fighting *inside* his establishment. Still, I felt my stomach clench with fear as we approached.

A young man, who looked no more than sixteen years of age, was being searched as his escorts stood waiting. The kid had two fighters, a massive Troll and a street rat, a sure sign that looking for trouble in the Den with minimal protection was still a trend. He was clad in full body armour, which was inscribed with Salvationist crew symbols. I recognised the markings of at least four rival crews on his back alone. Heaven knew where he got it from, but when he closed his visor he looked like a colourful drawing of a medieval knight. As we waited our turn, three concealed weapons were confiscated from him. Blasters and guns of any kind were forbidden, along with all Tarakan weapons. Official escorts were exempt, as a sign of respect, but even they were warned not to use a forbidden arsenal on pain of . . . well . . . severe pain.

When it was my turn I stepped in front of the goggle-eyed Troll guard, who stared for a moment at my tattoos, then nodded in camaraderie. Nevertheless, he took his sweet time searching me thoroughly with his enhanced vision. Watching him work, I admit I felt a hint of envy. The goggles were ugly, and whoever stitched them on was no artist, but the device enhanced the gift we both shared tenfold. I could see in the dark and, when pressed or panicked, through thin materials such as skin or cloth; but he could know what I ate for dinner from three streets away.

As I was searched, a second guard asked whether I was aware of the rules of the place and made sure I knew the penalty for killing someone the wrong way inside the Den. The goggled guard didn't find any weapons on me, which was so unusual, it made everyone a bit tense, but after a few more questions I was let through. When it was Galinak's turn to be inspected, we ran into a problem that I hadn't anticipated.

The Troll took one goggled look at my escort, nodded slightly, and extended an open cloth bag.

"Your blaster and throwing knives," he commanded drily, "and I'll need the power tubes for the gloves as well."

Galinak stood very still. "I'm an escort," he said and pointed at me.

"Not officially you're not," answered the Troll. "You're not affiliated with the syndicate anymore, and I know none of the other escort Companies will work with you after what happened the last time." The Troll pointed at Galinak's weapons and to the bag in his other hand. "You're a visitor here. Visitor rules and visitor prices." He sounded like he was enjoying himself. "That will be ten coins for entry, normal price at the bar."

Galinak didn't move. He blinked slowly, twice, then raised his right hand to his left gauntlet, a gesture which created a flurry of movement all around us. People dove for cover and guards raised their weapons. The clicks and whines of power-ups and the swooshing of weapons being unsheathed in haste created an odd cacophony of sound.

Galinak's hand twisted, and a glowing power tube slid out of a hidden socket into the palm of his hand. He did the same with the second gauntlet, and then took his time producing his personal weapons, which I noticed were small compared to the general style around us. The second Troll, who'd jumped back rather unprofessionally when Galinak raised his gauntlet, smiled in triumph as I paid the extra levy for my escort.

"My stuff better be here when I get back," Galinak said, and walked away.

"Enjoy your stay in the Den, old flesh!" the Troll spat at our backs as the double doors opened and we walked into the chaos.

"Rust," I swore quietly as the double doors closed behind us. If Vincha was really at the Den she most likely wouldn't be cooperative. And my only protection was a retired Salvationist with no weapons and, apparently, plenty of enemies. This was gearing up to be an interesting night, and not in a good way.

6

I'd never visited the Den before, but I'd made sure I had all the information I could gather about the place. I knew what to expect, had a good knowledge of the layout. I even knew the colours of the tapestries, but I was still awestruck when we walked past the second set of metal doors and into a green haze. My first instinct was to gag at the mix of body odour, Skint smoke, and deep-fried food, but I managed to suppress it. Even with my enhanced sight I could not see the back wall, which I knew for a fact was exactly seventy-five steps away. My mentor was right: no matter how many scrolls I'd read or stories I'd heard about this place, seeing the broken Tarakan artifacts hanging from the ceiling, some still attached to a skeleton arm, leg, or torso, was a different experience altogether.

Keg drums played a heart-racing beat, increasing the general noise level to the point you had to shout to be heard. The place could hold a few hundred people, and I estimated that it was close to full. Galinak guided me away from the doors, and as we carefully shoved our way through the crowd, a few patrons were openly sussing us out with challenging stares. Several armed

Company escorts nodded their acknowledgment to Galinak before turning their attention back to their tasks. Looking up I spotted makeshift guard towers with guards standing watch. It was easy to recognise the long nozzles of their sniper blasters. They were surveying the crowd expertly, and from what I had heard, they needed little motivation to act.

Galinak whispered something in my ear just as a large gong announced a challenge in the Arena.

"What?" I shouted back as the crowd surged to my right to participate in the action.

"Do you know where you want to go?" he yelled again.

I nodded and pointed to the far left. *Gambling den*, I mouthed. He nodded, relief plain in his face, and pushed me in the direction of the stairs.

We avoided getting too close to the centre bar, where an unfortunate was being kicked in the face by three men as his escort tried to pull him away. Several mug-girls passed us carrying trays of drinks. They were wearing metal armour studded with spikes and blades. If you wanted to grab one of them, you risked a deep cut or worse. The mug-girl who passed closest to me had two bleeding digits stuck on her torso and bosom. I gave her a wide berth.

We passed the steps leading down to the pleasure den. Several scantily clad women and a few men were hanging around there. These women's augmented hands brushed against me as I walked by, sending waves of pleasure through my body and making me momentarily forget the purpose of my visit. It was Galinak who propelled me forward. The prostitutes didn't bother to touch an escort with their vibrating hands.

Thanks, I mouthed.

He shrugged, then froze in place and looked past me, grimacing. I turned, followed the direction of his gaze, and saw a large Troll advancing toward us. He had four or five other men with him.

"Rust," I heard Galinak swear as he shoved me aside. "I really don't need this now." For once, I wholeheartedly agreed with him.

The Troll planted himself in front of us with such obvious aplomb that people must have immediately realised a confrontation was coming. We soon gathered a crowd. He was a brawler, a big one, built for close combat, and he looked much younger than Galinak. Several blunt instruments were hanging on the belt of his dent-free, dark steel power armour. It was a beautiful and obviously expensive piece of metal art, even the wires were protected by thin rubber tubes and attached to the armour in a way so it would not interfere during a fight. The spiked arm bracers looked razor sharp, and the metal gloves could most likely punch through walls.

"Galinak, you rust bucket," he said and clenched his steel hands into steel fists, "this must be my lucky day."

"Hello, fuse-brain," Galinak answered calmly, "did you lose your escort again, or did the Company finally realise you couldn't keep a disease on a whore, you incompetent lump of rust?"

Nasty laughter rippled all around us. Even the Troll's entourage sniggered at the insult.

"It's my day off, tower-head," the Troll barked, his face turning red, "so I'm free to wipe your metal all around the floor."

I eased sideways, but the people around us formed a tight circle and wouldn't let me through.

"How's your brother, by the way?" asked Galinak, though I could see his hands twitching, painfully aware of his lack of weaponry. "Is he *seeing* anyone?"

Someone at the back of the crowd burst out laughing, but only when the angry Troll answered did I understand why.

"You took his eye out, you piece of rotting flesh," the Troll roared, his eyes glancing briefly over Galinak's shoulder, a sure sign we were being outflanked.

"He was looking at my cards," Galinak explained patiently.

A mug-girl walked into the circle. Perhaps she was new or too preoccupied trying to avoid the drunk and the stupid to notice the confrontation. Galinak grabbed a mug from her and took a long sip from it. The girl opened her mouth to say something, but then her survival instinct kicked in and she hurried away without a word.

"Enjoy your last drink, Galinak," the Troll said.

Galinak shrugged and sipped again.

The Troll flexed his shoulders. "Where do you want it? Arena? Outside?"

Galinak shook his head. "I'm on an escort job. After I finish here, we can dance a bit, but I'll only stop if you ask nicely."

The Troll shook his metal-plated head and powered his gauntlets by banging his fists together; bright sparks erupted from both metal hands. "You're not an escort here, you're visiting, that's all. They even took your puny dart shooter at the door," he chuckled, brandishing his fists. "We can do it in the Arena, or I can tear you apart right here, or . . ." He turned his head towards me, obviously thinking of a better idea. "I can start with this fleshling here so you won't have to worry about your precious *escort*."

My mouth dried up. Losing an escort was bad for anyone's reputation, and the Troll had just decided this was the humiliation Galinak needed. I sensed a shift in the mood around me. People were jostling to get a better view. This was not an Arena challenge or a brawl staged for the benefit of the tower-heads. This was the real thing, and all around us people began betting real coin. The guards above also took notice, but were letting it play out, most likely assuming the fight would be finished quickly. I knew there was no talking my way out of this one. Galinak, old and empty-handed, was about to fight a fully armed, angry brawler Troll and his buddies. And then it would be my turn.

"So, is this a power chest piece?" asked Galinak casually, sipping his drink.

The question caught everyone off guard, including the Troll.

"Not that it's anything to you, flesh," he snarled, "but it is a triple-powered chest piece, with side protection, not that I'm going to waste power on the likes of you."

"Looks like a scrap job to me. I think someone sold you lead pipes and toughened clay."

The Troll stood taller with indignation.

"This is a genuine Tarakan item, rust-brain, bought it at the auction. I even have the certification from the guild of Gadgetiers. Your old hands will shatter on it, not that you're going to have the chance to throw a punch."

Galinak didn't look impressed. He swallowed and tilted his head as if to reexamine the armour.

"I think," he gestured with the mug, "that you bought yourself some scrap metal held together with lead strings, and the only thing funnier than knocking you out will be seeing your ugly face as I shove your worthless armour up your arse."

"We'll see about that," roared the Troll, his hand punching the button on his belt, which was exactly the time Galinak flung the contents of his mug into the Troll's unprotected face. The Troll staggered back, momentarily blind, his armour powering up but leaving a heartbeat of a gap. Galinak used that time to deliver a spectacular one-two to the Troll's exposed chin. The Troll stumbled backwards, his eyes rolling back in their sockets. A tooth actually flew out from his broken jaw in an arc of spittle and blood as he hit the ground. Galinak swooped forward, then abruptly reversed direction, bringing his elbow into the abdomen of a hammer-swinging, eye-patch-wearing Troll, who burst through the crowd behind us. The Troll staggered but remained standing, his armour taking the brunt of the blow. He swung his hammer again, knocking out an unsuspecting patron behind him, but Galinak was too close to him for the weapon to gain momentum. As the hammer brushed his shoulder, Galinak punched the Troll's healthy eye. He screamed and collapsed onto the floor, where he received a boot to the head.

It should have been over right then. But it was just the

beginning. Galinak picked up the hammer and turned quickly, surveying the people around us. The Troll's entourage, either out of duty or outrage, pushed their way forward.

Galinak stepped between them and me. "You'd better go now," he said. "This isn't your fight and I can't protect you."

"You should have told me people didn't like you down here." I tried to spot a safe place to hide but saw only a wall of flesh and metal.

"No one likes me anywhere," he muttered, more to himself than to me. "Go on, I'll catch up with you later."

Three men were closing in on us as I said, "What if you don't?"

Galinak shoved me forcefully sideways into the mass of people. "Then I'll give you a discount," he said, before turning and charging the advancing Trolls with a bloodcurdling roar.

7

I reached the stairs on my hands and knees, dirty but pretty much intact. Someone kicked me in the ribs and someone else stepped on my leg, but both actions were unintentional and left no permanent damage.

The fight behind me was developing into an all-you-can-hit kind of bar brawl. Two enthusiastic tower-heads, impressed by Galinak's combat abilities, joined the fray to even the odds and, as etiquette dictates in these circumstances, the violence quickly spilled in all directions. Soon, everyone in my immediate vicinity was swinging fists, weapons, or furniture at one another.

There were stains on the stairs in a colour I was hoping was just blood. I got up and brushed myself off the best I could as people hurried past me towards the centre of the fight. It was time for me to descend.

As the stairs spiralled down I could still hear the sounds of fighting, but the walls were thick and the Den was deep. What were once perhaps burial chambers were now the Pit's most notorious gambling hall. It was a surprisingly large underground room, divided by low walls and supporting beams into several open spaces, most of it taken up by playing tables featuring cards and dice games. Tapestries depicting beautiful scenes covered the outer walls, and the abundance of fireplaces, large oil lamps, and small fire urns, gave a definite feeling of calmness. The air was musty but breathable, thanks to the still-working Tarakan ventilation system. The guards were perhaps not as big as the Trolls upstairs but no less lethal. They must have realised a fight had erupted upstairs, but none of them moved from their posts. Instead, they eyed me with professional suspicion.

I bought a drink from a passing mug-girl and pretended to sip from it as if I were waiting for an opening at a table. I surveyed the crowd with my low-light vision, trying desperately to calm down.

I was sweaty, dirty, possibly suffering from a cracked rib cage, and carrying much less coin on me than I should have come in with, which was a problem since I had to play until I could spot her. After months of searching, I had a pretty good description of the woman I was looking for, yet as I stood with my back to the wall in the underground room I began doubting myself. While my eyes searched the room, my mind slipped back to the numerous informants and other lowlifes I had the displeasure of questioning. Some I had to bribe, others I had to threaten, and in a few instances, with hired muscle, I also had to hurt. More than half of them lied, and some lied well enough to send me chasing shadows. But she was here now, I was sure of it.

For the third time I moved to another position in the room, but I was already attracting the attention of the guards. No one liked spectators here. Soon I would have to find a place at a table and lose a bit of coin. Two men got up from a table, one swearing loudly. I began moving towards one of the vacant seats when I saw her coming off a table. It was so obviously her I almost laughed out loud.

The last description I had told me she wore her hair long, but now it was cut short, Troll style, and dyed black, hiding her skull tattoos to all but the keenest of eyes, such as myself. All of the other women at the gambling tables dressed in revealing outfits that were designed to take the players' minds off the cards or dice. She was wearing a long-sleeved grey outfit that covered her body from neck to toe, clearly hiding the scars of attached Tarakan artifacts and battle wounds, while numerous earrings covered the marks a Comm piece would have left on her ear. She used to be a communication Troll, but carried herself like a warrior. I briefly wondered what made her give the artifacts up and go vegan. Most likely it was because of the debts I knew she owed.

I began moving to intercept her, trying not to be noticed until I was within earshot, but her warrior sense kicked in and she turned to me, body tensing, long before I got close. I made eye contact and kept walking forward as she stood her ground.

I'd worked out what I wanted to say long before, playing it endlessly in my mind. Still, my throat felt suddenly dry as I managed a hoarse-sounding "I want to play." The look she gave me told me that my fake upper-tower accent wasn't completely convincing.

"The tables are over there, Milord," she said, indicating her head to the side. "I'm sure you can find some games to your taste and expertise."

I shook my head. "I want to play the house."

She eyed me again, openly assessing who was standing before her, a fool or a hustler. I did my best to look like the former who believes he is the latter.

"I've never seen you here before," she remarked, then remembering the Den's etiquette she added, "Milord," but with an insolent drawl.

"Not my usual place," I said as haughtily as I could. "I gamble in the upper middle spires. Played a few tournaments, too. I heard there's good gaming here." I made a show of looking around dismissively, "So far, I'm disappointed."

I guess I wasn't convincing enough, or perhaps she sensed something was wrong, because she shook her head slightly. "I suggest you start at the far tables, Milord, and work up from there. You might save yourself a fortune." She turned to leave.

She was older than she looked, I knew that, but I decided against grabbing her arm. She didn't seem the sort who would react kindly to such a gesture and I didn't want to find out how finely honed her combat reflexes still were.

Instead, I intercepted her again and flashed her the bags of coin I was carrying, letting their bulk do the persuading. She would be entitled to a small cut of the profit, I knew that for a fact.

"I want to play the house," I insisted, "one-on-one. Are you in or should I find someone else?"

She hesitated, sensing the trap, but just as I thought she would move away she leaned over and grabbed one of the bags, weighing it in her hand. The clink of the metal coins was audible enough. Satisfied, she straightened her back. "Follow me," she ordered, then turned and walked away without a glance to check whether I'd complied.

She walked over to the other end of the large room, where a very old tapestry that depicted a battle scene from the Pre-Catastrophe era was hanging. A guard nodded at her as we approached, then he grabbed the tapestry and moved it aside, revealing a short corridor and steps leading further down.

Using a key on a chain around her neck, she opened a wooden door and we stepped into a richly furnished room. Real oak furniture, and oil paintings hung from the walls. This was the private gambling room, and it was furnished to please the upper crust of society who came to lose a huge amount of coin and feel good about it. Looking around me, I immediately felt my anxiety level rise. I was way out of my league. Playing the house meant the odds were against you. I never knew why people chose to do this, but then again, I'd just passed several rich youths who descended to the Pit from the safety of the upper towers for the thrill and pleasure of getting beaten up and robbed.

"Anything to drink?" she asked casually, pointing at a well-stocked drink cabinet as I sat myself down in front of a gaming table. "We have Pre-Catastrophe moonshine."

At least that was an easy choice: there was no way I was going to accept any liquid on these premises. She was obviously still trying to assess whether I was as foolish as I seemed, or a professional cleverly masking himself as a fool.

I shook my head and sat down at the table. She positioned herself on the other side and produced a set of cards, laying them faceup so I could see it was a full deck. It was a rare set, large cards featuring elaborate illustrations and made with real cardboard rather than the usual wooden slates and crude markings. I estimated the set cost more than what I was about to lose at the table.

"Your game, Milord?" she asked me, this time with a polite tone of professional interest.

"Trolls," I answered.

That caught her off guard. "What's your game, Mister?" she asked me pointedly.

"Like I said, it's Tro—"

She cut me off. "No, what's your real game? No one plays Trolls here," she spat.

What could I have told her? That it was the only game I knew how to play? That it was the only game I had scrolls of strategy for?

"That is my game." I tried to sound as if the fact that no one plays a children's card game in the Den was the proprietor's oversight.

She shrugged and shook her head in disbelief. "Odds eight to six."

They weren't good odds, but they could have been worse. I threw one bag of coins at her. She spilled the contents of the bag onto the table's surface, counting the coins quickly with her fingers. She then shuffled the deck, offered me six cards, and drew eight for herself.

Her movements were not as fast or subtle as one would expect from a card dealer working at the Den, but they were precise. Each card flew in the air and landed exactly next to the other, facedown. She probably wasn't going to try and hustle me; with odds of eight to six she wouldn't need to.

"One friendly warning, Milord, as one tattooed to another," she said, locking her gaze with mine. "I see any hint of you using those interesting eye tattoos of yours to peek at the deck or see through my blouse and we are done. The guards usually take your coin on the way out and break a few bones to teach you a lesson, so, be advised . . ."

I nodded and swallowed hard, fighting hard to suppress a blush of the guilty. We began playing.

The first round was short and painful and cost me a quarter of my coin bag. The second round took longer, but I lost it nonetheless and had to bring out another bag of coin.

The third, fourth, and fifth rounds were inconclusive and the sixth a draw, which meant the seventh would be for a bigger pot. She was starting to relax a bit, I could sense it. I was just another idiot she was trying to part from his hard-earned coin. It was time to up the stakes.

"You've been doing this for long?" I asked casually as I looked at my cards.

She nodded and said "Long enough," almost as if talking to herself.

"But you did something else before," I said, pushing two cards back.

She didn't look at my eyes. Instead she changed three of her own cards and raised the pot.

"My older brother taught me this game," I continued casually. "He was a Salvationist." I saw her hand rise to touch her earlobe unintentionally, as if looking for the Tarakan earpiece that used to be wired into her brain.

She caught herself, grimaced, and threw two cards at me, which landed perfectly next to the others. I looked down and took a peek; a troll and a skull. The realisation dawned on me that perhaps I could win this hand, but time was running short. I had to leave soon, and I needed to know for sure.

I called for another card, and she threw it. Then I said, "Thank you, Vincha," and watched her reaction. There was none. She didn't even blink or look at me. She just raised the stakes with two more stacks of coins and threw one last card at me. The throw was a miss; the card began flying straight but then twisted midair and veered to my left. My eyes followed as it cleared the table, out of arm's reach, and landed on the thick carpet. It sat faceup, revealing another grinning skull. That card would have won me the hand.

When I looked back it was already too late. She was sliding across the table. Her knees hit me square in the chest. I flew backwards and, for the second time that night, hit my head, this time on the carpeted floor. For a moment I could only see swirling colours in front of my eyes as she pinned me down, her knees digging into my chest. I could feel a blade at my throat, pressed hard, the cold steel biting into my skin.

"Who sent you?" she hissed at me as I tried desperately to blink away tears of pain from my eyes.

"No one," I managed to croak while trying to breathe. The back of my head was hurting from the fall, and her weight was crushing my chest. Vincha was not a dainty woman, and she was holding a very sharp blade. I could feel blood tickling down the side of my neck and fought the instinct to try and push her away, a move that would have surely been my last.

"Go rust," she swore. She pressed a hand to my forehead, pinning my head and making it hard for me to blink. Suddenly the blade at my throat vanished but my feeling of relief was replaced with horror as I felt the cold steel again, this time just under my eyeball.

"I can cut your throat," she said menacingly, "or I can take out an eye. Tell me who sent you and it will be easier. Is it Fuazz?"

I steeled myself and tried to remain calm. One of my arms was expertly pinned down by an outstretched leg and quickly losing sensation. Trying to move my other arm was a mistake. The blade twitched and drew blood. I yelped.

"Talk now or we're going to start a long process," she said. Her cold voice was as sobering as the hot trickle of blood running down my cheek.

"Don't," I gasped. "I mean you no harm."

"No kidding," she chuckled bitterly. "Now who sent you? Was it that rust bucket Fuazz?"

"No." Though he had pointed me in the right direction.

"The Grapplers?"

"No, please—"

"Ex-guild?"

"No, it's not really lik—"

"The Omen Society."

I paused, surprised despite my state of mind at that moment. "Surely you didn't manage to get on their bad side as well?" I said, and surprisingly enough it made her laugh, though she didn't ease the pressure under my eye.

"Look," I tried again, using what I was hoping was a calm and reasonable voice, "when I said I came with no intention to harm you, I meant it. I'm not carrying any weapons."

Walking into the Den unarmed and staying alive long enough to boast about it was something even Vincha had to check. She began a thorough search, shifting positions expertly, changing her blade-holding hand several times without easing the pressure, leaving me vulnerable and exposed throughout the entire procedure. Under different circumstances it would have been almost enjoyable.

Finally she said, "Your eyes."

"What of it?" I kept my voice as light as possible. "I can see in the dark, cheat at cards, sometimes see through people or even thin walls, but what's the worst I could do, squint at you to death?"

She nodded more to herself than for my benefit and the blade eased up a bit.

"Talk," she commanded.

"I work for a small society of men and women," I blurted

quickly. "We are the Guild of Historians. We explore our past in order to know the present and prepare for the future." It came out like the superficial mantra it was. The Guild of Historians was as much about selling artifacts for hard coin as it was about helping humanity or finding out about the Catastrophe, but I didn't care—at least I was talking and Vincha was listening and no part of me was being prodded or cut. "I want to interview you, about what happened when you went into the ruins, with the boy . . ."

She looked down at me in disbelief. "You tracked me down to the Den for this?"

"Yes."

"Go rust in a corner."

"It's important to us. We need to know what happened."

"I don't remember. It's been a long time," she said, still hovering above me.

"We have ways to make you remember," I said, and added hurriedly when I saw her expression harden, "Just mind techniques, nothing intrusive."

She shook her head. "What's past is past." She got up, still holding her blade at the ready. "Don't make any sudden moves," she warned. "Now tell me how you know my real name and how you found me."

"I've been trying to track you down for almost two years now," I said, rubbing my dead arm back to life.

"I'm surprised you found me."

"There are some things I'm better at than cards," I said, managing a lighter tone of voice, and sat up as an involuntary groan escaped my lips. "You never stay more than a month in one place, you never go back to the same workplace when you come back to the same town, you never work the same line on a map for more than three spots, and you prefer to work and stay in older establishments, especially ex-Salvationist businesses. You're good, but there's a pattern to your movements. Once I figured it out, it was only a matter of trying the odds."

"And all this for a rusting interview?" she said, perching herself carefully on the side of the playing table, out of arm's reach but close enough for a kick or a stab.

"Yes. We just want to hear your version of what happened."

"Well tough luck, Twinkle Eyes. I ain't talking to you or to your weird rusting guild."

I got up on my feet, nice and slow, and picked up the overturned chair. "We're willing to pay," I said, then added when I saw her expression, "and pay well."

"I earn nicely, thank you. Now get out."

This was the moment. There wouldn't be another one. After tonight she would disappear, because if I could find her, so could others, and there were plenty of nasty individuals who were looking for her. I had to make her talk, I simply had to, so I said the next sentence despite knowing it would probably get me killed.

"I know why you travel in such a pattern."

I saw her freeze.

"I know why you travel the way you do. I know why you're still in debt and where the coin you earn goes. I know about your daughter."

Her expression went blank, which meant she was about to kill me.

"This is not a shakedown," I said hastily, throwing my hands in the air. "I don't care about your business, but I'm ready to make life easier for you and for your family. I will pay a lot for your story."

She paused, the blade dancing in her hand. I held my breath, thinking I might as well hold on to it as long as I still had a choice. I tried to avert my eyes from the dancing blade.

"How much?" she asked

"Enough to clear your debt and make your family easier to conceal."

"I paid my debts," she said. "It took me a long time but I paid them."

That was surprising, and probably untrue. "That's not what I heard," I said in a neutral tone, not sure if this turning point in the conversation could be used to my advantage.

"I paid my debt to the last metal coin," she insisted, as if she thought I cared, "but the bloodsuckers piled up the interest, you can never get away from them, and they just wanted more, kept coming for it, so I stopped paying."

I nodded. "Still, coin is coin. I'm offering you hard metal for no risk and no sex. How you use it is your business."

"How much?" she asked again.

I thought of a sum, divided it in my mind, divided it again, and then said it.

"You're kidding, right? For that sum I wouldn't even show you my birthmark."

I smiled. We were negotiating, and that was something I was very good at. I opened my mouth for a clever response, but there was a sudden commotion behind the door. Without realising how it was done, I was on my feet, facing the door, with Vincha's blade once again pressing against my throat.

There was a loud bang and then the door burst open. The guard who moved the tapestry came sailing through the air and now lay sprawled at our feet. He did not get up. Galinak, covered in perspiration and stained with blood, walked slowly but purposely through the open door. He was smiling peacefully, as if he'd just gone on a leisurely stroll.

He stopped when he saw me. "Well," he said, "what have we got here?"

"Galinak, you piece of rusting metal," said Vincha calmly, her face close to my neck. "I thought you'd been banned from here."

"It's nice to see you too, Vincha." Galinak tilted his head. "May I say that you sound better than when you were on Skint, but what the hell happened to your wirings?"

"Been clean and vegan for more than three years now," said Vincha, "but my reflexes are still good, better than those cat innards you have for wirings."

"You should release my guy," mused Galinak, "unless you wish to test those reflexes. And let me warn you, I am not the gentle soul I used to be."

"Perhaps we could negotiate? I could give him back to you one piece at a time," Vincha pressed the blade just to make a point. There was something really wrong about this encounter.

"Sooo," I intoned, trying to sound carefree, "you know each other, what a coincidence, and a pleasant surprise, saves me the introductions, now where were we? I believe we were negotiating."

Vincha paused, then said a price, which was exactly eight times what I offered her.

"Bukra's balls! What are you trying to buy, her soul?" asked Galinak. The guard groaned and moved and Galinak kicked him several times until he stopped.

"That's a lot of hard metal," I said. We could all hear the commotion coming closer. "It would be bad judgement for me to accept such an offer."

"You showed plenty lack of judgement in employing an old burned-out Troll like Galinak." I didn't see Vincha's face, but I could *feel* her smiling, "That's my offer, take it or go rust in Tarakan Valley."

"I'll do whatever she does for half the coin," suggested Galinak, "and I assume you're not asking for sex, unless you have a really weird sense of—"

"Vincha," I intervened, "it's against my principles to pay that much for anything, even for your story, but I'll accept it. Now put the damn blade away and let's go."

She obliged, releasing the blade from my throat but keeping it in her hand. Both warriors stared each other down, but Galinak was quick to smile and spread his arms wide.

"What? No hug?"

Vincha snorted a laugh, sheathed the blade, and busied herself gathering my lost coins from the table.

"You're stealing from the Den," remarked Galinak with the careful tone of voice one keeps for the suicidal.

"Never coming back here again, anyway," she answered curtly, pocketing my hard-lost fortune.

"How is it going up there?" I asked Galinak.

"Hmmm, let's see." Galinak scratched his head with a bloodied hand. "Someone smuggled in a shock grenade and threw it, and when they raided the bar, the guards stationed above started sniping—and let me tell you, these guys never even heard of the stun button, so . . . it's pretty bad, but I've seen worse."

Walking through a bar fight involving four hundred participants was not a pleasant notion. "Is there another way out of here?" I asked Vincha.

"Sure, there's a secret door leading to a safe house just around the corner. We can avoid all the fighting and mayhem," she said drily, pocketing the last coin.

We looked silently at each other for a few heartbeats. "Are you serious?" I asked hesitantly.

"Of course I ain't serious," she shook her head at my gullibility. "One way into the Den and one way out. We'll have to fight our way through."

Galinak puffed a theatrical sigh of relief. "I thought for a moment you were serious about the secret door," he admitted, and then we ran for it.

The gambling hall was now empty of patrons, but halfway across it we encountered a group of men disposing of the last standing guard. They homed in on us with greed and a lust for violence plain on their faces. Without saying a word, Galinak advanced casually to my left as Vincha took my right and the fight errupted. I paced cautiously between them, completely untouched, as if walking inside the eye of a storm, occasionally side stepping or ducking as people were flung, flailing and screaming, from one side of the room to the other. I couldn't help but notice the different fighting styles of the two veterans. For Vincha fighting was purely business; short, economical gestures, arms close to the body, hitting vulnerable points for maximum damage. She cut through them like a hot blade through butter, breaking, twisting, gouging, and kicking without hesitation. Galinak, on the other hand, fought like it was an art form. He danced around, making broad gestures and finishing moves that occasionally used the Den's few intact pieces of furniture and architecture as props. Very soon there was no one left standing but us. I suppressed the urge to clap my hands in appreciation as the pair brushed off dust and wiped off other people's blood. Galinak was grinning broadly again.

We climbed the stairs and entered the main hall, which was now completely wrecked and with far fewer people in it. I could see at least three places, including the central bar and the wooden cage of the arena, where fire had broken out, probably ignited by a missed sniper shot. A few enthusiastic patrons managed to climb up to the elevated guard posts and were now engaged in hand-to-hand combat with the snipers. On ground level the guards were earning their pay, taking control of the area bit by bit, pounding every standing person they saw into a state of bloody unconsciousness. We avoided them by staying low and moving in the shadows as we headed for the door, thankfully without incident.

Outside the Den things were not much better. Many of the guards were lying among the wounded and dead.

The goggled Troll was standing alone, looking around nervously. For all his enhanced vision, he didn't notice Galinak until he was tapped from behind on the shoulder, which caused him to spin around in fright, brandishing a blaster.

"I'll have my weapons now," said Galinak, surprisingly polite and calm.

"You can't," spluttered the Troll, "there's a clampdown until the fight is done. You'll get them back when it's over."

"I need them now," insisted Galinak.

The Troll eyed Galinak with a sneer of contempt and steadied his blaster, pointing it at Galinak's chest. "Rough rust, old snot. You'll just have to cross your wires and wait."

It was probably the wrong thing to say.

8

Sunlight rarely touches the Pit, so I lost track of time and it seemed like it took forever to get from the Den to Vincha's home. We had to climb several ladders and cross a rope bridge to reach her wooden shack. It was indistinguishable from the hundreds of such structures, a neighbourhood built up against the base of the Tarakan towers in rows that rose above the lower market halfway to the Central Plateau and was adequately called Shackville. The word *shack* was perhaps an overstatement. It was a small, windowless hut made of rotten wood. Between the gaps in the warped floorboards, you could see the drop below. Even with the protection from the elements that the City of Towers provided them with, shacks would occasionally collapse, and the Pit's residents would jump to help casualties—relieving them of the burden of their belongings at the same time, then using the leftover debris to build more shacks.

I sat down heavily on one of the only two stools available and massaged my temples. The air was hot, and there was a constant humming noise. Galinak wasted no time. He sat on the floor and began to dress a blaster burn with salve he bought from a

Mender's stall at the market, while Vincha poured us a drink from a flask she fished out from under her makeshift bed. To be precise, she poured two drinks, one for herself and one for Galinak, but did not offer me any, which, oddly, made me feel a little hurt. She downed the drink and busied herself chopping the eel we also bought on our way back. If the butcher in the ever-open food market thought there was anything odd about bloodied and bruised customers, she was wise enough not to show it.

There wasn't much to look at, so I end up eyeing Vincha's travelling bag while considering our current position. Vincha travelled light; her bag confirmed this. My guess was she planned to split town, but first she wanted to eat, gather her strength, and figure out the best way to hustle more coin out of me.

The cooker was powered by a cable she'd clearly attached without permission to a local power generator. Still, it was a blessing. Many residents of Shackville had no choice but to cook over open fires. Vincha brought two cracked ceramic plates to the small table. There were no forks or other forms of cutlery, only Vincha's blade, which carved the cooked eel with alarming ease. She served herself a hefty portion, then sat down in front of me and folded her arms across her chest.

"No instruments" was the first thing she said.

I nodded my compliance.

"No prodding of any kind, and if I see your eyes glow, or if they even so much as look funny, I'll carve them out." She made a show of looking meaningfully at her knife before carving a piece of eel for herself.

"Done." I tried not to stare at the blade as she cut through steaming flesh or dwell on how it had felt pressed up against my skin back in the Den.

"So where's my payment?" Vincha shoved the piece of eel into her mouth.

"First I need to know you were in the Valley when it all happened."

50

She snorted, swallowing. "Rust, yeah, I was there. Not many of us came out alive on that day, but I made it."

"And you remember what happened?"

"I remember." Her voice got uncharacteristically quiet. "I've been trying to forget ever since."

"You were close to him." It wasn't a question. I'd spoken to dozens of ex-Salvationists about that period. Actually, I'd coerced, drilled, begged, seduced, bribed, threatened, and occasionally beaten the stories out of them. They had all talked, eventually. Each had a personalized version of the same story, placing themselves at its epicentre, yet they all had one thing in common: Vincha, and how close she was to the boy.

"Yes, we were close," she admitted. "He was just a kid, small and skinny, frightened, surrounded by the worst Salvationist scumbags, a broken soul, like the rest of us. Somehow, we connected. I don't know why. We just did."

Galinak chuckled and said, "Woman's intuit—" then ducked the knife that flew past my face and embedded itself in the rotted wall behind him.

"Go rust, cheap wires," she spat at him, but without much zeal in her voice. Even the throw was halfhearted, although I was just guessing that, really.

Galinak and Vincha traded colourful insults for a while, but I didn't pay much attention to the poetry. I was too excited. My long search was over and the key to solving the mystery was sitting in front of me. This woman knew what had happened, she *knew*, and for all her bravado and greed, I sensed that like the rest of them, she wanted to tell me her version of the story; all I needed to do was ask the right questions.

I knew what I was going to ask first, but I just had to wait until Galinak fell silent.

"What was his name?" I asked.

Vincha smiled coyly. "Wouldn't you like to know."

I already knew, but that wasn't the point. "I've heard many names."

"Yes, they called him the Kid, or the Key, but mostly just the Puzzler. They never called him by his name, maybe because it would have reminded them that he was human. But I knew his name, he told me . . ."

"What was it?"

She *knew* . . .

"Where's my coin?"

I took out two diamonds from my pocket and put them on the table.

She looked at them, then at me. "What are those?" she demanded.

"These will fetch you a quarter of what you asked for."

She looked back at the diamonds with open suspicion on her face "Where?"

"Upper Towers will give you a fair price, or the East Coast traders if you want to make the trip. Most craftsmen would buy them as well, but for a reduced price."

Anticipating her protest, I added, "No one could carry that much coin around. The diamonds are sound, and worth a quarter of what we agreed upon."

She scooped up the diamonds into her hand in a fluid motion and inspected them before saying, "I'll tell you a quarter of the story, then."

"It's a start," I said, my heart pounding.

"His name was Rafik, but his friends called him Raff, a boy from one of the Wildener villages, you know, those who followed that weird Prophet who rejected technology. Of all the places he could have been born, fate chose for him the worst rusting place."

9

Rafik lay on the ground, trying to stay still and control his breathing. If his pursuers would hear him it would be his end. He heard shouts and the thumping of feet hitting the ground a few yards to his left, and he fought the urge to bolt. There were two of them. A third one moved farther away, searching, but Rafik guessed he was still within earshot.

"Did you see him? Are you sure?" It was one of the infidels.

"Yes, I'm sure," came the answer from such a close distance it made Rafik's heart jerk with fear. "We take him out and we'll have them all."

Rafik closed his eyes and dug his chin down in the dirt, willing himself to be grass, praying to the Prophet Reborn for help, berating himself for any blasphemous thoughts or deeds in his past, for surely his sinful ways had brought him to this predicament. If what the infidel said was true, all his friends were either captured or taken out. He could not make up his mind which fate was better; the infidels had their nasty ways with captives, and he knew that for a fact. Poor Eithan—Rafik had made efforts to protect his friend, but they'd split up in the woods and Eithan was among the first to fall.

One of the infidels took another step towards the shallow ditch, and Rafik shivered involuntarily as he heard the enemy's feet crushing the grass.

They were almost above him, standing on top of the mound. It was a sheer miracle neither of them looked down and spotted him practically lying under their feet.

After an eternity, he heard one of them say "Let's go. He probably kept running east. We'll find him soon enough—he can't be too far away."

The other infidel mumbled a defeated reply, and they began to move away. He was saved; thank the God and the Prophet Reborn. Rafik's body, suddenly realising he'd been holding his breath for far too long, exhaled quickly. The gesture was followed, naturally, by a large intake of breath, which carried dust from the plants or the earth. Before Rafik could control himself, he sneezed loudly.

The rest happened in kind of a blur. He heard shouts of discovery and running steps getting closer. Rafik's fist clenched over dirt and dead leaves as he uttered one last prayer to the Prophet Reborn. When they were on top of him, he jumped up and flung the handful of dirt into the face of the incoming infidel—who, bless the Prophet Reborn, was just opening his mouth in a shout of triumph. The result was pretty spectacular, but Rafik did not linger to watch. He was running again, this time faster than ever before, faster than he'd ever run in his life. He heard his pursuers behind him and bolted through the undergrowth, trying to lose them. There was no point in turning and fighting; he would be overwhelmed for sure. There was only one thing to do now: complete his mission or die trying.

Rafik altered his course midstride and burst through the undergrowth again. As luck would have it, he actually ran right between two surprised infidel guards, and before they managed to react he was already back in the foliage. Now there were four of them running after him. *Four, two, it doesn't matter,* the exhilarating thought flashed in his mind, *as long as they cannot catch me.*

The infidels probably realised what he was trying to do, as several cries rose from the areas he passed, and they began converging on him from all directions. In his peripheral vision, Rafik saw dark silhouettes rushing almost alongside him. Soon they would pounce. Instinctively, he abruptly altered his course again, which took him in a direction away from his goal but also traced an arc that would confuse his pursuers just a little while longer—at least that was what he hoped to accomplish.

Suddenly he was confronted by an infidel who stepped from behind a tree and tried to grab him. But he misjudged the power Rafik had accumulated in his mad dash. They collided, and the infidel fell back on the ground with a thump and a cry of surprise and pain. Rafik barely lost speed, but the little he lost was significant. They were almost upon him, and he was getting too tired to keep this pace much longer. It was now or never.

Rafik roughly calculated his position and changed his direction once more, ducking under the arm of a pursuing infidel, his bare feet feeling as if they were hardly touching the ground. He could see his mark now, getting closer, but also the infidels who were running towards him from all directions. He passed the bodies of his friends lying on the ground in neat rows, Eithan among them. It was over, he knew it. One infidel was in a better position and would intercept Rafik before he could reach his target. The others were only an arm's reach behind him; he heard the sound of their steps hitting the dirt and could almost feel their breath on his back.

There was no power in him anymore; his lungs were on fire, his feet were bleeding, and his body was in agony. In a few heartbeats, Rafik knew, it would be over. The unbelievers would triumph, yet it was something he was still unable to come to terms with. God was with the believers, and the infidels always lost. *Always.* It was something Rafik had known as a fact from the moment he could comprehend words from sound. Just as he felt himself slow into despair and defeat, his body already accepting the fate his heart was yet rejecting, the infidel who was about to intercept him stumbled on an invisible twig on the ground. An accident? Surely not! It was a miracle.

Rafik's spirit soared as he skipped over the body of the fallen infidel guard, galloped the last few yards, and wrapped his hands around the tree that was his target, shouting, "Boom!" again and again in ecstatic joy. He heard the infidels curse in defeat and his teammates, the holy warriors, shout in joyful triumph as he raised his hands and proclaimed victory.

When Rafik turned around he saw his teammates jumping up and down, roaring their excitement. Eithan ran forward and hugged his friend, picked him up from the ground, and spun him around in a circle. The infidel team looked disappointed, but many among them held Rafik's view on God's attitude towards the believers and were almost visibly relieved to lose.

The boys changed the name of the game often, sometimes to "Pure Blood and Tattooed" or "Guards and Bandits." The rules were pretty much the same, but when they called the game "Holy Warriors and Infidels" there was always an extra excitement in the game, much more at stake than a simple afternoon's honour. No matter what the odds, the holy warriors were the blessed sons of the Prophet Reborn. The Infidels had to lose, they *had* to, even if this time was too close for comfort.

Rafik squirmed and kicked a bit until Eithan finally lowered him down, though he was still full of excitement, and he kept hugging and thumping Rafik's chest with open palms even as the rest of the boys were calming down. That was typical Eithan; he always became completely engrossed in everything they did but remained a little *too* enthusiastic for too long. It annoyed Rafik, who found Eithan's company embarrassing at times, especially around girls. But when one chooses his best friend at the age of three and they swear to each other in blood at the age of seven, one does not break the friendship just because pretty Elriya keeps laughing whenever Eithan behaves like a fool. Nor do you walk away from a friendship because your sworn brother happens to be absolutely awful in any kind of physical game and sport, and you have to coerce your teammates with promises and threats so they pick Eithan for their team.

Rafik pushed his friend gently away before the others began taunting them. With his attention focused on Eithan, Rafik did not notice the two boys who emerged from the bush. One of them was Cnaan, the boy who had swallowed the dirt flung by Rafik. Strictly speaking, when the only rule of taking a combatant out of play was that his back had to touch the ground, Rafik's move was perfectly legal. Yet Cnaan was not trying to dispute the victory or debate the rules; he just wanted to get even. In his clenched fist, he held a massive ball of leaves and dirt, and he charged Rafik with the zeal of hurt pride and the confidence of someone who outweighs his opponent by a full stone.

Eithan called a warning, but Rafik only managed to turn before he was lifted off the ground for the second time. A heartbeat later the ground claimed him back with a cloud of dust and a blow that took the air out of his lungs. His right hand partially blocked the fall, and he felt the skin scratch and split open on the gravel.

Momentarily dazed, Rafik could only shield his face from the barrage of vicious blows Cnaan was landing on him. He twisted and managed to half-turn on the ground, but Cnaan turned him back with a vicious shove and sat firmly on Rafik's chest, pinning him down. As his eyes cleared, Rafik's vision was filled with Cnaan's heavyset frame. One chubby hand grabbed Rafik's jaw while another was poised, ready to shove a fistful of revenge into his mouth.

Suddenly Cnaan's overbearing weight was lifted off Rafik's chest. Rafik rolled to the left and rose unsteadily to his feet, wiping dirt off his face with his bloodied arm. Cnaan and Eithan were rolling on the ground, kicking, punching and, in Eithan's case, occasionally biting. That was another trait of the little guy; fearlessness and a blind loyalty to his blood friend. Rafik did not mind *that* side of Eithan's personality. The problem was that Cnaan had friends as well—perhaps more followers than friends, but boys ready to join in the fight, especially if Cnaan was winning. They set upon Eithan, and it was Rafik's turn to come to the rescue. Rafik had friends, too, boys who suffered from Cnaan's attention from time to time and were waiting for an opportunity for payback. In a few heartbeats, the entire group was brawling.

As the battle commenced, time slowed and the outside world vanished from existence. Rafik flung his limbs in all directions, hitting anyone he did not recognise as a friendly face. As in any battle of grand proportions, alliances were formed and promptly broken as one side lost heart. A few of Cnaan's entourage fled the fight, bleeding and crying. When Rafik saw the glint of fear in Cnaan's eyes, he knew he was going to win the day yet again, but victory was snatched away with cruel suddenness as a heavy set of hands clamped around his collar and he was hauled to his feet. Angry words were hurled at him from several grown-ups. He was slapped across his brow, and that was stronger and more humiliating than anything he'd suffered during the fight. The rest of the boys were held by other angry adults.

Rafik held his breath and tried as hard as he could not to cry. At the corner of his eye he caught Cnaan's frightened stare; like Rafik, he was trapped between two pairs of heavyset arms. A temporary alliance silently formed with that very glance, as a new common enemy was recognised: the grown-ups.

"Why were you fighting? Who started this?"

Rafik did not answer, nor did Cnaan, or Eithan.

"We thought it was a bandit attack; the entire village is up in arms," said another angry voice to his left. "The signals were fired, men are coming back from the fields, women and children are hiding, what were you thinking? I *will* tell your father, Rafik, and I hope he'll put his belt on you."

Many more grown-ups were now arriving, all of them carrying weapons. Rafik's heart sunk. It was true; now that the ringing noise in his ears had subsided, the ringing of the alarm bells was clearly audible. They were in trouble—worse, *he* was in trouble.

"Tell me who started this or . . ." The hand rose up again and Rafik flinched, knowing the slap was going to hurt and this time he would cry.

"That's enough, Rachmann."

The commanding voice of Fahid, Rafik's older brother, froze the threatening hand as it was poised to strike. Instead, Rafik was released.

The man called Rachmann turned to face Rafik's brother. "The boy's mischief frightened the entire village." He pointed an accusing finger at Rafik. "Is there no discipline in your household?"

"I do not see Rafik standing alone here, do you?" was the calm reply. "And he was not fighting with himself, yet I see your hand raised against only one boy."

"Well, we all know he is the one full of mischief," grunted Rachmann, who was many years older than Fahid and disliked being told off by someone who had just come of age.

"Even if what you claim is true, it is not your duty to discipline my brother. Only our father has this right. I assure you he will admonish Rafik for his misdeeds."

Perhaps it was the assured voice which calmed Rachmann down, or the rifle that was casually slung over Fahid's shoulder— the same rifle with which Fahid had single-handedly fought off the bandits only two months before and brought honour to the Banishra house. Rachmann grunted something mildly offensive under his breath and stepped aside.

At a gesture from his older sibling, Rafik began walking away from the group, but not before glancing meaningfully at Eithan and Cnaan. If their condition reflected his own, Rafik was a sight to behold. He felt the tickle of blood streaming gently from his hand, and his left cheekbone was already swollen and tender.

The siblings walked in silence for a while until they cleared the trees. Fahid stopped, put a hand on Rafik's shoulder, and said, "Now, let's take a look at you, little brother."

He turned Rafik this way and that, and after a brief inspection he proclaimed, "Goodness, your shirt is torn and you've got a nice black eye here. And look at your hand, it's bleeding all over the place. Mother will kill us both."

There was definite concern in Fahid's tone of voice. Rafik shuddered. Their father was a quiet and resolute man who rarely shouted and never hit his children. Their mother, on the other hand, was his fiery opposite, with a mighty forearm and a heavy-duty ladle, which she used to dish out her own painful version of the holy scripts.

Fahid smiled as they continued walking. "So who threw the first punch?"

When he grows up, Rafik wants to be just like his older brother: tall and strong and loyal, known to be a source of quiet strength and courage among the villagers even though he would only reach sixteen springs this year. Yet Fahid was a grown-up now, and one did not snitch to grown-ups, no matter who they were. Rafik shrugged and did not answer, not wishing to lie to his own brother nor betray his friends.

But although Fahid was about to be married soon, he had not forgotten the code of his own youth, and he laughed as he ruffled his younger brother's short hair. "At least tell me you gave as much as you got."

Rafik tried to smile but found the cut in his lower lip hurt too much.

"Eithan and I, we were winning."

Fahid let out a short chuckle. "You are a brave pair, the both of you, fighting those odds."

And that was the best compliment Rafik had ever gotten.

Pain all but forgotten, he walked on air after his older brother all the way home to be berated by their angry mother.

10

"Rafik, would you please repeat what I just said?"

Rafik blinked and his eyes focused on the familiar classroom. Heads were already turned, and Rafik saw malicious smiles spreading across a few faces.

"What . . . ?" was all he managed to utter, and a few boys giggled. From his place on the mat he could see the teacher's feet, wrapped in cloth sandals. Rafik shook his head slowly; it felt almost too heavy to lift.

"Rafik Banishra," Master Issak said, slowly punctuating every syllable, as if explaining the obvious, "Son of Sadre, could you please repeat the words of the Prophet Reborn, regarding the infidels?"

Rafik beamed, relieved. That was easy.

"They all burn in Hell, Master Issak," he answered confidently.

There was a wave of laughter in the room and the teacher had to raise his voice to be heard.

"The *exact* words of the Prophet Reborn, Rafik, regarding the *specific* creatures of Satan, if you please?"

On any other day Rafik would have remembered the words of the new holy book, which the Prophet Reborn received from God before the Catastrophe and was filled with prophecies about the demise of the Tarakan infidels. Rafik knew many of the verses by heart—the ones about the unholy and the terrible justice that awaited them were his favourite by far—but not today. His head felt as heavy as stone and his thoughts were lost in a fog.

"Uh . . ." Rafik tried to buy time. "He . . . who . . . falls . . . into . . . temptation . . . will . . . go to Hell?"

Laughter swept the entire class again and fuelled Master Issak's indignation.

"Rafik Banishra, on your feet and over here!" he shouted. Rafik rose unsteadily as the class shuffled to clear a path to the front of the room. Seeing another boy punished was much more interesting than reciting verse after holy verse.

Master Issak was dressed in white clothes of purity, but the look in his eyes was as dark as night. Even sitting down, he was taller than Rafik, and three times his width. The teacher shook his head as Rafik approached. When the boy stood two paces away the teacher brandished a short, flexible stick and watched with satisfaction as Rafik shuddered.

"Give me your hand," he demanded.

Rafik was still for a moment, then he slowly raised his right hand towards the teacher.

Master Issak looked at the hand with disdain; it was full of scabs, red scratches, and bruises.

"What happened to your hand?"

"I fell, Master Issak," Rafik said, unwilling to snitch about the boys' argument over the Warrior and Infidels game, which had quickly turned into a scrap. Blushing did not help his lie, and the teacher let out a mirthless laugh before frowning again.

Master Isaak was quite fond of Rafik, who had a superb memory for the verses and was an enthusiastic student of the holy scripts. Perhaps under different circumstances Master Issak would have let the boy off with a stern warning, as he'd done before, when Rafik's mischievousness had gotten him in trouble. But Rafik's hopes were dashed when Master Issak took a deep breath filled with righteous rage. He grabbed the boy's wounded hand and raised his stick. He began reciting the verses, delivering snapping blows with the stick every few words, Rafik wailed in pain with each accented word.

"Hear O the devout sons and daughters of Abraham. The Prophet Reborn, who rose from the days of fire, *said;* if you let temptation hold, you will *fail* your God. If you allow *vanity* and covet what humans must never have, you *will* fall the long way to all *hells*, where the impure are *punished* for their wish to be as powerful as the one *God. You . . . shall . . . not . . . attach.*"

Master Issak let go of Rafik's bleeding hand and watched the boy walk unsteadily back to his mat and collapse. Eithan was already there, and the two boys huddled together.

After Rafik's discipline, it was almost time for midday prayer, and the class needed to walk to the temple in the centre of the village. Master Isaak adjourned the class and stood by the door. As the boys walked up to him one by one, each kissed the book of the Prophet Reborn and bowed his head as the teacher inspected him for signs of the curse. Eithan fixed Master Issak with a defiant stare before bowing his head. Master Issak inspected him, then gave him a slap on the back of his head for good measure. Eithan suffered in silence, then stood by the open door and waited for Rafik, who was shuffling slowly and still holding his wounded hand.

Master Issak gently patted Rafik's head. "Let it be a lesson to you, boy. You're a good student, but forgetting the holy words of the Blessed Reborn demands retribution."

Rafik nodded and pursed his lips. Master Issak noticed that blood still dripped to the floor from his wounded hand. A look of concern passed his eyes.

"You're excused from prayer today, Rafik," Master Issak said. "Go straight home. Let Eithan walk you there."

He turned to Eithan. "You must swear by the Prophet to take

him straight home and return immediately to prayer, understood?"

Eithan nodded. "Yes, Master Isaak. I swear by the Prophet Reborn."

Satisfied, Master Issak turned and walked after the rest of the class without a glance back.

As soon as he was sure Master Isaak was out of earshot Eithan said, "Master Isaak was an ass to hit you like that."

Rafik leaned heavily on the wooden wall of the class hut, feeling shaky and tired. "All the grown-ups are still angry at us for causing the alarm."

"Yeah, I heard Cnaan got a good beating from his da. He said he didn't but did you see the way he was sitti—" Eithan stopped midsentence and caught Rafik before he fell to the ground.

"Prophet. You look bad, blood brother," Eithan put Rafik's arm around his shoulder and an arm around his waist. "Come on, let's go to your ma."

11

Rafik didn't remember the next four days of his life. He was feverish or asleep most of the time, and was moved to the barn to reduce the risk of infecting the rest of the household. He did remember being attended to by his mother and his older sister, Nisha, who tried to feed him hot lamb soup, washed him with hard soap, and constantly uttered prayers for his recovery.

A travelling healer came and went, looking like a ghost with his white mask and gloves as he poked and prodded the hallucinating boy. The healer talked to Rafik's worried parents as Rafik drifted in and out of consciousness. The word *infection* was repeated several times. His wounded left hand was smeared with foul-smelling salve, which stung and hurt, before being bandaged in cloth. The only other thing Rafik remembered was hearing his mother say, "No, you cannot see him, Eithan, not yet. But he is getting better and soon you can play together again."

On the fifth day he woke up feeling better. In fact, he sprang out of bed with a strength and vigour that surprised and delighted his mother. He ate all the food she served him—even the boiled cabbage, which he normally hated. Soon he was proclaimed healthy, and he was let out of the barn and promptly directed to a wooden keg filled with scalding hot water, in which he scrubbed off the residue of sickness that clung to his skin, being careful not to wet his still-bandaged hand.

Eithan was already waiting for him outside, and in no time at all Rafik was briefed about the gossip of the last four days. Three travelling merchants had arrived two days before. Eithan had caught and cooked a giant toad the size of a grown-up's fist. Cnaan was seen talking to Elriya again, and her parents complained to his parents. The village guards investigated some smoke coming from the edge of a field and frightened two vagabonds, who begged for their lives before being released with a warning. Eithan was a very good storyteller who could turn even the most mundane activity into an exciting tale.

Finally, Eithan pointed at the bandaged hand. "When are you taking it off?"

Rafik shrugged. "I have to wait until the healer visits again. It feels all right, though. It doesn't hurt anymore."

"Come on, let's see it. It was really bleeding when you fainted. I carried you all the way to your home." Eithan puffed his chest out with pride.

"It only happened four streets away." Rafik tried to hide his embarrassment, especially because he'd insisted on walking unaided only to faint once they'd passed the centre of the village.

"Yeah? You were bleeding all over my shirt. I think you fell on it when you fain—when you fell," Eithan said, quickly correcting himself when he caught Rafik's expression. "Come on, let me look at it."

"Maybe later."

"Are you scared you'll see your hand and faint again?"

"No, I didn't faint because I was scared. It was an infection."

"Maybe your hand got all twisted from the infection and now it'll look like a claw."

"No, it didn't. It feels all right."

"So . . . let's see it."

"I'm not supposed to. The healer said—"

"What are you, *scared* like a *girl*?"

"Fine, but if I bleed, I'm wiping my hand on *your* tunic."

Rafik got up on his feet and quickly began unravelling the bandage. He could see the back of his hand as the strips of stained cloth fell to the ground. The skin there was notably whiter than the rest of his body, but he didn't realise how different the colour was until it was completely free from the bandage.

"That's strange," commented Eithan, stepping closer.

"Maybe it's the salve. It smelled like cow shit when he put it on me." Rafik sniffed carefully. It smelled of soap.

"Well, it really healed your hand," remarked Eithan.

Rafik flexed his hand. "True, there isn't even a scratch on it."

His skin was perfect, or at least the back of his hand was. There were still scabs on the tips of his three middle fingers.

"Ugh," said Eithan, peeking from behind Rafik's shoulder, "The scabs are really black."

"It's because of the salve," Rafik said quickly. "I bet they'll peel off." He rubbed the tips of his fingers with his thumb, but the skin felt soft and whole, and he couldn't catch a scab edge to leverage a good peel. Annoyed, he brought the injured hand close to his face and began scratching it. It was right then Rafik realised the scabs had shapes. The scab on his forefinger was shaped like a triangle. The scab on his middle finger was shaped like two crescent moons, and the scab on his ring finger was shaped like three tiny balls, one on top of the other, connected by a string. Blood drained from his face.

"What is it?" Eithan asked.

"Nothing," Rafik closed his hand in a fist so tight his nails bit into his palm.

"No, I saw something." Eithan moved closer. "Let me see it again."

"No!" Rafik shouted. "No, get away. It's the medicine. I shouldn't have taken the bandages off."

"But the scabs, they looked like . . ." Eithan suddenly choked on his words, but Rafik didn't wait to see his friend's reaction; he was already running away as fast as his feet could carry him. He burst into the shed and plunged his hand into the still lukewarm water of his bath. Then he pulled his hand out and looked at it again. The marks were still there. Tears streaming down his cheeks, Rafik began scrubbing his fingers with all his might—but every time he checked, the scabs where still there. He searched the shed, whimpering in fear, until he found a sharpening stone, then he began rubbing his fingers until they began to bleed again.

It was Fahid who eventually found him, crying, shivering and holding his bloodied hand in a tight fist.

12

Sadre Banishra's expression was one of deep concern, barely held in check, as he entered the barn. He turned ashen when he saw the expressions on the faces of his wife and eldest son.

Rafik was standing in the middle of the barn. He shouted, "Papa!" and ran towards him.

Sadre laid a heavy hand on his son's small head. He looked uncertainly at his wife and older son. Fahid bit his lip and lowered his head. Rafik's mother slowly shook hers but held his gaze, tears trailing down her face.

"Fahid, go to the house and make sure the other children *do not talk to anyone.*"

"But father, he said Eithan saw—"

"Just do it!" Sadre snapped.

"Father," cried Rafik, "I didn't do it. It's not my fault. It's the medicine, right? It's only very small, look." He held his hand up to his father's face.

Sadre gasped and took a step back. "Blessed Prophet," he mumbled.

"Papa, I . . . I didn't . . . look . . . it's so small . . . if I put the bandage back, maybe . . ."

Ignoring the boy's words, Rafik's father gripped his son's arm and inspected it, before pushing it away and checking his other arm. He then grabbed Rafik's head with both hands and searched the boy's face, neck, and shaved head, even behind the ears, until he was satisfied there were no other tattoos.

"Take your clothes off," Sadre ordered. When Rafik hesitated, he lunged and tore them off his son's body in several violent movements.

"Sadre—" Rafik's mother took a step closer, trying to calm her husband.

But Rafik's father turned his head towards her and hissed, "Everything is lost, *everything,* unless we do something *quickly.*"

Rafik trembled from fear and the sudden cold as his father looked over his back, armpits, buttocks, genitals, and feet—he even checked between the toes. He found no other tattoos except for the three on Rafik's fingertips.

Sadre glanced at the corner of the barn where the tools were kept and then looked at his wife, who must have realised immediately what her husband was planning to do.

"No," she said in horror. "He is your *son.*"

"He is *our* son," Sadre said, his voice hard. He got up and grabbed Rafik's wrist. "And we have no choice. We do this for his sake, and for the sake of *our* family."

"What are you going to do, Papa?" asked Rafik, his voice rising with fear.

Sadre kept a firm hold of his naked son. "You must be brave, my boy. You must understand and pray to God and the Prophet Reborn, and you must forgive—" His voice cracked, and he turned and led Rafik to the chopping block.

Rafik saw his mother hand the heavy axe to his father while saying, "It's for your own good."

Rafik began to pull back with all his might, screaming, "No, no, please no, Mama, please don't!" But his struggle didn't slow his father down. Not even when he dropped to the floor.

His mother was already tearing the hem off her long dress, preparing bandages while his father opened the latch of the small oven and thrust the axe's blade into the flames. They waited, watching the metal turn red-hot. Rafik's soft whimpering punctuated the silence.

Sadre, still holding Rafik firmly, finally beckoned to his wife, and she bent down and brought the gleaming hot ax. This brought a new wave of panicked wails from Rafik, and although his wrist was pinned to the chopping block, he managed to curl his fingers into a tight fist.

Sadre watched the axe in his hand for a long moment, steadying his breath before slowly turning his attention back to his son. "Rafik," he said softly, "I need to chop the tops of your fingers off. Please son, I need you to be brave."

"No, Papa, please, no! I'll be good, I promise!"

Sadre grabbed his son's chin and forced him to look into his eyes. "You are cursed, *marked*." The softness was gone from his voice as he spat the words into Rafik's face. "This is an abomination, do you understand? If it is discovered, we are all finished. Your brother's wedding will be called off, your sisters will never marry, we will need to leave this village, and you will be killed. They will hang you and leave your body to rot. Now stop crying and repent for whatever God and his Prophet Reborn have punished you for, and if you do not help me and be still, I swear by the Prophet Reborn that I will chop off your entire hand."

It was that last threat which somehow calmed Rafik's hysteria. Losing the tips of your fingers was not as bad as losing your hand. He slowly uncurled his fingers and turned his head away. His father suddenly bent down and kissed the top of his head.

"You are brave, my Rafik," he whispered, "and you must remember, this was an *accident*."

Rafik felt his mother's arms around him, channelling warmth

and love even as she pinned him down. He didn't want to see what was going to happen, but after what seemed like an eternity he turned his head towards his father. It was exactly at that moment that Sadre must have gathered the courage to bring the axe down on his son's outstretched fingers. There was a flash of pain which completely blinded Rafik, the sound of searing flesh, and an awful smell. Rafik shrieked and then collapsed on the ground as his mother rushed to cover the smoking hand with cloth. The last thing he saw before losing consciousness was his father throwing the three digits into the flames, then collapsing to his knees and throwing up.

13

The voices woke Rafik up.

"How is he?" a man asked.

"He's better today, thank the Prophet Reborn," the familiar voice of Rafik's father answered, "the fever is gone. He drank some water this morning and fell asleep again."

"Thank the one God and the Blessed Reborn. What a horrible accident, and just after he got healthy. God saves us and protects us from harm."

Rafik stood up unsteadily. His knees were weak and trembling and his mouth dry.

"Is this what all the people are saying? That it was an accident?" Rafik's father lowered his voice.

"What else would they say? That is what you wrote in the message when you asked me to come. I traveled here, although I am no healer, so I do not know what help I could be. But Sadre, I only had to walk into the village to hear that you did not let the previous healer return or even let that pompous fool Isaak sit and pray at his bed. People are worried. They think that maybe Rafik has caught some kind of disease. What's going on?"

"It was no accident."

"What happened?"

"I chopped his fingers off, Simon. I took off my own son's fingers with my ax, and my beloved wife held him down so I could do so."

Simon was Rafik's uncle. He lived in another village and rarely came to visit.

"Are you mad? Tell me you are jesting."

"I am not jesting. Laughter will not touch my lips for the rest of my life."

"But why?"

"He was *marked*, Simon. He had it, the curse, on his fingers."

"No!" Simon gasped.

"They appeared on his fingertips after he fell and bled, after the sickness."

"God save us."

"I searched him, he did not have marks anywhere else on his body, so I . . . I had to . . . you should have heard him, Simon, my brave boy, he even stretched out his fingers for me . . . my little boy, why is God punishing me so?"

"Calm yourself. How is Fahtna taking it?"

"Badly. She's putting on a brave face for the kids, but she cries every night and blames herself."

Rafik leaned on the doorframe but his father and uncle, sitting at the kitchen table, did not notice him.

"What about Fahid?" Simon asked in a quieter tone

"He volunteered for extra guard duty. I don't think he wants to be here, with him."

"He has plenty to worry about."

"I know. If word of this gets out . . . the wedding . . . everything I worked for my entire life . . . my girls. Why is this happening to me? I'm a good man. I pray each day, even in the fields. I pray to the Prophet Reborn to keep us all safe and healthy."

"I don't know, brother. Does anyone else know about this?"

"I don't think so, but he shouted the name of his friend, Eithan, a few times in his dreams. These boys are inseparable, and Eithan brought Rafik home when he got sick the first time, and then sat by our door for four days until I had to chase him away. This time Eithan hasn't tried to visit even once."

"You think this Eithan knows?"

"Maybe, but if he saw the marks he hasn't told anyone yet. They would have been on my doorstep if he had."

Simon, Rafik's uncle, scratched his shaved head. "I hesitate to ask, but are there many cases of the curse in your village?"

"No. The last one was two months before I moved here and married Fahtna. She told me they hanged the boy, left his body to rot for three days, then burned his family's house and slaughtered all the livestock. That's the only one I know of, and it happened more than fifteen years ago. But now that I think about it, there were also two girls who went to the fields and disappeared. We looked for them for weeks but found nothing, not a trace of them. I think they ran away, maybe they were marked, too . . ."

After a long pause Simon said hesitantly, "The situation is grim, may the Prophet Reborn protect us. I don't know how I can help you."

"I need you to take Rafik away."

"What? Are you asking me to bring Rafik into *my* household?"

"No, of course not. I'm asking you to help me send him far away from here."

"But why? You said you chopped the fingers off. People will believe it was an accident. If you send him away, surely they'll suspect."

"I have to, Simon. I have to send him away as soon as he's able to walk."

"What are you are not telling me?"

It was in that moment that Sadre noticed Rafik leaning against the doorframe.

"Papa . . ."

Simon got up from his chair so quickly that it fell backwards to the floor with a clatter.

"You're awake! Say hello to your uncle Simon. You last met him two years ago at the spring festival."

Rafik nodded slowly. "Hello, Uncle."

"Prophet's blessings on your head, Rafik," Uncle Simon answered nervously.

"Show Uncle Simon your hands," Sadre said. "Go on, don't be afraid."

Rafik held out his right hand and Simon gasped, swore, then uttered a quick prayer of forgiveness to the Prophet Reborn.

Rafik's hand was whole. His fingers were all there, fleshy pink and perfect, without a mark on them save the same black tattoos, which now spread across half of his three middle fingers.

14

A whistle and a snap from a leather whip marked the beginning of their journey as their cart rocked back and forth on the muddy road out of the village. Rafik was wedged tightly between his uncle Simon and his older brother, Fahid, with his hand wrapped in bandages and once again hidden inside his tunic. People stared and waved as the small cart picked up its pace and exited the village's main gate. Two guards gestured to Fahid, who told Simon not to stop. One of the guards stepped aside only at the last moment, swearing. Fahid turned around and shouted a halfhearted apology as their pony went into a trot.

They were headed in the direction of Simon's village, less than a day's ride away, but it was a ruse. Shortly into their journey they would turn and head onto a narrow road that crossed the village and the fields. Rafik knew the area well; he had staged many glorious battles between warriors and infidels with Eithan on these very hills. Now he reckoned he would have to play on the infidel team, not that anyone would play with him anymore.

Rafik blinked away tears. His uncle said they were going to find a man who would know how to cure him. He clung to this hope with all his will. It would all be a great adventure and soon he would come back home, cured. Besides, he did not *feel* like an infidel; he still believed in God and the Prophet Reborn. He still prayed devoutly every morning. He didn't feel the need to attach anything to his body like the infidels did, or to maim and kill innocents. He concluded this was all some kind of misunderstanding. Clearly the Prophet Reborn was testing him in some way, the way the Prophet himself was tested. Rafik swore to himself that he would pass this test and remain pious and true to the faith no matter what happened.

"When are we going to stop and pray?" he asked, but received no reply.

When Rafik asked again, Fahid muttered something noncommittal just as a barrage of rocks rained down on their cart. Most of the stones fell short but one stung Rafik's back. The pony almost bolted in panic and Uncle Simon swore loudly. Fahid jumped off, leaving enough space for Rafik to turn around and see their attackers. There were nine boys spread across the hill, and Rafik knew them all. Half of them ran up the hill when they saw Fahid but a few stayed and picked up more rocks.

Normally Fahid had tolerance for pranks, but this was not a normal day. He cocked his gun and shot once over the boys' heads, causing them to drop the rocks they were holding and scurry away in panic. The cart jerked violently as the pony tried to bolt again.

"Why in the Reborn's name did you do that?" Simon bellowed. "They must have heard that shot in the village. Now we must hurry. Seriously, to waste good ammunition on such things . . ."

Rafik was once again wedged between the two nervous men. He did not watch the road ahead, or pay attention to his redfaced brother. He was still looking behind him at Eithan, who was the only boy who did not run away after the shot was fired.

They were close enough to recognise each other but too far away to meet each other's eyes. With a shout of rage, Eithan suddenly flung the stone he was holding at their cart. It fell short, rolling on the road until it came to a stop. Then Eithan turned and ran up the hill.

15

I shook my head in disbelief, even though I knew that Vincha was telling the truth. I had met too many liars on my journey, and I knew the difference. "I'm surprised they didn't kill him outright," I said.

"No, they just chopped his fingers off." Vincha's voice was venomous.

"You can't beat fatherly love," Galinak remarked from behind me. When I glanced back at him, he was shaking his head. "Rustfuckers."

Vincha shrugged. "Some people get all messed up and do all kinds of shit when they first find out they're marked. The worst is what they do to themselves. I knew a girl who plucked her own eyes out." She levelled a meaningful gaze at me.

"Yes, it's true these things happen, especially in rural areas," I said, "and most of the time the severed or maimed part does not heal itself or grow back, although this isn't the first time I've heard of such a thing."

I felt their attention on me almost as a physical sensation and added, "But I've never heard of it happening to an adult. Most likely the regeneration can only happen during adolescence."

Vincha nodded and stroked her cropped hair. Galinak broke the awkward silence.

"Are you going to finish the eel?" he pointed at both our plates. "They get poisonous once they're cold, and it would be a shame to throw good food away."

Without a word both of us handed our plates to Galinak.

"I guess we all have similar stories, every one of the tattooed," said Vincha softly.

I turned back to her and nodded. "For me it wasn't so bad," I said, feeling I should strengthen the bond I was slowly establishing with Vincha, in order to encourage her to continue with her story. "I was . . . I am from a well-off family, and Wilderners aside, the purges were already tapering off when my marks emerged. My family protected me." I looked straight at Vincha, thinking, *The way you protect your own*, but she didn't catch my eye.

"My mother tried to kill me when I was born," said Galinak suddenly, "but I think she was just on a bad Skint trip or something. Both of my parents were marked, so their fear was that I would be born, you know, a naturalist."

This time I wasn't sure whether he was bluffing or not, so I just shrugged and focussed my attention back to Vincha. "So the boy ends up here, and . . . ?"

"Hold your trigger, soldier," she said with a smirk. "You paid well and good to hear the story, so I'll tell it to you as it was told to me. When you reach my age, you learn to appreciate the slow things. Like Galinak over there."

Galinak grunted something rude under his breath and busied himself picking eel skin from between his teeth.

"When I came back from the Valley, I went cold natural," continued Vincha, "unplugged, vegan, call it whatever you like. As soon as I got over the craving sickness I went to the boy's village, to see what happened to his family. Even though I was without any augs, they shot at me. If you think they'll get used to us in time you're wrong, Twinkle Eyes. It's the same in all the outlying villages: some towns are dangerous, no matter what religion they follow. Makes me wonder how many of us got butchered out there just for having been marked."

"And how many died for having a simple skin rash." I nodded, trying to nudge her back to the story.

"And for a bunch of zealous religious freaks preaching the *Prophet Reborn* and trying to go back to the pure old ways, they sure packed some nice, modern weapons, if you get my drift. They don't mind that part at all, never did. Anyway, I didn't give up and finally caught up with this Eithan fella. He wasn't very cooperative at first, downright hostile, to be honest, but"—her eyes glinted mischievously—"I have ways of endearing myself to young men, with or without augs."

"You broke his ribs, didn't ya?" said Galinak, smacking his fist to his palm for effect.

Vincha shrugged, but her smile broadened. "I made him talk, shall we say, in various pitches of voice, and in the end he told me what I wanted to know. Even with the boy gone, the gossip was too much. Fahid's wedding was called off a half a year after Rafik left, the village spat the Banishras out." She spat on the floor to emphasise the point. "Bunch of backwater rust arses."

"Did Eithan ask about his friend's fate?" I asked.

"Not in the beginning, but before I left he asked me if I knew how Rafik was faring. I told him the truth. Eithan just shook his head and said, 'No, he is alive, I would know if he was dead.' I thought it was an odd statement, but I couldn't stay long enough to talk to him further since there was already a manhunt after me. I thought if I lingered any longer I might overstay my welcome."

"I would have stayed." Galinak's smile was full of eel and bad intentions.

"And that's why your skull is fractured in so many places.

Half of your brain leaks away in those rare moments when you shower, dear."

They began exchanging insults again, like bored children in the back of a cart.

"Vincha. The story!" I snapped. "Tell it your way, but tell it, rust."

That, for some reason, stopped their bickering. They glared at me for a moment, then burst out laughing.

"You know, you're cute when you're angry, Twinkle Eyes." Vincha reached over and ran her fingers softly down my cheek. "Don't worry, little cub," she purred, seeing me blush. "I don't think you have the strength or the stamina, to be honest." Galinak chortled in amusement.

They went back to their bickering and I watched the two lethal warriors trade insults like misbehaved children until I could bear it no more. My palm hit the wooden table and got their attention. I felt like an admonishing parent when I bellowed "Can you *please* tell me what happened to Rafik?"

I guess I said the magic word, because finally she did.

16

It took ten days to reach Newport, nicknamed Trucker's Heaven, a city Rafik had heard of but never truly believed he would ever visit. Under any other circumstances Rafik would have been ecstatic at the prospect of travelling so far, but when they caught their first glimpse of Newport he felt only anxiety. They were tired, dirty, and aching from the tough ride, and the rationing of supplies meant Rafik always felt either hungry or thirsty or both. With each passing mile the prospect of ever making it back home seemed more and more like wishful thinking.

On the second and third nights of their journey they stopped and bartered for supplies in two small hamlets. Rafik was ushered into a barn and was not allowed to go outside or speak to anyone, and as soon as the sun was up they moved on. The rest of the nights, they roughed it in the wilderness, pitching a make-shift tent off the road. To save time, they did not try to catch game or even cook on an open fire for fear of bandits. For obvious reasons, they did not purchase supplies in the village for a long journey; they had only taken whatever they could from Rafik's home. As a result, for several days their rations consisted of stale bread, smoked sausages, and hard cheese, which stank so badly Rafik gagged with each bite he took.

He suffered from hundreds of itching ant bites, and he spent the travel time wishing for a long hot bath and a soft cushion to rest his aching backside on. Worst of all was the terrible itch he felt in his bandaged hand, but his brother strictly forbade him from unwrapping the linen and even cuffed him over the head when he caught Rafik trying.

When they were younger, the two brothers used to play pretend games where they travelled together, defeated enemies, and discovered new lands. But it was obvious that Fahid was not enjoying the reality of this particular adventure. He never let go of his gun, obsessively cleaning it or counting and recounting his bullets. Worse, he did not join Simon and Rafik in prayer, excusing himself with the need to take care of the pony when it was obvious he easily could have tied it to a tree and joined them.

Simon and Fahid took turns guarding their little camp at night. The lack of proper sleep made them tired and irritable during the day, yet they flatly refused to share their burden with Rafik. Every time they exchanged words or even glances, Rafik could feel the resentment in his brother's eyes. It was not the trip Rafik had imagined when he'd daydreamed about exploring beyond the village's fields.

On the seventh day they met two woodcutters who traded a crude but sharp hand ax for a leather pouch and a cloth tunic, and agreed to share food around a tiny bonfire. They were a father and son, both unbelievably strong and incredibly drunk but otherwise friendly and knowledgeable about the way of the land. The son had a wooden flute and knew a few tunes, many of which Rafik had never heard before, but mainly the pair chose to entertain them with stories of the skirmishes and close calls they'd had with a savage local gang of bandits who robbed and murdered their victims, then made clothes from their skin and goblets from their hollowed skulls. That night, Rafik had trouble falling asleep.

On the eighth day they reached what the woodcutters called the Smooth Road, which used to connect Newport with another city that was now gone and forgotten. The Smooth Road was wider than anything Rafik had ever seen but nothing like its name implied. Its hard surface was so full of potholes that Rafik could not fathom why it was called smooth at all. From there on traffic became more frequent, even though they were approaching Newport from the forest side, which was supposed to be relatively untravelled. Every so often, four- and six-wheeled trucks passed them noisily, throwing dirt and raising dust and scaring their tired, old pony. A few truckers honked their horns or waved from their high seats, but most ignored them completely, leaving them wheezing amid black exhaust fumes and dust. None of the truckers stopped to trade, rightly assuming that so close to Newport, the three had nothing left to barter with.

The dust and pollution that lay over the valley were so thick it took Rafik a while to notice Newport sprawled in the valley below them. It was the biggest *thing* he had ever seen in his entire life. It seemed as if the thousands of buildings were part of a single mythical creature, a hundred times larger than his own village.

Newport had no protective walls. Instead, many roads led into its centre, like the tentacles of a giant beast. Simon explained as a matter of warning that everyone was welcome in Newport as long as you had coin to spend and weapons to protect your wares. Newport was a den of criminals, but the supplies and weapons it sold were crucial to the survival of Rafik's village and the other communities of the west.

As the made their way to the city, they caught a glimpse of the shimmering Tarakan highway. Simon explained that this was a road built by the Tarakan infidels to connect their nefarious cities. Only a few of these roads survived the Catastrophe intact. Rafik heard his father once comment that the Tarakan infidels' cities were so large they filled the horizon, reached the stars above, and were filled to the brim with the most hideous and unimaginable sins. He didn't really believe such a thing could exist until he saw Newport.

Truck merchants visited their village about once a month, or more during the harvest seasons and festivals, but only a handful of people from Rafik's village ever travelled to Newport, and none of them had done so more than once in their lifetime. *When I go back home,* Rafik thought, *Eithan will be so jealous.* He would beg Rafik to tell him every little detail of his adventure, with the grand finale being the tale of the curse being lifted. Eithan would apologize for throwing the stones at him, and Rafik would let his friend grovel and beg for forgiveness, but in the end, they would become blood brothers again. Rafik blinked away tears and quickly wiped his eyes with his bandaged hand.

Two nights before, when Fahid was not paying attention, Rafik had carefully loosened the blackened cloth bandages and took a peek at his fingers. If anything, the markings seemed to have grown larger. The skin on his hand was still whiter than the rest of his body and it tingled and itched. As they made their way towards Newport, Rafik began tugging nervously at the linen cloth until Fahid noticed and cuffed him on the back of his head again.

After that it took some time before Rafik dared to glance at his brother, who was sitting rigidly, staring wide-eyed at their destination. It was Fahid's first time in Newport, too, and probably his last. Rafik clenched his bandaged hand into a tight fist inside the dirty cloth. *There is a cure—there must be.*

Truck merchants made a living going from town to village, selling and buying whatever was available. Every time a truck arrived at Rafik's village the merchant would stop a few hundred yards away and signal with his horn. The guards would approach, and if everything looked safe the merchant would be let into the village. Women would hide in their houses while men would come out to the centre of the village and look as menacing as possible. It was important to show force, not only to lower prices but also because many truck merchants cooperated with bandits as a way of buying passage and protection, often selling vital information about a village's defences. Once business was concluded, men and even boys Rafik's age would carry merchandise back and forth from the truck.

When he was younger, Rafik was always amazed at the size and bulk of the trucks. They were immense and scary looking. Cnaan said it would take more horses than his village could gather to move a fully loaded truck, yet the merchant would simply get into it and the truck would move all by itself. On several occasions Eithan tried to explain about the dark magic of the truck's heart, called *engine,* but Rafik was almost sure his blood brother was making this up.

As their cart approached Newport and their road merged into an even wider one, he realised that the trucks that parked outside his village were small in comparison to the ones he saw now. When he finally came into the last stretch before Newport he saw a SuperTruck for the first time, a mammoth of steel that travelled on Tarakan highways at unimaginable speeds. The thirty-wheeler dwarfed all the other vehicles around it. Each of its wheels was bigger than their own wooden cart, pony and all.

They were forced to move off road as the vehicle rumbled past. Roughly the same shape and size, the SuperTrucks differed in almost every other aspect including colour, and the number of naked women painted on their exteriors. Rafik had never seen a drawing of a naked woman before, although once he peeked at his bathing sister, and perhaps that was why he was cursed now. He tried to avert his gaze from the drawings every time a truck rumbled past, but his eyes had an uncanny knack of finding their way back to things he was not supposed to look at.

Slowly the city emerged around them. At the end of the long stretch of road they reached a roadblock manned by a dozen heavily armed men. Fahid gripped his gun with both hands, but Simon told him these men were aligned with the truckers guild. Their job was to inspect and collect tax and then direct trucks to designated parking areas. As it happened, they were in luck; the leader of the men was from a village to the southwest of Simon's own village, and he had a soft spot for Wildeners, as he called them. He let them through for only a small amount of coin and gave them directions to a tavern called the Round Wheel, which he promised had an adjacent stable and lice-free beds.

The tavern was a formidable three-story wooden house but the stable looked and smelled as if it had not been cleaned in weeks. Simon went inside and haggled with the owner for a long time, and when he came back outside he was in a foul mood, grumbling that one night's stay cost enough coin to feed his family for a fortnight. That struck Rafik as odd; he imagined lifting the curse would take longer than one day. Maybe he'd get an ointment to rub on his fingers and then they could go home. Simon had to persuade and eventually threaten Fahid to holster his weapon before they walked out onto the street.

"You'll get us all killed, boy. In the name of the Prophet Reborn, try to calm yourself."

"These infidels have no honour. We must be ready," argued his older brother, but he eventually relented and hid the pistol under his garments.

It was midday, and Rafik wanted to pray before they left the Round Wheel, but Simon said there was no time for that, they needed to be back in the tavern before dark.

"This place is not like your village or mine, Rafik," he explained. "The guild's men are concerned with taxing you but not protecting the peace unless it is in their interest. We must not be caught out during darkness, or we might attract all manner of trouble."

It sounded reasonable, but still, there had been a lot of missed prayers, and Rafik was beginning to suspect his uncle was perhaps not as devoted to the Prophet Reborn as he should be. It was more than a bit unfair, since Rafik was the one who was cursed, and he needed prayer now more than ever.

When they were done with cleaning and feeding the pony, Rafik tried to argue again about the prayer, but Fahid snapped at him to shut up.

Rafik was positioned yet again between the two grown-ups and was ordered to walk between them, and keep his mouth shut and his bandaged hand in his pocket.

Soon all thoughts of prayer were gone from his mind as they made their way through the biggest crowd Rafik had ever seen. Everyone was armed, even the women. The second thing that struck Rafik regarding the people of Newport was their hair. Some men had hair as long as a woman's, and many of the women had hair as short as a man's. To Rafik, this fact alone was astonishing, and he caught his brother staring as well.

The streets were wide but covered with potholes full of dark, foul-smelling water. Most people walked, but every once in a while, a truck would drive through the crowd, which parted expertly, as people stepped to the side so as not to get run over or sprayed with muck.

"Just stay calm, both of you," Simon said quietly. "If I'm right, the place shouldn't be far from here."

The Prophet Reborn must have been angry at his uncle, because they had to ask people for directions and backtrack several times, but eventually they reached a door with a sign above it saying "Dominique's Bar." The name "Dominique" flashed red every so often but her last name stayed dark all the time.

"Follow me and . . . well . . . just keep close," Simon ordered and pushed open the door. They stepped into a kind of shop. As they walked in a group of men were laughing loudly, and one of them got up and immediately fell over for no apparent reason, which made everyone else laugh even harder. More than a few of the men turned and glared at them menacingly.

"Stay close and don't drink anything," warned Simon. "And in the name of God and the Prophet Reborn, put away that gun, Fahid. You are making people nervous."

Simon led them slowly through the room. People were standing or sitting, but every single one of them was drinking from a cup or a mug, which struck Rafik as odd. There was also a strange, rhythmic music emanating from nowhere and everywhere at once, but Rafik could not see any bards or musical instruments, so he assumed the musicians were upstairs or in the basement, which seemed a very strange place to put them. Rafik's village tolerated travelling bards, and they were allowed to sing and play to the men of the village and entertain them with news and stories from the world. Rafik and Eithan were fascinated by them and never failed to secure a secret vantage point from where they could enjoy the show. The biggest troupe that visited in Rafik's lifetime consisted of four musicians, and they came only once and had to leave in a hurry after one of them was caught talking to a woman. There must have been at least six or seven of them here, concluded Rafik, yet his brother and uncle didn't seem to pay any attention.

They walked farther inside. Rafik wondered if this was a den for Tarakan sinners, like the ones mentioned in the holy scripts sixteen times, a place that sold poisoned water, and all who drank from it would burn in hell for all eternity.

"I am looking for Khan Carr," Simon said to a burly man. The man turned and pointed sluggishly towards a table at the back corner, where a large group of men sat, surrounded by smoke and plenty of upturned jugs. When they approached the table, two of the men got up and moved towards them. Words were exchanged, bodies were patted, and weapons put aside for safe-keeping, but the situation was not tense, since a shaggy-looking man at the table recognised Simon.

"Banishla," he bellowed and moved away from the table to hug Rafik's uncle. The man was thin, almost gaunt, with short-cropped grey hair and black eyes that missed nothing. He wore a black tunic stained with grease and a pair of trousers like most truckers wore, made of a rough-looking blue material. His boots were the shiniest Rafik had ever seen.

"Banish*ra*," Rafik heard Simon mumble under his breath.

The man waved dismissively, "How are you, old dog? How's your dear brother, eh? We have to drink to his life and health."

"These are my nephews, Fahid and Rafik, sons of Sadre Banishra. Boys, this is Khan Carr, a *dear* friend of your father."

Khan Carr shook hands with Fahid and added a pat to Rafik's head. He stank of smoke and other less recognisable but equally repulsive odours.

"Fine boys, from a fine man," he declared with what Rafik thought was not a sincere voice, yet Fahid stuck out his chest with pride and stood a little taller.

"Master Carr," Simon began, looking nervously at the guards surrounding them.

"Call me Khan, my friend," Khan slapped Simon on his shoulder.

"As you wish . . ." Simon's unease was apparent.

"Sit down, have a drink with me, we'll get something for the boys to eat? They look hungry."

"Khan, I need to talk to you, *privately*," Simon said firmly, and stood his ground.

The small man paused for a few heartbeats, then his manner changed and he said quietly, "I see that you did not come here to sample my fine brews and reminisce. This is business, yes?" He glanced at the two brothers. "Or perhaps it is about something else altogether? Fine, follow me, then."

He led the three of them to a small room, which was less noisy and, just briefly, less smoky. Only one other man came into the room with them. Tall and lean, he had a short greying beard, which did not cover the ugly scar on his left cheek, and he carried a large handgun at his belt. He took his place by the door and focused his stare at a point on the far wall.

Khan produced a black pipe from his pocket, lit it with a silver fire maker, and blew stinking smoke from his mouth and nostrils. Several chairs and tables of various sizes were placed in the room without any logical design and after being prompted by Khan everyone sat down. Rafik sat on one of the smaller stools.

"I need your help, Khan," Simon said as soon as the door was closed. "Sadre needs your help."

Khan blew more smoke from his mouth and said, "What is it?" in a dry, calculating voice.

Simon turned to Rafik. "Show him your hand."

Hesitantly, Rafik took the bandage off.

Khan blew another puff of smoke, thankfully to the side this time, before placing the still-smoking pipe gently on a side table.

"Come closer, son," he ordered, but not unkindly. "Do not be afraid. I owe your father and uncle much and will not harm you."

Rafik walked cautiously closer, without raising his eyes from the floor, and thrust his hand forward. Only then did he dare look at the man's face.

Khan's eyes went wide. He swore under his breath and grasped Rafik's hand, spreading Rafik's fingers wide and staring at the markings for a long time. He kept breathing in and out and mumbling to himself so softly that even Rafik could not understand what he was saying.

Eventually Khan let go of his hand, and Rafik snatched it back and hid it in his tunic pocket.

"You understand our problem, yes?" Simon asked gently.

"Perhaps," Khan answered carefully, "you should spell it out for me, so we can avoid . . . any misunderstandings."

Rafik found his voice. "My father said that you could help me—that you could cure me." He slipped his hand from his pocket again and waved it in the air.

"Is that what you were told?" Khan asked, glancing sideways at Simon and Fahid. "That I could cure you?"

"Well? Can you, or can't you?" Rafik asked boldly but added in a softer tone, "I really want to go home. Please . . ."

Khan shook his head, a thin, sad smile touching his lips. He took his time fetching and relighting the pipe and placing it in his mouth again. The room remained quiet. After several puffs of smoke he said, "I can help you, Rafik, son of Sadre, and I know a few people who could help you even more. But I cannot *cure* you from this . . . condition of yours. No one can."

"We just want him to be safe," Fahid said, "to be—" he hesitated, glancing at his younger brother "—with his own kind."

"Is that what you want?" Khan got up and paced the room slowly.

The man near the door kept looking at Khan, as if waiting for some kind of a signal.

"How much, then?" asked Khan.

"How much what?" asked Simon.

Fahid jumped to his feet. "My father told me what he did for you," he said angrily, "and you yourself admitted that you owe a blood debt to my family. Yet you ask us to pay you for doing a decent thing. You are no friend of ours!"

"Fahid," Simon cautioned, as the man at the door began moving forward with obvious intent and was stopped only by a small hand gesture from Khan.

Khan turned his back to Fahid and walked to a cabinet. He opened the glass doors and came back to the table holding a bottle in one hand and three beautifully crafted small glass cups in the other. Khan carefully poured dark liquid from the bottle into the small cups and brought them to Simon and Fahid.

Fahid refused his glass, shaking his head, but their uncle accepted it, holding it tentatively in his hand. Khan bent down and picked up his own glass.

"You misunderstood me, Fahid," Khan said. "When I asked 'how much,' I meant it as 'How much do you want for the boy?'"

There was a stunned silence in the room.

Simon broke it with an almost inaudible "What do you mean?"

"I am no expert, but the markings on the boy's hand indicate that he is a—" he paused, then he shrugged and continued "—rare breed . . . and a *very* coveted one. All of the tattooed have powers. Some are stronger, some are quicker, but, if I am right, none of them can do what this boy could."

He turned to Rafik. "Do you have any other tattoos on your body?"

Rafik shook his head.

"Are you sure? I'll check later, you know."

"No, only on my fingers. My father chopped them off with an ax but they grew back and—"

"Shut up, Rafik," Fahid snapped.

Khan scratched his chin. "Interesting." He turned back to Fahid, measuring every word. "If what your brother says is true, he is worth hard coin. If it was not for my debt to your family, I would have let you walk out of here empty-handed and drink many toasts to your stupidity."

"We just want to get him to somewhere safe," Fahid said again, fidgeting nervously.

"Oh, he will be very safe, your little brother, I can vouch for that, and well provided for, and educated as well, in all manners of fields. Now about his price . . ."

"We do not want your coin, only your word of promise," Fahid hissed before Simon could say anything else.

"I'll tell you what." Khan picked up a glass cup again and presented it to Fahid. "I will give you my solemn oath that I'll take care of your brother if you drink with me."

Fahid looked at the small glass for what seemed to be an eternity. Rafik was sure his devout brother would refuse to sin, but eventually Fahid reached out and accepted the glass.

"In one go," said Khan, smiling.

"May God and the Prophet Reborn forgive me," Fahid murmured, and all three drank at once.

Rafik guessed his brother was too nervous and drank the water the wrong way because he became very red and began coughing and wheezing. Simon seemed to be fine, though. Khan and the other man laughed unpleasantly and suddenly there was a pistol in Khan's hand. Rafik saw his uncle's face turn white. Fahid tried to react but could only cough and wheeze. Rafik wanted to move, shout something, distract Khan, kick his legs from under him, or beg for mercy, but it was as if his legs were made of stone.

He could only gape in horror as Khan grasped his brother with one hand and pushed the gun to Fahid's forehead with the other.

"I am not normally accused of such things as honesty," he said calmly. "One does not stay in business with such a reputation. You, on the other hand, are a fool. A brave fool, perhaps, but a fool nonetheless, and in this town, you'd be a dead fool before the night is out. I should just kill you here and now and save you the trouble of growing up just to be killed by people who outsmart you." Khan waved the pistol in front of Fahid's bulging eyes. "But . . . I owe your father my life, and so instead I'll give you this." He lowered the weapon, turned it expertly in his hand and shoved it, butt first, into Fahid's trembling hands.

"Standard ammo, seven in a clip," he said as he released the young man and patted his shoulder paternally. "I'll give you some extra ammunition before you go, say a hundred bullets? Do we have a deal?"

Fahid gulped, and Khan clapped his hands. "What shall I do with you, boy? Driving such a hard bargain, I tell you what, I'll throw in a bag of black linen, and a barrel of my best mead! Yes, I know you are not allowed to drink, but you could trade it with someone who does. Once someone drinks my mead he never wants to drink anything else, so make sure you mention where it came from. What say you? Do we have a deal?"

Fahid looked at the gun in his hand, still red in the face, and nodded without a word.

"Good." Khan landed a heavy slap on Fahid's shoulder and turned to Simon. "We are done here. Tell your brother I honoured my debt, but don't spread any tales. If people knew I gave you an honest trade my reputation in this town would be ruined." He laughed again and did not wait for Simon to answer. "Have you met Dominique yet? She'll take care of you lads. Go downstairs and get some food. The kitchen is still open." He clapped his hands again and smiled to himself. "It's always open here."

They shuffled out of the room and went downstairs, where they ate the greasiest meal Rafik had ever tasted. It was glorious and disgusting at the same time, but he couldn't eat much because he was fighting waves of rising panic. Again and again he heard Khan's words in his mind: "I cannot *cure* you. No one can."

He was not going home.

17

Rafik watched as the symbols on his fingers stretched and grew in front of his eyes, until he fell into them, enveloped by darkness. For a brief moment, he lay suspended in warm nothingness, but soon he heard soft, distant voices whispering. He could not make out what they were saying, but it didn't bother him. He was comfortable, warm, and safe. The dots of light, which appeared before him in the darkness, drew his attention.

They grew into symbols, eventually becoming large enough for him to see their shapes clearly. Many reminded Rafik of his own tattoos, featuring crescent moons and dots, while others were completely different. He recognised numbers on a few symbols while others were completely alien. Once the wall of symbols eclipsed his horizon Rafik stopped falling and lay suspended, watching, mesmerized. It reminded him of an army of ants he and Eithan once discovered when digging in the garden of his home. The symbols kept moving next to and over each other, shuffling positions, rising and falling, disappearing as other symbols moved to the fore and reappeared elsewhere.

Rafik couldn't take his eyes off the symbols. He felt a strong desire to touch them, to move them around, and a growing, inexplicable urge to organize them into a pattern. He somehow knew that *this* symbol should stand next to *that* one and the *next* one should go *there*.

He heard voices again, up above him, from far away.

"Don't wake him up."

"We can't just leave him here like this."

"It won't make it any easier. Look at him, he is now at peace."

A deeper voice said, "You shouldn't have given him the spiked goat milk. We should have had the chance to say good-bye."

"It is for the best—"

A more familiar voice interjected angrily, "If you ever hurt him, I hope I never find out about it, because I will kill you."

"There aren't many who have threatened me and are still breathing, but I assure you I have no intentions of hur—"

Rafik drew away from the voices; they were spoken from such a distance they could have been from a different world. Perhaps the voices were a dream, and the symbols before him were the only reality. Besides, he'd just realised something very exciting: there *was* a pattern hidden among the symbols. You only had to stop *that one* and move *this one* and cancel *this line here*. Rafik watched his hand stretch and extend to an impossible length, towards the wall of moving symbols. He couldn't see his own fingers, but he was not afraid.

This is what is supposed to happen, this is how it should feel.

His hand plunged into the symbols, and Rafik discovered he could now stop some of them in their tracks. He exposed part of the pattern by holding down specific symbols with his fingers, but whenever he would take hold of one symbol the others began moving again, and since the symbols all had different patterns of movement he kept losing the pattern. Only after what seemed to be an eternity, Rafik discovered the symbols would stay in their places if he *concentrated* just enough on keeping them where he wanted them. It took him a while longer to figure out how to maintain control over several symbols at once. The more he concentrated, the better his control over a growing number of symbols became. He managed two symbols with relative ease, then three, then five, but soon after he realised it was fruitless. There were thousands of moving symbols in front of him, and he could stop only several at once. Rafik withdrew his hand, feeling disappointed. He could sense the pattern, but he could not control a large enough amount of symbols to reveal it. Feeling suddenly very tired, Rafik floated slowly upwards, away from the wall of symbols and towards the light above him.

The growl of a heavy engine and a horrendous blast from a passing truck's horn startled Rafik from a very deep sleep. He found himself lying on a mat in a small room, naked under a thin linen sheet. His clothes were neatly folded on a sheepskin cushion, which matched the pillow under his head. At a glance, he saw several mats spread out evenly in the room, but they were unoccupied. Rafik's heart lurched in his chest as he realised his brother and uncle were not with him. The only other person in the room was the scary-looking man who guarded Khan before and was now sitting on a stool with his back resting up against the wall. Upon seeing Rafik sit up the man became fully alert, got up from the stool, and shoved the pistol he was cleaning into his belt. "Finally," he said, "I tried to wake you several times but you were out like a burned fuse."

"Where are my brother and my uncle?" Rafik asked, his heart filled with dread.

"They went out to shop for stuff, they'll be back soon," the man said, but something in his eyes told Rafik he was lying.

"I want to see them." Rafik jumped up and started to put on his clothes. He had to stop himself from bursting into tears. He remembered pleading with his brother to take him home with them, but Fahid kept promising they would come back for him when he was cured. But there was no cure. That was what Khan had said. Rafik didn't remember who gave him the cup of sweetened goat milk, but his last memory was quenching his thirst with it. Now his uncle and brother were gone.

He had to run after them; they had to take him home. There was no cure, so there was no need for him to stay here with the man who puffed smoke from his mouth and drank cursed water and threatened his brother with a pistol. He would keep his hand in his pocket the whole time, he would never bring it out, he'd promise them. Perhaps his father could chop his fingers off again—maybe they wouldn't grow back this time.

"You're supposed to wait here," the guard said. "Khan will be here soon."

Rafik bolted towards the door.

"Hey, hey, hey!" The guard moved to intercept him with cat-like speed, and he caught Rafik's arm. But he underestimated Rafik, who was fed by the sheer terror of abandonment. The boy lashed out with all his might at the guard's groin. The man swore in a surprised, tightly choked voice and folded over, releasing his grip on Rafik as he toppled over onto the stool behind him.

Rafik made it through the door and down a short corridor when Khan appeared in front of him, grabbed him with both hands, and dragged him kicking and screaming back to the room. The guard was still there and was not looking happy, but Khan didn't pay him any attention. He plonked Rafik firmly on a stool, pulled over a second one using his leg, and sat himself down, letting out a heavy sigh.

"Look at me, boy," he demanded.

"I want my brother, I want my uncle," Rafik wailed.

Khan grabbed Rafik's chin roughly, "I said *look at me*. Now tell me, how old are you?" Khan's eyes were almost night-dark and his breath stank.

"I'm twelve." Rafik's voice trembled, "Where are—"

Khan leaned forward and dug bony fingers into Rafik's cheeks. "Shut up and listen," he said. "When I was your age I killed my old man. Do you believe me? I see in your eyes that you do. Good, now pay attention: I'm a bad guy, I am *the* bad guy, do you understand what I'm saying? I'm the kind of man your mummy warned you about, and the good news is that I'm on *your* side.

I'm protecting you now, because I owe your father a favour and I promised your idiot brother that I'd take care of you." Khan released his grip and sat up, still looking at him intently. "Now, as I said, I'm a nasty, bad man, and I won't think twice about breaking my word, so don't do anything that will convince me not to be on your side, like trying to run away, do you understand? And stop crying. I have no use for tears."

"But where are my—"

"They're *gone*. They left you here with me and ran back to the backwards village you were unlucky enough to be born in. They left you because—and listen to me well and stop crying, because this is important—they left you because they do not *want you anymore*. Because if they brought you back home you would be hanged and quartered and burned, and so would they. They *abandoned* you here with me, and now I need to take care of you. From this day on I am your father, and your mother, and uncle and brother and whatever other extended family you might be stupid enough to miss, Rafik. Those fools are so backwards they do not realise what a blessing you are. You may not believe it now, but one day you will look at this as the happiest moment of your life. You can never go back to your village, ever. I can see you don't want to believe me, and perhaps you are already thinking about running back to the mud huts and the bearded fanatics there. But I'm going to stop you, not only because you wouldn't last two strides in *this* town before a big, fat trucker turned you into his love doll, but because when I find you—and have no doubt that I *will* find you—I will make you beg for the trucker. Understood?"

Rafik did not know what a love doll was, or what a fat trucker would do to him, but he understood the threatening tone clearly. He nodded, too afraid to speak, but Khan seemed satisfied.

"On the bright side, if we play our cards right, you and I are going to be rich and live a nice, comfortable life. Do as I say, and I'm going to take care of you, understand? Nod if you can't talk. Good. Now do you want some food? You need some food in you.

Martinn here will bring you some food, and you *will* eat it all and you will not leave this room unless I give you permission to do so, are we clear?"

"I want to go to the bathroom, and I want to wash," Rafik said suddenly, realising how many days it had been since his skin last felt fresh water.

"The shit shed is outside. Martinn will take you there. Be careful not to fall in. I'll bring up a basin and some soap. If you're good I'll take you to the bathhouse in a couple of days."

Rafik was taken to the shed outside, which was a hole in the ground boxed in by thin wooden planks. It was there that he discovered what had been left in the inside pocket of his tunic. It was the knife his brother had taken as a trophy from one of the bandits he'd killed. The sharp blade sprang in and out of its sheath with the pressing of a button. Rafik always envied Fahid for owning such a blade. He'd even stolen it once and played with it all afternoon, earning a hiding from his brother when he was discovered. Now he held the weapon in his hand and knew he would never see Fahid again.

But with this realisation, a certain calmness washed over him. This was the will of the Prophet Reborn. He was on an adventure, and in his hand he held a knife. When he came out of the shack the knife was hidden again.

Martinn gave Rafik permission to go and wash his hands and face in the basin rooms. Rafik opened one of the doors only to find the biggest man he ever saw, with a woman half his size crushed between him and the wall, her legs wrapped around the man's mighty waist. They were doing something Rafik had only ever heard about in whispers. He did not see much because the woman, in a feat of impressive flexibility, leaned over and slammed the door in his face, muttering, "See something you want, boy?"

Rafik completely forgot about washing himself as he ran back to his room, knelt down on his knees on the sticky floor, clasped his hands before him, closed his eyes, and prayed to the Prophet Reborn with all his might.

18

Rafik was not a stranger to routine. His life in the village was defined by a tight schedule made up of daily chores, prayers, school, housework, and designated playtime. His new life meant a new routine, filled with chores and errands from before sunrise until way after sundown. There was no playtime, nor did he have anyone to play with. The only part of his old life he stuck to with vigilance was his regimen of daily prayers.

After a while he lost count of the days. Khan came and went, sometimes for hours and sometimes for days, promising Rafik he was "looking for a good contact." He didn't come through with the promise to take Rafik to the bathhouse but Rafik managed with what he had; a bucket and lukewarm water.

Eventually even Martinn got bored guarding the boy and let him have the freedom of the place. Half a day later Rafik was already serving cursed water to customers, cleaning tables, and even collecting coins for Dominique, the heavyset woman who kept the rowdy truckers in order with a sharp word and occasionally a hearty slap. She was the fattest lady he had ever seen, but she displayed the pink flesh of her middle for all to see without shame. From the first moment they met, Dominique took a shine to Rafik and, despite working him constantly, she made sure he ate, sent him to sleep early, even washed and dried his clothes, and made sure he changed the bandages on his hand every day. After Rafik complained about the bandages, Dominique knitted a colourful glove to cover his tattooed hand, and made sure the boy wore it at all times. Rafik believed she was married to Khan, because she shared his bed at night and they fought constantly.

Truckers were a rough bunch, but mostly they treated Rafik well, calling him a "mutt" and "pup" and sometimes giving him what Dominique called "a lousy tip" in order to impress their women. Very soon he discovered the basement, where rows of wooden barrels were stacked. "This is how we make the drink we sell upstairs," Dominique answered when he asked what they were.

"It's an art form, kid, and I'm the artist. Make it the wrong way and people will go blind or die. Make it the right way and they will part with all their metal to get their hands on my products. And I ain't talking about these." She hefted at her huge breasts with both hands and laughed when Rafik blushed purple.

Rafik had the sense not to point out that Dominique herself was drinking at least as much as the customers. She was nice to him, for the most part, when she wasn't shouting or cursing or cuffing him over the head. She was as close to his mother as he could get, so he kept quiet and tried to be as helpful as possible.

Mornings were the hardest. He missed home terribly, and many times he thought of running, yet he dared not, remembering Khan's words. He would not last long alone in the city, and even if he somehow made it back, in his heart he knew what it would mean: his dad, the ax, the stones . . . he was cursed, he had been sent away by his own family and shunned by his friends. They did not want him anymore. When he thought about that, tears would fill his eyes, and he would find a dark corner and choke his misery into his stained sleeves.

His dreams on the other hand, were a sharp contrast to his harsh reality. They were filled with images of twinkling, ever-changing symbols. He was now able to hold a dozen of them at once, still a fraction of the control he knew he needed to see the hidden patterns. Even when awake, Rafik was seeing symbols and patterns everywhere he turned; they were in the circles of the wheels on the trucks he saw through the window, in the different types of cups in the area downstairs called the bar, and even in the shapes of buttons sewed onto the clothes the truckers wore. He looked at everything differently, watching shapes, categorizing them, lining them up in his mind, joining them together, manipulating them, and exploring possibilities. He didn't know why he was doing it, but it soothed him and kept his tears at bay, most of the time.

After what seemed to Rafik like an eternity, but was probably only a month, he was ordered to put on fresh clothes, and taken on a trip around Newport by Khan and Martinn. It was an even more fascinating place the second time around, because now he saw shapes and patterns everywhere he looked. Many parts of the city were in ruins, but some buildings were so high they had more stories than Rafik could count. When they climbed over hills made of broken stones, Martinn hoisted Rafik on his shoulders, the way Rafik's father used to do when he was back home. It made him happy and sad at the same time, and Rafik was glad when they reached the top of the hill and Martinn let him down. Soon, they passed a large metal tower, which dwarfed the guard tower in his village ten times over. Engraved on one side of the tower was a symbol that was exactly like one that Rafik remembered from his dreams; five circles intertwined, with three dots in the centre. It was the first time he saw such a symbol while he was awake, and the realisation filled him with excitement.

"What is that?" he pointed. "That symbol over there?"

"This?" Khan said, squinting. "I don't know what it means; it's a symbol in the Tarakan language."

"What is Tarakan?" Rafik asked. He kept hearing this word.

Even the music in the bar was coming out of a small, yet surprisingly loud, Tarakan device.

"You mean you don't know about the Tarkanians?" Khan looked genuinely surprised.

"Arse rusts, that's what they were," muttered Martinn, but Khan ignored him. "They were an evil race who used to live here but now they're gone."

"What happened to them?"

"Dead," Martinn replied, "and good riddance." He spat on the ground in the direction of the tower.

"We had a war with them," said Khan, "and before they lost, they caused the Catastrophe."

"Why did we fight them?"

"Because the Tarkanians enslaved humans, made us do all their work."

"Like Dominique makes me do stuff?" asked Rafik, sensing the comment would be funny. It worked—both men laughed, and Khan ruffled Rafik's growing hair. "The woman asks nicely, my boy. You are just wise enough to obey all her requests. I should learn from you. But no, the rumors were that the Tarkanians used the human slaves' bodies for their weird experiments and even food."

Rafik shuddered.

Martinn was still chuckling when he said, "Well, the Tarkanians are gone now, and we are free."

"But they left us a legacy," continued Khan, as they began climbing another rubble hill. He pointed at the remains of the buildings around them, "Their architecture, their cities, buildings, and roads, but most important: the remains of their technology, Tarakan devices that still work even though we have no idea how. Of course," he said, patting Rafik lightly on the shoulder, "they also left us people like you."

"Like me? What do you mean? I'm *not* a Tarkanian," he said.

"We are going to find out what you are soon enough," Khan answered, just as Martinn announced, "We're here."

They were on top of an enormous hill made of rubble, or perhaps it was a ruined tower, Rafik couldn't tell. There was a large, redbrick building before them. Although it was not tall by Newport standards, it was still taller and wider than anything in Rafik's village. They were standing high enough to be on the same level as the top floor. It was an exhilarating height.

Even from far away the sound emanating from inside the building was loud. There were harsh and fast drumbeats repeated again and again in a simple pattern, and from somewhere inside came the distinct sound of a brawl in full swing. Rafik noticed there were many cracks in the walls and none of the windows had glass.

The two men checked their pistols and looked at each other.

Khan turned to Rafik and looked him straight in the eye. "This guy we're going to see, Jakov, he had an . . . accident." He stalled, looking for words, then said with a shrug, "Some parts of his body are replaced by metal, okay? Don't be scared, I just want him to have a look at you."

Rafik nodded. Compared to being told you might be a member of an evil race who caused the destruction of the world, seeing a man made of metal sounded like a blessed distraction.

"You're to call me Uncle, okay? You understand me? Do exactly what I tell you and nothing else. If I tell you to run, run; if I tell you to dive to the floor, you do just that, yes?"

Rafik nodded again.

"Good. Now let's go."

They made their way in silence down the hill of rubble towards the building.

More than a dozen men and a few women were sitting idly outside. With their weapons and wild, unkempt look, they reminded Rafik of the bandits who had attacked his village the previous spring, though they were a bit better dressed, mostly in leather or sheepskin, and equipped with guns instead of the rusty swords and wooden clubs. All were smoking or drinking, but they stopped what they were doing when they saw Khan, Rafik, and Martinn approach.

Rafik's attention was immediately drawn to the strange bicycles. In his village there were only two bicycles, one for the village elder and one used by the messenger, and they were much, much smaller than the ones he saw now. There were at least ten of these great bicycles standing in a neat row. Some were making a strange humming noise all by themselves. Reluctantly Rafik followed Khan and Martinn away from the great bicycles, but when they turned the corner he was glad he did.

They saw two men in a clearing, each riding on a great bicycle, which somehow moved without any pedals. Both men held very large poles in one hand and maneouvered the great bicycles with the other. They were surrounded by large piles of stacked tires and a cheering crowd of spectators. The riders circled around a few times, then suddenly charged, levelling the poles down and passing each other at blinding speed. There was a large crack as the poles clashed, but the riders passed each other without anyone being hurt.

The crowd whooped, and even Khan grinned and said, "A fiver on the red-bearded fellow."

Martinn cocked his head, then nodded. "Done."

The men rode two more passes and cracked poles but didn't manage to hit one another. The red-bearded rider's pole snapped and was quickly replaced before the final pass, which left the other rider writhing in pain in a cloud of dust, as his vehicle skidded on the ground until it crashed into a pile of tires. The crowd cheered, and the red-bearded rider raised his pole in a victory salute. Martinn cursed under his breath, and Khan laughed.

They resumed walking, but after only a few dozen paces their way was blocked by four men and a woman, all brandishing weapons. The noise around them was deafening, and Rafik covered his ears with his hands and stopped paying attention to what was being said. Soon they were led inside. They walked through the lower level, filled with sprawling bodies engaged in all kinds of activities. Four guys were in the midst of a bloody fight, but no one tried to stop them. Rafik was drawn to the patterns on the side of their high boots. Martinn put a protective hand on Rafik's shoulder and drew him close. Soon they were climbing up, walking over hazardous looking wooden boards placed over the gaps where stairs had once been. Rafik counted the stairs between the holes and tried to find a pattern; it was a nice little game that occupied his mind all the way to the top floor. The music was not as loud as downstairs but still loud enough to be uncomfortable.

There were more people standing around a large open area, holding, checking, cleaning, comparing, or just playing with all kinds of weaponry. Khan, Martinn and Rafik walked past them towards a doorway at the far end of the floor, this one with an actual door in its frame. Two guards stood there, holding even larger guns and wearing more metal than anyone else. They wore distinctive black cloaks. One of the guards stepped forward.

"Tell Jakov that Khan Carr is here to see him, with the boy."

The guard nodded silently and kept watch as the other guard opened the door and stuck his head inside. After a brief, awkward pause, one guard said, "You and the boy go in, leave your weapons with your friend here."

Khan gave his pistol to Martinn without argument, but the guard who talked to them insisted on a search and found another pistol hidden in one of Khan's boots and a knife in the other. Khan apologized profusely, claiming he had forgotten all about "*those* little toys." The guard didn't look convinced, but he let them in. He didn't search Rafik—which was a blessing, because Rafik didn't want to give up his brother's knife to anyone. He snuck his hand in his pocket and gripped it hard. He did this every time he was afraid, which was often.

They walked into the next room where another pair of identically clad guards stood. The man called Jakov was sitting between them. Just looking at him made Rafik grip Fahid's knife even tighter than he had before. Master Issak's stern voice rang in his ears, joined by the voices of his father, brother, Eithan, and eventually his entire village, repeated again and again, in sermons, lessons, and prayers, warning Rafik from the greatest sin of all: *You shall not attach.*

If it was not for Khan's grip on the back of Rafik's neck he surely would have tried to run away. The entire left side of Jakov's face was hidden behind a grim-looking metal mask, with a protruding metallic eyepiece where his eye should have been. He wore a hood, which covered his head, and a plate of chest armour. Instead of a human left arm he had a metallic arm with seven fingers and two thumbs. The hand was picking and prodding at several weapons and other objects which were spread on the large table in front of him, and it kept going even when Jakov looked up at Khan and Rafik.

The room was large but filled with crates, barrels, and weapons to the point that there was not a lot of room to manoeuvre.

For some reason, the music from downstairs was louder in this room, and the floor was humming and shaking with the beat under Rafik's soft sandals.

"Ah, Khan," said Jakov in a raspy, metallic voice. Only the parts of his lips which were flesh twisted and moved as he spoke. "You came with the boy." He didn't offer them a seat, and all the while his metallic hand kept working on a pistol on the table.

"Hello again." Khan's smile was thin and brief. "Glad to see things are still well oiled." When Jakov did not reply, Khan turned to Rafik. "Show him your hand, *nephew*."

Rafik obliged. He released his grip on the knife inside his pocket as Khan propelled him forward until he stood so close to the man called Jakov that he could hear the soft whine of metal from his metallic arm. Hesitantly, Rafik pulled his hand out of his pocket and peeled Dominique's glove off with his other hand. Jakov leaned forward and took Rafik's hand in his, studying his fingers intently. After a while his metal hand stopped moving.

"Radja," he said softly, not lifting his eyes from Rafik's hand, "I can't hear myself think. Please ask our hosts *again* to quiet their damn noise, and make sure you are *polite* about it." Rafik heard heavy footsteps behind him and the opening and shutting of the door. Jakov released Rafik's hand and patted his head in what was obviously an unfamiliar gesture, then leaned back and nodded at Khan.

The metal arm disappeared briefly under the table and came up holding a bottle, A moment later, two small glasses appeared as well. "This is a rare one," Jakov said as his hand manoeuvred and poured. "Pre-Catastrophe. You would not believe how much metal I spent on only two crates, but it was worth it." The liquid settled in the small glass and Khan accepted it. The part of Jakov's face that was made of flesh twisted into a smile as he lifted his own glass. "Freedom, Metal," he announced, and then there was the sound of a shot, followed by a woman's shriek, which caused Khan to spill half his drink and swear. A series of shots followed, after which the music stopped abruptly.

"Much better," commented Jakov and with a quick toss, drained his glass through the corner of his mouth. Khan hastily followed suit with what was left in his own glass. Jakov poured them another round.

When the liquid was gulped and the glasses knocked resolutely down on the table Khan asked, "So, is my nephew here the real deal?"

"We shall see shortly," said Jakov. Again, his metal hand dove under the table and brought up a metal box, roughly the size of a hand. There were three holes on the side of the box, each roughly the size of a finger. Rafik was ordered to stand closer to Jakov, who turned his seat so he could face Rafik. His metal hand gripped the boy's shoulder as he brought himself even closer.

"Now, young man, I want you to put your fingers *here, here,* and *here.*"

With every *here* Jakov's human finger poined at a different hole and the metallic hand squeezed Rafik's shoulder lightly, with just enough pressure to cause discomfort, silently promising crushing pain if the boy did not comply.

Heart thumping in terror, Rafik placed his fingers where he was shown. The metallic hand released its grip on his shoulder. "Good, now sit down over here and relax," Jakov said. A guard slid a comfortable-looking chair over and guided Rafik with a gentle push to sit in it. Rafik tried to pull his fingers out of the box, but found that it was impossible. The metal grip on his shoulder was back. Jakov was standing too close for comfort.

"I *said* relax," said Jakov as he pressed several buttons on the lid of the box. "This will not hurt, *much*."

As he pressed the last button the box hummed, and Rafik felt a strong jolt of pain hitting his fingers and travelling up his arm. He must have screamed—he certainly heard something resembling his own voice—but it was as if he were screaming from a long distance away. He was somewhere else, somewhere safe, enveloped by darkness and staring into emptiness, happy to be away from the people and the noise. They were all bad people, he knew, even Khan, even Dominique—they were like the Tarakan infidels he was warned about, and Jakov was the worst of them. He was a metal man. *The man who lets metal be a part of him is cursed for eternity. He and all of his shall perish in holy fire.*

In the darkness, shapes and symbols began to form. They were closer than the symbols in his dreams, much less numerous and all drawn in a faint greyish colour. The symbols moved sluggishly around and in obvious patterns. Rafik stopped one symbol from moving the wrong way before he realised what he was doing. Then he did it with another symbol, and another, again and again. The pattern was so evident that Rafik almost laughed. He quickly stopped the symbols to form half the pattern, and then, with a surge of inexplicable pride, he exposed the entire pattern. There was a soft buzzing sound and a flash of light, and he was suddenly in the room again, with his fingers out of the box.

"I did it," he said excitedly, "I solved the puzzle."

"Yes, you did." Jakov's half grin was as wide as it was unpleasant.

"Are you sure?" asked Khan. "It was only a couple of seconds. What do you mean, 'puzzle'? What did you see in there?"

Rafik was too confused to answer, but he heard Jakov say, "Yes, I'm sure, only his kind can do this, anyone else gets a mighty jolt, believe me. What you have here, *my friend*, is a genuine Puzzler."

Khan whooped and even clapped his hands, unable to contain his joy, but Jakov kept calm and turned back to the boy. "Tell me, Rafik, who is Khan to you?"

Rafik turned his head towards Khan and said, "He is my uncle."

"Really? Uncle?" Jakov's made a show of turning his gaze back and forth from boy to man. "Strange, you don't look alike at all. Even your skin colour is different."

"Uncle twice removed," Khan said quickly. "Or even three times. I don't know, my family's history is a bit . . . eh . . . complex, shall we say."

"Interesting. Well, I can take him off your hands for a fair price, my friend."

Khan shook his head vigorously at that. "No, no, no, I'm sorry I can't. I promised the boy's mother, you know how it is . . ."

Jakov leaned back in his chair. "Oh, well, of course. *Promised,* you say. Very important, a man's word, that is. I can get you connected with someone, then, how about that, twenty-five percent of the agreed purchase?"

Khan spread his hands wide, "I'm sorry Jakov, but the family is in debt and desperately need the coin. I could do fifteen."

Jakov's human face hardened as if it were the metal part. He leaned slowly forward and gently brushed some dirt from Rafik's shoulders. The boy was too scared to move away.

"Twenty-two, and you are making me look bad in front of my own men."

"Eight—nineteen is what I can do," said Khan hastily.

"Let's agree on a nice round twenty, shall we?"

Khan spat on his hand and thrusted it forward before realising he was offering to shake Jakov's metal hand. He dropped the hand to his lap and stuttered, "That's a deal, Jakov, thank you."

"Good man, good man." Jakov smiled without humour. "Why shake hands when we could drink to our success, my friend? You should try this cheese I have. There's a farm I stop in every time I come here. They are all cousins or something, some of them can barely speak, but they make the best cheese I've ever tasted. It's really an art form."

Khan turned his head, "You hear this, Rafik? You're a lucky boy. There are some important people who want to see you, far, far away from this rust hole."

Rafik did not understand too much of what was happening. He was still in a daze from what he had gone through only moments before. Everything around him seemed distant and sharp at the same time. The guard at the door had an interesting pattern engraved in the belt of his power armour; there were seven chairs in the room but only three of them were grey. Jakov's metallic hand had long fingers with four joints each and two thumb-like digits with two joints each for a total of thirty-two joints . . .

At the front of his mind though, above all else, was the answer to the question he'd been searching for since the day the tattoos appeared on his fingers. These men told him what was wrong with him; they named his malady. He was a Puzzler. Now he had to find out what that meant.

19

The way back to the bar was a blur, but Rafik did remember Khan hugging him and pinching his cheeks. Khan hailed one of the small metal carts that could drive without a pony and paid the driver coin to bring them back to the bar faster. Rafik never sat on or in anything that could move so fast. Cold air blew through the open windows, and the setting sun warmed his face. The seat was soft and comfortable, and he was suddenly very tired from the excitement of the day. Rafik saw symbols dancing in front of his eyes. They merged into the Tarakan symbol that marked the tower they'd passed on their way to see Jakov. He was startled when Martinn shook him awake.

"We're here. Now you can sleep on your own mat."

As soon as they got into the bar, Dominique came charging at them and peppered Khan with questions. Every time Khan tried to deflect she became angry, and every time he answered truthfully she became furious. It was quite peculiar, really.

"You went to meet *that* tin head? Have you lost your mind, Khan? That man is more vicious than a rabid dog with hot peppers stuck up his hole."

"Everything is under control," Khan said. "We've been handed a truck load of of metal."

Dominique shoved Khan aside and pointed at Rafik. "What are you going to do about the little mutt now?"

"I'm going to arrange transport for us—you, me, Martinn, and the boy. We will go to Regeneration, maybe even visit my brother Gandir, and take the long tube to the City of Towers. I know someone there, a contact. He can arrange things, he knows some influencial people. We'll get the guilds interested, maybe even set up an auction."

Dominique was not impressed. "Any plans involving your idiot of a brother is as foolish as you are."

Khan spread his hands. "Who said anything about involving the lard bucket on this? I just want to see his face when he sees us chest deep in metal. I'll even buy that stupid house he stole from me and toss him to the streets, that's what I'll do."

"And who is going to take care of the bar?" Dominique shook her head at Khan. "Or did you forget the amount of coin you owe or the *kind of people* you owe to?"

"Dominique, bane of my existence, thorn in my side, sweet unreachable lips"—Khan lowered his voice to an almost inaudible whisper—"if this deal goes the way I think it will, there is no coming back to this lousy bar. There are far better places to live than Newport. I hear the coast has some wonderful ruined cities that are being reconstructed. We could build a house there, maybe even on the seashore like you always tell me that you dream of . . ."

Dominique glared at Khan and grunted something about him being too much of a miser to buy passage for four. "You'll be lucky if he takes you with him," she said to Martinn when Khan left, "and that will only be because he needs you to watch his back."

Martinn shrugged and escorted Rafik to his room upstairs. Rafik was left alone to wash and pray. He silently apologised to the Prophet Reborn for having missed his midday prayers. Lately

Rafik's prayers had become less frequent. He felt bad about it, but truth be told, Rafik was also angry with the Reborn for inflicting this curse upon him. These new symbols and patterns were fascinating, and Dominique was nice, despite her gruff ways, but he missed home and he wanted his family back. He was surrounded by unbelievers, ruffians, ladies who walked about with their bits showing and kissed men who were not their husbands. The bar was full of drunks and sinners, but somehow—and this was what irked Rafik to no end—they were all *nicer* than most of the people back in his village, and definitely happier. How could that be? Could it be that Master Issak was wrong about the scriptures?

Rafik tried to chase from his mind these blasphemous thoughts and dutifully completed his nighttime prayers. He undressed, washed his upper body, and tried to fall asleep. Yet somehow, the fatigue that had hounded him all day was replaced by restlessness.

After tossing and turning for a while, Rafik got up and paced the room, looking for patterns in the floorboards and the walls. Eventually he got bored, opened the door, and asked Martinn if he could go downstairs. Martinn relented, and they both went downstairs to the bar.

There were a few regular patrons and a few new ones. Soon Martinn was talking animatedly to a young woman he apparently knew and seemed eager to get to know again. Rafik spent his time making a few coins by bringing drinks to drunks.

He was so used to the sounds of the passing trucks now that he didn't pay attention to the roaring noise of the engines, and maybe that was why no one else noticed Jakov and the great bicycle riders until they were inside the bar. They were dressed in black and carried guns, except Jakov, who carried a power pistol in his human arm.

It took precious time for people inside the bar to realise that the armed men who'd just walked in were not coming for a drink. Jakov spotted Rafik handing brew filled mugs to two fat truckers and pointed a metallic finger at him.

"Grab him."

That was the only order his guards needed.

One of the men approached Rafik, snatched him by his collar, and began pulling him towards the exit. Rafik's squeal of alarm alerted even the two very drunk truckers nearby that something was amiss.

"Hey man, where're you takin' the boy, I ain't tipped him yet," one of the truckers said as he rose lazily to his feet. The man pulling Rafik stopped and turned, and with a casual motion he shot both truckers in the chest. The blasts completely deafened Rafik, so he didn't hear the cracking noise of a bottle as it smashed into the shooter's face. He ducked instinctively as broken glass mingled with drops of blood and beer that cascaded on top of him. The shooter let go of Rafik, who turned to see Jakov and another man shoot Dominique. There was movement, flashes of light, and bits of glass flying everywhere in a deadly chaotic swirl, which had no pattern.

Rafik ran without looking back. He rushed upstairs and, without remembering how, found himself in the room where his uncle and brother had negotiated with Khan. It was the wrong place to be, he realised, as there were no windows and no place to hide. Rafik leaned on the door, breathing hard and trembling, tears running freely from his eyes as images from the carnage below kept playing in his mind. He bit his own fist to stop the whimpers escaping his mouth.

Hide.

Rafik took several steps into the room, trying to find somewhere that would conceal him, but before he could get his bearings the door burst open and Radja, Jakov's bodyguard, filled the door frame, a heavy gun in his hands. Rafik froze. All he could do was just stand there, his entire vision focused on the bloodstains on Radja's leather armour. When he was satisfied that the room was empty save for the boy, Radja hefted his gun, extended his arm towards Rafik, and said something. At least his mouth opened and closed several times, but for some reason, no sound came out. Rafik awoke from his stupor only when Radja took several steps and grabbed him, but by then it was too late to escape. Still he resisted, but it was like trying to stop a horse midgallop. Radja trapped Rafik in a one-armed choke hold. Putting a knee to Rafik's back, he pushed the boy forward one step at a time.

Rafik fought for air, but the man's arm was like steel. He could not recall later how Fahid's knife was suddenly in his hand. He pressed the small button, felt the handle shake as the blade sprung out, and stabbed with all his might at the arm that was choking him. Radja roared with pain and loosened his grip. Rafik ducked his head under the arm and was suddenly free.

He bolted forward, just when Martinn stepped through the door, holding a pistol in each hand and firing them in unison above Rafik's head. As he passed by Martinn, Rafik saw a flash of bright light scorching the wall near the door. He heard more shots, and Martinn howled in agony. But Rafik did not look back. He kept on running and was almost at the stairs when someone grabbed him from behind and pulled him into a room. "Don't make a sound!" he heard Khan's voice in his ear. "Where's Martinn?"

Rafik pointed towards the broken doorway.

"Don't move, kid," Khan whispered. He peeked around the corner, holding a pistol with both hands, then signalled for Rafik to follow him. They stopped near the broken door, and Khan bent down and quickly looked inside. What he saw, however briefly, was enough to make him pull back and gag, holding a hand over his mouth.

Khan swore several times, then turned and pushed Rafik through another doorway and into the room he slept in. They made for the window, but when Khan looked out he saw that one man was already climbing up to it. He leaned out and shot twice, missed, then ducked back inside as a barrage of bullets blasted through the thin walls and ceiling.

"We'll have to do it the hard way," he said, more to himself than to Rafik. They moved back to the corridor and edged towards the stairs. They were halfway to ground level when the man who had first grabbed Rafik appeared. He was holding a combat rifle and pointed it straight at Khan. Half of the guard's face was a bloody mess, but he still managed to say, "Let go of the kid, Rustfuck."

Before they could react, the man jerked violently, bits of his flesh spraying everywhere as his body flew sideways and through the kitchen's swinging door. A shotgun appeared, followed by the bulk of Dominique. She pumped it using her left arm and kicked open the kitchen door. "No one aims a weapon at my man but me," she said and shot again, then looked up at Khan and Rafik. "I need a vacation," she said, breathing hoarsely and leaning on the wall next to the still-swinging kitchen door.

Only when they were standing next to her did Rafik and Khan realise how badly hurt she was. Her blouse was torn and drenched in blood, and her shoulder was dislocated. There were cuts and burns all over her face, and a part of her right ear was missing.

"Rust," Khan swore softly, "let's get you to a Mender."

They turned around, and Rafik got a glimpse of the carnage. It was the worst thing he'd ever seen.

"Damn, woman," Khan whispered under his breath, "I told you to clean the place up."

If Dominique heard him, she didn't have time to react, because three more men came through the broken front door. They were followed by Jakov. Khan darted to the kitchen and came back with a rifle, and Dominique and Rafik crouched behind the wall of the stairway. It took only four shots before Khan's rifle jammed. "Don't shoot the kid!" Jakov shouted as bits of wall went flying all around them but he could barely be heard above the noise.

"The basement," Dominique ordered. She fired her own shotgun, hitting one of Jakov's men in the leg, as the three of them retreated into the kitchen. Rafik made every effort not to look at the mess on the floor. Dominique threw down the shotgun and picked up a pistol from the belt of the man she'd shot in the head.

They moved as fast as they could between the barrels until they reached a steel door. Dominique produced a key. Blood and sweat were coming out of her in quantities far too large for one person to sustain for long. She leaned heavily against the wall and urged them to get out. Their pursuers were coming down the stairs. Dominique detached herself from the wall, leaving an alarmingly large bloodstain behind her, and fired a few shots at the stairs, keeping their pursuers at bay.

"Remember the explosives we stashed?" she asked and fired again at the empty stairs. "That would slow the bastards down for good."

"No time," answered Khan as he fired his own pistol once, moving through the open door and pulling Rafik behind him. "Let's rust out of here and get you to a Mender."

Rafik quickly turned to check their surroundings, so he only heard Dominique's voice and never saw the expression on her face when she said, "You always were a lazy lover, Khan." She slammed the door, trapping herself inside.

Khan jumped and grabbed the handle but the security bolt was already down. He slammed his fist against the door screaming, "Dominique, open the damn door! Open the fucking door, you fat, crazy bitch, don't do this!"

Faintly above the racket they both heard the receding footsteps and the voice of Dominique shouting, "Come on down, boys, I have a special brew here, just for you!" More shots were fired. Khan grabbed Rafik's hand, and they ran. When they were only a street away, a set of explosions blew the entire bar into a mushroom of flame, which engulfed the adjacent buildings.

They stopped and turned to look, despite the urgent need to run, and, for what felt like a long time they watched the flames take what was left of the building. For a while all Rafik could do was stand there and watch the bar go up in flames. Khan shouted profanities and kicked things, but after a while his outburst subsided. He wiped his face and shook his head, shoved his pistol into his belt, then grabbed Rafik by the hand and led him away from the burning buildings and into the night.

20

The Backside Burner was not as wild or famous as Margat's Den; nevertheless, it was a place everyone knew. The establishment proudly claimed to produce the spiciest food in the known world, hence its name, and had even hosted annual food competitions that were reputed to have claimed several lives. Located just outside of Newport at the SuperTruck depot, where SuperTrucks too huge to enter Newport parked, it catered to the taste of truckers with gut-wrenching food, unwatered drinks, playing tables, and an array of prostitutes.

In theory, SuperTruck owners could become very rich relatively quickly. A decade of hard labour and a bit of luck could earn a Tarakan highway driver enough coin to live in modest comfort for the rest of his life. The problem was that truckers seemed to spend at least as much as they earned, and usually much more than they earned, and by the time they paid their debts they were too set in their ways and too addicted to the dangerous and carefree way of life that the Tarakan roads dictated.

The Backside Burner might not be considered a rough establishment, yet it was still not the sort of place to bring a young boy.

Heads turned, but whether it was some truckers' code of "minding your own business" or the sight of a man and a boy in blood-stained attire, they kept their curiosity at bay.

The man Khan was looking for was sitting at the main card table on a deep-cushioned playing chair, which barely held his girth. On his head was a cap long faded into dirty beige that covered most of his upper face. His card-holding hand was tucked under a waist-length, food-stained beard.

Running for your life from a violent gang led by an angry half-man, half-metal murderer was by no means an everyday occurrence. Yet even under such circumstances, you did not approach a trucker from behind while he was playing cards, not unless you were looking to deepen the serious trouble you were already in. Kahn and Rafik waited at a respectable distance until his hand was played and his coins were gathered before they made a tentative approach in plain view.

"Captain."

The trucker leaned back from the table.

"Khan Carr, you son of a who—" He stopped when he spotted Rafik and nodded to himself. "Hell, it's no matter to you if I curse your mother, you never knew the woman."

"I need to talk to you, Sam," Khan said.

"You want to talk to the Captain?" The man turned in his seat and lifted his cap up to his brow. "Well, Khan, the way you're looking right now, I hope you haven't come to propose to me."

People laughed and thumped their tables.

"I need to speak to you, *Captain*, privately," Khan pleaded.

The trucker must have decided that the man had suffered enough abuse, because he pointed at a far booth as he got up from his seat. Captain Sam was not tall, but he was wide. His trousers were held up by four strong ropes that looped around his belly and shoulders. His walk was slow but confident as they made their way to a table and sat themselves on dirty wooden seats. Captain Sam ordered a large quantity of mead, and after looking at Rafik, he ordered a steak for the young boy. He then busied himself by stuffing black leaves into his mouth and chewing them thoroughly, adding a long gulp of mead every few chews. Khan twitched nervously, waiting for his cue to speak.

Finally, the trucker leaned forward and asked, "What's rusting your metal?"

Khan was beyond pleasantries. "I need you to drive me . . . us . . . away from here, tonight. We need to get to Regeneration."

Captain Sam didn't even stop chewing as he said, "No can do, amigo. I'm only half full."

"Sam . . . *Captain*, it's urgent that we both get out of here tonight."

The man turned his head and spat a long arc of black goo at a nearby bucket. "What's wrong with you? Didn't you hear? *I am half full*. Means I am half *empty*, and a half-empty load barely pays for power tubes to feed my Sweetheart. She gets slow and irritated if she has to run on road power alone."

"I'll pay you," Khan said quickly, then gulped and added, "as soon as I get my hands on the coin or kind in Regeneration."

The food arrived, and for a few moments Rafik forgot all about the grown-up talk. He hadn't eaten anything all day and was absolutely ravenous. He didn't even utter a blessing on the food, and only later admonished himself for forgetting.

Halfway through the steak, Rafik saw Captain Sam sliding away from his seat. "Nice meeting you, son," he told Rafik and winked. "Apologies for ordering the small steak portion. You look a bit hungry."

Khan leaned forward and grabbed the trucker's arm. "I beg you. Please sit down and hear me out. Please."

Captain Sam glanced casually down at his forearm and Khan let go. The trucker paused, then shrugged and sat back down.

"One wrong word, wise guy," he warned, "and I'll make dessert out of you and serve it to the kid. Look at him, don't you feed the boy?"

"It's the kid I'm talking about. Look, he's . . . special . . . and he would bring me . . . us . . . shitloads of coin, I mean buckets of—"

"Brake and reverse right there. Are you sitting here, telling me you are going to get rich by selling this kid like a load of wood? Are you a fucking slaver now, Khan?" His voice was still calm but his tone made more than a few heads turn from halfway across the bar.

"Me? No, no, no, I'm not selling the boy. I'm just the middle man for the boy's family, once I get my cut—"

Captain Sam thumped the table as he rose again to his feet. Truckers were hastily vacating the surrounding tables.

"Khan," Captain Sam said evenly and gestured with his callused hand in a broad arc. "I like this place. They treat me with respect and bring me clean food and strong drinks. I would not want to cause damage to this fine establishment, so you and I are going to step outside, and then I am going to break a few bones of your spineless little body until I can shove your own heel up your arse."

"Oh, in the name of—" Khan turned to Rafik. "Just show him your hand."

Only then did Rafik realise he was still wearing Dominique's glove. Mid-chew, he slowly peeled it off, raised his right arm, and spread his fingers.

The trucker stared at the hand for a long while then let out a sigh and shoved a new batch of chewing leaves into his mouth.

The mood around them eased.

"What's the story here?" said the Captain.

"It's tragic," Khan said, obviously relieved. "The boy was born in one of those Wildener villages, you know, where they kill you if they even suspect you have tattoos. I owe this boy's father my life, so his family smuggled him to Newport and I promised to help bring him to safety. Now Jakov the weapon's dealer, that nasty piece of rust, heard about the boy and tried to take him, burned my bar, killed my girlfriend, and we barely got out of there alive. I'm sure he's still after me, and there are only a few places in this town I can hide. I don't mind taking care of my own business, but I have to look after the boy. It's a matter of honour."

"Khan, you wouldn't recognise honour if it was your own ugly love child." The trucker looked at Rafik. "Tell me the truth—is this man treating you well?"

Rafik looked up at Khan and felt for a brief moment what it was like to hold the power of life over death. He prolonged the moment as long as he could, then nodded twice for good measure and heard Khan's sigh of relief.

"Fine," said the Captain. "I'll do it. I'll drive you to Regeneration, and then you'll pay me whatever I decide you owe me."

"Oh, good." All the air seemed to come out of Khan all at once, and he slumped back in his seat. Rafik silently slid his leftover steak towards him. Khan looked at the plate and slowly picked up a piece of meat with his fingers and shoved it in his mouth. Captain Sam watched them intently, so Rafik guessed that he timed what he said next, perfectly.

"There's one more thing."

Khan was just opening his mouth to take another bite. "What's that?" He closed his mouth and lowered the meat.

"I need an advance."

Khan put the piece of meat down. "An advance?"

"Yes, I swore long ago that I would never take freeloaders. I need an advance, something of worth."

"*Captain*, my bar just burned down, everything I own is gone, and I have nothing of value on me except a gun."

"Don't need a gun. Don't believe in 'em," said the trucker.

"That's good, because I wasn't going to part with it. Sentimental value."

"Well, Khan, you'd better find something of value to give me or all your hovering and grovelling will have been in vain."

"Captain, please—"

"Sorry, Khan, I know we go back a little, but I gave my word."

"Who did you promise?"

"I gave an oath to my Sweetheart."

"You swore an oath to your truck?"

"I'd be very careful what I say next, if I were you."

Khan bit his lip and began patting his pockets, emptying their contents onto the table. There were bits and bobs and a few low-value tin coins but nothing else. Then Khan's eyes lit up when he produced a ring from his pocket. The ring was plain and had a flat surface. It didn't look like much.

"What are you showing me?"

"Look at this," Khan said and turned the flat surface. A miniature female appeared, scantily clad, with all anatomical features very much in place. She was dancing in a circle on top of the ring, her arms stretched above her head, then shifting down to caress her own moving body. It was the most beautiful thing Rafik had ever seen.

"And look here," Khan said, turning the surface again. Another woman replaced the previous one, dancing in a different way, but in the same mesmerizing style.

"Avert your eyes, boy." Captain Sam barked a laugh, and Rafik found himself obeying although instinct told him not to.

"Fifteen different ladies," Khan said in a throaty voice, "all dance on the ring."

"Where did you get that?"

"It . . . was given to me . . . by . . . my mother . . . passed down the generations . . . of my family."

"I'm not interested in filth."

"But why?" wailed Khan in desperation.

"My heart belongs to one and only one."

"You don't mean . . . it's a damn *truck*."

"Watch what you say, Khan. It's my last warning."

The men were staring at each other intently so it took them a while to notice Rafik's hand, which was presenting a different object to the trucker.

"What is that, boy?" Captain Sam glared at him.

"It's a knife." Rafik pressed the button twice and the blade sprung out. There was still dried blood on the metal.

"I'm sorry," said the trucker. "I cannot accept that. I don't believe in weapons."

"Oh, for the love of—"

"It's not a weapon," Rafik said quietly. "It's the only thing my brother gave me before he left, the only item I have left from my family. It's important to me, but I will give it to you if you take us away from here."

Captain Sam went silent for a moment. Then he accepted the knife in his leathery palm. He pushed the button several times and watched the blade spring in and out of its case.

"Well, it's a rare enough item," he remarked, testing the sharpness of the metal with his thumb, then spitting directly on the blade and cleaning it on the hem of his tunic before pocketing the item. "If you cross me I'll use this knife to cut your balls off, Khan."

Khan nodded.

"And I'll make sure you live through the whole process, too."

"I get it, Captain," Khan snapped. "You'll get more than your fair share. Do we have a deal?"

"Yup, done deal," the Captain said. "Let's go."

They got up from their seats, and Captain Sam cleared his throat before bellowing, "Gentlemen, may I have your attention."

The room fell silent almost immediately.

"I'm leaving now, heading southeast with a hull half full," he said, surveying the bar. "So there will be more business for you and there's no need to thank me, unless you want to buy me a drink." Sporadic laughter rippled among the truckers.

"Now, there may be a few men coming here later, might be looking for people who resemble my companions here. I would see it as a personal favor if you not cooperate with these men, even if they are persuasive with coin or otherwise. Have a nice evening."

Without waiting for a reaction the trucker turned and strode out of the bar. When they were out of the Backside Burner, Khan asked, "Do you trust them?"

The Captain shrugged and said, "Trucker's honour." He shoved more chewing leaves into his mouth, his grin as black as it was mischievous. "And besides, we'll be driving northeast."

21

Though it was close to impossible to steal a SuperTruck, the parking area was heavily guarded by guild members, who also doubled as bouncers when fights got out of hand in the Backside Burner. Each parked truck was guarded by at least four armed guards.

Rafik was mesmerized by the sheer size of the SuperTrucks and the fact that they were as different as they were big. No one thirty-wheeler had the same pattern. He mentioned that fact to Captain Sam as they walked towards Sweetheart.

"Ah, they do not look the same, boy, because every trucker puts a little of himself into his ride. But wait until you see Sweetheart, boy, she is magnificent." He patted the boy on the shoulder, urging him gently to move on.

"Is your truck the biggest?" Rafik asked, but the Captain shook his head.

"There are three things you never really own, boy: women, liquor, and a SuperTruck. You just get to have them for a while. And you don't start your driving on a SuperTruck, either. You work your way up, learn the lingo, earn your wheels the hard way, and then one day, if you're lucky, you get to place your hands on the wheel of a real SuperTruck."

Rafik thought about the Captain's answer as they walked among men and machines, then asked, "Why are you called Captain?"

"Well, boy, have you ever heard of ships?"

"No."

"They were like Trucks, but they floated on water and roamed the seas a long time ago. We do have some boats left today, on the coast, but no ships. Anyway, long ago, ships were manned by a group of people called sailors and led by a captain. Every ship had a unique name, and the sailors and captain lived and died on its deck and took pride at keeping her the ship in excellent condition. Sweetheart told me that many times the ship would be treated by the crew like a lady. Sailors would talk or sing to her, and the captain would treat her as his missus. When that happened, the stories say, the ship would never take water and sink or lose a battle. I'm called a captain because—"

The trucker stopped in his tracks.

"Well, water my oil and flatten my tyres," he said softly to no one in particular. He strode towards a huge silvery truck guarded by six men. They all shifted position on their feet as he walked past them, saying, "Good evening, lads. At ease, just checking on her now. I see all is well." He passed five of them, and when he reached the sixth guard, who was leaning on one of the machine's large wheels, Captain Sam suddenly charged and landed a heavy fist into the guard's jaw. The man went down with a heavy, if somewhat surprised-sounding grunt, where the Captain proceeded to kick him, accentuating each strike with, "How . . . many . . . times . . . do I have to say . . . never . . . ever . . . touch her."

On any other day, such violence would have branded Rafik's soul, but this day had been too full of bloodshed for Rafik to care—and besides, there were interesting patterns on the Super-Truck. Eventually Captain Sam stopped kicking the guard and turned to the other guards, who had stood watching. He threw a small bag of coins at one of them, pointed at the guard at his feet, and said, "Take care of him, and tell him that when I get back, if I see him guarding *any* of the SuperTrucks again, he'd better have a spare set of legs."

The men helped their friend up and walked away without another word. When they were far enough away, Captain Sam brought out a small rectangular object and pressed it once. High up, the door of the truck opened with a hissing sound and a ladder extended itself down.

"Here she is," he declared with pride, and spat aside the chewing leaves before ordering them to "climb aboard."

They climbed up into a surprisingly spacious cabin, which had two levels—one with a seat for the driver and a passenger, and a second, lower level, with three comfortable-looking seats. At the back of the cabin hung a row of dried sausages and a stack of several barrels, which reminded Rafik of the cellar of Dominique's bar. The very same thought must have crossed Khan's mind, because he swore softly as he leaned back into a chair and closed his eyes. Before Rafik had the time to take it all in, a pleasant woman's voice filled the cabin, startling both Khan and the boy.

"Good evening, handsome," the voice said.

"Hello, Sweetheart," answered the Captain, climbing up into the driver's seat with surprising agility. He turned and said to Khan, "She wouldn't move without checking it's me."

"I see you have guests with you tonight."

"Oh, this is Khan and his little pup, Rafik. They'll be travelling with us." He leaned over in his seat, beaming with pride, "She can detect a fly on the back of the hood."

"How was your steak tonight?"

Captain Sam's face turned serious as he said in an even tone, "It was very tender, dear, albeit a bit too spicy for my gut." He winked at Rafik.

A strange-looking slate with glowing numbers drawn on it slid forward towards Captain Sam. "Please enter the code, Captain."

Captain Sam hid the slate with one hand and touched a series of numbers with the other. As the slate slid back and the floor began to slightly vibrate, he turned back to Khan. "Press the wrong code, and Sweetheart would know this was a kidnapping and act accordingly. And trust me, you do not want to see her angry."

"I'm warming your seat up just the way you like it." The SuperTruck's voice was calm and pleasant.

"Thank you, Sweetheart. Set a course for Regeneration, love."

"May I remind you, Captain, that I am half empty, and our schedule tells me Regeneration is our destination in a month and three days."

"I know, darling," Captain Sam said as he busied himself pushing a few more buttons, "but we must change the schedule and travel early this time. *Look* what I have for you."

He fished a glowing power tube out of his pocket and shoved it gently into a compartment in the machine's enormous steering wheel. "I was waiting for a special occasion, but I thought this would be a good time."

"You are so considerate, *Captain*," the truck's humm increased slightly, "I assume you want to drive manually until we reach the Tarakan highway?"

"Not this time. Sound the horn, dear, and take it all the way." The Captain leaned back and crossed his hands behind his neck as lights of various colours began flashing all around them. The engine roared into life, and as the SuperTruck began to move forward an ear-piercing horn was sounded. It was probably much louder outside, but it was enough to startle Rafik and Khan yet again. The captain laughed in merriment and said, "Need to tell them all we're leaving." He swivelled his chair back to Rafik. "So, you never been on a SuperTruck before?"

Rafik, lost for words, could only shake his head.

"Well hang on, boy." Captain Sam grinned and wiggled his bushy eyebrows. "You're in for the ride of your life."

22

The SuperTruck called Sweetheart moved its incredible bulk slowly but with precision and ease. Inside, there were more than half a dozen slates—Captain Sam called them screens—from which they could see what was going on outside the Super-Truck. The images changed every so often, from the back of the vehicle to the sides and bottom, and even to the roof. Rafik watched, fascinated, as alien symbols crossed the top of the screens. Captain Sam explained they were measurements and distances and "other stuff you don't have to worry about. She's taking us nice and easy to the highway, ain't it so, Sweetheart?" He thumped the enormous steering wheel fondly.

"Of course, Sam," the soothing woman's voice filled the cabin from all directions, "and I suggest you relax and rest and let me navigate. Analyzing your breath, I detect that you've had too much to drink to be able to drive safely."

"Nonsense, lass, I'm as sober as an . . . an . . ." Captain Sam was momentarily lost for words. He covered the embarrassment by releasing a mighty belch.

"Exactly," said Sweetheart calmly with only a hint of satisfaction in her voice.

Despite the horrors of the day, Rafik's excitement surged. He'd woken up in the morning thinking his life would be filled with backbreaking chores, and here he was, inside a SuperTruck. It was more than satisfactory to imagine what Eithan, who got all round-eyed at the sight of a simple six-wheeler merchant wagon, would say about *that*.

Rafik wanted to look out from the high windows. He tried to climb on his chair. To his uneasy surprise, he found himself bound to the chair by two straps which looped around his middle and across the chest.

"Relax, boy," the Captain said when he sensed Rafik's discomfort. "It's for your own good. If we make a sudden stop it's either you're strapped down or we have to scrape you off the windshield. But look over there, you see that set of buttons? You can move your seat up and down and sideways." The Captain was right. After a bit of experimenting, Rafik figured out how to raise his seat so he could look outside. They were as high as a two-story building, perhaps even higher, and already travelling at unimaginable speed.

After turning away from Newport, the SuperTruck steered itself onto a wide road that was lit by powerful Tarakan lights perched on impossibly high metal poles.

"Those are still working," Captain Sam said, pointing at the metal towers from which the light emanated. "Almost no other place has them anymore. They used to be everywhere, but now this row is a wonder of the world."

"Why is that so?" Rafik asked, turning his head from the window.

Khan, who'd been quiet for such a long time that Rafik thought he was asleep, suddenly answered, "In many cities they were taken apart by looters, for the metal, but in Newport there are many truckers who drive at night and want an easy ride in and out of town. So the guild hires guards to make sure no one tries to steal the poles."

"Yeah," grunted the Captain. He pointed at one of the poles as they passed by. Rafik could clearly see there were several skeletons hanging from it.

"Every once in a while, some bandits get ballsy and try and steal one of them. We catch them, cut their balls off, hang them by the straps of their belts and leave them to rot until there's nothing left of their bodies. Sends a message, if you know what I mean."

This quieted everyone for a while, and they drove in silence until they reached a part of the road that was completely dark. The Captain said chirpily, "Time to light up the gloom, Sweetheart."

"Aye-aye, Captain," said the SuperTruck, and the vehicle's surroundings were suddenly bathed in bright light.

"Any company?" asked the Captain.

Sweetheart answered, "One type-three class, seven miles ahead, heading north an average of ninety-seven miles per hour. We will not meet it unless one of us alters course."

"Can you scan it?"

There was a short pause, after which the answer came: "I bypassed the vehicle's elementary firewall. It is an artificial platinum-plated fourteen-wheeler, carrying wood, three weapons systems, one heat-tracking missile, one male driver, a female companion, and a canine whose exact breed I cannot define. The vehicle's height and weight are—"

"That's enough Sweetheart, that'll do," the Captain said, his hands resting on the steering wheel, but only following its movement not controlling it. "That dumb rust-arse trucker," he said to Khan. "He spent half his life's savings getting a Gadgetier to install enough salvaged Tarakan weaponry to start a war, wasted half his hull space on it, too, but didn't bother to turn his anti-scan system on. I know when he scratches himself and where."

"Why is that important?" Khan's voice was flat, as if he was keeping the conversation going but was preoccupied by something else.

"Well, first of all, you should never let the bad guys know what you're carrying in your hull, and second, all the weapons in the world won't help you if the bad guys hack into your system and turn it off." He busied himself stuffing more leaves into his mouth. "At least that was the explanation Sweetheart gave me. Been with her for years, but I still don't know all the technical terms she uses."

"Who are the bad guys, do they ride great bicycles?" asked Rafik, suddenly anxious again. He'd already convinced himself that they'd left the bad guys back in Newport.

"'The great what?" Captain Sam chuckled, "No, no no, kid. Two wheelers can't scratch a SuperTruck. What we have here, we call them pirates, like the ones who used to attack ships on seas, but they're nothing more than bandits on wheels, really. Some are ex-truckers who think they can do it the easy way—they do the driving—the others are just thugs who do the killing and looting. But don't worry, son, we know how to deal with those road roaches if we ever come across them, don't we, Sweetheart?"

"We do, my Captain," answered the SuperTruck, and the Captain laughed, exposing blackened teeth. As the heavy truck rumbled on, Sam took pleasure in showing Rafik some of Sweetheart's secrets, pointing out screens and quoting numbers and measurements that meant nothing to the boy but were fascinating nonetheless.

"Did you build this truck . . . I mean Sweetheart, yourself?" he asked.

The Captain laughed and shook his head.

"Me? No, boy, I did not," he said ruefully. Then he lowered his tone and added in a pretend whisper, "She doesn't like to hear this, but she's older than you and me together, and not a simple lass, either. Hell, I laid my hands on every part of her and I still don't understand how she works."

"Is she really . . . alive?" Rafik was fascinated. The people in his village used weapons and a few primitive machines, like the generator that powered a cooling storage device, or the dangerous harvester used in the fields during the spring. The machines had a tendency to break down, needed constant attention, and none of them were even close to having the sophistication of a SuperTruck. Rafik was repeatedly warned of the dangers of *attaching*, mixing human and machine, yet here he was inside a machine that seemed to be part human, running away from a human who was part machine.

The Captain didn't seem to mind the question, or perhaps he was just indulging Rafik.

"She's alive to me," he said in all seriousness, "and I never tell her how or when to talk to me, like some of the other boys do. She speaks when she wants and says what she wants, and believe me, boy, she has a large, what d'ya call it, vocabulary. She speaks better than I do, that's for sure. So yes, I think she is alive, as alive as she can be."

They sat in silence for a few moments before Captain Sam began talking again.

"I never really *bought* Sweetheart," he mused. "Sure, there's an old trucker out there who never needs to worry about coin again, but it wasn't about her price. His name's Brinks; we called him Brinks the Brick because he was as flexible as one and could hit you as hard." Sam snorted a laugh. "He used to call her 'little daughter,' and believe me, boy, I had to get on his good side before he even let me touch her. Before Sweetheart, I drove a fourteen-wheeler for twenty seasons, and thought I knew what I was doing. Then I met Brinks. He needed a second, and I made good of an opportunity. It took one trip with Brinks the Brick for me to realise I'd stayed alive on the road out of pure luck. He taught me how to drive and how to take care of her. We spent forty seasons driving together, Brinks, Sweetheart, and I."

"And you don't have a wife, or kids?"

"Well . . ." Captain Sam said into his beard, "you can't be a trucker without having a few offspring spread all over your route, if you know what I mean." He glanced over his shoulder at Rafik and added, "Actually I'm guessing you didn't know that. What I mean is that Brinks and Sweetheart, they were my real family, and when Brinks got so blind he couldn't see the road no more we struck a deal, but like a father-and-son deal. He retired, and now I drive Sweetheart and send him a third of my earnings. Now, Brinks was a man who knew his rig, every last metal coil in her, and he knew his roads, and let me tell ya, he knew how to handle himself in a tight spot. But even Brinks didn't build Sweetheart."

The Captain drummed a slow beat with his fingers, "Now my Sweetheart ain't talking much about her past, but I reckon she is a mix built of Tarakan and human know-how. I don't know how the SuperTrucks survived the Catastrophe, but they're built for resilience, especially Sweetheart's type"—he thumped his hand lovingly on the wheel—"the SuperTruck Z class, and not many of them left. There are a few good truckers and mechanics out there who have the skill to piece back together a normal fourteen-wheeler, but most of 'em wouldn't know much about SuperTrucks."

The Captain shot a glance at Rafik. "I know that some people don't like the tattooed very much, but other than the Super-Truck's self-repair systems, Gadgetiers are the only ones I know that could do serious maintenances on a SuperTruck, and I know a few who could even add a weapons system to it. That makes the tattooed solid in my eyes, but no one can really *build* a Super-Truck no more. *That* knowledge is gone, dead, and don't let anyone flatten your tyre with nonsense about the coming of the Mechanic or other such religious crap." Captain Sam pointed a stubby finger at Rafik, "No matter what they say about them Tarakans and how evil and terrible they were, remember that they built the SuperTrucks and those roads, boy, I am sure of it. They must have been very similar to us, and how bad could they be if they built Sweetheart, eh?"

He stroked the steering wheel gently. "I've asked her about

them Tarkanians but she doesn't like to talk about them." He smiled. "Remember this for the future, boy: every woman needs a few secrets from her man, but not the other way around." When Rafik's face stayed blank, Captain Sam shrugged and chuckled to himself. "Well, the road you pass is behind you, that's what we truckers say. Each SuperTruck is unique, and we lose one or two every year." He shook his head. "Why anyone would try to stop a SuperTruck is beyond me. People are just plain stupid, or crazy, or both."

They lapsed back into silence. Captain Sam asked Sweetheart for the controls, and he drove himself for a while, steering the huge wheel. It seemed to Rafik the speech made Captain Sam sad, so he resisted the urge to ask more questions. There was not much for him to watch except trees and vegetation, and soon his mind started to replay the dramatic scenes of the day.

"Khan? Are you asleep?" he asked softly.

Khan, who'd had his eyes closed during the entire conversation, stirred a bit before answering reluctantly, "What is it?"

"Is Dominique in heaven?"

There was a long pause, during which both men were silent, then Khan said, "She's in heaven, Rafik. I'm sure she is."

Rafik thought about it for a while. He didn't want to upset Khan, but he was worried about Dominique. The holy scripts were very clear about letting only virtuous women into heaven, and he was pretty sure that Dominique did not fit that description. She drank cursed water all the time, wore far too little, and although she was loyal to her man literally to the end, she was in the habit of speaking so suggestively to the other men in her bar that she made even a few of the hardened truckers blush and many of their women angry. Rafik didn't believe that Dominique would easily be admitted into heaven, but he desperately wanted her to be let in. He heard the Captain say, "Sorry about your gal," and Khan replied something in a voice too low to discern. Perhaps Dominique was waiting to be judged by the Reborn Prophet right now, her life of sin weighed against her last heroic act. It suddenly occurred to Rafik that perhaps there was something he could do to help.

"Can you tell me which way is east?" he asked aloud. A screen near his seat flashed an arrow pointing in the right direction, although Sweetheart warned him that the direction would change in a short while.

For the first time since they began the journey, Rafik decided to speak to the Sweetheart directly. "Please let me out of my seat," he asked, turning his head to the speaking tube.

"Why do you need to move?" Sweetheart asked.

Rafik touched the glove he was wearing. "I need to pray for my friend Dominique, so she can go to heaven."

"I'm afraid it's too dangerous to let you do that now, Rafik, if we come to a sudden halt—"

"Oh, slow down and let the boy pray," the Captain said while keeping his gaze levelled at the road.

The binds uncoiled themselves from around his body, and Rafik knelt down inside the SuperTruck, under the array of hanging sausages and beside the barrels. He did not have the holy book of the New Prophecies with him, of course, and he would have been forbidden from touching the book with his hands even if he did, so he just crossed his arms over his heart and uttered the words he could remember in the ancient tongue he'd never truly mastered. After the prayer he reverted to the secular tongue and begged softly, in his own words, to the one God and his Prophet Reborn to let Dominique's soul into heaven because she was a good person and gave her life to save others, and surely that was a great deed worth far more than any small sins she might have committed.

During his prayer, neither of the two men uttered a single word.

Rafik was suddenly tired. He climbed back into his seat and found out to his surprise that it turned into a very comfortable bed. But as soon as he closed his eyes he saw Jakov walking into the bar and the two truckers falling down with blood spurting from their open chest wounds. He could smell the blood and hear the gunshots and Martinn screaming and Dominique's muffled voice behind the closed iron door. He desperately tried to think of something else. The wall of symbols sprang to life in front of his closed eyes. It was soothing. He could block out all the other memories by concentrating on the wall and playing with the symbols.

The next thing he remembered was Captain Sam waking them up, cheerfully declaring that they'd arrived at the Tarakan highway. The SuperTruck tilted at a sharp angle as it climbed up to the new surface. The only thing that Rafik knew about the highway was that it had been built by the Tarakan infidels to help vanquish and enslave all of the surrounding people. Looking at the glowing yellow road, ten times as wide as Sweetheart's hull and stretching as far as the eye could see, he could not feel anything but awe and curiosity.

"Pure Tarakan built," said the Captain, as if reading the boy's mind, "still as smooth as a baby's bottom and specifically made to get SuperTrucks where they need to go as fast as possible. Without these roads Newport would be a hamlet no one would bother to visit, and people would have no way to carry out commerce beyond the next village. The north has steel and the oil refineries—that used to be the human's way of getting their trucks to drive. You know about fuel, don't you, boy?"

He glanced down at Rafik, who nodded. You don't get to serve tables in a bar filled with truckers without picking up a thing or two. Captain Sam nodded in satisfaction. "Well, problem is, the north has oil but the cold makes it hard to grow enough food. The south, on the other hand, has plenty of crops but no oil to feed their machines. The west has wood and coal and the east is good for sulphur, tin, and silver." Captain Sam thumped his thick hand on the steering wheel. "Everyone has something to sell and something to buy, so this is where we come in. Unfortunately, in some parts of the land the Tarakan highway was destroyed, and we have to drive on human roads, but without the Tarakan highway and the SuperTrucks it would take days instead of hours, or weeks rather than days to go from place to place, and everyone would be left to fend for themselves."

Rafik looked out again. Except where the road met the Tarakan highway, it curved upwards on both sides, and a wall, about half the height of Sweetheart, divided it in the centre. Even though the Captain told him that Sweetheart's windows were cancelling out most of the glare, the entire Tarakan highway glowed bright.

"You need a special cover for your eyes if you stop too close to the Tarakan highway at night," explained the Captain. "It stores energy from the sun during the day and somehow makes light into energy, which actually powers up the SuperTrucks as you drive on it. If you know your truck and are smart about the way you handle it, as long as you drive on the Tarakan highway you'll never run dry. I'm telling you, those Tarkanians knew their business. Now watch this, boy." He pressed a few buttons. "Let's move, Sweetheart, the highway is calling."

"Initiating, Captain." The humming noise grew into a loud growl.

Watching the screens, Rafik saw how eight large plates lowered themselves from underneath Sweetheart, lodged themselves into the surface of the highway and pushed the entire SuperTruck up in the air. The giant wheels turned inwards and from their centres sprouted large metal tubes.

Rafik gripped his seat as the SuperTruck rocked and heaved, but then Sweetheart announced something regarding internal stabilizers, and the movement soon subsided, leaving the vehicle suspended on nothing but air. "Beats me how this happens," the Captain declared with unconcealed pride as the plates withdrew back into the truck. "Sweetheart told me it was something called a magnetic field, but I don't care if it is Tarkanian voodoo. After Sweetheart here, it is the most amazing thing I have ever seen. And now comes the fun part."

Through the screens Rafik watched in awe as all around the SuperTruck several large metal tubes emerged. For a few heartbeats everything seemed to freeze in its place as the normally soft humming sound grew into a roar, and then a burst and a flash of blue light came out of the metal tubes, and the entire bulk of Sweetheart shot forward so fast, Rafik's body crashed back into his seat.

"Groovy, eh?" bellowed the Captain above the noise. "I just love that part!"

"How . . . fast are we going?" asked Khan, his own hands gripping the sides of his seat. It was the first time he'd talked in a long while.

"Oh, eighty at the moment, but we're just warming up," answered the Captain happily. "Don't worry, the noise level will calm down in a few minutes, then we'll go faster, much, much faster."

Rafik's jaw dropped as he tried to imagine the distance they were travelling. The south fields of his village were the farthest he'd travelled before setting off to Newport, and that would take an hour of walking. He tried to calculate how long it would take him to go back to his village and realised that without Captain Sam and his Sweetheart it would take him a year or even a lifetime to get back. Would he ever be able to go back home? Images of his family and friends flashed before Rafik's eyes. He felt his throat tighten and fought for control as Fahid's voice berated him: *Don't cry like a little girl, Rafik, how do you want to fight bandits? Real men never cry.* With a quick gesture he wiped away a few tears that managed to escape and bit his lower lip hard.

Captain Sam pressed a few buttons, then swung out of the driver's seat, leaving the wheel of the SuperTruck under Sweetheart's control. "Are you okay, boy?" he asked. When the boy nodded, he added "I know *exactly* what you need" in a cheerful voice. He climbed down to the main cabin, plucked a giant sausage from behind Rafiks's seat, and threw it at the boy's lap before getting one for himself. He took a ravenous bite from it before pouring cursed water from one of the barrels into a metal mug and gulping it down so fast it wet his long beard. With meat in one hand and a sloshing mug in the other, Captain Sam turned back to Rafik and Khan.

"Now boys," he asked, his grin full of sausage. "Who wants some entertainment?"

23

So engrossed was Rafik with what Captain Sam called Sweetheart's Internal Entertainment System, that he hardly noticed how the next five days passed them by. At first it was just the stories on the screen, which showed real people doing very exciting things and sometimes also kissing. They were made a long time ago, before the forces of God drove the Tarakan infidels away and the Prophet was Reborn. Each screen story was different, although a few had the same people in them. Rafik couldn't figure out everything he saw, but he did learn that people used to live in huge cities, chased each other a lot in small, horseless vehicles called cars, constantly shot at each other, and kissed in public a lot, something that was forbidden in Rafik's village even between husband and wife, but in the stories no one seemed to mind.

There were 3,073 such screen stories in Sweetheart's memory. Captain Sam didn't know how all of them got into Sweetheart's mind, but he knew them all by heart, sometimes mouthing the words to himself as they were uttered by the people on the screen. He told Rafik he could choose any story he wanted to see from the long list of names, except for some that he said were only for grown-ups. The movies were exciting, and although some of the actions reminded Rafik of his last day in Newport, all the people he liked seemed to be okay in the end. This made him think of Dominique again, and he became sad.

Still, Rafik thought screen stories were the best thing he ever saw, until he discovered that Sweetheart's entertainment system contained seven thousand games . . .

Games were like the screen stories, but you got to be the hero and move about and do things by touching the screen, flailing with your hands, or moving in your chair, and Rafik thought *that* was by far the best thing he'd ever experienced, far better than warriors and infidels, but then he found the puzzle games. They were not like the wall of symbols in his dreams, but some worked on the same principles. There was a game in which you could manipulate falling objects and create whole lines, which then disappeared with a satisfying popping sound. Later he found a game where you had to press colours and symbols in long sequences, and another in which you touched a multitude of sequences among meaningless yet ever accelerating flashing symbols. Rafik got so absorbed in the puzzles he forgot all about the screen stories and the other games and even stopped thinking about Dominique and Martinn.

At the beginning Rafik played these games one after another, alternating every so often, until, to his delight, Sweetheart suggested he divide the screen into several smaller sections so he could play them all simultaneously. Captain Sam showed genuine amazement at this, although Rafik did not think it was such a great feat. He played until his eyes hurt, then slept, but kept playing with the wall of symbols in his dreams. In one such dream he managed to hold twenty symbols at once. This gave Rafik enormous satisfaction and peace of mind. He was getting better. Life was getting better. On the third day of travel, he completely forgot to pray.

Apparently, they were driving very fast now, covering in one day a distance that would take many months via pony cart and years on foot. The land around them was mostly wilderness, but they passed the occasional abandoned city, places so wrecked by the Catastrophe that no one but the most desperate looters and greediest of Salvationists dared visit. The ruined cities were too far to see in detail, but the sight of them made Rafik feel uneasy, and he would go back to the puzzle games. Every once in a while, the Captain would try to get Rafik's attention by pointing out an interesting landmark, such as a mountain range or a river, but Rafik was too absorbed in his games to really care where he was. He even politely refused to learn Captain Sam's card game, but the trucker didn't seem to mind, saying, "Ah well, better that you don't know about those things. Bring you only grief, those cards, unless you really know how to play."

They didn't drive all the time on the Tarakan highway, because, Rafik learned, it was broken in many places. The Catastrophe destroyed parts of the highway, and floods, storms, and earthquakes had left their marks over the years. Captain Sam even told stories about a group he called "a bunch of crazy flat tyres" who, for reasons known only to themselves, destroyed a whole section of the southern road with ancient explosives before being demolished themselves. When Sweetheart exited the Tarakan highway, travelling felt pony-cart slow, although Captain Sam assured Rafik they were still going faster than any cart could travel.

Every few hours the Captain insisted on stopping somewhere "for a rest," although it seemed to Rafik that he was not doing anything resembling hard work during the drive. Khan tried to dissuade the Captain from making too many stops, but the trucker insisted it was good for Sweetheart to rest every couple of hours. "And with her, I always think long-term."

The scheduled stops annoyed Rafik, as he had to stop playing games. He joined Khan in urging the Captain to continue the voyage simply so he could get back to his puzzles. But the trucker wouldn't budge. Even if they were on the Tarakan highway he would ask Sweetheart to exit to a normal road, drive a bit until they found a remote area, and stop there. Captain Sam would insist that Rafik give Sweetheart's entertainment system a rest and "stretch his bones." It was by far the most boring part of the journey, except for the time they stopped near a forest and Sweetheart forbade them from going out because of roaming wild hogs. Rafik was happy to stay inside, especially because Sweetheart had her very own shit shed. It was very small but really clean, and it even smelled nice.

Two or three times a day, Sweetheart would announce that they were being hailed by another SuperTruck; this would be followed by mutual scans and then there would be a conversation between the Captain and the other trucker. They could even see each other on-screen, and although Sweetheart protested every time, saying it wasn't true, the Captain kept telling the other drivers that his visual equipment was faulty and didn't let them see the interior of his SuperTruck. The other truckers seemed to be taking the Captain at his word and didn't mind. They had colourful and imaginative names such as Oil Rat Larry, Buttocks Brian, and Sunshine Suzette, who was Captain Sam's favourite lady trucker.

The other SuperTrucks had names, too. The first one was called Road Cutter, the other Wolf Leader, and Sunshine Suzette called hers Hope Wagon, but that was because she was carrying with her something she called "the light of belief."

The truckers exchanged gossip, news of the road, warnings of pirate activity, and weather reports. All topics of conversation were spiced with rude jokes, halfhearted insults, and a rich variety of colourful profanities, especially from Buttocks Brian.

Captain Sam tried to keep the dirty talk to a minimum, glancing worriedly at Rafik and smiling apologetically at Khan, even though Khan was mostly pretending to be asleep or staring off into the distance. The boy wasn't paying the slightest attention to the conversations—he was completely fixated on Sweetheart's most challenging puzzles.

When the SuperTrucks finally passed each other they would slow their speeds and honk their horns and flash their lights, but even at the slower speed they were going it was over in a blink of an eye.

It was no wonder that Rafik didn't even lift his head from the screen when Sweetheart first announced that they were being scanned.

"Well . . . that's not polite," muttered the Captain. "Scan back and ask for identification."

"Our scanner is out of reach," announced Sweetheart matter-of-factly.

"Rust," said the Captain. "I should have upgraded you, love."

There was an odd moment where everyone in the cabin was tense and silent, until Sweetheart suddenly declared "Scanner dropped off."

The Captain checked the screens. "Nothing on our radar?"

"Nothing, Captain. The scanner was more than ten miles away."

"Trouble?" Khan straightened in his seat, looking alert for the first time in days.

"No, it's probably nothing, just a rude trucker, trying to peep into my hull and see if he can undercut my prices," the Captain explained. But he still looked uneasy and he increased their speed to 240.

Khan was just settling back into his usual stupor when Sweetheart announced suddenly, "We are being scanned again, two miles behind, five vehicles—shark class of unrecognised type—closing in." Her voice was calm and pleasant but its effect on the two men was dramatic.

"Bring up the back shield, turn on the jammer," the Captain shouted and went into a flurry of activity.

This time Khan did not make inquiries, instead he turned to Rafik and ordered, "Buckle up." The coils wraped themselves around Khan and Rafik, who was already pinned to his seat by the sudden increase of speed. He looked around in confusion.

"What's going on? Who's after us?"

"Looks like highway pirates," Khan answered briskly and turned to the Captain. "How come you didn't detect them before?"

"They were smart," grunted the Captain. "Shark class can sometimes use a system they call 'stealth,' although it costs a huge amount of energy. So they detected us, scanned out of reach, and went in with jammers and stealth." He turned his head to the screen, which was showing five red dots progressing fast in the lower part of the screen.

"Sweetheart, increase speed to two ninety. Are they scanning again?" he asked.

"They are trying to," answered Sweetheart above the growing hum. "I am blocking them, although it takes seventeen percent more energy, and—"

"Let them through, briefly, do it as if they found a gap in our defences—let them scan just the hull and then close them off."

"Why are you doing that?" shouted Khan. The noise level was now too high to maintain a normal conversation.

"They are using a lot of power, and I am at half hull and not about to stop, so they might give up if they think it's not worth spending all their power tubes on the junk I'm hauling."

"They are scanning us," announced Sweetheart, "once . . . twice . . . they have lock . . . closing off gap . . . they are out."

The two adults watched the screen with intense concentration. "Come on, roaches," the Captain whispered under his breath. "I'm not worth it, drop off."

"They maintain course, increase speed, a mile off," announced Sweetheart, "you can see them on the left screen now."

The three of them turned their heads and watched the five slick-looking vehicles, flying in arrow formation across the highway. Their metal glinted in the sunlight as they closed the distance between themselves and the SuperTruck.

"That's not right," the Captain said, scratching his beard in bewilderment. "They must realise they're spending more on driving at this speed than they can possibly get from what I'm hauling."

"Captain, their scan was not concentrated on the haul at all," Sweetheart said. "In fact, they only scanned the cabin and a few auxiliary systems."

Both men looked at each other and swore in unison.

"It's Jakov," Khan paled. "How did he find us?"

"Not too hard, come to think of it." The Captain pressed many flashing buttons as he answered. "From what you told me, this Jakov of yours had a pretty good idea where you might be heading, and of course he would eventually find the guards who saw us leave Newport. I shouldn't have hit that oil smear," he added regretfully, "but he was touching her."

"Sharks, half a mile and closing," announced Sweetheart. "They are entering missile range."

Rafik could now clearly see the five vehicles on the screens. They were small in comparison to the SuperTruck, with black windows and huge back engines. Various weapons were mounted on their roofs and hanging from short metal wings at their sides.

Khan turned to Captain Sam, "Tell me you were jesting when you said you have no weapons on this truck."

"I was not. I don't believe in weapons," answered the Captain, not bothering to look back at Khan. "Any other trucks on radar? Anyone at all? Spread the word, love, find me someone, anyone."

"No, Captain," Sweetheart adjusted her volume, but she still sounded calm above the roaring of the engine.

"Throw an emergency call in a loop, say we have pirates on our tail and ask for help."

"I can't believe you have no weapons on this lump of rusting metal," Khan shouted.

This time Captain Sam did turn his head to Khan and opened his mouth but before he could say anything Sweetheart announced there was an incoming message.

"Only sound, don't waste energy on visuals," commanded the Captain.

"Hello again, Khan," Jakov's voice filled the cabin and caused Rafik to shiver. "Sorry about your bar and your lady, but you were being *very* unreasonable. I hope you can be reasonable now."

"You fuck," Khan screamed. "I will piss on your rusty metal corpse, Jakov."

"Save your breath for when you need to beg for your life," Jakov intoned calmly. "I only want the kid, so if you just st—" Captain Sam flicked a switch and the voice was cut off.

"I ain't wasting power talking to that rusting crowbar," he growled.

"Three hundred yards and closing," announced Sweetheart, then she corrected, "Two hundred yards, gun range, shooting—"

There was a flash of bright light to their right. "Warning shot," said the Captain. "Good, waste your power tubes, boys."

"What are we going to do?" Khan shouted, "This . . . truck . . . cannot outrun five sharks."

"Oh yeah?" answered the Captain, a thin smile appearing under his beard. "I could have filled half her haul space with weapons, and every time I met pirates, I could have gone in guns blazing. And you know what? Instead of becoming a slow-moving, half-full, weaponised gargantuan, I invested in two extra engines, so hold on to your seats, boys." He busied himself briefly. There was a series of loud clicks and whirls as two more long tubes emerged from the sides of the SuperTruck and it suddenly surged forward with incredible speed.

"Three hundred twenty-five . . . three hundred fifty," announced Sweetheart. Then she added, "Sharks matching speed, four hundred yards, missiles locked, three fired."

"Flares," shouted the Captain just as they were rocked violently forward and then to the side.

"Hull damage," announced Sweetheart calmly. "No energy to self-repair, another missile launched."

The truck rocked again. "Lower right anti-gravity hoop is down, lower left is damaged to eighty percent." The truck tilted to the right and Rafik's head snapped forward, his body pressing hard against his restraints, before the vehicle stabilized itself.

"Losing energy, three hundred forty miles an hour and falling, sharks at a hundred fifty yards, hundred twen—"

Jakov's voice filled the cabin again, "Nice try, Captain, but you cannot outrun me. I'm going to take your truck apart piece by piece if I have to." There was a series of shooting noises as he spoke, and Rafik could feel soft pings as the bullets hit.

"Hull at seventy percent," said Sweetheart as they slowed down even further.

"I'm going to kill him." The Captain's voice was thick with cold fury. "Turn off all unnecessary power."

The air flow in the cabin ceased and the bright light of day suddenly penetrated the windows.

"That added six percent to sp—"

"Including your voice announcements. Just show me the data on-screen," snapped the Captain.

Sweetheart's voice was cut off, and a number appeared on the screen: seven.

"Take off buffer as well."

The number changed to eleven percent, but the SuperTruck began to vibrate violently.

"And give me manual control," shouted the Captain above the increasing noise as he clamped heavy hands on the steering wheel.

They surged forward again; this time the flashing red numbers on the screen reached 350. The SuperTruck was shaking so violently that Rafik was trying with all his willpower not to be sick. Khan was noisily losing his lunch beside his seat.

"They will have to switch to manual steering to keep up with us"—Captain Sam seemed to be talking to himself—"so now it's an even field, let's see who . . . Khan, you rust pot, don't fall apart on me, and you'll be cleaning tha—" The rest of the sentence was lost as the Captain aggressively swivelled the steering wheel, trying to crush the sharks which were making an attempt to surround the SuperTruck, but they were too nimble to be caught with such a move.

"Khan, I need you on auxiliary controls!"

There was no answer from Khan. He was slumped unconscious in his seat.

"Damn speed fright," cursed the Captain as another set of explosions pushed them to the side curve of the highway. Rafik saw a brief spark from the screen, which showed an explosion on their left before it suddenly went blank.

Correcting their course again, the Captain looked back briefly and met Rafik's gaze. With one hand still holding the steering wheel, he pressed two buttons on the dashboard. Khan's and Rafik's seats began changing positions, and in a few heartbeats the boy found himself sitting next to the Captain and in front of the dashboard, which now displayed blinking buttons and flashing screens. Khan's seat was pushed to the back of the cabin.

"We're going to show these guys how to drive, boy," roared the Captain. "Press the yellow button second row to the left, yes, that one."

Rafik found the button, leaned over, and pressed it.

"Hold on tight, I call this one 'the worm.'"

Suddenly the screen showing the back of the truck was filled with a cloud of thick smoke. But a moment later the five sharks cut through the smoke cloud, weapons blazing.

"Do it again," roared Captain Sam.

Rafik complied, feeling the SuperTruck slow down a bit as he pressed the button.

The cloud of smoke did not slow down the pursuing vehicles; in fact, they were closer than before.

Jakov's voice filled the cabin again. "If that's all you've got, Captain, stopping you would be as easy as hacking your comm.

You really should have invested in a proper weapons system. Maybe after you give me the boy we could make a deal. I'll give you a discount on what's left of your haul."

Captain Sam swore as he pressed a button and cut Jakov's voice off. "He ain't coming inside you again, Sweetheart," he said, pressing several more. "Rafik, press that button one more time, but then press the red one, third to the right, a line below, yes, that one."

Another cloud of smoke blew, and this time the Captain pulled a lever just as Rafik pressed the second button. The Super-Truck slowed down abruptly, and Rafik's body slammed against the restraints as the SuperTruck flew up several yards in the air. The first shark drove through the smoke just as the SuperTruck came crashing down on it. There was a sea of sparks as metal screamed beneath them and an explosion that rocked them upwards again.

"That was a perfect worm, boy," roared the Captain as he slapped the wheel in triumph. "If Brinks the Brick could see me now, he would be a proud son of a rust bucket." He flicked several switches and said, "You're on, Sweetheart, screens on as well. We're not running anymore."

Captain Sam's joy was premature; the manoeuvre slowed Sweetheart significantly. As the numbers on the screen went down to close to two hundred, Captain Sam pressed on a large pedal underneath the steering wheel, and they began accelerating again. But one of the sharks had managed to squeeze past, and now it drove in front of them, its large cannon pointed at the cabin. The other two sharks were on either side of the Supertruck, while the fourth stayed at the back. They were surrounded.

"Hull at fifty-seven percent," said Sweetheart. "We are at two hundred thirty miles an hour."

"This is not a race anymore, love. This is war. We're going to play with magnets now, Sweetheart."

"That might damage power relays—"

"On my mark!" roared the Captain. "To the right side, now!"

The SuperTruck jerked upwards and tilted sharply to the right. Rafik, shouting in surprise and fear, grabbed his seat with both hands as his body slammed sideways against the restraints yet again.

For a heartbeat the SuperTruck's entire bottom was facing the shark as it sailed through the air purely on momentum. Rafik thought he heard Sweetheart's voice mentioning something about "reversing polarity." but he wasn't sure if those were her exact words.

What he knew for sure was that just as Sweetheart was about to crash the SuperTruck tilted back, extremely close to the highway surface, and the Shark to their left was gone. Instead there was another display of sparks and fire underneath them.

"I call that 'tilt and swallow,'" whooped the Captain, but their jubilation was cut short when Sweetheart informed them that four antigravity plates were damaged.

Another explosion behind them caused the SuperTruck to tilt yet again, this time upwards, losing power to its rear antigravity plates. Rafik saw sparks flying from the back of the SuperTruck— its rear now dragging on the highway surface.

Captain Sam's cheers turned into a tirade of profanities, and he shouted at Sweetheart to "lose the haul." It took only a few heartbeats before the back doors of the metal mammoth opened and several huge metal crates slid down from inside and out onto the freeway. One of the crates hit the shark behind the truck, tearing it in half.

With its weight off, the SuperTruck hull rose from the ground again as another shark closed in from the left. When it was at the same level as Captain Sam's seat, the black window of the shark flew open and the thick muzzle of a formidable-looking gun emerged.

"Duck!" shouted the Captain.

Rafik lowered his head just as the window to his left exploded and bullets filled the hull and the roof of the cabin.

The Captain tried to crush the shark but it accelerated, then slowed back down again and fired another load. Rafik covered his head and bent as low as he could, as pieces of dried sausages and spouts of cursed water sprayed the cabin. All he could think of was the carnage he had witnessed at the bar. He wanted to crawl somewhere dark and safe and hide forever.

When he finally gathered the courage to lift his head, the shark was coming in for a third pass, this time from Sweetheart's right side. Rafik heard Captain Sam shouting at him to duck, but all he could do was watch as the masked driver trained his gun straight on him. From behind his head a hand holding a gun stuck out from the broken window, and a series of deafening shots erupted. One of the shots must have hit its mark, because the shark wavered, then drove full speed straight into the road's curve, spinning through the air before crushing behind them. Only the front shark remained.

Khan fell back into his seat, still pale but with a look of satisfaction spread across his face.

Jakov's furious voice filled the cabin again: "I'm going to kill your truck and I'm going to kill you."

The mounted gun on the shark swivelled towards them and barked fire. Everyone ducked, but this time the bullets were not aimed at the cabin but lower, into the SuperTruck's engine.

"Receiving damage," announced Sweetheart.

"Can you crush him?" shouted Khan, crouching behind Rafik's seat.

"He's too fast," answered the Captain, beads of sweat pouring down his face.

"Exit in two miles, damage alert, forward engine flooding." The SuperTruck's voice was becoming distorted.

"Hold on, Sweetheart," roared the Captain, desperation in his voice. He slammed the brakes hard. With a terrible, high-pitched whine, the SuperTruck lurched forward as it came to a complete halt so abruptly that Khan flew forward, smashing his shoulder into Rafik's seat before falling down to the cabin floor with a heavy grunt.

Caught by surprise, the last shark kept driving. But after a short while they could see the small vehicle slowing down, then turning around and heading back.

"How's your gun?" the Captain said.

"Empty," winced Khan, getting up from the floor.

"Maybe I should reconsider my no-weapons policy," the Captain muttered into his beard.

"No kidding." Khan got up slowly, massaging his bruised shoulder. There was blood coming out of his nose.

The shark stopped at a distance—short enough to shoot at them, but not so close that the SuperTruck could suddenly surge forward and crush it.

"Send the kid out, and I'll let you live." Jakov's voice filled the cabin. "I'm not going to ask you again."

The two men looked at each other.

The shark slowly progressed towards them.

"There is a crowbar somewhere in the back," said Captain Sam. "Search behind the kegs." As Khan rummaged through the mess, the Captain pressed a button and the seat restraints withdrew. "It ain't over yet, boy," he said with a tight smile.

Rafik took a deep breath. "Captain, let me out. Please."

"No way, boy, there is still fight in this trucker," Captain Sam clenched a mighty fist but his brow was wrinkled with worry.

Khan came back empty-handed, looking despaired. "What now?"

Captain Sam turned to watch the shark in front of them "We fight that rust face."

Rafik shook his head. "Jakov has guns, Captain; he killed Dominique and Martinn, too. Let me out. Maybe I could convince him . . ."

Khan was the only one to respond this time. "No, there must be another way."

But the trucker's expression had suddenly lost resolve.

"Captain, he will kill Sweetheart," said Rafik urgently as the shark came closer.

"Rust," Captain Sam swore as he pressed a button. The passenger door began to slowly open with a loud puff of hydraulics.

"No, Captain." Kahn surged forward to grab Rafik, but Captain Sam's open palm slammed into his chest.

Khan turned his eyes to the boy. They were full of defeat and anger. "Rafik . . ." he pleaded, as the boy slid out of the truck and climbed down. As soon as his feet touched the road, Rafik moved away from Sweetheart, waving his hands in the air in the hope of attracting Jakov's attention. The shark turned away from the truck and began moving towards the boy.

Just then, the shark jerked sideways as a mushroom of glowing fire exploded to its side. It accelerated past Rafik, its side door sliding upwards. Rafik threw himself out of the reach of Jakov's outstretched metallic arm, and as the shark drove away he rolled onto his back and caught a glimpse of Jakov's scowl. For a moment he was afraid the shark would turn back, but it sped away.

The ground was surprisingly cool to the touch. Rafik got to his feet and ran back to Sweetheart, just as a large SuperTruck came into view. As Rafik climbed back to the cabin, he heard a voice saying, "Did you say you were having trouble with *pirates*, Sam? Cause I ain't seeing many of them here."

"Warhead Steve," the Captain thumped his hands on his wheel, whooping with joy, "speaking of the wrong guy at the right time."

"I believe it was you who told me I was a fool for carrying weapons on my rig, Captain," said the trucker.

"I believe I owe you an apology and enough drink to fill your haul," answered Captain Sam. "I owe you, trucker, big time." He turned to Khan, who was slumped in his seat, looking pale, sweat dripping down his face. "And I think you owe an apology as well."

"Me?" Khan raised his head from his hands, "I don't even know the guy."

"Not to Warhead Steve. You called Sweetheart 'a lump of rusty metal,'" the Captain said in all seriousness.

Khan took several deep breaths to steady himself before saying, "I wasn't thinking straight, Captain. I apologize sincerely."

"Don't apologize to me, apologize to *her*."

To Khan's credit, he did.

24

It took them three more days to reach New Denver, one of the larger towns bordering the Tarakan highway. According to Captain Sam, it had a family of competent mechanics. Warhead Steve and his co-driver, Krunk, helped the Captain with the initial repairs before two other truckers showed up and escorted the damaged Sweetheart off the Tarakan highway. It felt like a funeral procession. Sweetheart was in a sorry state, barely able to communicate, and when she did, her voice was broken and distorted. She had almost no auxiliary power, and one of her engines was dead. Her body was torn where blasters had scorched her hull, and she was riddled with bullet holes. Surprisingly, it was Captain Sam who had a cheerful demeanour throughout the journey. He told Rafik he felt like someone who'd found out that his beloved had a terrible accident but was going to pull through, so he didn't dwell on anything but the necessary steps that would make recovery possible.

"She can partly heal herself," he said, as Sweetheart was towed into a large garage, surrounded by repairmen and mechanical moving boxes called bots.

"All SuperTrucks have self-repair systems, so with enough power tubes she could regenerate her own hull. We truckers look after each other. I'll get the power tubes quick enough."

They watched as the mechanics and the bots moved around Sweetheart like flies around a corpse. Captain Sam sighed, then shrugged to no one in particular.

"I'll need help with the rest of the repairs. It'll cost me an arm and a leg, but there's a gal up the East Coast who's a genius with the internal mechanics of SuperTrucks. I'll drive up to her as soon as Sweetheart feels well enough. It'll take a couple weeks, but if I get lucky with some merchandise to haul, the trip might even pay for itself. After all that, when she's ready, myself and some of the boys are going to find this Jakov . . ." He didn't complete the sentence, but Rafik knew he wouldn't want to be in the weapon merchant's shoes when Captain Sam came for revenge.

Khan approached and stood next to them. "Captain, I say this with all sincerity: I can never repay you for this."

Captain Sam snorted and laughed, then spat on the ground and twirled his long beard. "Ah, no, Khan, I took the job. All I want is my original payment when you get your hands on some coin."

"I will repay my debt," promised Khan as he extended his hand.

Captain Sam did not look convinced, but nevertheless he shook Khan's hand and said, "I talked to a guy I know, Jeremiah, he's a youngster driving a ten-wheeler. He'll be going up the narrow backroads tomorrow, and doesn't mind the extra company. It will take you longer, and it'll be a bumpy ride, but you'll reach Regeneration eventually. And if you ask me, with this Jakov after you, it's probably better that you stay off the highway for now."

Khan nodded as the Captain continued. "This Jeremiah's quite a character, but as we truckers say, 'his oil checks out,' and he even has a few weapons on board, so you'll be safe."

"You're not coming with us?" asked Rafik.

Captain Sam turned his head to meet the boy's eyes. "No," he said, not unkindly. "I have to stay with Sweetheart and make sure she recovers, but I hope our roads will cross again."

Rafik nodded and said what his father would say when he wished for something to happen: "I will pray to the Prophet Reborn for that."

The Captain chuckled. "You do that, Rafik, you pray for all of us, and one day we shall meet again and you can solve all of Sweetheart's puzzles." He fished Fahid's knife out of his pocket and handed it back to Rafik. "I didn't bring you to Regeneration, so I'm giving you your blade back. I even cleaned it for you. Sharpened it, too."

Khan and Captain Sam talked some more. Rafik, palming his brother's blade and feeling guilty and happy at the same time, made an excuse and left the two men.

Later, when Khan found the boy, he was sitting on a large rock and staring off into the distance.

"Come on, Rafik," Khan said gently, "let's find somewhere to lay our heads tonight."

Rafik blinked, as if coming out of a dream, then turned to Khan and spread his fingers wide. "Is this why you're taking me away?" he asked. "Is this why Jakov is after me?"

"Put your hand away," Khan hissed.

Rafik shook his head and waved his hand in defiance. "Why? Why did I have to leave my village? Why are you and Jakov fighting over me? Why did Dominique and Martinn have to die? Why did Jakov shoot at Sweetheart and Captain Sam? Is it because I can solve puzzles? Why is that so important? Tell me, Khan!"

"Lower your voice, rust." Khan looked around nervously.

"I will not, I want to know." Rafik was now standing, facing Khan, looking at him with resolve mixed with anger. "Tell me why my family took me away from my village. Why Eithan, my blood brother, threw rocks at me? Why do people shoot at each other over me? Why? I can't do anything special—why am I so important?"

Rafik was crying now. Small fists of rage pounded Khan relentlessly until the man had had enough. He caught one of Rafik's hands, and then the other.

"Rafik, listen to me," he said between gritted teeth. "Rust, stop misbehaving or I'll smack you. As far as anyone here is concerned you are my nephew, so I could break every bone in your body and no one would mind. Look at me."

Exhausted from the ordeal on the highway, Rafik gave up struggling. He sagged in place, shoulders hunched, eyes downcast.

Khan checked their surroundings. When he was satisfied that no one got curious enough to find out what their little drama was about, he spoke in a hushed tone. "You're a very special boy, Rafik. You can do things that very few people can do. You can solve puzzles. That's what makes you special. In the truck, you tried those weird puzzle games and after one day you were playing them at the highest levels of difficulty. I know, because Captain Sam told me so."

"Those puzzles weren't difficult for me," Rafik mumbled.

"Exactly. That is why there are people who are looking for anyone with your gift. These folks want to find someone like you so much that even people like me know about it. They will take care of you, and teach you wonderful things that I know nothing about. Then it will all make sense. I promise, son, it will all eventually make sense."

Khan gently pried Dominique's glove from the boy's grip and put it on Rafik's hand. "We need to go now," he said, as Rafik got slowly to his feet.

It didn't take long for Khan to find a woman who would give them lodging and dinner in exchange for a few coins and Khan's offer to chop wood. The meal was greasy; they shared it on one plate and had to eat with their hands, but Rafik didn't mind.

Afterwards, they shared a room that had two itchy cots. Rafik whispered his prayers and washed in a small tub while Khan counted and recounted their remaining coins. When Rafik was done, Khan said he was going out to look for supplies. He left Rafik in the room and locked the door from the outside. Rafik lay on a cot and tried not to think about the last few days. He played with his brother's blade, and though it was not the right thing to do, he engraved his name on the wooden wall near his bed, and added the name of the Prophet Reborn in the holy language.

Memories of the violence he'd experienced in Dominique's bar and on the Tarakan highway kept invading his thoughts, and his fear came back to haunt him. To keep his mind off things, he busied himself searching for patterns in the room. He counted the stains on the walls and the wooden planks of the floor and even the circles the flies made around the closed shutters. The sounds of footsteps and short bursts of laughter came from below. He counted the number of steps taken between the outbursts of laughter. Eventually all the patterns merged into one, and Rafik found himself floating in the familiar void again.

He played his game on the wall of symbols, ignoring the voices which occasionally penetrated the peaceful bubble surrounding him.

". . . You did not tell me you have a boy."

"He's not my boy. He's someone I'm escorting as a favour."

"He's cute."

"You're cute."

". . . What if he wakes up?"

"He never wakes up, sleeps like a log, this one, believe me, now come here."

There was more laughter and murmuring and sounds, which Rafik chose to ignore. He was by the wall of symbols, playing his puzzle, and the world made sense.

25

Jeremiah's ten-wheeler was in a sorry state; its body was so patched you couldn't tell which metal was part of the original vehicle. The cabin was tiny in comparison to Sweetheart's: only one row of soft, worn-out seats, with the driver sitting in the middle. The air flowed only when the windows were open, and whenever the truck stopped or slowed down, the cabin would get unbearably hot. There were no flashing screens, no stories to watch or puzzles to solve. Considering its condition, it was no surprise that the vehicle didn't speak, and if it had a name, Jeremiah never mentioned it.

They drove at a speed that would have impressed Rafik two or three months before but now seemed like crawling. When they were driving uphill, the truck would slow to a walking speed and cough and bellow clouds of black smoke that would linger behind them. Rafik could not imagine what it would be like to stand behind the truck when it moved past; the farmers they passed held cloths over their faces for protection and waved their hands in the air to disperse the residue. Apparently the truck had a special engine, which in the eyes of Jeremiah compensated for its slow speed and the smog it created. It could have been fuelled by almost anything: oil, wood, grain, and even certain types of crushed stones. Jeremiah claimed he would never swap places with the SuperTruck drivers, or even the fourteen-wheelers, and, as he said, "have to choose between being a slave to the Oil Baron of the north or bowing to the City of Towers."

Despite having a faithful wife, four sons, and three daughters, Jeremiah seemed to be on a single-minded mission to spread his seed throughout his route. Their journey was filled with tales of the trucker's various conquests, and each village or hamlet brought a new series of such stories, which, Rafik had to admit, were very educational. Rafik wondered how Jeremiah ever had time to actually drive. When not telling stories, Jeremiah sang at the top of his lungs, accompanying himself with a tiny four string guitar while steering the truck with his left leg. The songs were not the kind of poetry you found in the holy scripts, but were more like Dominique's banter. Rafik's vocabulary would be greatly enriched by the end of the trip.

All the villages they visited were closely guarded, with high wooden fences and sentry towers, but once Jeremiah was identified, they were always allowed to drive through the gate and spend the night inside the protective walls.

"It's my route," explained Jeremiah as he checked his appearance in a broken glass, running his hand through greasy, thinning blond hair and spraying himself with a liquid he called "love water." "They knew my father and now they know me, so I get special prices." He winked and grinned as he slid out of his seat. "And special treatment, too . . ."

On their fifth day of travel they arrived at a small town called New Jerusalem. The name excited Rafik greatly, since it was very similar to a city mentioned many times in the holy scripts. The guards seemed to know Jeremiah very well and waved them through in a friendly manner. As soon as they were through the gate, Khan turned to Rafik and made sure he was wearing Dominique's glove.

Rafik watched with interest as people moved out of the truck's way or just stood and watched it manoeuvre through the narrow streets. A few waved at them, and Rafik waved back, although he made sure not to use the gloved hand, just to be on the safe side.

The village felt similar to his home, but there were certain obvious differences: women wore short sleeves and did not cover their heads, men had short beards and wore their hair long, and the few boys and girls he saw mixed freely. Yet the overall feeling of community was a painful reminder of the family and friends he'd left behind. Jeremiah parked the truck expertly, and he and Khan went out to the awaiting crowd. Bartering took time, and the heat inside the truck was uncomfortable, but every once in a while Khan made sure Rafik was still inside and warned him about getting out.

Once the business was concluded, and although it was only midday, Jeremiah declared they would be stopping for the night. His gaze drifted to a woman who was standing inconspicuously near one of the small huts with a large, yellow-haired baby in her arms. Khan tried to argue for a speedy departure, but Jeremiah was quick to remind him who was in charge; since both Khan and Rafik had been taken as a personal favour to Captain Sam, they should just shut the rust up. After that Jeremiah actually ordered Kahn to help him unload several items, including a huge wedge of smelly cheese and a smoked leg of lamb. Then he walked away towards the woman without glancing back.

Jeremiah disappeared into the hut, and the door quickly slammed shut behind him. Khan kicked the dirt in frustration and spat on the ground. He checked again that Rafik wore Dominique's glove, then ordered the boy to stay inside the truck while he went to look for a place to stay.

Soon it got unbearably hot inside the cabin. Rafik lowered his window and leaned out, keeping himself busy by looking for patterns. He was too engrossed in his own world to notice a group of boys and girls until they marched past the truck and towards a small, fenced-in field. They were talking loudly among themselves. Just like in Rafik's village, the boys were constantly teasing one another, pushing and shoving playfully, getting into mock fights, or challenging one another in different ways. The only difference was that there were plenty of girls in this group, and Rafik watched them with fascination as they passed by.

One boy, obviously the leader of the group, was holding a ball made of leather patches sewn together. They quickly formed two teams, and soon they were competing against each other, each term taking turns kicking the ball around the field with the intent of sending it into a marked area on the opposite side of the field. It didn't take long for Rafik to figure out the rules. He was fascinated by the game. The best player was a squat boy who charged powerfully through the defence of the rival team to score point after point for his team, but almost equally skilled was a girl who was faster and nimbler than any of the boys and was quickest to cover the length of the field.

After a while a woman came and ordered one of the boys to stop playing and come with her. Subsequently, his team began losing badly. Once it was obvious that it would be unfair to continue playing in such uneven circumstances, the kids huddled together and tried to re-form the teams. There was much arguing and shouting, and it seemed they would soon come to blows.

Then one pointed at the truck and said something. They all turned and looked straight at Rafik, who immediately withdrew to the inside of the cabin. The fast girl detached herself from the group and strode purposefully to Jeremiah's truck. As opposed to the girls in Rafik's village, she did not avert her eyes but sought his, looking up at him with an open, challenging stare.

"Can you play?" she asked. Her accent was strange, but Rafik could still understand her words.

He shrugged, not trusting himself to speak.

"Well? Can you or can't you?" she snapped, impatiently tapping her foot.

When he failed to answer she said, "Oh, never mind," and turned to leave.

"Wait." He heard himself say and pushed his body forward. "I've never played this game before, but I think I know how."

She stopped and turned back, "Really? You think it's that easy?"

He thought about it for a moment and then nodded, accepting the unspoken challenge.

"Then you're on my team," she said.

Rafik pushed the door open and jumped down. She stood almost a head taller than him, with short black hair, light green eyes, and a narrow face. She stuck her hand out and said, "I'm Rijana."

He hesitated, understanding instinctively what he needed to do. But his hand must have had a mind of its own, as he found himself shaking hands with the girl. "Rafik," he said weakly, realising too late he was wearing Dominique's colourful glove on his other hand.

She looked down with open curiosity, but a few impatient shouts from the awaiting group stopped any questions about it. Without another word he followed her back to the waiting group, shoving his hand deep into his pocket.

Luckily, no one else wanted to shake hands or greet him in any other way when he was introduced. Many of the boys glared at him, and Rafik instinctively understood why. He was a stranger, and his presence was tolerated only for the sake of the game.

The game resumed, and Rafik quickly found out it was harder to master than it looked. He had to fight his instinct to touch the ball with his hands, and quickly realised that the game was as tough and physically demanding as Warriors and Infidels. Soon his team was down five points, mostly because of his mistakes. It was obvious his teammates were not happy. Rijana reassured Rafik that it was okay and that "These things happen," which made matters even worse. Eventually she told him to move to the far end of the field, and almost immediately the ball landed at his feet. A boy from the rival team turned and charged. With growing panic Rafik tried to figure out who to kick the ball to. His teammates were running in different directions, trying to block, move, or open up a space, but there was no one available. And just then, in a blink of an eye, Rafik saw the pattern. The boys and girls were still running around the field, but to Rafik they became the moving symbols on the puzzle wall of his dreams.

There, I can see it.

The boy who challenged Rafik was almost upon him. Rafik saw his legs moving one after another, thumping the ground and raising small clouds of dust. He waited for the boy's right leg to hit the ground and then he turned quickly to the left, passing the boy before he could turn and moving to the middle of the playing field. He could now see everything that was happening around him clearly, as if they were all moving slower than he was. Each player was a symbol moving in a different direction, and Rijana was running at him.

Rafik kicked the ball just as another boy slammed into him, sending them both sprawling to the ground. He rolled on the ground several times. Within a heartbeat he was on his feet again, and he saw Rijana manoeuvring with the ball exactly where he thought she would be. She turned, kicked, and scored easily.

That was the turning point of the game. Rafik realised that each player had a moving pattern, and he acted on reflex to find the weakest point of the pattern and snatch the ball away cleanly from under their feet and pass it to Rijana. The rival team was beginning to show frustration, and the game became rougher, but Rafik didn't mind at all. He was a kid again, playing with other kids who didn't know about his curse. It was so long since he'd actually run as fast as he could, and he dodged, moved, pushed, kicked, and even once won a point for his team.

At some point it became too hot to wear Dominique's glove. Without thinking, Rafik peeled the glove off and shoved it in his pocket. He didn't care anymore—he was playing, running, sweating, laughing, and for a moment all felt as it should be.

Perhaps Khan would agree to stay in this village for a while. He could play this game and maybe talk to Rijana, who beamed at him every time he passed the ball to her.

Rafik's team had just won another point when Khan came charging into the field. He grabbed Rafik by the collar and, without saying a word, hauled him back into the truck.

"What do you think you're doing?" he shouted, his face red, after he slammed shut the truck's door.

"You can't tell me what to do! You're not my father!" Rafik heard himself shout back. "We were just playing."

Khan took three apples out of his pocket and threw one at him. "I just spent the entire afternoon haggling for some food for you, and I come back to see you running around without anything covering your hand. Do you know what would happen if they saw your tattoos? These people are no better than the rust buckets back at your village. Put on your glove. Now. I can't believe you were so irres . . ."

Rafik blocked out Khan's angry words, leaned back in his seat and looked outside. Losing another member of the team to grown-up interference must have signalled the end of the game. The kids were already dispersing, with the exception of Rijana, who was staring at the truck, close enough to perhaps see the two silhouettes behind the dirty front window.

As Khan kept berating him, Rafik lowered his gaze, spreading his fingers in front of his face. His hand was trapped in Dominique's glove for so long he only saw then that the markings were larger since the last time he'd examined them. The triangle, two crescent moons, and three balls were still there, just larger and more distinct, covering his fingertips and stretching down to his palm. To a casual observer it might have looked like a blotchy ink stain, but it took only one clear glance to see that it was more than that. It was due only to the intensity of the ball game and perhaps sheer luck that the other kids did not notice his markings. What would they have done if they had? The image of Eithan, his best friend, throwing a rock at the pony cart flashed before Rafik's eyes and he shook the memory away with disgust. When Rafik looked out again, Rijana moved a little closer to the truck, looking hesitant, as if waiting for something to happen. He wanted to talk to her, to explain why . . . or just to talk to her, but he couldn't, not now, or ever.

With a new surge of anger, Rafik suddenly leaned forward and pressed his hand against the dirty glass. "Why should I keep it a secret?" he shouted, "I've done nothing wrong, and you just want to keep me so you can sell me later."

Khan was dumbstruck for a moment, then he snatched Rafik's hand away from the window. "Rust, boy, did anyone see you?"

Rijana was already running away. There was no way to know if she saw the markings. "Let me go, let me go!" screamed Rafik, still struggling.

Khan let go of one of his hands and then struck Rafik, hard. "You bastard! You freak! You left me with nothing, nothing, you hear? My bar, my house, my Dominique, Martinn, you took it all from me, and now you're going to get me killed!" He hit the cowering boy once more. "I have the right, you hear? I have all the rights in this goddamn rusting world. Your family threw you out because they didn't have the guts to kill you themselves. I took care of you, I fed you, I gave you a bed, and you cost me everything!"

Khan opened the door, climbed out of the truck, and pulled Rafik after him so violently that he fell down and scraped his knees. Khan dragged him between the villagers, who were now openly staring at them. When he got to the hut that Jeremiah was in, he kicked the door repeatedly until it opened and the trucker came out, looking as if he had to get dressed in a hurry.

"What do you want?" he barked angrily.

"We're leaving. Now." Khan was panting with rage.

"Go rust. You don't tell me where and when to go."

"The kid, someone—" Khan hesitated only briefly. "In a matter of moments we might all get lynched."

The look on Khan's face must have been convincing enough,

because Jeremiah swore and ducked inside for a moment, then came back with his boots in his hands. A baby was crying inside, and a woman swore at the top of her lungs as the door slammed shut. They ran back to the truck, climbed into it, and Jeremiah began manoeuvring the heavy vehicle while shouting obscenities at Khan and Rafik. They were already driving up the main street when they saw the gathering of men walking towards them, led by Rijana.

Jeremiah stepped on the acceleration pedal, and the truck coughed black smoke and lurched forward. The mob began to run down the street shouting angrily. Rafik heard "Show him to us!" "You brought a fiend into the village!" and even one "Hang them" before another cloud of black smoke reduced the shouting mob to coughing fits. Fortunately, the guards were still unaware of the situation, and they opened the gates as the truck approached.

A few miles later, Jeremiah stopped the truck, and an angry shouting match between him and Khan ensued. Jeremiah accused Khan of being the cause of their situation, while Khan claimed he could not have been in two places at once and if the trucker would have kept his "damned rod" in his pants for a little while longer, all of this could have been avoided. They were shouting and swearing. At some point, the trucker threatened to leave them both at the side of the road, to which Khan replied that he would then find his way to Jeremiah's village and have a word with Jeremiah's wife. Both men ran out of steam shortly after that and went quiet. Sometime later Jeremiah cursed the world in general and his bad luck in particular and resumed driving. The rest of their journey was much quieter.

26

Khan woke up Rafik with a light squeeze to his shoulder. "See this?" He pointed at the silhouettes of the town's buildings on top of the hill. "This is Regeneration." For the first time since the fight at Dominique's bar, Khan actually smiled as he added, "My fat little hog of a brother lives here. He and I do not get along too well, but we'll pay him a visit," he patted Rafik on the head. "You know the old saying, 'Blood's thicker than lard, eh?'" He chuckled at his own joke. "From here on it's gonna be an easy ride all the way."

Jeremiah snorted to himself but said nothing, busying himself with manoeuvring up the hill and around the multitude of trucks, carts, and people walking on the the narrow road. Khan, on the other hand, was in a rare chatty mood, and so Rafik learned that Regeneration was not just the biggest human-built, post-Catastrophe town; it was also the closest one to the Tarakan City of Towers. On a good day you could even see the outlines of the south towers melding into the heavens. It must have been a foreboding sight for the new, desperate settlers, for it was common knowledge that many babies born close to the Tarakan city would have terrible deformities or bear the mark. So much so that other communities dubbed Regeneration "freak town."

In the old days, when the invisible barrier surrounding the City of Towers still barred humanity from entrance, people got sick and died just from foraging food too close to the city. Yet the founders of Regeneration were as resilient as they were desperate, for most of them simply had no other place to live. Life on the edge meant the people of Regeneration had to work together and accept everyone who was willing to help. For a time, it became the only place where humans who bore the mark could walk freely, a fact that Khan repeated to Rafik several times.

"You mean I could walk around without wearing Dominique's glove?" Rafik asked, still struggling with the idea.

"Oh, no," Khan quickly replied, patting lightly on Rafik's gloved hand. "Keep it on, kid. Even in this town, you never know . . . you just never know . . ."

Surprisingly enough, Regeneration had no protective walls but the natural defence of the hill it was built on. It was far enough away from other settlements and close enough to the dangerous air and soil of the City of Towers to deter raiders. Yet, even without walls, Regeneration had heavily armed guards, a roadblock, a gate, and something called a toll, which Jeremiah had to pay. This all took time, so it wasn't until midday that they drove into town.

"Look up." Khan pointed once they entered the narrow streets of Regeneration.

Rafik had to lean out from the open window to see Regeneration's most prominent feature. In the past few weeks he had seen a man whose face was half metal, and ridden in a SuperTruck on a Tarakan highway. He was sure he had seen it all, but what Rafik saw now left him speechless. Two long rows of metal bars, human-sized in length and twice a man's width in thickness, were miraculously suspended in midair above the town. Facing each other in pairs and evenly spaced, the rows of metal bars began above a high metal platform in Regeneration and disappeared into the distance.

"Amazing, isn't it?" Khan remarked. "They go all the way to the City of Towers. Of course, when the first settlers discovered the platform, they didn't know of it. They only wanted the metal." He chuckled. "But they soon discovered you don't mess with Tarakan devices. The platform was charged with some kind of energy that could fry a man in a heartbeat, and the bars were too high for anyone to reach, so after they made a few attempts the people of Regeneration left the platform and the metallic bars alone.

"Then one day, this long tube appeared on the platform and opened its doors. A few dozen fools walked in, and the doors suddenly closed and the they found themselves flying all the way to the City of Towers.

"From then on, the Long Tube continued to go back and forth, connecting Regeneration with the City of Towers. This really changed things around here. From a place no one wanted to visit, Regeneration became the easiest way to get in and out of the City of Towers. I mean, on a good day, you can even see the city from here. You wouldn't believe the house prices now . . ."

Unfortunately, Rafik missed the view of the City of Towers when they finally arrived at the center of Regeneration, because the skies were thick with grey clouds. Jeremiah didn't even bother to say farewell. As soon as they were out of the truck he sped off, leaving them hopping in thick mud, trying to escape the polluted cloud he left behind.

Regeneration reminded Rafik of Newport, except it was even bigger and dirtier. They walked in the rain for what seemed like an eternity until finally, soaked to the bone and shivering, they reached a small wooden house with a large backyard filled with all kinds of junk. A scary-looking dog warned them off until its owner came out to see who was loitering in his yard.

Gandir turned out to be a fatter, balder, older, and meaner

version of Khan, and if any brotherly love still remained between the two, it was too subtle for Rafik to detect. He reluctantly let them into his crumbling house and did not react well when Khan asked him for a very large sum of coin. In fact, he was so angry, Rafik was afraid he might set his dog, aptly named Fangs, on them. Rafik, still wet, was sent to another room so the two brothers could argue.

The smaller room doubled as both a bedroom and a bathroom with the help of a hole in the floor, which was obviously too small for its intended use. The smell was so bad he gagged several times and would have thrown up if he'd had any food in his stomach. Rafik ended up standing with his back to the door, as far away as possible from the bog hole. He wanted to pray, but he was too disgusted to touch the floor. Instead he leaned on the door and took his mind off the cold and hunger by listening to the two brothers shouting obscenities at each other.

"You can't march in here after all these years and with a boy and demand coin."

"I ain't demanding. Brother, I am asking. Blood is thicker than la . . . water."

"Oh, now you are telling me about blood? I piss on your blood. You took off with that fat bitch and left me with Ma, and never a coin did I see from you."

"Say another word on Dominique and I'll break all of what's left of your teeth. And don't whine about Ma. I remember she died very quickly after I left, from the *cold*, you said, and you live in *our* home now. Did I see a rusting coin from you? No. But I need my cut now."

There was a sound of furniture being moved and a chair falling on the floor, as the two brothers must have gotten up to their feet. "You rusting gob, you think you can tell me what to do anymore? I'll tear you limb from limb and let my dog chew on your scrawny bones. I'll feed him that ugly kid of yours too."

Khan was obviously trying to keep control of himself. "Oh, sit the fuck down, Gandir, or you'll hurt yourself. Look, you're already sweating like a hog. Let's eat something. Fine, if you don't want to help me out of brotherly love, I got a business proposition for you."

It took some time but Gandir eventually relented and agreed to give Khan the coin, only after being promised double in return. He even had the level-headed idea of buying the travel slips to the City of Towers himself so that Khan and Rafik would not need to spend too much time out in the open, but he flatly refused when Khan tried to press for extra coin.

"I need food and shelter for the boy," argued Khan, "as well as ammunition for my pistol. I'm out of bullets."

Gandir snorted dismissively. "You were always quick to pull the trigger." This led to yet another bout of shouting, but eventually Gandir relented and gave Khan twenty steel coins, promising to buy ammunition as well as Long Tube tickets.

After that things calmed down, and soon the brothers got very drunk. Khan spun his own version of their adventures, which made him look courageous and just. There were also some differences between the way he described the chase on the highway and the way Rafik remembered it, but he was hardly listening anymore. He found a fairly clean rag, spread it in the corner of the bedroom farthest from the hole, and lay down. Soon sleep conquered hunger.

Morning came late, as both brothers were sprawled on the floor in a stupor. Rafik tiptoed between empty casks and rolling mugs and found a few smoked strips of dried meat. They tasted as if they might have been meant for the dog, but he was too hungry to be fussy about what he ate. By midday the brothers woke up and Khan went out "on business." Soon after that, Gandir went out as well, locking Rafik inside the hut and warning him that Fangs would tear him apart if he tried to get out.

Time slowed, and eventually, out of sheer boredom, Rafik began cleaning the house. Both brothers came home in the middle of the night, completely drunk and barely standing. They immediately resumed their bickering and completely ignored Rafik, who curled up in his corner and tried to fall asleep. All in all, it had been a boring day, but just before he fell asleep, Rafik decided it had been a good day because nothing really bad had happened. The following day would be very different.

27

At high noon the next day Kahn and Rafik were standing close enough to see the Long Tube arriving at the platform, which was about 250 paces away. Even after the wonders of the SuperTruck, Rafik's mouth opened in awe when he saw the silvery tube sail between floating metal bars as blue and red lightning bolts jumped from one floating bar to its top surface and the tube descended silently from the top of the platform.

"Where is he? Rust," muttered Khan impatiently as he searched the crowd.

The Long Tube had an unfailing daily schedule, but it still attracted what seemed like the entire population of Regeneration. All Rafik could see from his vantage point at the ground level was a forest of legs, carts laden with goods, and plenty of weapons. Then the Long Tube's doors opened and several uniformed warriors stepped out, immediately drawing Rafik's attention with their menacing mechanical presence.

Rafik's heart fluttered in fear and awe as he watched them descend the platform, easily cutting through the thick of the crowd, which hastened to move out of their way. There was no question who and what these warriors were, for the armour and metal attached to various parts of their bodies, and the formidable weapons they carried, marked them as the abominations mentioned countless of times in the holy scripts. Rafik stood in his place so rigidly that even Khan noticed something was wrong with the boy. When he realised what Rafik was staring at, he waved his hand dismissively. "Oh, don't worry, those are just Trolls. You'll get to see a lot of them in the City of Towers."

Rafik considered this for a long moment. He was brought up with the absolute knowledge that these . . . Trolls were to be feared and despised, but so were the marked, those who wore the tattoos and attached metal to their marks. It never occurred to him before that he, Rafik, might actually be one of them. A shiver ran up his spine, and he pushed the thought away, unable to deal with the possible consequences of such a reality. Instead he asked, "Are we going to travel on the Long Tube?"

Khan was so preoccupied looking for Gandir, that Rafik had to ask three times before he got Khan's attention.

"What? Oh yeah, as soon as my fat, lazy brother brings us the travel slips," Khan said as he kept searching. "Since the Long Tube works all by itself, you would think it should be free for all to ride, but even the oldest Regeneration dwellers don't remember a time when one faction or another didn't tax passengers for the privilege. I've lost count of the amount of bloody confrontations over who controls the platform. These days, the Council of the City of Towers is in charge of the platform, so now at least the travel slips and taxes are well organized. Ah . . . here's my miserable excuse for a brother."

Gandir shouldered his way back, huffing and puffing, as beads of sweat dripped from his brow.

"Where were you, you fat hog?" Khan spat as soon as his brother was in sight.

"It took forever to get these," Gandir snarled back, waving the slips. "And you owe me thirty extra, you bony mule fucker."

Khan snatched the slips, "And where is the ammunition I told you to get?"

Gandir shrugged, "Couldn't get that in time, and the travel passes were costly enough, so find something else to do with your trigger finger, for once."

"You lying, sad excuse for a lard bucket," Khan clenched his fists, "you probably spent the coin eating those disgusting pies you're always stuffing your face with. Don't deny it, I can smell them on your stinking breath."

Any further response Gandir tried to offer was drowned out by the bellowing horn blast, and the awaiting crowd immediately surged forward.

Without saying a word of good-bye, Khan grabbed Rafik by the arm and moved forward, elbowing his way to the platform while pulling the boy after him. Rafik kept bumping into torsos and elbows, which he endured in silence. The flow of people must have led them the wrong way because they ended up being turned away from the cargo loading area. Khan swore loudly and changed directions abruptly. Rafik turned to follow Khan when the crowd behind them parted briefly and he saw a distinctive metal hand move between the people.

Terror swept through Rafik, as the image of Dominique being shot flashed in front of his eyes. He felt his body begin to tremble uncontrollably and pulled hard on Khan's hand, trying to shout a warning, but it was like a hand gripped his throat and no sound came out. The pull was enough for Khan to stop, and as people quickly passed them in the chaotic cue, he turned back to Rafik. This time Rafik found his voice but a second blast from the platform swallowed his words completely. Khan shrugged irritably, turned back and yanked Rafik after him with a force that could not be resisted.

They were only a few paces away from the platform when Khan suddenly realised the trap. He froze, his eyes wide with comprehension, then turned and shouldered himself and Rafik away from the platform gate. But by then, Jakov and his men were already upon them. A man stepped from among the crowd and grabbed Rafik's shoulder. Rafik shouted a warning and Khan whirled around, punching the man in the face, then turned to kick another in the groin.

They ran for their lives. Several times Rafik felt a hand closing in on his shoulder or arm, but every time he managed to slip away. Khan changed directions abruptly. They burst into and through a tavern and ran past the slippery ground of the privy stalls outside, skidding around a corner and pushing an unfortunate man back into the shit shed. Doors were kicked open, people shouted in a mixture of surprise and fear, and Rafik jumped over a man twisting in pain on the floor after being hit in the face by Khan. They ran through small streets, backyards, and over a wooden fence. It was like the game of Warriors and Infidels, but so much scarier.

Eventually though, exhausted and lost, Khan miscalculated, and they found themselves at a dead end. They tried to climb, but two shots buried themselves into the stone wall, forcing them to jump back down. A volley of shots sent pieces of rock and dust down on their heads. Khan shot back, pushed Rafik into a groove on the side wall, and leaned against him, practically pinning the boy. Rafik saw Khan checking the number of bullets in his pistol, his face contorted with fury, as he tried to think of a way out of the mess. Unfortunately, there were no easy solutions. After another volley of shots, they heard Jakov.

"You cost me a lot of time and plenty of coin, my best bodyguard Radja, and a few good men whom I unfortunately paid in advance, so excuse me if I'm running out of patience here."

Khan looked around, his eyes wide with fear, but they were trapped.

"Do I need to do the counting-to-three part?" Jakov mocked. "Or can we skip over the boring etiquette and finish this farce?"

"Jakov, you backstabbling rusthead," Khan shouted back, "you took everything from me."

"I gave you a fair offer and you chose to disregard it. You

should have known the consequences." Jakov's voice was hard. "Now be a good businessman, cut your losses or die trying to keep something you can't handle."

"Fine," shouted Khan, banging his head softly against the wall behind him and shutting his eyes. "Let's make a deal, then. I'll give you forty percent."

"No deals, Khan. You're going to give me the boy now or you will die here in the gutter." Jakov was clearly losing his patience.

Khan turned his head slowly to Rafik. "Sorry for doing this," he said. Then he thrust the boy in front of him and placed the muzzle of his gun at the back of Rafik's head. He stepped away from the groove, pushing Rafik forward.

"Leave us alone or I shoot the boy."

Rafik saw Jakov and five other men aiming a rich arsenal of weaponry at Khan, who was taking cover behind him.

"This has always been your problem, Khan." Jakov looked Rafik right in the eye as he talked. "You always had ambition beyond your capabilities. You never knew when to cut your losses and walk away."

After that, everyone stood in silence for a moment, trying to figure out what to do. Rafik could hear Kahn breathing behind him. He felt the muzzle of the gun shaking against his skull. "How do I know you won't shoot me as soon as I give you the boy?" Khan said, defeat in his voice.

"I give you my word," Jakov said. But even Rafik knew that he was lying.

"You double-crossed me before, and now you expect me to take your word?"

"That's all you're going to get. You don't have any other options."

"No game."

"So you will die."

"I'll shoot the boy."

"And I'll cut my losses and move on, the same way you still could do."

"You don't understand." Khan's voice was close to hysteria. "I have nothing—no coin, no bar, no woman, no house. I have nothing to lose, Jakov, nothing."

"Stop your whining, Khan. Just walk away."

"I'll shoot the boy."

"Then you'll die."

Rafik felt the pressure of the muzzle increase against the back of his head.

"Wait," he heard himself shout. "I have a deal for you both." He paused briefly but when there was no reaction, he continued. "I will go with you, Jakov, and you will let Khan go—" he took a deep breath and added "—and in return I will do as you ask me. I will not try to run away. I will obey you and I will solve all the puzzles you give me. Isn't that what you want?"

This time the silence was longer. Jakov's expression turned from mild amusement to deep calculation. Until that moment, he probably didn't think about the possibility that a resentful and uncooperative boy could endanger his profit. He eventually said, "Fine. I agree to your terms. Come with me and Khan won't be harmed."

"No deal," Khan shook his head. "I'm the one with the gun here, and I say no deal!"

"I'm going to turn around now, Khan," Rafik said quietly and did just that. The muzzle of the gun was now pressed against his forehead.

Khan's face was wet from sweat and tears. He stared at Rafik, blinking, eyes red-rimmed. "You're not going anywhere," he repeated.

"When we travelled in Sweetheart, Captain Sam told me about the game he likes to play," Rafik said, "the one with kings and queens painted on cards?"

Khan nodded slowly, confused.

"Captain Sam said that sometimes you can bluff, even if you do not hold the right cards. If the other guy keeps going you can sometimes double-bluff, but you have to be lucky. This is like that card game, but you cannot double-bluff here."

Rafik saw Khan's eyes widen with comprehension.

"I'm going to go now, Khan," Rafik said softly. He walked one step backwards, still facing the pistol. "I will pray for you." He took another step away from Khan, who was still pointing the trembling weapon at him.

Rafik turned and walked slowly towards Jakov and his companions. Everyone's eyes were completely focused on the boy. When he reached Jakov, the merchant patted the boy on his shoulder with his human hand, a look of newly found appreciation in his eyes. The rest of the men formed a protective wall around them, facing Khan, who stood still with his gun held with both hands. Jakov picked up Rafik's right hand with his human hand and his metal fingers slowly peeled off Dominique's glove. The merchant took a long look at Rafik's marked fingers, and finally his human face twisted in a mirthless half smile.

"Good," he said. With a snap of his metallic fingers he shredded the glove, letting the remains drop gently to the muddy ground. "You won't need *that* where we are going."

Rafik's watched the pieces of Dominique's glove land on the ground before the heavy leather boot of the merchant buried them completely in the mud. He felt Jakov's razor-sharp fingers close on his shoulders and heard his raspy voice as the merchant bent down.

"You will keep your promise, won't you?" he whispered in the boy's ear.

Rafik, still looking at the ground, could only nod.

"Good," Jakov said again and straightened, turning his attention back to Khan.

"Just because I'm impressed with the kid, I will give you something to live for, Khan. It's called *revenge*." Jakov was now grinning triumphantly behind his metal mask. "You see, it was your own brother who betrayed you. He sold you out."

"You lie!" Khan's face turned red. "You lie!" The words flew out of his mouth with a wad of spittle.

"He sold you out for a hundred coins and three onion pies," said the merchant calmly. "He might still have the coin if he hasn't spent it all on whores."

By the look on Khan's face, comprehension was dawning on him. He lowered his gun and a strange, menacing look entered his eyes.

"Go get your revenge, Khan," Jakov said, "and then start a new life, somewhere far away from here, and for your sake, let us never meet again." He turned and walked away, motioning for Rafik to follow. The boy shot a parting glance at the man who was as close to family as he had at that moment, before turning and walking silently after Jakov.

28

The Long Tube was still at the platform. It was a stark reminder to Rafik of how fast his fortune was changing. He was being passed from hand to hand like a piece of merchandise with no regard for his own desires or feelings. He still did not know why his talent for puzzles made him so valuable to everyone.

He was lost in gloomy thoughts until the group reached the platform. From up close, the Troll guards looked even more imposing; their weapons and Tarakan devices clearly separated them from the rest of humanity. Rafik watched them with open curiosity while Jakov bought them passage. Jakov even purchased rations for the way—round bread and rock-hard cheese, but also salted and fried lizards on a stick, which turned out to be a surprising delicacy.

Before getting into the Long Tube, they were thoroughly searched and their weapons were taken and stored. A uniformed Troll guard checked each issued travel slip and pointed them brusquely towards their seats, not before warning them not to start a fight on pain of death. Each compartment had seats for a hundred people, and they were almost full.

It smelled like a latrine inside, and there was a depressing accumulation of garbage on the floor and on some of the seats. Jakov's two guards cleared their designated seats, which were facing each other, and shoved some of the junk on the floor with their feet towards the passengers they deemed too weak to protest. Instinctively, Rafik shoved his hand deep into his pocket, but people did not pay the slightest attention to him. A few stared briefly at Jakov but turned away as soon as their gazes were met.

Almost as soon as they were settled, the doors of the Long Tube closed, to the cheers of many of its occupants, and the Tube began moving up and, from Rafik's point of view, backwards. They accelerated, the twin metal bars flashing past Rafik every few heartbeats until they were too fast to focus on. It was then that he realised that the openings in the wall were actually blocking the wind. He moved his hand and touched an invisible surface that felt cold and tingly.

Jakov nodded at the boy's expression of wonderment, leaned over, and knocked on the transparent wall with a metallic finger, "Amazing, isn't it? Makes glass look like a brick wall in comparison."

He ordered the guard to change seats with Rafik so the boy could have a better view. For the rest of the journey, he was happy just to sit quietly and look outside as he chewed on dried fruit.

The Long Tube was moving high up in the air and apparently at an incredibly fast speed, but the inside of the compartment was calm and stable. For part of their journey, Rafik could see the bright Tarakan highway mirroring their path. Trucks could sometimes be seen travelling exactly under them, and it was a measure of how fast the Long Tube was travelling that the trucks disappeared in the blink of an eye. Rafik hoped Captain Sam had managed to fix Sweetheart, and his mood turned sombre as he remembered that the man who chased them was now sitting beside him.

When the roads disappeared, they travelled above farms and fields of corn and wheat, and sometimes Rafik could make out men working in the fields. The farms and pastures formed a pattern, and as he watched them flash by, he began playing a little game in his mind where he manoeuvred the farms and fields around for better use of the road. Jakov told him that before the Catastrophe people used to get into metal Sky Birds and fly around in them from one part of the world to another. Rafik would not have believed this story on any other day, but now it seemed like anything was possible. He asked why anyone would place their fields so far away from home, but Jakov just laughed and called him a stupid mutt.

After seeing the look on the boy's face, or maybe just to pass the time, Jakov relented with an explanation of sorts: "When the City of Towers lowered its barriers and opened itself to humans, one of the first problems was lack of food. Several of the city's Tubes reached a few farms and villages, but what was brought back was simply not enough to feed the growing numbers of people coming into the city."

Jakov gesticulated with his metal hand. "So it was every Troll for himself. That, together with the unfriendly competition between the various factions, which are called guilds, meant that the Tube's platforms were a constant war zone. This caused two bouts of famine and almost depleted the city. It was then that Mauricious Altenna, a visionary guild boss, managed to convince his rivals that there were higher gains to be had by joining forces to create stability. Those who joined formed the Council, which was led by a mutually agreed upon puppet leader named Sirbin Sammuel."

Jakov smiled when he said, "Those who did not join, died. The city's ShieldGuard was formed, and soon after, the Council took control of all the platforms, then the city, and eventually the surrounding areas all the way to Regeneration and beyond. Successful raids brought plenty of captives, and together with the prisoners of the guilds who resisted the Council, they were sent to cultivate the wild lands surrounding the city. I hear that every once in a while these new farmers stage a revolt, but they are no match for the Council's power."

Jakov shoved a piece of hard cheese into the side of his mouth and chewed slowly before continuing.

"Now things are as they should be. The Council is so powerful you can buy stuff in the surrounding villages with slips marked by the city's merchant guild instead of hard coin. The guilds are busy salvaging all they can from Tarakan technology to stage another war, and best of all, a new Tarakan city was discovered deep in the mountains of Tarakan Valley. They say this city dwarfs the City of Towers ten times over and contains the most powerful artifacts and weapons. Now everyone is busy sending Salvationist crews to Tarakan Valley and selling what they find there, instead of fighting each other."

Jakov leaned towards Rafik, who withdrew back into his chair, but the merchant only waved a metallic finger at the boy, "But there is one thing that everyone needs, one thing they all want. Without it the wonders of Tarakan Valley are beyond their grasp. Do you know what it is?"

Rafik shook his head, mesmerized.

Jakov was about to tell him when a chime sounded and the Long Tube began to descend. "Ah, well, we are approaching. You'd better take a look through the window—it's a magnificent view. Here, take my seat."

As the Long Tube entered the City of Towers, Rafik felt as if he had just discovered the centre of the universe. All his questions regarding Jakov's story forgotten, Rafik pressed his face against the cool, invisible surface, trying to see everything at once. The towers penetrated the clouds above them, their silhouettes marked by a row of blinking lights that looked to Rafik like little stars on a clear night. Jakov pointed out the Eastern and Guilds Plateaus as they passed them, and Rafik could clearly see great buildings, paved streets, even large clusters of trees Jakov called parks, all on a plateau suspended high above the ground. The fantastic sight soon disappeared as they descended down the middle spires and to the Central Plateau. The Long Tube cruised slowly above the lower levels of the city, which Jakov called the Pit and was filled with humanity, machines, and livestock. The Tube turned around two more towers whose bases were each far bigger than Rafik's whole village before climbing back to the Middle Plateau.

The platform was bustling with activity as people shouldered past each other in a hurry. Everywhere Rafik looked, he saw menacing-looking ShieldGuards and Trolls carrying metal devices, weapons, and augmentations without fear or shame. People like Jakov's guards, clean of marks and without Tarakan hardware, were the minority. But Jakov seemed to relax, as if he were arriving at a safe haven instead of coming to a city that had more killings in a fortnight than the estimated annual birth rate—a fact he mentioned in passing to Rafik as they walked towards the row of cart drivers.

Even with the Council's firm control over the Tube platform, the place seemed to be in complete chaos. Thousands of people moved in different directions all at once. The sheer size of it all made Rafik lose his bearings, and Jakov's metal hand propelled the boy in the right direction.

"Watch yourself here," he warned sternly after the third time he stopped the boy from walking the wrong way. "You'll get lost, and this is not a forgiving city."

As soon as they cleared the platform, Jakov waved to one of the numerous cart drivers, who took them to the gates of the upper towers, where they climbed on a Tarakan lift to the top plateau. It was there, on a metal disc that was ascending so high the people below seemed like ants, that Rafik felt a strange combination of awe and familiarity, as if he had come to a place where he truly belonged. Everywhere he looked he recognised symbols and markings, either embedded into the walls or on marked weapons and artifacts. What all this meant, he didn't know, but he was eager to find out.

Jakov secured two large rooms in a guest house inside one of the top towers of the Upper Middle Plateau, overlooking the most beautiful garden Rafik had ever seen. The rooms were large and furnished with odd but high-quality furniture, and the beds were soft and clean. The meals served were something Rafik had never tasted the likes of in his entire life. The table was loaded with hot, sweet buns, different types of meat in rich gravy, fruits Rafik had never heard of, and six different kinds of cheese. Jakov drank wine, but Rafik could not have imagined a better beverage than the clean, fresh water that was brought to the table. When he went to wash, Rafik found out that instead of a water well, clean water magically came out of pipes, one hot and one cold. Jakov paid a man to help Rafik wash properly, cut his mangled hair short, and even bring him fresh clothes in bright green and red colours and soft boots made of leather. It must have cost him a fortune, but Jakov mentioned that he was interested in the two other main amenities of the place: unparalleled security and a reliable messaging service.

The rooms Jakov rented took up the entire floor. He placed one of his own guards at the top of the stairs, and Rafik was allowed to wander within those parameters. After an initial exploration of the facilities, Rafik resigned himself to his own room, where he spent most of his time dreaming of the wall of symbols.

The following day, most of Jakov's guards were dispatched with a long list of errands. Rafik had to stay in Jakov's room. He watched with fascination as the merchant removed and maintained his metal arm, cleaning and oiling the joints with a clean leather cloth. Seeing the boy's open curiosity, Jakov began telling the story of how he was injured in a weapons deal gone bad and was left for dead.

"I'm not like you." He nodded toward Rafik's hand as his own free arm circled slowly across joints and metal. "I don't have the mark, but I was brought to a Mender who was just beginning to experiment with Tarakan augmentations, and the bastard was a genius, an artist, even." He cocked his head to its metal side. "Too bad he's dead now, but he saved my life, reconstructed my face, and made me this arm."

"I thought only people with marks could attach devices," Rafik said, remembering something Khan had told him a few days before.

"No." Jakov reattached his arm by pushing it hard into his empty shoulder socket, then he flexed the metal hand several times. "In principle, almost anyone can use Tarakan attachments, but those with the mark have better uses for them. Don't know why, but the tattooed can attach Tarakan devices more easily, and they might be stronger, or faster, than the unmarked using the same attachment. There is also significantly less pain, or so I'm told." He smiled thinly.

"It hurts?"

"Don't let anyone tell you it doesn't—it hurts a lot."

"So why do you do it?"

Jakov looked straight at Rafik, then picked up a fruit from a bowl with his metal hand and held it up to the boy's face. Then he picked up a glass bowl with his other hand. With one snap of his metal fingers Jakov sliced the fruit neatly into several smaller pieces, and they fell into the bowl.

"You have two choices." He put the bowl down, picked up one of the slices of fruit, and brought it to his mouth. "You can either take Skint to dull the pain, and eventually your brain leaks out of your ears, or—" He paused, put the slice of fruit into his mouth, chewed slowly and swallowed, then wiped his chin with his healthy hand. "Or you can just suffer, my young friend. Conquer pain with the force of your will, and you shall triumph."

Rafik thought about it for a while, then, judging the timing right, he asked, "Why am I so important? What is a Puzzler?"

Jakov began shaking his head but stopped. He was in a rare mood, having won the day and walked away with his prize. "I can't tell you what I don't know, boy. What I do know, without a doubt, is that you are worth a small fortune. It has something to do with codes and puzzles, and something to do with the Tarakan cities, even the City of Towers, and the secrets they hold. My guess is that you will find out the answer to your question soon enough."

Rafik wanted to ask more, but one of Jakov's bodyguards returned and the men got busy talking to each other. The bodyguard had brought a black box, not unlike the one Jakov had tested Rafik with in Newport, but it was slightly bigger and with more buttons on the front. "He was not happy parting with it," remarked the man who brought the box. "I had to use . . . tough diplomacy."

That brought a soft chuckle from Jakov, who replied, "Why, my friend, you are a natural ambassador!" He then called Rafik over and made him try the box in the same way he'd tried the first one, by putting his fingers in the allotted slots.

The first few puzzles were too simple, with very few rows of symbols and a laughably apparent pattern. For Rafik, who could now manipulate and control almost fifty symbols when dreaming, it was as easy as breathing. But the box had other puzzles that were more of a challenge, and the box counted the time it took him to solve each one. When Rafik completed the last puzzle, sweat was pouring down his face, his head hurt, and he felt very tired.

Jakov looked at the digits displayed on the box and said, "Too slow. You need to do it in less time, at least a third less."

"But I solved the puzzles," Rafik said defensively, hurt by Jakov's comment.

The merchant only shook his head. "They will test you at the auction house, and the faster you are, the more you'll be worth."

Earlier, Jakov was having a pleasant conversation with the boy, and now he was treating Rafik like a piece of merchandise. Rafik withdrew his hand in sudden anger. "So this is why you do this, to get a better price for me?"

"Remember your promise to me, Rafik." There was no more warmth in Jakov's voice, and although he was still reclining on the soft leather chair his body seemed to tense.

Rafik got up on his feet, grabbed the puzzle box, and was about to throw it at the wall when a strong grip blocked his arm. Jakov's metal fingers closed over his throat, squeezing hard and lifting him up until he was standing on the tips of his toes. The image of the sliced fruit swam in front of his eyes in a haze of pain.

"Remember your promise, Rafik," Jakov hissed. The metal side of his face was so close to Rafik's cheeks, he could not even see the merchant's healthy eye. "Consider this: the more you're worth, the better you're going to be treated by whoever buys you."

Rafik was dumped on the floor, where he stayed, wheezing and gasping for air.

"Now get up and try a few more times," Jakov walked back to the table and picked up another fruit as Rafik slowly got up from the floor. "This machine has twenty levels," the merchant sat back down on the comfortable reclining chair, "and I want you to master them all by the time we go to auction. You have five days. Get to work."

29

The auction house was the third-biggest building in the city. There was enough evidence to support the historians who claimed the building used to be a hub of financial activity before the Catastrophe. Among the clues were the steel vaults filled with gold bars, suggesting the great importance of such useless metal in the past. The great building was now used both as an auction house and as the centre for the Guild of Merchants. The bidding began every Saturday exactly at noon, marked by the huge clock embedded in the wall, but commerce was already in full swing at sunrise. Much like market day in Rafik's village, stalls were erected outside the auction house and the merchandise about to be auctioned was presented for prospective buyers. Trolls and other fortune-seeking mercenaries stood in designated areas, hoping to obtain a contract from one of the guilds. They were constantly showing off their Tarakan attachments, brandishing weapons and trophies, and performing physical feats such as lifting or crushing heavy stones with their augmented hands. There were also several mechanics for hire, and a heavily tattooed Gadgetier who claimed he could fix, attach, or enhance any Tarakan device.

Rafik sat on a stool near the entrance of their lavish tent and kept peering out with curiosity. He saw Jakov paying a hefty sum to the tent owner. As if reading Rafik's mind, he remarked, "Do you think I will just present you out in the open like a street vendor? No, business such as this should be done in private, away from the gawkers and the riffraff."

Throughout the morning, Jakov admitted the prospective merchants and guild representatives who showed up one by one and only by presenting Jakov's own written invitations. The curious and the few who thought their reputation placed them above such formalities were left outside, expressing their indignation with words that could have made Dominique smile. Each delegation brought its own puzzle box and Rafik was thoroughly tested, solving puzzle after puzzle as men and women watched him intently.

Jakov claimed to be Rafik's custodian, and no one seemed to question that; certainly no one asked Rafik any personal questions or for proof that the boy was in Jakov's legal custody. With one exception, the only thing that interested the merchants and guild representatives was his puzzle-solving ability. They kept examining his hand and making him solve increasingly difficult puzzles.

There was one woman, though, Mistress Furukawa of the Keenan guild, who examined him differently. She was stern looking, with short, cropped black hair who, despite looking very different, reminded Rafik of his mother. She let two members of her delegation examine Rafik's hand, and watched him solve the puzzle box from a short distance. Her comments about Rafik being too young and inexperienced were said in a tone of voice suggesting final judgement. She certainly did not let Jakov sweet-talk her, and she completely ignored his clumsy attempts at flattery. After her delegation was done she began asking Jakov questions about his health, then turned and directed her questions at Rafik, to the merchant's annoyance. The woman asked him where he came from, his age, and whether he was happy. The last question puzzled the boy and he merely shrugged. After listening to Jakov's final pitch, the woman simply turned and left the tent, nodding politely to the representatives of the rival guilds who were waiting for their turn to see the boy. Jakov cursed softly after she left, and he shared a few sly comments regarding the woman's lack of femininity with his guards, who chuckled obediently.

By the time the bells rang, marking the beginning of the auction, Rafik was completely exhausted, and Jakov was smiling as broadly as his mask allowed.

"That Furukawa hag said you were too young just to scare off the competition and lower your price," he told Rafik, patting his shoulder paternally. "Well, that little trick didn't work for her. They are all interested, all of them, I saw it in their eyes."

A while later, as Rafik lay on a bear fur in the tent, with a wet cloth on his forehead to sooth his headache, an auction house steward, dressed in a black-and-bloodred uniform, entered and announced that it was Rafik's turn. He led the boy and Jakov past other tents and through a great oak door, which swung open all by itself. The darkness inside the labyrinth of corridors they walked through was lit by small oil lamps. They walked past many heads made of stone and countless drawings hanging from the walls, moving too fast for Rafik to understand what they depicted. Eventually they emerged in the main hall. There were more than a hundred people standing around the central podium. The auctioneer, a tall, gaunt man with an incredibly strong voice, was introducing a Troll standing next to him, flexing his huge shoulders, and striking a pose with a large blaster rifle.

"The next contract is for Barim Karssel of the lower spires and is for one year, starting today, with the option to extend the contract by mutual decision." The auctioneer, dressed in silver and wearing a heavy-looking metal chain of office, turned and pointed at the Troll while still maintaining eye contact with the surrounding audience.

"Now, I want you to look carefully at this perfect combination of man and machine. Featuring three genuine Tarakan devices and seven more battle-proven augmentations, this experienced warrior will bring you loot. He is a veteran of eight shallow and two deep salvation expeditions in the City within the Mountain, Master Karssel's total haul last year was more than forty thousand in coin and kind."

Jakov snorted in disbelief and shook his head slightly. "Yeah, right," he whispered to no one but himself, "he no doubt attached a few augmentations to his imagination."

"Master Barim Karssel's starting price is three hundred in hard coin paid in advance plus five percent of the future haul. Do I get three hundred and five? Right there, thank you, do I get three hundred plus six percent? Yes, Madam, a fine choice. Look at that body armour, ladies and gentlemen. Genuine Tarakan artifacts, do I hear three fifty plus seven percent?"

The auction continued for a while and eventually was stopped at a cut of ten percent, and 650 coins. Jakov remarked to no one in particular that the Troll's contract was grossly overpriced. By now the merchant was fretting nervously, and when his name was called to the platform, he pushed Rafik so roughly that the boy stumbled forward.

The auctioneer waited as Rafik climbed the stairs and stood in the middle of the platform. There was a ripple of excited chatter in the crowd. Like any auction house, it was filled with both professionals and chancers who came only to see a good show and perhaps get lucky and pick up a dropped deal. A lone boy without any visible augmentations meant something exciting was about to happen, and the rumors had been spreading all day.

"Lords and ladies, gentlemen and fine folk," bellowed the auctioneer in a slow, rich voice, "we have someone very special here with us today."

Suddenly there was a commotion from the main doors and the auctioneer stopped. Several armed Trolls marched in, followed by a figure whose presence caused everyone to turn and gasp. Many bowed their heads in respect, and more than a few merchants shuffled backwards and away from the centre of the hall, creating a sort of a corridor to the platform. From his high vantage point Rafik could see the man clearly, and it was obvious why he struck such an imposing figure; he was as tall as the biggest Troll Rafik had ever seen, and almost as wide. He was dressed in full black battle armour with a heavy fur cloak draped around his shoulders. His face was long and thin, and his dark eyes looked like they were set deep in their sockets. The man surveyed the crowd briefly, but his gaze quickly centred on Rafik. This caused a shiver to run up the boy's spine.

The auctioneer was the first to regain his composure, "Lords and Ladies, Gentlemen, the auction house, and the Guild of Merchants welcome the Honourable Council Voice and head of the Sabarra merchant guild and salvage company, Mauricious Altenna." Everyone bowed their heads. There was a weak ripple of applause, which died quickly as the man waved for silence with his right hand.

Mauricious Altenna nodded to a bald man who stood to his left, leaving him in the centre of the crowd before moving with his entourage to a far corner.

The auctioneer continued: "Lords and Ladies, Gentlemen, Honourable Council, this young man here, Rafik, was tested by the Guild of Merchants and several respected representatives of other guilds, and his gift has proven to be genuine. This is, Lords and Ladies, a genuine Puzzler of the highest talent and ability." As instructed to by Jakov, Rafik raised his right hand, palm out and fingers spread, and waved his hand slowly in all directions.

There was a murmur of excitement from the crowd, yet the auctioneer's voice rose above it to declare, "This is a private, four-year contract with the boy's custodian, with an option for extension into a permanent contract with no percentage of the haul. Housing and training and other expenses are required. We start at twelve hundred in coin, no kind."

It was only then that Rafik truly realised what was happening. He turned his head and saw Jakov standing a few paces away, watching the crowd with a gleam in his eye. When Rafik turned his head back to the crowd his price was already at seventeen hundred. A few heartbeats later it crossed the two thousand mark and did not slow down. Rafik was still holding his hand up, frozen in air. He let it drop slowly to his side and glanced around, looking for an escape route, but knowing in his heart that he would never make it to the door. Everywhere he looked he saw ShieldGuards and Trolls. Even if he could somehow make it out, how far could a boy worth above three thousand in hard coin manage to go before someone snatched him again?

The chancers and private entrepreneurs were soon out of the bidding race, as well as two smaller mercenary firms that probably had been hoping to pool resources and share Rafik between them. This was now strictly a competition between the more powerful guilds. All those who'd quit the auction moved away from the main floor, and when Rafik's price reached five thousand there were only two people standing in front of the dais: the bald man standing for the Sabarra guild; and the Keenan guild, represented by the stern-looking woman who had asked Rafik personal questions back in the tent.

The bidding did not slow down before the price crossed the seven-thousand mark, and by now the crowd was completely silent. Before accepting every raised bid, the man representing Sabarra glanced back to Mauricious Altenna, who nodded his approval with the tiniest of gestures. It was a testimony to the man's power that the auctioneer gave time to the Sabarra, and even paused his constant urging for a higher bid in order for the exchange to take place. He did not grant the woman representing the Keenan guild the same courtesy.

As the crowd withdrew from around her, she never let her

eyes wander from Rafik as she raised her hand again and again without hesitation, accepting every bid. Yet even her resolve was wavering when the price rose above eight thousand, and several times she waited until the final warning to raise her price again. The dynamics were such that Rafik, the auctioneer, and the entire audience turned their heads in unison between the woman, the bald man, and Mauricious Altenna every time it was their turn to bid. As his price rose even higher, Rafik could feel the growing tension in the crowd. People whispered to one another, moved to get a better view, even cheered or clapped whenever a sum was raised and accepted.

"Nine thousand coins for the honourable representative of the Sabarra guild." Rafik heard the auctioneer's voice behind him. "Do I hear nine thousand, two hundred and fifty from the Keenan guild?"

As excited chatter flowed around the corners of the hall, the woman stood stone rigid, and this time even the auctioneer took a bit longer before giving first warning. She waited till the last moment, when the auctioneer drew a breath to announce a Sabarra win, before raising her hand again. The crowd sighed in unison and turned their heads to the Sabarra guild's leader, but as soon as her bid was accepted Mauricious Altenna suddenly turned and walked out of the hall, his entourage rushing behind him, causing a small commotion. The Sabarra representative immediately bowed to the dais and then to the woman beside him before withdrawing without saying a word.

"This auction is sold to Mistress Furukawa of the Keenan guild, for . . ."

The crowd erupted in cheers as the hammer fell and the sum and winner were announced by the jubilant auctioneer. People surged forward to congratulate the woman. She ignored them and walked over to Jakov, who, despite his metal mask, was looking visibly stunned.

Rafik was immediately surrounded by armed Trolls and escorted off the dais, where a young man and a woman, dressed in the purple cloaks of the Guild of Merchants, led the way through several long corridors and a flight of stairs to a spacious and richly furnished hall, which even had a burning fireplace in the far wall. The armed Trolls stayed by the door while Rafik followed the man and woman. At least a dozen men and women dressed in white and purple were busy transferring books and scrolls to different tables. Rafik and his escorts approached one of the tables, which was piled with bound books, rolled-up scrolls, parchments, scroll cases, several ink tubes, and three enormous wax seals. An elderly woman, whose purple dress was marked by silver adornments, was sitting by the table. As soon as they approached, she immediately began asking questions regarding Rafik's auction and diligently inscribed it on a scroll and in two other books. Rafik's final sum of purchase caused a stir in the room and even made the scribe lift her head up to check she'd heard right.

When the sum was confirmed she looked at Rafik. "Congratulations, son," she said with a nod of respect, "you just broke the yearly record for a single transaction. For that, your name will be written in gold."

Rafik did not know how to react, nor did he understand what was being said to him, so he respectfully nodded back.

The young man who escorted Rafik from the dais could not contain his excitement. "With all that coin, that metal-armed merchant is going to need extra protection," he commented. "He is going to be marked by every gang in this city, but if you ask me, the real story of the day is how the Sabarra baited the Keenans to financial ruin."

"I did not see anyone asking you for anything, Fendar," the older scribe said drily as she scratched words and numbers onto the scroll.

But the young man did not get the hint. He turned to the woman standing on the other side of Rafik, puffing his chest out in self-importance.

"The Sabarra is rumored to have enough Puzzlers for their

Salvationist crews," he lectured in a tone that reminded Rafik of Master Issak. "But for the third season now, the Keenans hauled in the second-largest amount of loot after the Sabarra. So it is only logical that Mauricious Altenna would find a way to weaken the competition without an open conflict."

"That's enough, Fendar, and it's *Councilman* Altenna to you, young man. He has eyes and ears everywhere"—the scribe made a show of looking around—"and he is *very* concerned about how people address him, even behind his back."

Fendar paled and pursed his lips.

"Good." The scribe turned to Rafik and softened her tone. "I bet this was quite an ordeal for you, young Master, and a scroll of purchase takes time to prepare. Why don't you sit over there until we all go upstairs to sign the contract?" She indicated a soft-looking chair. "And help yourself to some refreshments. I'm sure Fendar here will see to all your needs."

The scribe was right about the tediousness of the process. Rafik ate fruit and drank fresh water and entertained himself by finding patterns in the bindings on the rows of shelved books on the walls. Soon the bindings changed shape and he found himself by the wall of symbols in his dreams, where he felt at peace.

Rafik did not remember until much later that night that today was also his birthday. He was now thirteen.

30

"Nine thousand?" Galinak shook his head incredulously. "I know times were crazy but . . . they paid nine thousand in coin for the little mutt?"

"Nine thousand, two hundred and fifty hard C.o.T. coins," Vincha said.

"Bukra's balls . . ."

"Well." I waved my hand in emphasis. "You have to remember it was the height of what my LoreMaster calls the Tarakan Rush. The new outpost in Tarakan Valley was filled with crews such as yours, Galinak, and literally tons of artifacts were being sent back via the Northern Long Tube. Everyone wanted a piece of the take. Private mercenary companies were all the rage, and the guilds were raking it in. Combat Trolls' contracts doubled in value with each passing season. Mechanics, Gadgetiers, and Menders were tripling their prices, and a Puzzler—"

"Yep, they were rare all right," admitted Galinak, "and mad as they come." After reflection he added, "That scribe boy was right. I wouldn't want to be this Jakov guy—he might as well have tattooed a huge target on his back."

"Well." Vincha began packing her few belongings, retrieving the hunting knife from the wall. "When I first came back to the city, *I* went looking for him—" she paused "—to have words about the way he treated the boy." Galinak chuckled, no doubt imagining how that conversation would have gone. "But I couldn't find the rustfucker, no matter where I looked, and believe me, I tried. That half man disappeared. My guess, he split to the East Coast."

I knew I wouldn't be able to keep a straight face, so I pretended to cough so I could cover it with my hands. Throughout the night, I was looking for a way to get Vincha to stay in the city. My coin bag was almost empty, and I knew she wouldn't accept my promises as currency. And suddenly, just as I was losing hope, here it was, the hook I needed. Vincha's mention of Jakov proved to me that she was telling the truth, for many segments of her tale tailored together snippets of information I already gathered in my years of investigations. But the most important element of her story revealed that she *cared* enough to risk her life looking for the boy's family after she came back from Tarakan Valley, and to try and find an obviously dangerous man such as Jakov and exact revenge. That was leverage I could perhaps use, with delicate manipulation, to keep her talking. It would be better than using the other tools in my possession.

When I felt I'd regained my composure, I got up and stretched. The hut's wooden shutters were closed, but I could sense it was already midmorning. From the way Vincha was packing I guessed she thought she'd fulfilled her side of the bargain and was now ready to leave. I had to think fast. How could I get Vincha to keep talking? Between what I'd already paid her and what she stole from the Den, she had enough coin to keep her going for a long while.

As it turned out, someone else managed to stop Vincha from leaving. Unfortunately, it was at my expense. Vincha had been metal clean for years now, but some things stay with you even when there are no more wires coming out of your skull. She snapped her head up suddenly and whispered, "Something's wrong," and before I had time to react she added, "Rust, we're being scanned."

We all turned to the only wall connecting us to a walkway. I concentrated and part of the wall became transparent to me.

"Five men," I said, my voice only slightly trembling, "two already at the door and three crossing the rope bridge." They had their weapons drawn, and it seemed clear they weren't looking for a friendly chat.

Vincha kicked her bedding aside and removed two loose planks from the floor, exposing a hole big enough to squeeze through. It looked to me like a long drop, but Vincha had planned ahead, and there was a rope tucked underneath the beddings as well. Galinak, on the other hand, powered his gauntlets and moved straight to the door—the odds didn't seem to bother him much. I was beginning to appreciate the aging Troll, but at that moment I was desperately trying to say or do something that would stop Vincha from using that rope. I didn't have the faintest clue how, but I was not going to let her escape without me. So instead of taking cover I began moving towards her, which was, in hindsight, yet another mistake on the list of errors I'd made that day.

The door burst open and a large Troll holding a hand gun filled the door frame. Galinak was only two steps away from him and immediately rolled forward, trying to duck under a possible shot, but the Troll at the door knew who he was looking for. His gun was immediately trained on me, and he pulled the trigger without hesitation.

Had I possessed honed combat reflexes I could have dived for cover, or shot him before he managed to shoot me, but I'm not a man of action. Instead, I froze in panic and felt a flash of hot pain in my middle. The world turned upside down as I collapsed to the wooden floor.

31

Had it been a live round, there would have been a hole the size of one of Galinak's fists in my rib cage. Were it a blaster I would have died screaming in agony as my inner organs sizzled and burned. Instead, a stun ray made my body seize up, and, since it caught me as I was moving toward Vincha, the momentum caused me to crash headfirst to the floor. On the bright side, I didn't feel the pain of impact beyond a dull thud, which would eventually become yet another painful bump on my poor skull. I could see Vincha's head disappearing as she descended, and I heard the first sounds of hand-to-hand combat behind me. Lying there, helpless, I was experiencing a curious cocktail of euphoria mixed with panic. The mere fact I was still alive mixed with a rising sense of fear as I realised I was unable to breathe.

A Gadgetier once explained to me that a stun ray somehow stopped all the muscles of your body for a short time, enough to make you experience near death before your survival reflexes overcame whatever the ray was doing to you. It was obviously unpleasant but usually didn't harm the target beyond temporary incapacitation. It was by far the most humane of the Tarakan weapons, though that was not much of a consolation at the moment. My sight was getting blurry, and the light dimmed as the air refused to fill my lungs. The sounds of fighting were eventually drowned out by the singular crescendo of my slowing heart.

I don't know exactly what happened next or how long it took, but suddenly I felt my body heave and tremble and I was breathing again. I was still unable to move, but it was surprising how momentarily blissful swallowing and blinking became.

From the noise around me I gathered that the fighting had moved outside the hut, but there was nothing I could do to help, and I was not able to run. The only thing I could do was think. Whoever sent these men wanted me alive, which was good, but I concluded it would not be a polite conversation. Galinak was an impressive warrior, but there were five trained men, at least one of them a Troll, and it was to his credit that the fight was even taking this long. Soon they would come into the hut, injured and pissed off, but victorious nonetheless. They would tie me up or simply hold me down, and then they would ask me questions. Regardless of my answers, I knew I was about to experience a lot of pain.

I had to get out of this hut, but there was only one way out: down, through the hole Vincha had created. Some degree of feeling came back to my body, and I found I was able to crawl. It was pathetically slow, but I nevertheless inched my way to the gaping hole with absolutely no idea what I was going to do once I reached it. By the time I managed to get to the hole, my eyesight returned to normal and I saw the rope dangling down from a supporting beam below me, ending at a precarious height above another hut. Even if I managed to squeeze through the hole, balance my weight on the supporting beam, grab the rope and support my own weight on the way down, I would have to let go when I reached the end of the rope and hope that the makeshift roof would take my weight—or that I would not miss the roof altogether and plummet to my death. If I was lucky, maybe I would survive the fall with nothing more than a broken leg or broken ribs. If I wasn't lucky . . .

I decided to try and reach the swaying rope from where I was, but that proved to be more difficult than I'd anticipated. I kept inching forward above the gaping hole, fully aware that the noise of the battle had now subsided. When I heard heavy footsteps behind me I knew there was no time to finesse my exit. I stopped trying to grasp the rope, leaned forward, and felt my body slide out to what would have most likely been my death had two pairs of hands not grasped my legs, pulled me back onto the hut's floor, and roughly flipped me over.

"You all right, fella?" Galinak had a long red gash on his forehead, but he didn't seem to mind that blood was streaming down his face.

"Still unable to speak, eh? I think I like you this way." Vincha, who was sporting a bruise of her own on her right cheek, was otherwise unharmed. "Nice going, by the way," she said nonchalantly to Galinak. "I haven't seen that over-the-side hip throw used in a very long time."

"Couldn't have done it without you," he answered politely, but he was clearly smug. "The way you swung from that rope and landed on top of those two, Bukra's balls, it was like a show from that famous wandering circus troupe. And don't get me wrong, but I would never want you to wrap your legs around me like that."

"It was inspiring, wasn't it?" Vincha's smile was almost sweet as she looked back down at me, "Oh, he's moving. Can you talk, Twinkle Eyes?"

I managed a moan.

"That's good, little fella, you took one right in your—"

"Gg . . . ee . . ." I gasped.

"Take it easy, fella, no need to run. Those boys are all down for the count."

"Ggg . . . get back, Galinak," I finally got out. "You're bleeding all over me."

"Oh, sorry." He disappeared from my line of vision.

Vincha helped me up. By the time I had full control of my body, Galinak had brought in the last of our assailants and dumped them unceremoniously on the hut's floor.

"That's the last one." He began collecting his darts and rummaging through their pockets.

"That's only four, I saw five," I said, rubbing my head with both hands, trying to ignore the painful throb.

"That's right. But unless the fifth one was wearing a grav suit," said Vincha, "he's at the bottom of the pit, compliments of Galinak's signature hip throw."

Galinak bowed and touched an invisible cap.

I swore, trying to calculate the possible trajectory of such a fall. There was a good chance the man landed on a stall below or even on an innocent passerby. If so, there was also a good chance those below could calculate or guess where he'd fallen from, which meant we had to leave now. But first we had to find out who these men were and, more important, who sent them.

The four turned out to be packing quite a treasure trove of weapons, scanning devices, fully charged power tubes, and bags full of coins. One of them was obviously dead. The other three were probably alive, though they didn't look much better than the dead one. With odds of five to two and only a moment's warning, Galinak and Vincha came out victorious. For some strange reason I felt really proud. These two warriors were old-school, true Salvationists. I noted to myself that I had to keep them on my side.

"These guys look like a crew or something," Galinak said. "Rusting amateurs, is what they are. If the Troll had shot me first we would have been all wires and spare parts by now." He turned to Vincha, his hand still rummaging through one of their pockets. "You pissed someone off, Vincha, someone with coin."

"Could be anyone, really." Vincha shrugged. "I've been pissing off more than a few people, and if this fleshling—no offence, Twinkle Eyes—managed to find me, I'm sure others could, too."

"Maybe they're a rogue crew who got a lead on us?"

"They're not rogues. They're employed by a guild, or the Council," I said with enough confidence to get their attention.

"Rust, are you sure? How do you know?"

"A talent. I never forget a face, and I've seen this one before." I pointed at the dead man. "He's Sabarra, I'll bet hard coin on it."

Galinak whistled in appreciation, turning to Vincha. "Bukra's balls, what did you do to cross wires with the most powerful guild in the city? They practically run this city now."

Vincha tried but failed to look nonchalant. "Nothing that I know of," she answered. "I thought they came because of you, Galinak. How much debt are you in?"

Galinak snorted and spat at one of the unconscious figures. "Yeah, well . . . Let's wake one of them up and find out who they were looking for, shall we? I have this new thumb twist I'm dying to try . . ."

"They were coming for me," I said, nipping the argument in the bud. The look on my face made it clear that I wasn't bluffing.

"Well, well." Vincha sent me a look of reappraisal. "But you're just a harmless historian, aren't you, Twinkle Eyes? How does someone like you attract the attention of the Sabarra? Unpaid library fines?"

I shook my head. The knowledge that I had been compromised left me uncharacteristically mute.

"Do you know why these men are after you?" Galinak asked.

"Would you like us to find out?" Vincha added, and remembering her interrogation technique in the Den, I could not help but shiver. I shook my head. I was pretty sure why they were after me and had no desire to confront them about it in front of Vincha.

"Have it your way." She shrugged, pulled her hunting knife from its sheath, and bent over.

"What are you doing?" I cried out.

"Oh, I thought I'd give them a shave," she said, pulling on the scalp of one of the men and putting the blade to his throat. "You won't have to worry about them chasing you again."

"No. Stop," I ordered and was actually surprised when she obeyed. "They wanted to talk to me, not to kill me."

"Maybe true, but I assure you if we wake them up they will try to kill us all," said Galinak. "Might have used a stunner on you, buddy, but they were using real rusting weapons on us. I say we give them what they deserve and get it over with."

"No," I said again, more forcefully. The Sabarra were after me for business, and I didn't want to add revenge to their motivation.

"They're going to hunt *us all* down when they wake up," Vincha said hotly. "These guys always do."

"Although I can make sure they will only be able to crawl," Galinak suggested. He bent over and grabbed the leg of one of the unconscious guild fighters. "If you crack their knee at the right angle . . ."

I shook my head until they gave up. Vincha shouldered her bag and moved out quickly. I caught up with her at the rope bridge. "Where are you going?"

"Somewhere far away from you," she said. "You're trouble, Twinkle Eyes, and I have enough of my own."

"Wait." My hand stopped her shoulder. She only turned to me, although I was sure she was contemplating throwing me off the bridge. "I will pay you to continue telling your story," I said urgently. "I need to know what you know."

"Need?" she repeated with disgust. "What's your story, Twinkle Eyes? Don't rust my metal about history and all that crap. History doesn't bring a Sabarra interrogation crew to my doorstep."

"I promise I'll tell you my story, too," I said, knowing I would have to sooner or later. Sensing Galinak was now on the bridge as well, I said without turning, "Galinak, you are officially hired to protect us . . . well, me."

"You can sweet talk the old fool to escort you, Twinkle Eyes," Vincha said, "but if you want me to stick around, you better put some hard coin in my hand."

I took a deep breath. "I don't carry that kind of coin on me."

Before Vincha could react, I hastily added, "Would you? But we can go somewhere, where I can fetch some . . ."

Vincha looked as if she was about to argue, but Galinak suddenly barked, "This rope bridge isn't getting any more stable—how about we let the boss bring us the coin and then we see, eh?"

"Fine," Vincha turned, "but you better not double cross me, Twinkle Eyes." I let her warning hang unanswered as we crossed the bridge and moved on. This time I led the way. And to be honest, I liked the way Galinak called me "boss."

32

In retrospect, it was probably foolish of me to conceive a plan in which our emergency meeting spot was a tavern called the Blade. I was still feeling slightly ill from the eel, and the Blade was on the city's smallest cluster of spires, a mile or so west of the Central Plateau. We needed to find a way up, and now I knew for sure that someone was looking for me, and not just anyone. The Sabarra guild was known to be run with a firm hand. If one of their crews was after me it meant that the head of the guild, the man who won the goriest of the guild wars, now presided over the Council and was taking a personal interest in me.

I decided to walk through the Pit and hire a cart to bring us up through Cart's Way. My less brilliant idea was to send Galinak on his own first. He almost got into two fights before failing to fulfil my simple request: that he hail us one rusting donkey cart and do it without attracting too much attention. He even began haggling loudly over the price and was still doing so when Vincha and I finally joined him. The cart driver was in a foul mood and would have simply driven away if not for the fact that Galinak was holding the donkey firmly in place. At least when the weather turned sour I had a good reason to hide my face in my cowl.

Whether it was out of frustration or fear, Galinak managed to lower the price to a more agreeable sum, but upon seeing the extra passengers the driver declared that the agreed sum was per person, effectively tripling his rate. I was in no mood to haggle, so I agreed to the outrageous price. I didn't envy the poor donkey that had to pull us the entire way up to the middle spire in the rain.

When we arrived at the Blade, I found one of those orphan boys who looked eager enough for work and sent a coded message to my contact, River. Then we had nothing to do but sit down and shame Vincha into buying us a drink, since I was completely out of hard coin. After a while she softened up and ordered some food as well, and we retreated to a side room, sitting in silence and sipping our drinks while listening to a troupe of local bards play some old tunes in the main room. At some point Galinak asked Vincha if she'd like to dance. He was not rewarded with a response. As I sat back and tried to relax, my body decided to remind me that I hadn't slept the night before, and that I'd survived several violent, not to mention emotionally draining, encounters. In short, I dozed off and was not aware that Vincha felt us being scanned again. The door to the room opened, and by the time I realised what was going on, the other two were already up and struggling with a third person—River, my contact. He was not a Troll or even a warrior—but he was no pushover, either.

I got everyone to calm down and made sure they were properly introduced to one another. No one apologised—except me, several times, to everyone—but at least I felt some sense of grudging respect from the two warriors towards my contact. After all, it had taken me a few heartbeats to gain control of the situation, and he was still conscious and breathing when I stopped the fight.

River was a middle-aged man who in his prime and with the right gear could have been a Troll, or even a crew leader like Galinak. But River's love and talent for all things Tarakan had made him into a Tinker, an inventor, and an avid collector of Tarakan technologies. It was true irony that no guild would hire him for expeditions because he was unmarked by tattoos. I knew he was bitter about his fate and would have given anything to explore Tarakan Valley and the City within the Mountain.

His loss was our gain, for River ended up working for my LoreMaster and proved to be trustworthy and competent, and so far he had never let me down. In other words, River was one of the good guys. So when he took me aside discreetly and gave me a fifth of the funds I'd asked for, I didn't assume right away that he was stealing from me.

He shook his head. "Sorry, coffers are empty. You guys been spending it like the second Catastrophe's coming."

I asked him to stay and walked back to the room, thinking, as it were, on my feet.

I took the coin pouch, moved a quarter of the funds to my own pocket, and tossed the pouch to Galinak, who hefted it expertly in his hand and smiled.

"Two months' escort," I told him. "You go where I go, you watch my back."

Galinak made a show of thinking about it, then shrugged and smiled his acceptance.

I sat down and looked at Vincha, who returned my gaze with a calculating stare. She was going to be disappointed, and what I was about to do was far from chivalrous, but I was not going to let her get away, not after all I'd been through.

"You're going to tell me the rest of the story," I told her. "That was the last of my coin, and I already paid you enough."

When she realised I was serious, she got up, picking up her gear in one swoop, and said, "You just wasted my day, Twinkle Eyes. Good-bye."

I am not proud of what I did next.

"Not so fast." My tone of voice made her turn her head to me just as she was at the door. "I don't know what you did to Fuazz,"

I said slowly and deliberately, "but he is *seriously* pissed off. I know so, because he told me in his own words what he would do to you when he finds you."

She froze in her tracks, her hand on the door's handle.

I heard Galinak swear softly to himself.

"And Grapplers have notoriously long memories," I continued, carefully assessing the distance between us. "I believe they're looking for you as well. You step out of this room and I will give them the exact location of your *daughter*."

It was a gambit. I didn't know how Galinak would react to my threat, even though I had just officially hired him to protect me. You had to be blind not to see that he was fond of Vincha, so the gamble I took with my life was that when Vincha tried to kill me, Galinak's twisted code of professionalism would overcome any personal feelings he might have for the woman.

My words caught Vincha when she was already at the door, but she still managed to hit me twice before River and Galinak dragged her off me. She struggled like a wounded lioness, but thankfully Galinak had made his decision in my favour. With some effort, Vincha's arms were pinned to her back and her head was shoved to the table, held down by the angle of her twisted arm and Galinak's raised knee pressing on the back of her neck with his full weight behind it. This painful submission hold took the wind out of her, but still she struggled until River slapped something round and metallic on her back, which made her legs crumple. A grim-looking Galinak eased off and lifted her into a chair while maintaining a controlled choke hold.

"I'm going to kill you," she breathed in fury above his arm. "I didn't tell you the truth. I did find Jakov and when I found him, I killed him, slowly. And if you harm my family I will tear you apart. I will find you and cut your eyes out, and then your balls, and then . . ."

I didn't know if she was telling the truth about killing Jakov, I certainly hadn't heard a solid lead that he was still alive, but I knew she was angry enough to threaten me with slow death, even when pinned down and theoretically at my mercy. I realised, too late, that I'd made a mistake.

"Enough," I said. "Galinak, let her go." I knew I was skating on thin ice with him and I didn't want to push it. "River, take your damn Gadgets out of her system."

I turned to her. "Now you listen to me, Vincha. I never wanted it to be like this. I paid you for the story and didn't threaten you before, but you milked me dry. I have no more coin, and I need you to tell me this story. Time is running out. I can't mess around anymore." I was angry, hurting, tired, desperate, and broke. No more Mister Nice Guy—he was good only for sitting in libraries and reading history books and Salvo-novels. Here and now, I needed results.

I was not giving her much of a choice, but under the circumstances, she was still getting a good deal of coin out of me.

She didn't rise from her chair, but I could see she was considering her options, rubbing her wrists and shooting Galinak looks, which didn't give me hope for future reconciliation.

"So, I tell you the full story and then I'm free to go?" she asked, carefully enunciating every word while looking me in the eye.

I held her stare, knowing that this woman was at the end of her tether, and were she given the opportunity, I wouldn't blame her for attempting to cut my throat.

"Yes," I lied. "You can go when you're done with your tale. I have no wish to cause you or your family harm."

"You will forget where my family is?"

"I promise you, though I am sure you will move your daughter somewhere else by then anyway." *And I will find her again if I need to.*

"You might betray me before I manage to do it."

I shrugged "Why should I do that? As you know, my contract with Galinak is over in several weeks, and I am metal dry. You could easily track me down if I betrayed you."

"I might just do that," she said slowly and shot a glare at Galinak. "I might not wait several weeks to do it."

Galinak spread his arms wide and winked. "I guess we'll end up dancing after all."

"You filthy old rusting f—"

"Shut up, both of you," I snapped angrily. "I suggest that you both find an appropriate time in the future to get this sexual frustration out of the way, but right now I want to hear what happened to Rafik after he was bought by the Keenan guild, and then I want you to take us there."

33

"Welcome to your new home, Rafik," Mistress Furukawa said, as the guards closed the large gates behind them. They were standing in a very large courtyard, in front of the entrance to the main house. It was almost impossible for Rafik to imagine that they were all standing on a huge disc so high above the ground that the people below them looked like ants. The dais was covered in trees, and the gentle breeze touched his face. He later learned that the freezing wind that should have been blowing at this height was somehow blocked by the mysterious Tarakan technology.

"This building and all you see around it is the property of the Keenan guild," Mistress Furukawa said, gesturing with one hand while nudging him forward with the other.

Just like me, thought Rafik, looking around nervously. He had not yet come to terms with the fact that Jakov was no longer controlling his life. In fact, Rafik was still half-expecting the merchant to show up again. The idea made him shiver, and he pushed that thought away by looking around.

Rafik had to admit the place was impressive, and Mistress

Furukawa, perhaps sensing the boy's awe, described the premises as they walked through it. The whole compound was built in the style of an ancient fort, with six towers, three buildings—the main one being four stories high—several courtyards, and even a large garden and an extensive underground level.

Mistress Furukawa nudged him gently when he slowed down to take it all in. "Come, it's almost time for dinner. Time to meet your new family."

They walked through several halls and crossed an inner courtyard filled with human-sized dummies made of wood and straw. Mistress Furukawa explained this was the practice area for combat training. Once they reached a side door they slipped into a maze of short corridors that led them to the main dining hall. Never in his life had Rafik been inside a building so large and imposing.

The corridors were richly furnished, lined with tapestries depicting ancient battles and several statues of sword-wielding warriors. Their footsteps were muffled by the bloodred carpeting. As they came closer to the hall Rafik heard a booming voice, but the words were distorted, swallowed up by the heavy curtains that surrounded them. When they stepped into the dining hall, in the shadow of the large columns that supported the room's high ceiling, the words took shape and meaning.

A man was standing on a low dais and lecturing several dozen youth who sat at three very long tables laden with food. Rafik could see only the man's back; his body was shrouded in a grey cloak. The man's voice was deep and powerful. The youth seemed completely entranced by his words, because no one moved or braved a whisper. Sitting at a smaller table closer to Rafik were several men and women who were also listening attentively. The scene reminded Rafik of the scripture lessons in his home village, though the listeners were not sitting on the floor, the food on the table was clearly of higher quality, and it soon became obvious that the man was not speaking of the holy scripts.

"We, the Keenan guild, found each and every one of you,

sometimes when it was almost too late. We saved your lives, brought you here, gave you food and shelter, and taught you how to use your special abilities. Where your families and friends showed you fear and violence, we gave you acceptance, understanding, and respect. We will always support you. We will never abandon you, unlike the people who you once thought of as family. The Keenans are your real family now, in action and virtue instead of just blood.

"Look around! You are surrounded by brothers and sisters, closer to you than the blood kin who betrayed you. Sitting behind me are your guild mothers and fathers; give them the respect, love, and obedience they deserve. And most of all, our leader, Master Keenan himself."

As if on cue, everyone bellowed the word "Respect!" in perfect unison, and the word echoed among the walls and columns. Only when it finally died down did the speaker continue.

"Soon you will be called to serve the guild, to repay your debt. Remember, you are the new humanity. You are the future, the representatives of the civilisation we once were and what we will one day become."

The man would have continued his speech if not for a boy who spotted them lurking in the shadows. He immediately sprang to his feet and shouted, "Mistress Furukawa. Respect."

The entire room rose to attention and turned to face the woman, who walked slowly and deliberately to the centre of the room. With a light touch she made sure Rafik moved with her. The man who was speaking turned as well. His eyes were the brightest shade of green Rafik had ever seen. He focused his gaze on the woman and then stared at Rafik. Slowly, as if doing something against his better judgement, he bowed to Mistress Furukawa, and the room followed suit. He climbed carefully down from the dais. He was limping heavily, like Grandpa Suhd from Rafik's village, but without the walking stick Grandpa used to hold. When he came closer he declared out loud, "Welcome, Mistress of the House of Keenan," but even as his words echoed throughout the hall, and with his back to everyone else, he hissed under his breath, "Are you *insane*? What have you done?"

"I trust the representative of the merchant guild arrived before me, Master Goran?" Mistress Furukawa answered in a loud, clear voice and tilted her head in the direction of the "mothers and fathers" who were watching the situation intently.

The man nodded and whispered, "Three of them came, with several carts. I sent a courier to the auction house to check that the sum they were asking for was genuine. How could you do this? We never gave our consent, and now we're almost depleted of coin." He looked down at Rafik. "And look at him. A lifetime of wealth—a year's worth of supplies, for an untrained boy!"

Rafik was standing next to Mistress Furukawa, but his eyes darted around the dining hall. With the exception of the game in New Denver, Rafik hadn't seen children his own age since leaving his village. Newport was a hub for truckers and gangsters, he was only in Regeneration briefly, and then he'd been locked in a room since he arrived in the City of Towers. In the previous few weeks Rafik had experienced battles and violence and had escaped death several times. But facing this large group of boys and girls, all looking at him with open curiosity, made him nervous in a way he hadn't been in a very long time.

He heard Mistress Furukawa speaking under her breath: ". . . decision was for the good of this guild. It is not your place to question my judgement."

She turned and addressed the room. "It is a good day for the Keenan guild. Please welcome the newest member of our family, Rafik!"

"Rafik, Respect!" they shouted, and the sound left his ears ringing.

"I'm sure there's a lot of gossip about him already, so let me be the one to dispel the rumours. Rafik is a genuine, certified Puzzler."

People moved excitedly in their places, exchanging meaningful looks.

Mistress Furukawa locked stares with Master Goran as she continued, "For the first time in years, the Keenan guild has a Puzzler of its own. It is a sign of our rejuvenation and growing strength. It also means that sooner or later, all of you will be called to serve your Keenan family in deep runs."

Another audible commotion of excitement swept the hall, but it quickly subsided as the Mistress continued her speech. "I want you to double your training. Learn more and work harder than you ever have before, because deep runs are as dangerous as they are rewarding. In a few days we will be honoured by a visit from Lord Keenan himself."

"Keenan, Respect!" the shout filled the hall.

"He will be inspecting our progress, personally." She let the implication of her words sink in before adding, "And now, let us eat. Then you will all resume training. Please be seated."

There was a sudden commotion in the room as everyone sat down. Rafik was told to sit at the end of a faraway table. He complied, filling his plate with food while trying not to catch anyone's eye, which was difficult because everyone was ogling him.

He lowered his eyes and as he uttered a blessing over the meal in the softest of whispers, he heard a girl's voice, "Look, he still prays, how cute!" A few sniggers followed.

"Hey you, Puzzler!" someone called.

"His name is Rafik," it was the girl's voice again.

"Whatever. Hey, Puzzler, look at me."

He had no choice but to turn his head in the direction of the voice. The boy who was talking to him was sitting a few seats away. He was big, grossly muscled, and sporting a shaved head with clear tattoos marking his arms, chest and neck.

"Show us your hand," he said, chewing a mouthful of meat.

"Stop bothering him, Kurk," said a girl with red hair tied back in a long braid. "Can't you see he's scared?"

It might have been an alien place in a strange city, but Rafik's instincts told him the rules here where the same as his home vilage. He was the new boy, and had to show that he was not afraid. Failure would mean future bullying. He raised his hand and spread his fingers.

Kurk looked at the symbols on his hand, then smiled broadly at another boy.

"Yes! We finally got one, a rusting Puzzler, praise Keenan! We are going deep!" He turned back to Rafik. "Don't be afraid," he said in a high-pitched voice, as if talking to a baby. "We won't hurt you. You are our key, we need you."

Rafik did not understand, but his hand acted on its own accord, turning itself around and slowly lowering all his fingers but the middle one, to create a gesture that he'd learned from a drunken trucker in Newport. He was rewarded by a burst of laughter.

Kurk's condescending smile turned into an angry smirk. "Watch it, boy," he sneered. "We only need one of your hands to open doors."

There were a few more sniggers at the table. Rafik still didn't understand what Kurk was saying about doors, so he kept quiet and chewed his food. Kurk's honour seemed to be satisfied, though, and the rest of the meal went smoothly.

Dinner was concluded with yet another loud pledge to the Keenan guild, after which Rafik was invited to meet the rest of the Keenan leaders. Mistress Furukawa was obviously in charge; only her conversation with Master Goran indicated there was any kind of discontent within the high rank of the guild. The rest of the grown-ups were too numerous for Rafik to remember by name, especially since he was practically exhausted from the events of the day. They all looked at him like owners checking a newly acquired, prize racing dog. One of them even wondered out loud how soon Rafik would bring a return on their investment.

By the time the introductions were over the rest of the kids were already gone. Rafik was led to the dormitories by House Master Prushnik, a balding man who was fond of his pipe. Rafik's cot was at the end of a long row of twenty. The beds were

Tarakan built—they floated in the air with no support whatsoever and adjusted themselves to the knee level of the person standing next to them.

"Nice, eh?" the House Master relit his pipe, puffing energetically. "You won't get that in Tarakan Valley. Over here you can store your clothes and any other items you need. When you receive your trainee pistol, make sure you place it in weapons storage every night. Are you ready to hear the rules for staying here?"

Rafik nodded; he was hardly in a position to argue.

House Master Prushnik took the pipe out of his mouth and pointed the chewed end at Rafik. "You need to remember only the most important rule: do as you're told. No more, no less. Fail and you'll spend the night in a rat-infested cellar below. Not something I would recommend, though it does build character. If you don't believe me, ask some of the boys—they can show you the teeth marks."

Rafik promised to obey. The House Master nodded with satisfaction and placed the pipe back in his mouth. "Good. Now, give me your arm, no, not the one with the mark, the other one."

House Master Prushnik locked a thin silver bracelet over Rafik's right arm. The bracelet was incredibly light and adjusted itself in size to fit perfectly.

"Leave your belongings here and let's go to the common room," he said. "The other trainees are probably eager to get to know you better."

Rafik could not tell by the House Master's tone if this was a good or bad thing.

They walked together to the common room, which was yet another large hall. It was the hub of social activity for the trainees. Everyone turned and stared as they entered, except Kurk, who was busy doing one-handed push-ups as another boy sat on his back counting loudly. Now that he was wearing the silver bracelet on his arm, Rafik noticed that everyone was wearing bracelets.

"This is it," House Master Prushnik said as he patted Rafik

on the shoulder. "You may stay here when you're not training or doing chores, so you probably won't be seeing much of this hall in the next few months. Enjoy it while you can."

As soon as Rafik was alone a mob of trainees accosted him, firing questions from all directions:

"Show us your hand again!"

"Can you do something else?"

"Did they tell you what your training is going to be like?"

"I can feel his mind; it's full of weird symbols and numbers."

"How weird!"

"Do we have to do what he tells us?"

"Of course not, rust brain, we're just supposed to protect him."

It was actually Kurk, shouldering his way through the crowd, who came to the boy's rescue.

"Stop bothering the puppy," he barked loud enough for everyone to hear. "Leave him be, can't you see he knows nothing?"

That was a challenge Rafik could not let pass. "I know more than you think," he spat back, "and I'm worth ten of you in auction."

There was a collective gasp at this, and Kurk walked slowly over to face Rafik. Even with the knowledge that the young Troll would probably not dare hurt him, it was an intimidating moment. It took all of Rafik's courage not to back away.

"You may be worth a lot of coin, puppy," Kurk mocked, "but you ain't good at anything other than opening doors. You're just a key. And we"—he gestured around to the boys and girls, who were obviously only a few months from becoming full Trolls—"are the ones who need to keep the Lizards off you on a deep run." He leaned forward, towering over Rafik. "Show some respect, or I will let them chew on your face a bit, just to teach you a lesson."

Rafik shuddered. No one had told him anything about deep runs or Lizards or face chewing. It seemed as if everyone knew who he was and what he was supposed to be doing, but Rafik knew nothing. His emotions must have been plain on his face, because Kurk laughed and turned away. Everyone else dispersed, and Rafik was left alone. No one approached him anymore, but everyone kept glancing in his direction and whispering among themselves, to the point that he felt uncomfortable and left the hall.

There was a new set of grey clothes waiting for him on his cot with the Keenan insignia stitched onto them. They felt rougher on his skin than the garments he was wearing, and were a size too large, but Rafik felt relieved to change into them, as if stripping away his old clothes meant he was changing from a miserable past into a better future.

With nothing else to do, and nowhere to go, Rafik lay down on the only spot that was marked as his. To his surprise, the mattress moulded itself to him, and he immediately felt waves of warmth caressing his body—it was the most comfortable bed he'd ever slept in, and it raised his spirits a little. As Rafik shut his eyes, recent events began playing in his mind. Being examined in the lavish tent, the auction, the scribe's comment about breaking a yearly record, the signing of the contract between Mistress Furukawa and Jakov—the merchant didn't even bother to say good-bye when he left the room—arriving at the Keenan guild house, hearing Master Goran's whispered admonition, and, of course, meeting the other boys and girls. Rafik tried to make sense of it all. Like the great wall of his dreams, he could sense there was a pattern lurking in the background but it was too complex for him to understand.

Before sleep finally claimed him, Rafik comforted himself with the thought that even if he was just a key for the Keenans like Kurk said, he was a very expensive one. The guild would want to protect their investment, just like Khan and Jakov did. So right now, he was safe, and that would have to do.

34

"Are you ready, young Puzzler?" House Master Prushnik smiled at Rafik while still holding the pipe between his yellowing teeth.

Rafik nodded, as he checked his appearance one more time, making sure all was in order. He ran his hand over his neatly shaved head.

"Good, I suggest we make haste then. Master Goran does *not* like waiting. Here, take this coat with you." He handed Rafik the garment. "You'll need it where we are going."

House Master Prushnik led the way through the guild's premises, occasionally greeting a passerby with a nod or a word, and stopping to check that household duties were done.

They crossed the courtyard, where the rest of the Keenan trainees were going through morning drills. As they passed by, many eyed Rafik with a mix of curiosity and envy, for it was announced during morning meal that Rafik would be exempt from all drills as well as chores. This did not make the rest of the trainees friendlier towards Rafik. Kurk, going through the motions of one of the drills, sent him a dirty look, and after he made sure no one else saw, accompanied it with a rude gesture.

"Here, we are," House Master Prushnik declared as they reached the stairs leading to a heavy door. "Let us descend to Master Goran's lair." He chuckled to himself, choosing a large iron key from the enormous key ring he carried on his belt and unlocking the door. "Only Master Goran and myself have the key for this door," he said proudly, opening the heavy door. "Master Goran is a stickler for privacy. He has a room on the top of the guild house, of course, but if you want to find him at any time, even at night, he will most likely be down here."

As they entered, House Master Prushnik picked up an oil lamp and lit it before closing and locking the heavy door behind them. He took the lead, walking down the set of wide steps as he rubbed his hands together for warmth. "There are actually working Tarakan lights here," he explained, "and heating too, but Master Goran likes it this way. Keeps visitors at a minimum, he tells me."

Walking down the stairs felt like venturing deep underground, though House Master Prushnik reminded Rafik that they were still walking inside a Tarakan-built plateau, which was suspended in midair. They passed through several dozen large rooms containing everything from furniture covered in cloth to chopped wood, neatly piled up, then they climbed down even farther until they reached another door leading into a large hall, which was lit up so strongly Rafik was momentarily blinded.

The House Master hung the oil lamp on the wall and patted Rafik kindly on his shoulder, signalling for him to follow.

It turned out to be not one hall but four, each filled with all kinds of machinery and metal piled on rows of shelves and sometimes just on top of each other. Rafik followed the House Master, carefully navigating past, around, and sometimes under until they reached a slightly more spacious fifth hall, where Master Goran was bending over a large table clogged with wires and metal, his arm deep within a silvery looking orb.

House Master Prushnik took his pipe in his hand and cleared his throat, "Master Goran, I have brought you the young Puzzler."

"Good, thank you, House Master." Master Goran didn't bother to lift his head from the table. "That will be all."

Despite the fact that Master Goran was not paying attention, House Master Pushnik bowed slightly, but as he turned to leave Master Goran spoke again.

"Oh, and House Master?"

"Yes?"

"Leave your key with the boy. I trust he will be able to make his way by himself from now on, as well as keep the oil lamp full."

The House Master looked stunned. He opened his mouth to speak but closed it again without saying a word. Finally, he turned, took Rafik's hand in his, and slapped the iron key into his palm. "Don't lose it, or I'll have your hide," he growled and stomped away. Moments later, there was a distant sound of a door being slammed.

Master Goran straightened up and turned around, removing a metallic visor he was wearing over his face with only a small slit allowing him to see. "Ah, the new talent," he intoned and gently laid the visor on the table. "Follow me." He beckoned with a hand enclosed in a semitransparent white glove, then turned and limped away.

Rafik hurried after Master Goran until they reached a metal door at the far wall.

"This is the first thing I want you to see." Master Goran peeled the glove off his right hand and positioned his palm above a small metal plate at the side of the metal door. The plate shone blue and the metal door slid open, revealing a shaft with enough space to hold several people.

"This is a lift," Master Goran said as he donned the transparent white glove again. "It can take you up to several key locations in the guild house, including my private chambers on the top floor. It makes coming and going much, much easier." The metal doors slid shut and Master Goran looked down, locking gazes with Rafik as he slowly said, "*You . . . will . . . never . . . use . . . this . . . lift.*"

"Yes, Master Goran," Rafik answered in a small voice.

Satisfied, Master Goran led Rafik to a nearby table and sat down.

He poured himself a drink and offered Rafik a mug of cold water.

"So, *our* newly acquired talent . . ." Master Goran said once more, watching Rafik as the boy drained his mug. Then he slammed his own mug down on the table. "I think it was a grave mistake to spend all of our resources on you. A *grave* mistake."

Rafik didn't know what to say, so he remained silent, holding his empty mug.

Master Goran sighed and shook his head. "What's done is done. Now, come show me your hand."

Rafik obeyed without thinking; so many people had examined his hand in the past few weeks that he'd overcome the instinct to conceal his marks. Master Goran held Rafik's tattooed hand and examined his three fingers closely under a pair of glasses he balanced on the bridge of his nose, which, he explained, made objects look bigger. The white gloves felt extremely odd on Rafik's skin—he'd never felt such material before but decided not to try and satisfy his curiosity. Master Goran examined Rafik's tattoos closely, taking measurements of them, his fingers, his hand, and his arm with a measurement rope. Rafik didn't need glasses or a measurement rope to know that the symbols on his fingertips had doubled in size since he'd left his home village, covering all his fingers and the middle one reaching into his palm.

After each measurement, Master Goran turned and tapped his fingers over a thin slate that reminded Rafik of Sweetheart's screens. He kept asking Rafik many questions about his tattoos:

how big they were when he first saw them, when did they start to grow, did they tingle, and even how many puzzles had he solved. Rafik tried to answer each question quickly and correctly, because every time he hesitated Master Goran tapped his foot impatiently.

Eventually Master Goran let go of Rafik's hand, got up from his chair, and walked slowly to a set of shelves filled with all kinds of metal, where he rummaged for a while. Rafik was left alone at the table. For some reason, his thoughts wandered to his home village, his family and best friend, and the autumn festivities that would be going on now. He felt his heart sinking into his chest, and a bitter taste filled his mouth. Rafik was so deep in his memories that he didn't notice Master Goran's return to the table.

"Missing home?"

The question startled Rafik. Could Master Goran read his thoughts as well?

"I was thinking about my brother's wedding," he answered. "It must have happened by now."

"No use trying to hold on to the past, Rafik. What you should worry about is the future." Master Goran held a rectangular puzzle box. Rafik could easily recognise them by now. Like Jakov's puzzle boxes, it had a time-measuring display, but this particular box also had two dozen thin wires coming out of it. Master Goran followed Rafik's gaze.

"By now you know that you are different even from the tattooed, Rafik, and what this is." Master Goran laid the puzzle box gently on the table. "You know you are a Puzzler, that you can solve puzzles, and that people find you valuable, but this is all you know, nothing else. You are a raw talent, unskilled, untrained, unrefined, blind to the subtleties of puzzling, innocent in the face of what you will be up against—which means you will be dead less than an hour into your first shallow run, and it would take even less time for you to perish in a deep run, into the City within the Mountain, something Lord Keenan will undoubtedly push for as soon as possible. You are a novice, even worse than a novice, because you know so little and think you know a lot, and everyone's enthusiasm is misleading you. You know nothing of what you are expected to do. Unfortunately, since we have spent all of our wealth acquiring you, your death would mean the destruction of this guild. I must train you as hard as I can, because your fate entwines with ours."

Rafik was too frightened to speak, but something in his eyes must have radiated defiance. "You think I'm lying." Master Goran's smile was not kind. "You think I'm just trying to hurt your feelings? You think I'm just an old fool, perhaps?"

"No, I don—" The slap caught Rafik midsentence and brought him to his knees. His eyes filled with tears. His face was burning.

Master Goran hovered above him. "Get up." It was an order. Rafik's legs worked of their own accord.

"Good. Did the slap hurt?"

Rafik shook his head. *Was it out of pride?*

The second slap caught him on the other side of the face and was even more powerful. This time he stayed sprawled on the cool floor, tasting blood in his mouth, whimpering softly. But still the order penetrated the ringing in his ears: "Get up!"

Trembling with fear, he pulled himself up again.

"Did it hurt?"

He nodded, his face feeling as if it was on fire.

"Good. The first slap was to make a point; the second one was for lying. Lie again and you will suffer consequences graver than what you just experienced." Master Goran grabbed Rafik's arm and pinned it to the table with a metal brace that was screwed into the tabletop.

"The pain you are feeling now is a soft tickle compared with the pain you will feel just before you die on a deep run. Hold on to that, Rafik, let it be your inspiration to excel in what I am about to teach you."

Master Goran slid the puzzle box onto Rafik's fingers. He then attached the wires to different parts of Rafik's hand and arm, speaking calmly as he worked, as if he had not violently hit the boy twice just a few moments before.

"There are too many things to teach you and too little time, so I will begin from the end. The Tarkanians had cities and outposts all over this world, but what is called 'the City within the Mountain' was their centre of power. As its name suggests, it is built inside a mountain range, overlooking Tarakan Valley. We do not know how many Tarkanians lived in the City within the Mountain, but there are millions of Tarakan buildings just in the Valley itself, from the smallest cottage to towers as high as the ones we have here in this city. Whatever terrible weapon killed the Tarkanians, it left most of those buildings standing, and in almost every such building you can find puzzle boxes. Why? Your guess is as good as mine. Maybe it was a way to educate people, or something to do with their religion, or maybe they just liked games, but here's the important bit: the Tarkanians must have known that the Catastrophe was imminent, and they prepared for it.

"Throughout the Valley there are underground bunkers—we call them nodes—filled with all kinds of equipment that would help the survivors of such a war, from sophisticated and lethal weapons to pills that can nourish your body for days, power tubes and clips, all kinds of ammunition, goggles that allow you to see in the dark, vehicles, and all manner of technology we can still use but have no idea how to make ourselves. These nodes replenish themselves periodically—we have no idea how, or why, but they do.

"To the best of my knowledge, the City of Towers has seven such nodes, which are barely able to supply the ShieldGuards and the upper crust of society. The Council makes sure there are always at least two Puzzlers in custody at all times to keep the flow of supplies going. Tarakan Valley, on the other hand, has hundreds of nodes that supply everything you could possibly dream of and more. But the real treasure troves lie deep in the City within the Mountain. Armoured vehicles, communication devices that let you speak to other people hundreds of miles away, and many artifacts we still have no idea how to use, are all there, waiting for us.

"So here's the catch." Master Goran leaned closer, his mouth uncomfortably close to Rafik's ear. "Each node has a door, and each door has a lock, and that lock is a puzzle, and only a Puzzler can open these locks." He chuckled without merriment. "Believe me, they've tried looking into alternatives. There are none. Only a Puzzler will do, and this is what they will expect you to do: to open the magic doors so they can collect the goodies." As he hooked up the last of the wires Master Goran added, "The puzzle locks in the City of Towers and even in the Valley can be difficult, but the ones in the City within the Mountain are lethal." Satisfied, he straightened up. "Now let's see how good you really are."

Master Goran pressed a button on the puzzle box, and Rafik felt the initial sting before finding himself in the familiar black void. For a few heartbeats he floated in complete darkness, trying to calm himself. But in the blink of an eye a puzzle appeared before him and Rafik did not hesitate. The first few puzzles were easy, and his fear turned into excitement, even into a cautious confidence. He managed to solve the first strain of puzzles and woke up feeling good about himself, but Master Goran's face was sombre. He shook his head as his hand moved over a Tarakan pad. Rafik had only a few moments to recuperate.

"This next set has a time limit," warned Master Goran, "so complete them as quickly as you can." With the press of a button the world winked away.

It was a more complex version of the last puzzle, not as big as some that Rafik had tackled during his time on Sweetheart, but its three dimensions made it confusing. All he could do for a while was hover above the sea of symbols, trying desperately to latch on to a pattern. He managed to grasp half of the pattern when a sudden flash of pain coursed through his entire body. He heard his own voice shouting in agony from afar, increasing in volume until it was ringing in his ears when the hall suddenly reappeared.

Rafik found himself doubled over the large table, gasping in pain, desperately trying to pull his fingers free from the puzzle box. But it was impossible to do so with his arm pinned to the table. Master Goran's face filled Rafik's field of vision.

"You know what's the difference between a Gadgetier and a Tinker?" Master Goran did not wait for a reply. "A Gadgetier is marked, he has the talent, the raw instinct, the knowledge is already inside him, while a Tinker is just someone who likes to shove his nose into alien machinery. I am a Tinker but you are a Puzzler, you have the talent."

Master Goran's voice calmed, and his eyes became distant, flat, as he continued. "Our last Puzzler also had talent, and he thought the boxes were just games—fun, fascinating games, but not very important. He was too preoccupied with learning to use his gun to spend time training like he should have. Then we went to the Valley, and he still pulled through, because he was very talented. When we entered the City within the Mountain he even bested the first lock, and a few locks after that, but what happened next . . ." Master Goran looked away from Rafik. "Most of us died there, or got severely wounded, and what was left of our crew brought the Puzzler back foaming at the mouth. He screamed for days and had to be force-fed. When he finally awoke, he was a shadow of what he once was, and his natural ability was burnt out of him." Master Goran turned his head and looked deeply into the boy's eyes. "Are you scared now?" he asked.

Rafik swallowed hard and nodded.

"Good. Try the puzzle again." Master Goran quickly pressed the puzzle box and Rafik was inside the puzzle again. This time his mind froze in terror. The memory of the terrible pain was still fresh. He did worse than his first attempt. He couldn't focus on the task, and the puzzle was far from being complete when pain jolted through his body yet again.

"Again," ordered Master Goran.

"No, please," Rafik begged, but it was too late. He lost precious time trying to find a way out of the puzzle dimension, and the pain he suffered made even breathing an agony.

He was too weak even to try and pull away this time. He just laid his head on the table, panting, tears of fear and shame running down his face.

"Again."

After two more failed attempts Master Goran decided it was enough and released Rafik from the puzzle box. The boy withdrew his hand as if it were on fire and fell backwards onto the floor, then crawled away from the table until his back hit the wall. He inspected his hand, expecting his fingers to be bleeding or burned, but his hand seemed whole and intact, and there were no marks on his forearm.

Master Goran limped over until he towered above the boy. "That was a level-five lock at three minutes," he said, looking down. "A shallow run, to a Tarakan node in the valley, would bring you to locks up to level eight with around the same time limit. The outer doors of a deep run are level fourteen with less than a minute to work out what to do. The Tarkanians were no fools. The better the loot, the harder the lock."

Rafik looked up, still holding his hand to his chest. "But why would they do that?" he wailed. "Why would they want to hurt you if you do not succeed?"

"Most of the puzzle locks will just freeze for a fortnight if you fail," admitted Master Goran, "and then you can go back and try again. But some puzzles are lethal. The pain you felt is my own addition, to put you under pressure, and it worked. Every time you tried you did worse than before." Master Goran walked back to the table and picked up the puzzle box. For a moment Rafik thought he was going to make him try again, and only sheer terror kept him from jumping to his feet and running away. But Master Goran walked slowly to the shelves. He didn't stop talking as he placed the box among the other objects.

"During a shallow run you might have to open a lock while

your crew is fighting. Don't be fooled by the word 'Lizards.' They are called this because of their green skin colour and long snouts—but these are extremely lethal creatures, almost an adult human in size, much more powerful and often very cunning. They have claws and teeth that would rip you to shreds, and are able to kill an unarmed man in a heartbeat. Many of the nodes are in Lizard-infested areas, and even with the cleaning crews we send out, somehow they reproduce fast enough to come back again and again.

"And they are not the only danger in the Valley; there are lethal traps, wild animals, even rogue crews who prey on each other. You might need to solve a puzzle while you are surrounded by enemies, under fire, or even wounded. The knowledge that your life and the lives of your group are in your hands must not cause you to make mistakes."

Master Goran came back, leaned down, and grasped Rafik's shoulders with his hands. "Your training here will make the difference between life and agonizing death," he growled, "yours and your crew's."

"I don't want to do this," Rafik said, trying not to burst into tears. "I never wanted to do this. I just wanted to stay home, in my village." He sniffed and felt his chin tremble uncontrollably.

Master Goran simply shook his head, still holding Rafik by his shoulders. "You cannot go home," he said gravely and gestured at Rafik's silver bracelet. "This bracelet tells the training officers exactly where you are, and it can even incapacitate you if you try to leave the training grounds. You think you're the first recruit who wanted to leave? The only difference between you and the others is that the guild will not ceremonially cut this bracelet off your arm after a month or two. You are too valuable. Our war with the Sabarra has cost us a fortune, and Mistress Furukawa bought you with all we have left." Master Goran sighed softly, "It was a bold move, I admit, but it has brought our guild to the edge. We might soar or we might fall, depending on the outcome of your training. Worse, the guild needs a return on its investment as soon as possible, otherwise we are exposed. Lord Keenan is a great warrior, but perhaps exactly for that reason he is a firm believer in trial by fire. You're going to be sent to the outpost soon, much too soon. I bought you a couple of months, maybe ten, maybe a year, but no more. Your only chance of survival is to train with me as hard as you can before they send you to Tarakan Valley."

Master Goran sought Rafik's eyes with his own. "You have to understand, it's not about discovering where we came from, or figuring out who the Tarkanians were, or what happened in the Catastrophe—it's about coin and power and who controls the future." He walked back to the table and leaned heavily on the high stool.

"Still thinking about escaping?"

Rafik didn't dare lie, so he nodded.

"I don't blame you, but you won't do it, and not just because of the bracelet. You might just be resourceful enough to find a solution to your problem, the same way I did." Master Goran's smile was genuine this time. "But even if you escape this place and find your way down to the ground level, and somehow escape the manhunt and manage to leave the city, you will eventually end up back in Tarakan Valley. You know why?"

Rafik shook his head as Master Goran slowly peeled the glove off his left hand and spread his fingers in front of the boy's face. Rafik could just make out the markings. Master Goran's tattoos were so small they fit on his fingertips and were so faded you could have mistaken them for an ink smudge. Still, Rafik could make out a triangle and one crescent moon.

"Because you are a Puzzler, Rafik, just like I was, before my mistakes killed my crew and I became a mere Tinker. My talent was burned out of me that day, but I still remember the pull of the Valley. You cannot run away, because Tarakan Valley draws you in, the same way it drew me and others of our kind. Only in Tarakan Valley will you feel at peace, as if you belong there, even if the place ends up killing you."

35

Rafik tried to move as quietly as possible and still gain ground, a difficult task considering the corridor was almost completely dark. A battle was still raging outside, and although he was already well inside the building, explosions, gunfire, and even an occasional scream reached his ears. It was not a good sign.

At least his cut finally stopped bleeding. He gingerly felt the bloodstained cloth wrapped around his forearm before continuing to inch forward, feeling the wall with his free hand while holding a blaster with the other.

There was occasional chatter in his earpiece but it was too garbled to be understood. It could have been either the thick walls that blocked the weak signal or, as he feared, enemy interference, which meant he had to move fast and find the door. Rafik turned into another corridor, which was thankfully slightly more lit than the one he came out of. A few paces later he saw the puzzle lock, smiled to himself with relief, and uttered a soft prayer to the Prophet Reborn for his good luck. He did not forget caution, though, and found the pressure plate just as he was about to step on it. There was no time to waste, nor did he trust his rudimentary skills in disarming traps. Instead he approached the puzzle-locked door from a different angle, marking the pressure plate with a cloth torn from his blood-soaked bandages.

When in position, Rafik tapped his wristpiece twice, sending his crew a signal and probably alerting everyone else to his whereabouts as well. Now it was only a matter of time against skill. He took off his gauntlet and flexed his fingers several times and placed them at the edge of the holes. Then he drew a deep breath and closed his eyes before pushing his fingers all the way in. It was a technique he'd found to be helpful in minimizing disorientation when changing into what Master Goran called "the puzzle dimension."

This was a difficult lock, Rafik realised as soon as he settled in, a puzzle of a magnitude and size he'd succeeded in solving only two times before. Even as he went to work, shifting and holding patterns, Rafik was acutely aware of his defencelessness, sitting on his knees with his eyes closed and his fingers shoved inside the lock. If the enemy found Rafik before his crew, he was done for. The wall of symbols changed and moved as everything swam before his eyes. He lost two strains, and for the life of him he could not latch on to any other pattern. As panic began to rise in his chest, a memory from training echoed in his mind.

"See this symbol?"

"The snake with three heads?"

"Yes, I can see why you would call it that, yes, the hydra. Have you seen it before?"

"I . . . I'm not sure . . . maybe . . ."

"Try to remember . . . look . . . here . . . here, and here, each is a part of the whole symbol."

"Yes, I see it now."

"I have studied thousands of puzzles, Rafik, and I have found that patterns are not just a game of random chance, they are more like a language. Perhaps the pattern is a sentence we do not yet know how to read, or a formula, or a name. Whenever you see this particular symbol know that there are only six possible combinations. One of them is the triangle with the ellipse inside, see? Over here . . ."

"Yes, I see it now."

"Good boy. Now the next part is easier, but the end of the pattern keeps changing, so I guess we'll have to rely on your instinct, look here . . . and here . . ."

And suddenly Rafik saw the full pattern of the puzzle lock clearly before his eyes. Heart pounding with excitement, Rafik took hold of the pattern and watched as it converged before him into one symbol.

When he opened his eyes, the door was slowly swinging open. The corridor behind him was still empty. He had to move forward and hope that his crew would find him before the enemy did. He got to his feet and rubbed the stiffness out of his knees as he walked through the door. Then a sudden whining noise came from within the darkness of the room. Too late, he realised what it was and tried to duck, but the blast hit him straight in the chest, lifting him up in the air and then pounding him against the door.

Lying on his back, Rafik experienced the familiar feeling of paralysis he'd come to know in the past few months. But familiarity did not make it any more comfortable. He lay there, gasping for breath, and kept trying to blink and not panic. Heavy steps echoed in the room, and Kurk came into view, grinning broadly.

"You're an oil smear, Puzzler," he said. With an expert flick of his thumb he recharged the stun gun and aimed it at Rafik. "Maybe I should shoot you again, though, just to be sure."

A second hit from the stun gun would not only hurt like hell, it would also extend the paralysis, perhaps even cause Rafik to faint from lack of air. He knew this because he'd already experienced the feeling a few times before. Kurk was Rafik's bane, never missing an opportunity to show the younger boy exactly who was inferior. Now it seemed that Kurk was about to make his point again, and there was nothing Rafik could do to stop him.

Just as Kurk's finger touched the trigger, Rafik heard Naava's voice coming from where he guessed was the entrance: "What's going on here?" There was a short pause, and then Rafik's team leader spoke again. "Rafik's down, it's over."

Kurk shouldered his weapon, looking disappointed as Rafik's crew came into the room, followed by two training teachers. By the time the others arrived, Rafik could move again. He rose slowly only to be confronted by his angry teammates.

"What did I tell you to do?" Naava poked Rafik in the chest hard enough to make him stagger back. "What were the orders?"

"To stay in the safe zone," admitted Rafik. Then he tried to explain. "But I had to move. Kurk's team was too close and had at least two snipers on me, and no one could find Donn—he just vanished."

"Well, thin wires, you just earned us two weeks of kitchen duty," someone muttered behind Naava.

The training teachers were already calling the rest of the teams for the posttraining briefing, but Rafik was still upset. "It's completely unfair," he complained loudly. "Kurk was waiting behind a puzzle-locked door, which I solved, and he"—Rafik pointed at Kurk—"was not part of the yellow team, he was just a trap. I solved the puzzle and entered the node, so we won."

The tactical combat teacher, a squat woman with fiery red hair named Mistress Havanna, turned to Rafik. "Stop making excuses. Your actions today were nothing short of a disgrace."

Rafik felt a blush paint his face as she recounted his blunders: "First you disobeyed a direct order from your crew leader. Second, you moved away from the safe zone without any protection, then you tried to open the lock without waiting for your crew, and finally, for some reason which I can't even imagine, you decided to enter the node. What did I tell you time and time again? *Never* walk into a node. Solving a puzzle does not mean you are free to walk in, and even if, for some reason, you must walk in, you do not walk in the way you did." Mistress Havanna turned to Master Goran, who'd entered the room during her speech. "Your boy might be able to solve puzzles but he will die on his first shallow run. What he needs is some serious combat training with emphasis on discipline."

Master Goran shook his head. "I'm sorry. You may be right about Rafik's poor combat skills and lack of discipline, but we cannot afford to take any more time away from his studies."

"He'll be no use to us dead."

"And he'll be no use to us if he fails to pass the puzzle locks," Master Goran responded calmly. "If Rafik moved away from the designated safe zone, it was because someone left him unguarded. The crew needs to learn to control and protect their Puzzler better. Everything else is secondary."

Mistress Havanna grunted her disapproval but didn't argue further. Instead, she congratulated Kurk and announced the reward for the winning team: a one-week curfew extension and a gate pass for one afternoon. Rafik's team was assigned extra kitchen duty and, as usual, had to clean and tidy the entire combat zone from the remnants of the battle. Rafik wouldn't have minded sharing the burden with his crew. After all, in his heart he knew Mistress Havanna was right: it was his fault they'd lost. But as usual, Master Goran intervened and excused him from the punishment in favor of more puzzle training. It happened every time, and Rafik knew that it alienated him from the other trainees and even a few of the teachers, who thought Rafik was getting undeserved privileges for being a Puzzler. No one seemed to remember that he was also forbidden to enjoy the perks—that leaving the premises of the guild school, the usual reward, was forbidden to Rafik under any circumstances.

They were about to disperse when they heard a commotion coming from the direction of the main gates. For a moment everyone froze, then Mistress Havanna, hand pressed against her ear Comm, ordered, "To the main courtyard, on the double, now!" They all ran, except Master Goran, who limped calmly behind them.

Lord Keenan was already waiting, surrounded by a large

entourage of guards and advisors. The trainees quickly got into formation and, at the signal from Master Hopp, the gatekeeper, bowed in unison and shouted, "Keenan, Respect!" three times. Lord Keenan nodded his approval and returned salutes before moving to inspect the trainees. It amazed Rafik how short and fat the man was, for stories about Lord Keenan's ferocity in battle made Rafik imagine him as a hulking giant of a Troll. In real life, he barely reached Kurk's shoulders, but power radiated from him, and Rafik found himself bending on one knee and rising up, shouting, "Respect!" as loud as he could, then sticking his chest out as he stood at attention.

Lord Keenan nodded to Master Hopp and asked for a report on the day's progress. Rafik's heart sank as he heard the brief summary of the mock run, but Lord Keenan did not react at all. Instead, he moved on to inspect the boys and girls, stopping beside each one to listen to a report about their personal conduct during the battle. Occasionally the Guildlord would nod his approval or say something to the boy or girl standing at attention in front of him. Kurk was informed that soon he would be ready for his first augmentation operation, and Bernard was ordered to sharpen his shooting skills. When the Guildlord reached Rafik he lingered longer than he did with all the other trainees, asking for a full report from Master Goran, Mistress Havanna, and Master Fu, who specialized in hand-to-hand combat. Master Goran praised Rafik's progress but readily admitted that even a shallow run could still prove difficult for the boy and a deep run would surely be fatal. The combat teachers were even more adamant about Rafik's poor chances of survival.

"Why is that so?" the Guildlord asked.

"There is no time to train the boy, Guildlord," Master Fu said softly, but his voice carried enough for Rafik to hear it. "He's studying with Master Goran all the time."

Master Goran did not wait for an acknowledgment from his Guildlord to defend his position, "The boy's focus should be opening the puzzle locks of the nodes," he said hotly. "He is the only one who can do so, and he is training for that purpose. He will have a crew to protect him. That is their job."

"He didn't survive an easy mock run in training," remarked the Guildlord.

"That's because he didn't follow orders," Mistress Havanna intervened.

The Guildlord shook his head. "Combat is a chaotic business, and his ability to solve puzzles is not going to help the guild if he dies on the first shallow run."

Master Goran looked as if he was about to argue but thought better of it and pursed his lips instead.

"The boy needs to know how to defend himself," Lord Keenan continued, his voice hardening in resolution. "I want him to be trained in evasive manoeuvres and light weaponry as well as work to improve his stamina." He looked at Rafik. "He looks pale and weak to me. He needs more exercise, and some muscle-building nourishment. Find time for it. Redouble your efforts, and I will check back in on the boy soon. The Keenan guild has invested dearly in this venture and we need to see results, not ineptitude."

The three teachers paled at this, but the Guildlord did not press further. He conducted a short meeting with the staff, attended the midday meal in the hall, and left soon after that.

From that day on, Rafik's routine changed dramatically. He rose at dawn for a personal training session with Master Fu and collapsed, exhausted, in the middle of the night, usually on a makeshift bed in Master Goran's lair. All of the Keenan masters took the Guildlord's words seriously and pushed Rafik with every practice session. Light-weapons combat was intense, but hand-to-hand combat was gruesome. Master Fu was relentless and demanding, and Rafik's body became a mosaic of red, black, and blue.

"Don't think. Move!" Master Fu shouted at Rafik, as fists and kicks connected with his body. But it seemed that the boy's natural reflex to try and find patterns kept hindering his progress. It didn't help that Master Fu always made Rafik face overwhelming opponents. Needless to say, Kurk took great pleasure at these training sessions, and Rafik breathed a deep sigh of relief when the brute was finally shipped away to be augmented and then sent to guard the fields outside the City of Towers.

Others replaced him, though, and no day passed without Rafik limping back to Master Goran, who would then challenge Rafik with puzzle after puzzle, constantly increasing their difficulty. It was no surprise that Rafik lost all track of time, and his recollection of the many weeks that followed was hazy. Winter came and went and he barely noticed. Rafik did not grow much stronger, as he'd secretly hoped he would, but by spring, he could run and climb faster and managed to avoid most of the punches and kicks in hand-to-hand combat.

He was also making good progress with his puzzle studies, and even Master Goran grudgingly admitted that the physical training benefitted Rafik's concentration. His shooting ability was still dismal. The power blaster felt clumsy in his hand, and his vision blurred when he aimed. Any larger weapon was too heavy for him to control properly. He consoled himself that at least the other trainees left him alone, but it could have been because he barely spoke to anyone or even had time to take meals together with them. Lord Keenan visited every few weeks to learn of Rafik's progress, and it was late spring when he finally decided to test Rafik further.

It was during combat drills that a warrior, dressed in battered and worn power armour and carrying his gear in a sack over his shoulder, strolled in. He stopped, dropped his sack on the floor, then slowly unfastened his helmet and removed it, revealing a bald pate with Comm wirings pinned to the back of his head, warrior style, and a Comm attached to the top of his scalp. He had a short, cropped black beard and wore no ornaments or trinkets.

Master Fu immediately ordered the trainees to stand at attention in a semicircle around the combat ring as the man unfastened his power armour from the waist up and proceeded to remove his gloves, bracers, and a forearm pad, dropping them to the ground as well. Master Fu turned to face the bald man as he stepped into the combat ring. Despite not being very tall, the man was a mountain of body mass and muscle. He had a short, wide neck, which he cracked to each side as he moved towards Master Fu, and skin the colour of baked stone.

Rafik held his breath as the two faced each other, staring intently into each other's eyes for an uncomfortably long time. Then the man banged a meaty fist into his palm and they both bowed slowly and deliberately, keeping eye contact the entire time. When they straightened up the man held up his hands and closed them into a pair of enormous fists, assuming a combat position. He towered over Master Fu, who held up his own hands as well but kept his palms open. They stood like that for several heartbeats, when suddenly the man burst out laughing and bowed deeply again to Master Fu. Rafik saw the combat teacher grin for the first time as the two embraced.

"This is Commander Doro," Master Fu said as he turned to the stunned trainees. "He's in charge of the Keenan guild's crew at the Valley outpost."

"Keenan, Respect!" Rafik joined the collective shout with enthusiasm.

After that short introduction Commander Doro asked to join the training session and proceeded to complete all the exercises to the letter, refusing Master Fu's invitation to comment or demonstrate. Word carried fast, and soon all the Masters and Mistresses came out to the sunny courtyard. Even Master Goran eventually showed up, although he kept his distance. Last came the ever-stern Mistress Furukawa, who stood with Master Goran, watching the end of the training with what could have been interpreted as a shadow of a smile on her lips. Rafik had never trained harder in his life, and by the looks of it, this was true for the other trainees as well.

After the training was over, the now-sweating Commander

Doro and Master Fu hugged again, then the Commander proceeded to warmly greet each and every one of the teachers.

"We did not expect you for at least another week," Mistress Havanna said.

"You know me." Commander Doro smiled mischieviously. "I like to surprise." He turned and bowed his head in acknowledgment to Mistress Furukawa.

"It is good to see you, Commander."

"Ah, Mistress Furukawa, your smile always brightens my day—" he tilted his head and waved "—and I see Master Goran still likes to play odd man out."

Rafik caught Mistress Havanna turning to hide her own smile. Mistress Furukawa's expression remained stony as ever. "Come, Commander." Her eyes wandered towards Rafik. "We have much to speak about."

Master Fu ordered two trainees to gather Commander Doro's gear and bring it to his room, and the group of instructors followed Mistress Furukawa. As soon as the trainees were given leave they began talking excitedly among themselves about nothing else but Commander Doro. Even Rafik was included this time.

"You know what this means," said Bernard, who was now the leading Troll after Kurk had shipped out. "He came to test us, those who do well might be shipped out straight to the Valley instead of doing field guard duty. And of course"—he looked straight at Rafik—"he came for the Puzzler."

The group's attention turned to Rafik, and as always, he felt his throat tighten.

"I wouldn't mind if he tested me," a curly headed Troll named Lizza mumbled to herself. She blushed deeply when she realised what she'd said. The group laughed and immediately began mocking and teasing each other. Even Rafik noticed the misty looks in the eyes of all the girls when they mentioned Commander Doro.

No one paid further attention to Rafik as he withdrew himself from the group and made his way down to Master Goran's lair.

Master Goran wasn't there to train Rafik, but a new puzzle box was standing ready on the table. Rafik spent the rest of the afternoon training, although he did not attach the pain-delivering wires to his forearm.

When House Master Prushnik failed to deliver his evening meal, Rafik decided to go up and join everyone in the mess hall. Perhaps he would see Master Goran there. To his surprise, he found Commander Doro sitting on the bench at the trainees' table, eating and chatting enthusiastically with them, and not at the instructor's table. A glance to the table on the dais showed Rafik that Mistress Furukawa and Master Goran were the only ones not there. All the other seats were taken at the trainees' table. Rafik hesitated before deciding to turn back. He would fetch something from the kitchen and go back to the lair. Master Goran would not be pleased if he came down and found Rafik gone.

"Hey, Rafik" he heard Commander Doro call.

He found himself turning before he knew what he was doing. He saw the commander looking straight at him.

"There's space over here," Commander Doro pointed next to himself, where Bernard was sitting. "Come." He beckoned.

When Rafik reached the bench, Commander Doro made everyone shuffle so Rafik could squeeze is between himself and Bernard.

When Rafik was seated, Commander Doro turned and extended his hand in greeting. "So you are the Puzzler everyone is talking about. Respect."

"Respect, Commander," Rafik answered weakly and watched as his hand was encased by Doro's enormous palm. He was half-expecting the Commander to begin examining his markings in front of everyone, but Doro let go of his hand and offered Rafik some hot bread instead.

Despite sitting next to each other, they did not exchange any further words before the Commander got up and bid everyone good night.

All the trainees spontaneously got to their feet.

"Keenan, Respect!" the hall rang with the cry as Commander Doro left.

On the second day of the Commander's visit, the teachers held several demonstrations to show off Rafik's capabilities. The demonstrations weren't fake, but even Rafik knew that he'd already tackled harder puzzle locks and that he would never have succeeded in beating Naava in hand-to-hand combat if she'd been allowed to attack at will. Master Goran watched the demonstrations but did not comment about them when they met in the lair. Actually, he didn't say more than he needed to for Rafik to understand his will. He seemed distant and preoccupied, and the training was finished earlier than expected.

On the third day of Commander Doro's visit, just as Rafik and Master Goran were beginning their Puzzler practice, the metal door of the lift slid open and House Master Prushnik stepped out.

"I'm sorry to disturb you, Master Goran," he said coolly, "but I was asked to bring the young Puzzler for an interview with Commander Doro."

"That is impossible," Master Goran replied immediately. "I need the boy here, for training. Tell the Commander he can interview the boy later, when I'm done."

House Master Prushnik nodded, and there might have been a hint of satisfaction on his face when he said, "Commander Doro anticipated your reaction, Master Goran, and with Mistress Furukawa's blessing has asked me to inform you that either I bring the young Puzzler to his chambers or he will make his way down here now."

Master Goran's face hardened. There was a short pause, where the three of them stood in silence, but finally Master Goran snapped, "Fine, take the boy."

With several sharp movements he unfastened Rafik from the

metal brace and called after him as the boy began following the House Master, "You'd better come back immediately after your *chat*. No idling about, you hear?"

It was the first time Rafik had entered the lift, and he watched with curiosity as House Master Prushnik hovered his finger above one of the buttons, which lit up blue as the door slid soundlessly closed. He felt the slight upward surge, and in no time he found himself on the upper floor of the guild house for the first time.

Heart pounding with excitement, Rafik followed the House Master until they reached a set of double doors. The House Master knocked lightly. Immediately there was a buzz, and the doors slid apart. Commander Doro was just turning around from the fireplace, a steaming teapot in his hand.

"Ah, thank you, Prushnik. I see that my threat worked wonders on the old goat."

The House Master tried his best to hide his smile "Yes, Commander. It was exactly as you anticipated. I will come back to fetch the boy." He turned and left the room.

"Come, join me at the table," Commander Doro said to Rafik as he moved towards the small, round, stone table standing near the window.

Commander Doro's room was the largest Rafik had ever seen. He passed a large double bed; on top of it lay several personal weapons, all cleaned and oiled, together with several dozen power clips. The blanket was on the floor near the bed.

"Don't mind that," the Commander laughed when he caught Rafik's stare. "Spend two moons in the Valley and you won't be able to sleep in anything as comfortable as this, either." He extended his hand and, as before, they shook as equals.

"I see you still have the bracelet on," he added.

Rafik blushed. It was as Master Goran had anticipated. All of the trainees had passed the removing of the bracelet ceremony, meaning they became sworn members of the Keenan guild and were trusted not to run away anymore. All but Rafik. He was too valuable to be trusted.

Commander Doro patted the boy's shoulder. "Don't worry about it. Sit down and let's have a talk."

When Rafik was seated, Commander Doro poured liquid from the pot into Rafik's cup.

"This is called Tea," he explained. "It's very rare in the Valley, so I make sure I purchase a large stock of dried leaves when I'm here. With all respect to the nourishment pills, this keeps me warm . . ." Commander Doro smiled to himself as he poured into his own cup, "and sane."

Rafik peered into his cup. "I know what this is. In my village the elders brew herbs." He tasted the liquid, it was bitter in his mouth and it must have showed, because Commander Doro laughed.

"You'll get used to it quick. They say it's more addictive than Skint." He took a long draught from his own cup, closed his eyes, and sighed, "That's better. Now, Rafik, tell me about your home village."

The question surprised Rafik. "Master Goran keeps saying the past is not important, only the future."

The same applied to praying to the Prophet Reborn. Rafik now understood that life outside his village was very different from the way he'd been raised, especially regarding Tarakan infidels such as Dominique, Captain Sam, and even Khan and Master Goran. But praying to the Reborn was something he still felt a deep need to do. It was not strictly forbidden but was definitely frowned upon by his peers. Master Goran thought that praying wasted precious time that should be devoted to "real study," and he allowed Rafik to pray only before bedtime.

Commander Doro shook his head. "The old goat might be right about many things, but all that we do here, all of this"—he gestured towards the weapons on the bed—"is about finding out about our past. So how about we start with you telling me about yours."

Rafik was uncomfortable and wary at first, but Commander Doro was patient and kept asking questions. In a short while

Rafik found himself talking about Eithan, their silly games of Warriors and Infidels, and the tattoos that suddenly appeared. He even found himself recounting the incident with his father in the barn. When he spoke about the way to Newport, Rafik realised he was finding it hard to remember his brother's face. Without thinking about it, his hand slipped into his pocket and touched Fahid's blade.

The story continued to flow. Some details he told while others he kept to himself. When he was done he felt sad but also, oddly, relieved. Commander Doro stayed quiet for a while. Eventually he got up, moved his chair, and placed it in front of Rafik's. When he sat back down, his huge frame completely filled Rafik's vision.

"I do not need to tell you who you are or that soon you will be shipped out of here," he said evenly, his dark eyes searching Rafik's. "You have some good instructors, but even if you stayed here for another three years you would still find the Valley to be a challenge. By now you've figured out that the guild bought you like merchandise and seeks a return on its investment." He waited for Rafik to nod, then continued. "I want to tell you that what I do—" he lowered his voice and leaned forward "—what *we* are about to do, is even more important than refilling the guild's coffers. When we open a node or go on a deep run we find medicine, technology, schematics, books containing knowledge we can't even begin to comprehend, machines that repair other machines, weapons, and energy clips and tubes. But more important, we find pieces of history—with every item we salvage, we learn about who we once were."

The Commander's eyes shone with excitement as he continued, "You hear stories about the time before the Catastrophe when ordinary people could do extraordinary things. They could fly high in the sky and drive carts deep into the ocean. Any person could communicate with almost any other person, anywhere in the world, and all questions had answers. People lived for a hundred years or more, and there was no sickness. I know it sounds too good to be true, but when you come to the Valley, when you see the buildings—the vast number of them, the sheer height of some of them, the awesome technology that was used to create them—it crosses your wires. When I come back to this city, to this building"—his hand gestured to the room—"what do I see?"

His hand clenched into a formidable fist. "Parasites. That's what I see. This city operates itself, and we live on it, not in it. We latch ourselves onto it and suck every bit of energy from it that we can, but we cannot build another city like it. We salvage the technology, learn how to use it, but only a few of the marked know how to manipulate it, and not one of the marked that I've met can duplicate it. Even the nodes we raid, we have no idea how they work, how or even why they get replenished, nothing. We live off the carcass of a destroyed civilisation, slowly devouring what's left of it. If the nodes stopped functioning, we would all go back to using sticks and stones. But as long as we are in the Valley, there is hope for the future. Our chances rise with every item we salvage, with every schematic or info pad we ship back. Maybe someday, someone, somewhere, will truly understand and we could become the people who our ancestors were."

"Everyone tells me I'm going to die there," Rafik said weakly. "They say I'm not ready, that I'm too weak."

Commander Doro nodded slowly. "I cannot promise you a peaceful life, but if you trust me and do as I say, I can promise you a life worth living." He got up and Rafik jumped to attention, almost toppling the small table beside him.

The Commander smiled and extended his hand again. Rafik gingerly shook it.

"Go back to your duties. I'm sure the old goat is waiting for you with all kinds of questions and comments. Learn from him and from the others as much as you can. I'm afraid I will be seeing you sooner rather than later."

Rafik hesitated, then saluted in Keenan fashion, turned smartly on his heel and left the room. He descended to the lair the normal way, still thinking of Commander Doro's words when he entered. To his relief, Master Goran was not there. Rafik rummaged through the countless puzzle boxes until he picked a box he knew to be a challenge and hooked himself up. This time he connected the pain-delivering wires, even though Master Goran forbade him from using them alone. When he came out he was completely exhausted. Master Goran still wasn't there— which was odd—but Rafik was too tired to be curious. He lay down on the narrow bed in the corner, and soon sleep came. He half-expected to find himself in front of a wall of symbols or, considering his conversation with Commander Doro, in a visit to his village. Instead, on that night, and every night from then on, he experienced a terrible nightmare.

36

The four of us stopped at the entrance to the Keenan compound. "What was the nightmare about?" I asked.

"Tell me what we're doing here and I might answer your question." Vincha looked around suspiciously.

I couldn't blame her. The Guilds Plateau was once where the most powerful guild houses were located and no doubt used to be the most popular area of the city, with some of the best taverns and definitely the best brothel, but no more. The last guild war and the mountain of shit that erupted in Tarakan Valley took care of that.

The Plateau was now practically deserted. The once famous steel gates to the Keenan compound were missing, taken down long ago for their metal. My vision made it easier for me to see the scorch marks and bullet holes that bruised its walls. After the massacre in the Valley the guilds began to lose power, and it took very little time for their weakness to turn into aggression. Accusations flew back and forth, delicate alliances were broken, and even more delicate egos were bruised. Assassination attempts followed. Some succeeded, others failed, and in the blink of an eye the City of Towers was in the midst of the last, and bloodiest, guild war ever. It decimated the entire Plateau and drove half the population away from the city.

It was then that Sirbin Sammuel, the rubber stamp Council leader, finally grew a pair. He allegedly offed the former head of Sabarra, Mauricious Altenna, then took charge and restored order to the city, using the troops given to him by the guilds themselves. The majority of the ShieldGuards held their vow to the Council and took hold of the city when the surviving guilds were too weak to pose a threat anymore. The guild leaders were forced to bow their heads to the Council and never regained their former status. When the guards were called back from the fields to fight the war, it took the farmers only a week to stage a revolt. Weakened as it was, the Council had to sign an agreement with the farmers that gave them freedom and rights and also made it impossible for any guild to completely control the food supply. By then the Keenan guild was already decimated. Lord Keenan himself died from a lethal poison dart as he dined, as the rumours go, with several of his concubines.

After the onslaught no one bothered to try and rebuild the Guilds Plateau. It was too far up from the city centre, and the guilds that survived the war were ordered to move to the Upper Towers, where they could be better protected—or, in other words, easier to watch.

By the following season, even the vagrants had left the ruins. There was simply nothing to steal and no one left to rob.

River busied himself with one of his gadgets, and the area lit up so suddenly I was momentarily blinded. I blinked and looked away from the light as he busied himself scanning the area ahead. I turned to Vincha. "Have you been here before?"

She shrugged. "Why would I have? I was never a Keenan, never got along with the whole guild-rusting propaganda, you know, the whole lord worshipping and political infighting. I was an independent"—she smiled to herself—"you know, playing all sides of the table."

"I just thought, well, you went and looked for Jakov after you came back, and went to his village . . ." I let my voice die long before the sentence was done.

She shook her head and laughed bitterly. "By the time I shook off all my addictions, the war was over and so was the Keenan guild. Besides, I had no quarrel with them. They bought the boy fairly, treated him like a prized possession, and tried to train him to do the job he was born to do. The way he told it, he was not mistreated or abused here. Sure, they were tough, and that Goran guy sounded like a real ass-rust, but you didn't survive the Valley by being nice and cuddly."

"Clear," River announced, looking more relaxed as he pocketed the scanning gadget. "Not a damn soul."

Vincha turned back to me. "You still haven't told us why we're here."

"We're here to meet someone," I said. "Someone who can explain things better than I can."

"Fine." Vincha made a point of rolling her eyes. "Be dramatic if you wish, but can I at least have my weapons back?"

"No," all three of us answered in unison, as I walked past the entrance.

Nothing in the compound but its size hinted of former glory. There was barely a trace of the upper level on the main building, and all that was left of five guard towers were mounds of rubble. The sixth tower was barely standing, with battle damage scorching its features. The place reeked of gloom and death and the aura of emptiness you get in places where bloody battles occurred. We walked in silence to the main courtyard, and River placed an oblong heating stone on the ground. The dark metal began to glow red and eventually conveyed enough heat and light to make us a little more comfortable. We gathered around it and sat on the ground while River placed a few more of his arsenal of dangerous toys around the perimeter, just to be on the safe side. I liked River. He was a thorough kind of guy.

I could have easily fallen asleep right there and then. The

events of the last two days and nights had used up every reserve of energy I had and then some. The last part of my journey actually felt like a dream. Galinak was the first to lie on his back in the dirt, hands supporting his head. He closed his eyes, his breath already slowing. I didn't know if he was awake or not but guessed, or hoped, that he still retained some form of battle awareness, even in his sleep.

As tired as I was, I could not afford a rest. The last time I dozed off, at the Blade, it almost cost me River's life. Instead I asked Vincha about Rafik's nightmares, knowing that her story would keep me from succumbing to exhaustion. I knew she was testing me with half truths, checking to see how far she could manipulate me. I certainly didn't buy her claim about not having visited this place before. Something in the way she'd walked in betrayed familiarity. At first Vincha didn't answer my question. She kept staring at the heating stone, hugging her knees to her chest and rocking gently back and forth. When I persisted, she tried to toy with me, rebargaining for her weapons, but it came down to the fact that Vincha was as tired as I was. Talking about Rafik and visiting this place had mellowed her just enough, which was the main reason I chose to bring all of us to this godforsaken ruin.

"He didn't tell me about the dream immediately," she said suddenly. "It took him a while to open up, to trust me enough." I caught her smiling bitterly to herself as shadows danced across her face. "But to be honest, his dream made me anxious. He told me it began with a figure of a man standing far away from him. The man was covered in a dark robe and his head was hidden in a hood. Only a four-fingered, scaly hand with sharp talons hinted at what was hidden from view, and that human claw was grasping a thick staff. Rafik always felt absolute terror when he saw the figure, which was usually standing in the midst of a mighty sandstorm, but sometimes also in a dark cave. Rafik said he would try to turn and run away in his dreams, but an invisible hand would grab him from behind and drag him kicking and screaming toward the figure until he was close enough to grasp its dark robe. The figure would then lean down, and Rafik could see his face."

Vincha shook her head as if trying to wipe the memory from her mind.

"Who was the man?" I asked, trying to keep her talking. "Did Rafik describe him to you?"

"He would wake up screaming every time," said Vincha quietly. "He told me the man had a 'melting face.'"

"Melting?" I looked at River, who was already back and listening intently, but he shrugged.

I looked back at Vincha and knew with certainty that she was holding something back, and that something was really important. I also knew there was no way I could fish this one out of her now, exhausted as we both were. This one cut too close to the bone. Still, I tried.

"Do you think this man really existed?" I asked, but before I got an answer something blipped.

River rose to his feet. "Company," he said quietly.

Vincha stood up, then immediately crouched low, swearing softly when she realised she had no weapons. Galinak didn't even bother opening his eyes; he simply rolled away, out of the circle of light.

"Relax, everyone," I said, coming up on my feet. I didn't want another unnecessary fight like the one in the Blade. "I'm expecting company, don't worry. Over here!" I shouted and waved. River opened his mouth to say something, but I didn't need to hear him to realise that once again I was so very wrong.

The heat stone exploded into smithereens, and the power of the blast sent me flying backwards. A voice shouted, "Give up, you are surrounded, this is the—" There was an abrupt gurgle followed by silence, as Galinak's knife found its mark in the darkness. I was still sprawled on the ground when the attackers came. I saw silhouettes moving in the darkness, and I guessed I was the only one seeing them clearly. In the last few days I'd witnessed violence and been its victim several times, yet I had retained a cool head and clarity of thought.

This time panic grasped me by the throat. I could only lie there, gasping for air, unable to speak, my heart pounding in my chest, until Galinak came rushing out of the darkness and lifted me off the ground without slowing down. They probably would have gotten us then, but River's blessed gadgets were doing what they were meant to do: explode and flash, disorienting the offensive enough to cover our retreat to the last remaining guard tower.

"Give me my weapons back!" Vincha shouted, as we took shelter inside the empty shell of the guard tower.

I found my voice. "How many?"

"One short of twelve, now," Galinak said and added, "Tell me they aren't who they seemed to be."

I nodded grimly and watched his expression harden.

"This should cost you extra," he said. "You're a real trouble magnet, Twinkle Eyes."

"Who are they?" Vincha asked, then added, "Someone give me my rusting weapons back, *now*."

Another explosion, this time a big one, lit up the entire courtyard behind us. River came running, crouching low as bullets and death beams crisscrossed after him.

He dove for cover, panting, and rolled around to put out the fire that was licking at his clothes. When I turned back Galinak was handing Vincha her full arsenal.

"I didn't give you permission to give her her weapons," I said. I knew I sounded petty at that particular moment, but frustration and fear were clouding my judgement.

"Well, you should have told me the rusting ShieldGuards were after you as well," he answered dryly.

Vincha's jaw actually dropped. "ShieldGuards?" she repeated, "You have shock troops after you as well as the guild mercs? Rust, what have you *done*?"

"I don't know," I said truthfully, but my skills of persuasion were not in their prime. I noted that her weapons, together with Galinak's, were suddenly aimed at me.

"I suggest we turn him in," she said.

I looked at Galinak, but he shrugged and shook his head. "ShieldGuards," he said. "Who'd have rusting believed it?"

River was still coughing from the smoke, but against these odds I didn't want him to have to choose sides.

"They're not after me," I said.

"Oh really?" Vincha grabbed me by the collar. "I guess they're just here for a picnic? Well then, shall we go and have a chat?"

"They're here for you," I said, just as she was about to propel me forward.

She froze. "You lie."

"No, I just didn't tell you all the whole truth," another explosion caused us all to duck, but Vincha did not let go of me.

"Why do you think I was searching for you all this time?" I blurted as fast as I could. "Why am I paying you a fortune to hear about a long-dead boy? Why are the guilds and the Council after us? You're important, Vincha—you may not be a Puzzler like Rafik was, but you are, in a way, a key."

"How am I a rusting key?" Her shout of frustration probably helped the ShieldGuards pinpoint our location because we were suddenly blasted to the floor again.

We ended up crawling up the crumbling stairs of the guard tower as everything around us exploded to bits of burning stone. My guess was that the ShieldGuards' orders included the words "dead or alive," and that we were way past paying attention to the "alive" bit. In a weird, distorted way, it was actually a good sign. The Council was spying on the guilds, and the guilds were spying on everyone, including us, so the information they had was probably vague. If they really knew how important Vincha was they would have used nonlethal weapons—unless, of course, the ShieldGuard captain was just a trigger-happy Troll.

Our position was far from ideal. We were forced to climb

to the second floor, which was half ruined, exposed from two sides, and isolated. There was nowhere left to run. Three Shield-Guards rushed us but soon retreated, two of them carrying their wounded comrade. Now they were doing it by the book: spreading out, taking position, waiting for reinforcements, and blasting the upper part of the tower brick by brick. A constant trickle of dust and debris rained down on our heads.

"What now?" Vincha asked.

"Maybe you could complete your story," I said, quickly adding, "Just kidding!" when I saw the look on her face.

River was more pragmatic. "I have two smoke grenades and one flash."

"Can those help get us to the gate?" I asked.

Galinak shook his head. The courtyard was a killing zone, and the grenades would not suffice to cover our sides the entire way, not to mention that four guards were now covering the tower's exit. With my sight I detected six guards moving around the tower in close proximity, so there was also no chance of sneaking out.

Vincha patted dust off her hair. "Do we have a choice?"

I shook my head. "My LoreMaster told me to spare no expense in finding you so you could tell me about Rafik. I don't know why he or you are so important to everyone, but if the ShieldGuards catch you they will eventually find out what you know, and if you survive the interrogation, they will kill you just to cover their asses. Vincha, I'm sorry, but they will, because they can't take the chance that things could get even worse in the Valley."

I could sense she wanted to strike me with frustration. "How does my rusting story relate to the shit storm that is the Valley?"

"I don't know," I said, and that, for once, was the truth.

I could see that this information didn't sink in, which was fine, I was not in the mood to answer any more questions.

Vincha summarized the obvious. "Then we have no choice—

we jump." She pointed at a hole in the wall, then turned to River. "Once we are out, throw your grenades to the left. We shoot to the right and run straight to the gate."

I looked through part of the wall to measure the distance of the fall. With an even ground on a lit day it would have been simple to accomplish with perhaps a few minor bruises. But the debris under the tower meant twisted ankles and a few broken bones at best. As if listening to my thoughts, Vincha ordered River to throw down the flash bomb before we jumped. "That will clear some bits from the area of the fall," she explained.

"And alert everyone to our attempt at collective suicide," completed Galinak smoothly.

"On my mark," Vincha ordered, ignoring Galinak. "Last one at the gate is left for dead, go."

Galinak and River jumped first, straight into the bright flash of light. Vincha grabbed me and we jumped a heartbeat later, so close that I was expecting to land on someone's back. I was always an optimist. Instead, I landed on the hard ground, rolled, hit my chin hard on my knee, felt my elbow bash against a brick, and heard my own grunt of pain.

I have no idea how I got up, but I found myself running. The area to my left was full of smoke, and rays of death tore through it, trying to find targets and several times giving me a close shave. I could see Vincha ahead of me, which meant I was last, and that meant I was the dead one. I tried to speed up, but I guess I was going as fast as I could. Then I stumbled and almost fell, bending down to prevent a full sprawl just as a death ray that would have cut me in half flashed above me.

Terror made my feet find new traction. I rose like one of the sprinters in a Pre-Catastrophe sporting competition and ran for my life. I saw the gate ahead of us, then I saw a ShieldGuard coming through the smoke cloud to our left, like a horned fiend. He was in front of me and was aiming a rifle, nice and steady, straight at Vincha's back. She didn't see him and kept on running, but the outline of her body was plain. The ShieldGuard was tracing her movement with ease, his finger already on the trigger, his head-gear leaning against the butt of the weapon. There would be nothing left of her.

The ShieldGuard was left-handed, so the weapon and his own arm were blocking his peripheral view from his left side, which was the side I was coming from. I can't recall exactly when I decided to commit suicide, or the thought process involved, or even how I ordered my legs to hurtle me towards the ShieldGuard, but I slammed into him just as he pulled the trigger. His power armour took the brunt of the blow, but the momentum was enough to topple us both. Punching him in the body was useless, and his head was in a helmet, so all I could do was try to slow him down, which I did to the best of my very limited ability.

It didn't last long. The man was not a ShieldGuard for nothing. Soon he was pinning my head down with one hand while raising a metal fist to finish the job. They say that your entire life flashes before your eyes just before you die. Well, best I can tell, they're wrong. The only thing I saw was the flash of a big metal fist rushing towards my exposed face. He let go of my head too early, and I managed to move it and his fist hit the ground instead of my face, the side of his gauntlet cutting a deep gash on my cheek. The ShieldGuard grasped my head again and raised his arm, which then exploded in front of my eyes. I was sprayed with blood and flesh, and I heard muffled screams from within the helmet. The ShieldGuard fell to the side and thrashed around in pain.

There was another flash of light crossing the space just above me, and this time I was quick enough to roll to the other side. Everything got a bit more confusing after that. Half blinded, gasping for breath, and trying to wipe off the gunk I was covered in, I was suddenly grabbed by a hand and dragged for a while before being rolled into a shallow ditch. I saw a familiar figure standing above me, firing a rifle just above my head before disappearing from view. There was more noise, but it was receding as if the fight were fading into nothingness.

I turned my head and saw River lying next to me. He was completely still, blood covering his face. I found that he still had a pulse, and then I realised the cavalry had come. My next thought was that Vincha and Galinak, if still alive, might not be in a very discerning state of mind. I have no idea how I did it, but I was up on my feet again and moving forward. I found Galinak and Vincha standing back-to-back, holding weapons in their hands. They were surrounded by five figures, and four of them held much heavier weapons.

"Stop!" I shouted with all my reserved strength. "They're on our side," and for no reason at all I added, "for a change."

Then I fainted.

37

They didn't wake me up gently, and I couldn't blame them for it. Vincha must have refused to give me the kiss of life, but Galinak had kindly administered the slaps of awakening, and it was his grinning face I saw when I first regained consciousness.

I rolled to my side, then got up on my knees. And eventually, on the third try, I got to my feet and looked around. The remaining ShieldGuards had retreated, but they would be coming back in force, probably soon. We had to get out of the Keenan guild house, but before that, I had to make some introductions. River, who'd regained consciousness before me, had already smoothed things out a bit. Vincha and Galinak luckily decided to stay with the armed strangers who'd helped them in battle rather than try and sneak past the ShieldGuards at the gates. There was a sharp pain in my ribs when I got up. I wiped my face and neck with a piece of cloth given to me by one of our rescuers, but it was too bloody to give back when I was done with it, so I shoved it in my pocket.

I turned to Vincha. "This is LoreMaster Harim," I said and gestured towards an older-looking man who patiently stood nearby. "Head of the Guild of Historians. He is my teacher and mentor, and the man who can give you the answers you seek." I turned to my master and bowed as deeply as I dared without risking toppling over. "Thank you for coming, LoreMaster. You didn't come a moment too late, and you certainly saved our lives."

LoreMaster Harim smiled sadly as he bent his head in acknowledgement. "I'm afraid the opposite is true," he said. "I have betrayed you, my friend. I deserve nothing but contempt."

I saw Vincha and Galinak exchange meaningful looks. My master sighed deeply, sagging a bit where he stood. "We were compromised, perhaps from the very beginning," he spoke slowly, "and whoever spied on us alerted the Council about your mission. We were raided tonight."

The implications raced through my mind.

"They took everything, notes, letters, Tarakan pads, and arrested everyone they did not kill." He gestured around us. "We are all that is left of the Guild of Historians."

"What about Genix?" I asked about the language expert. "Saviar? Paullina?"

My mentor shook his head sadly. "Taken or dead," he said, "and I am sorry to say, those who died got off lightly."

I looked at the others. They were guards, not scholars, and I recognised only two faces. Their expressions reflected their realisation of the bad choices they'd made tonight. Being questioned by ShieldGuards was a bad experience, but killing a ShieldGuard was something you never walked away from.

LoreMaster Harim turned to Vincha and Galinak and said, "I owe you a great apology, Vincha. I sent my assistant looking for you because you are important to understanding our recent past—" he paused and tilted his head in a familiar gesture that meant he was considering his words carefully "—as well as our future. But by finding you we have put your life and the lives of your family at risk, and for this I apologize dearly, for what it's worth."

"It's not worth much," Vincha spat. "So you can stuff your

apology and start explaining why this is happening and why the entire rusting city is trying to kill me."

I winced at her tone of voice, but LoreMaster Harim didn't seem to take offense. "I understand your anger," he said quietly, "and there is no point in asking you to trust me, but let me spell out your options right now. You can try to sneak past the Shield-Guards, or you can hide here for a while and hope you're not found when they come back in force and with scanners. If you manage to escape, you'll need to get out of the city to reach your family. The tube lines and the bridge of light are crawling with guards. You'll have to sneak out on foot through the Pit, climb the walls, cross the swamp, and hope you reach your family before the others do."

I could see Vincha's eyes narrow.

"The other option is to follow me out of here." LoreMaster Harim's voice was calm, logical. "I will take you to a safe place, tell you why this is happening, and send a messenger on the next tube with a warning to the caretakers of your daughter."

Vincha breathed twice before saying, "I'm not promising anything, but how do we get out of here?"

"The same way we came down from the Upper Towers," said Master Harim, as we all turned our heads to the Upper Plateau. "We'll have to jump."

38

I had no idea how my master managed to get his hands on so many precious Tarakan antigrav suits. But between escaping a second attack, blowing a hole in the wall surrounding the Plateau wide enough for us to jump through, and falling into the pit, I never got a chance to ask.

In retrospect, I shouldn't have been surprised. LoreMaster Harim was exploring the remnants of our world long before I was born. He was what was once called a Renaissance man; knowledgeable, resourceful, and with an innate understanding of human nature. He'd travelled as far and wide as many truckers and he even took a sea voyage, though it only hugged the coastline. One persistent rumour claimed he'd been approached by the guilds and offered the leadership of the Council but had declined the honour. He certainly never said a good word about politics and did only the minimum required to win the Council's recognition of his own Guild of Historians. In short, if anyone could secure a dozen antigrav suits, it would probably be Lore-Master Harim.

I remember reading that in Pre-Catastrophe time, the suits

might have been used by the military for reconnaissance or infiltration, though LoreMaster Harim theorized about them being used for some kind of perverted leisure. There was definitely not enough power in them to support a fully loaded warrior, let alone a Troll. Falling at high speed through the city's complicated architecture, not to mention landing, was not something the Council encouraged, although the suits were never actually decreed illegal, and if someone was resourceful enough to find one and rich enough to feed the huge amount of power it consumed, law would not have been a deterrent. The fact that we were not actually breaking any laws felt like small consolation as we fell to the Pit at stomach-churning speed. Even with the antigrav suit, the best way to move down was to let gravity do most of the work, using the power only to steer and, hopefully, stop.

The crude goggles I wore were disorienting, and the mouthpiece only partially blocked the smoke that wafted up. At best I would have had a heartbeat to avoid collision with a moving Tarakan lift or be sheered in half by a cable. I focused on Vincha, who was just below me, and, as instructed, kept my arms and legs spread wide to maintain stability. I humbly disagree with my LoreMaster about people doing this for fun in the Pre-Catastrophe era. This was not easy or exhilarating. It was an awful, frightening experience in which too many things could have gone wrong. But somehow, this time, we were lucky. I pressed the button in the palm of my hand a little too late, almost hitting Vincha, but stopping a hair's breadth from solid ground. She glided majestically until she landed next to me and helped me up.

"Now that was fun," for once, her eyes were shining with laughter.

Even in the Pit, whose inhabitants were naturally tolerant to the uncommon events, the landing of nine people wearing antigrav suits caused a stir, which meant we had to move fast. The ShieldGuards would soon venture into the Pit to find us, and certainly a bounty would be set.

LoreMaster Harim led us, walking briskly and with the assurance of someone who knew these streets well. Again, although I'd only ever seen him in the stately halls of the Upper Towers, I was not surprised.

I have no idea how we got to our destination, but we ended up in the smallest, smelliest little cabin I'd ever seen. It was not a human-built makeshift hut like the one I'd interviewed Vincha in only a day before, but a Tarakan-built structure of a sort I did not recognise. Originally it must have been partly open, with only three walls and a roof, but someone added a wooden wall and a door and did a decent enough job of it. It was now empty, and I had a pretty good guess why. The residents of the upper parts of the City of Towers enjoy the superb amenities of Tarakan plumbing. Refuse flowed away from the upper parts of the city to somewhere else, and by the smell of things it surfaced right beneath us. Nine of us barely had room to stand. Blissfully, two were quickly dispatched for guard duty and a third man was sent off on some other mission with barely a nod. They all looked relieved to leave and we ended up with a little more leg room.

LoreMaster Harim was lighting an oil lamp and I was getting my bearings, trying to figure out what would be the next plan, when Vincha spoke. "I know you," she said to my mentor. "I've seen you before in the Valley. I wasn't sure before, but now that I can see you better, I'm sure of it."

"Yes, we met, a long time ago." LoreMaster Harim smiled and carefully shut the oil lamp cover. The light in the room was barely enough to see faces at arm's reach, and I was too damn tired to use my sight, so I sat down in the gloom and listened.

"I was leading an investigation team; we needed protection and interviewed a few individuals. You were one of them."

"I remember," Vincha said. "You chose a cheaper escort."

"As I remember it, we chose individuals not pumped up on Skint."

Vincha inhaled deeply, and I thought she was going to retaliate, but instead she spoke again, calmly.

"Ain't blaming you for passing. I was off my wires then. New gear, implants in my head, background noise, everything was too much. If you managed to hire a clean crew then good for you, because pretty much everyone at the outpost was riding the green dragon."

"Yes." LoreMaster Harim's silhouette nodded. "It was not an easy task, and in the end it turned out to be an expensive waste of time, since we didn't find what we were looking for. But I remembered you and that chance meeting is the reason we are here today. I am glad you chose to come with me, Vincha, but now you have to make another difficult decision."

We all looked at each other but no one said anything until Vincha spoke again.

"Why do I get the feeling I won't really have a choice?"

"Oh, but you will. No one is going to coerce you or make any threats."

I lowered my face but somehow knew LoreMaster Harim was looking reproachfully in my direction.

"You are going to need to explain yourself better, Lore-Master, or whatever the fuck your name is." Vincha was reaching the end of her patience.

"Indeed. I will try to explain things to you. It won't be the whole story but you'll be able to see the outline of what lies ahead." My mentor shook his head. "It's only my theory, based on what I've been able to deduce from ruined archives, books, Tarakan pads, and a lifetime of travel and research."

Galinak stretched on the floor and yawned, closing his eyes.

"First, we must understand who the Tarkanians actually were," he began, "and surprisingly, it is easier to find books and reliable sources about events that happened five hundred years ago than occurrences that led to the Catastrophe. Many people today, especially in far-off places, believe that they were creatures from some kind of hell sent by God to punish us for our sins. I have heard the claim the Tarkanians came from the stars and enslaved us. The popular belief is that the Catastrophe was the result of a brave but perhaps foolhardy human uprising against the Tarkanians, yet my own research has led me to the conclusion that this is not what really happened. I believe the Tarkanians were human, but they were so far advanced, compared even to other people in *Pre-Catastrophe time*, that the Tarkanians could very well have become something that was more than just human."

LoreMaster Harim began to pace back and forth in the tiny cabin. "Throughout history people did not just live like we do today, in tribes, villages, or even independent cities, but rather joined together in larger entities called kingdoms, which then evolved into states. The strongest of states, with the most land, military might, and metal, were called empires, and they usually emerged when a technological breakthrough was reached. You invented something that gave you an edge over all others: steel-tipped spears, a war chariot, longbows, a cart that moved without horses, and suddenly the world fell at your feet. That is, until another nation found a better technological advancement, and your own empire crumbled to dust. That happened through thousands of years of human advancement, and in essence it's also what happened to the Tarkanians. But when Tarakan fell, it resulted in the Catastrophe.

LoreMaster Harim surveyed the gloom, either to focus his thoughts or to make sure we were still awake. "According to my research, the earliest mention of the word 'Tarakan' is close to two hundred years before the Catastrophe and refers to a guild or a company, but after a few decades it was referred to as a state, then as one of the strongest of states, and eventually stronger than all of the other states combined, a true empire.

"What makes Tarakan different from most other empires in history is that it was comparatively small in size, yet still immensely powerful. Its influence was felt everywhere. Tarakan used this influence to attract the best and the brightest from the other nations, tempting them with metal, better living conditions, and other such promises. There was nothing they could not do, from curing disease to making crops grow faster or even creating machines that could think for themselves."

My master paused for a short spell before continuing. "I know this sounds like a legend or a children's tale, but if the City of Towers and the wonders of the Valley and City within the Mountain are not enough proof of Tarakan power, then I suggest you make a trip to the far south, as I did. It is a dangerous voyage and you'll have to keep your distance, because the air is still poisonous. But when you see the Tarakan Star Pillar, which reaches the heavens, you'll know that there was nothing they couldn't have done."

I heard the enthusiasm in LoreMaster Harim's voice as he talked about the Star Pillar, and I made a mental promise to myself to visit that place one day, a laughable notion considering our current situation.

My master continued, "The transition of Tarakan from a company to a state is actually an interesting tale that could hint at possible reasons for the conflict which resulted in the Catastrophe. A deadly disease known as the purple plague broke out in several corners of the world. Tarakan scientists quickly found a cure—some said *too quickly*—but for their help, the Tarakan leader, a man I believe was called Falkner or Folkner, demanded that Tarakan would become independent, free from paying tribute to any other state. Tarakan Valley, the City within the Mountain, and even the relatively distant City of Towers became a part of the Tarakan state. Not everyone was happy about this change, and I believe the seeds for the events that destroyed the world were planted at that time.

"At the height of its power, Tarakan developed a series of tests in the form of puzzles, which they believed helped find the most gifted, smart, and creative people. I imagine that parents all over the world trained their kids from infancy, using Tarakan puzzle boxes. The puzzles were such a success that Tarakan soon began testing their veteran citizens as well. If you wanted to get ahead in Tarakan, you had to solve puzzles.

"Jump forward another century, and Tarakan is now feared as much as it is adored. This is where I started to read about references to 'Angels.' Some kind of people, or machines, or a mix of both, who were not conceived in the natural way people are made. I do not know what they did—maybe they replaced manual workers. What I *do* know is that their militant version were called Guardian Angels, and they were formidable, Troll-like warriors, possessing powers that make the tattooed pale in comparison. The Guardian Angels were fitted with many augmentations, and despite their relatively small size, they were an army to be reckoned with. There is enough evidence to suggest that Tarakan fought several wars outside its territory and that the Guardian Angels were especially feared and despised.

"To protect itself even further, Tarakan produced terrible weapons that could kill millions of people in a heartbeat. I believe many of Tarakan's enemies also possessed such weapons. We've all heard and read the stories of the Catastrophe. How fire and death rained from the skies. We've visited the ruined cities and learned to avoid the lands where, even after all these years, the air and water are still poisonous. These are the remnants of the terrible effects of these weapons.

"I don't know what actually triggered the Catastrophe, who decided to attack and why. Maybe it was a miscalculation, a terrible mistake, or, more likely, one side feeling it had a chance to deal a mortal blow to the other. But we live in the aftermath of that war. Our ancestors who somehow survived the onslaught soon discovered that most of their technology was destroyed. Machines everywhere simply ceased functioning, and the knowledge to rebuild them was gone. There are plenty of those machines even in the City of Towers, intact but dead and useless, like frozen corpses.

"In my experience, the farther I travelled from Tarakan centres, the worse the damage became. I've been to places where people live in caves and on the tops of trees, reduced to using sticks and stones for tools. The Tarakan cities remained whole, but as far as we know, every living Tarkanian perished in the Catastrophe. Yet I believe the Tarkanians had a plan in place in case of such a disaster."

"I don't get what this has to do with me," Vincha exclaimed. "I mean, your lecture is interesting, Master of the Lore, but—"

LoreMaster Harim didn't wait for Vincha to complete her sentence. "Have you ever asked yourself why the nodes were created, or why the items we salvage replenish themselves? Or why tattooed individuals keep showing up, all over the world, even in the most remote places? In all my research I have not read even once about them appearing before the Catastrophe."

Vincha fell silent again.

"Someone is still fiercely defending the inner sanctum. Someone is replenishing the nodes, making sure only puzzle-solving people can benefit from them. I believe Tarakan is alive, and the Tarkanians will come back. They will rebuild what we cannot."

I held my breath. Never before had I heard my Master connect all the dots this way.

"If what you say is true, then they should already be walking among us," Vincha countered. "But that hasn't happened."

My LoreMaster shrugged in the gloom. "I don't know why they haven't reemerged. I can only guess that the Catastrophe was more powerful and devastating than they expected it to be.

"I once asked a Gadgetier how she learned to decipher the mechanical codes on the Tarakan devices. She said she had no explanation; somehow, she just knew what the item was and how to manipulate it. Sometimes she felt her marks tingle when she touched Tarakan devices and artifacts. That sensation always made her feel at peace. It is obvious that the Gadgetiers, as well as all the marked, are intrinsically connected to the Tarakan artifacts, but Puzzlers are the only marked who can open puzzle-locked nodes. They must be the key, the first step in the return of the Tarkanians. Only with the Puzzlers can we hope to restore humanity to what it once was."

"Fine," Vincha interrupted again. "Let's say your wild tale

and assumptions are true. I still don't understand what it has to do with me."

"The Salvationist era was as close as we got to glory." There was true regret in the LoreMaster's voice. "Thousands of artifacts were coming into the city every month. We were opening nodes on a regular basis, conducting research, attaching Tarakan artifacts to our bodies, and manipulating technology. Some used this newly found power to gain influence and rule over others—this is human nature—but others studied the technology, and little by little, we were ascending. Then a young Puzzler came to the City of Towers and was sent to an outpost in Tarakan Valley, and everything changed."

I realised LoreMaster Harim was the only person still standing in the cabin when he stepped forward and stood just above Vincha.

"And now I need to ask you a question, Vincha. What happened to that Puzzler?"

Vincha looked up at my mentor. I couldn't see her eyes, but her voice was thick with emotion when she said, "He died, along with the rest of my crew."

LoreMaster Harim shook his head in frustration and blew air through his nose, the way he always did when thinking about an unsolvable problem.

"Did you see him die?"

"Like I told you, I was there." But there was a subtle change in her tone of voice, and I suddenly knew she wasn't telling the *entire* truth.

LoreMaster Harim must have felt the same, because he pleaded quietly, "Please, Vincha, it is important, more than you know."

"It was years ago. The boy is dead."

"How did he die?" LoreMaster Harim implored. "Please, Vincha, I need to know . . ."

Vincha leaned forward and hid her face in her hands for a

long moment before uttering a soft sigh of acceptance and leaning back again. Looking at my mentor she whispered, "I didn't see it happen. I was running for my life. But I heard him scream one last time, and I'm telling you, no one who screams like that survives."

39

Rafik's thumb hovered above the hilt of his brother's knife. He was about to touch the button that would spring the sharp blade yet again, a habit he'd acquired in rare moments of solitude in the Keenan guild house, when Bayne, the lead guard of Rafik's escort, suddenly snapped.

"Stop it, boy." Then he added in a low tone, "You've been playing with that rusting blade since we sat down."

Rafik shrugged and tried to hide his annoyance, but he still said, "It's not rusty. I keep it clean and sharp."

Bayne breathed out slowly, regaining his composure, "I appreciate that, boy, but you've been drawing too much attention as it is." Rafik turned his head around, catching fleeting glimpses in his direction. He pocketed the blade, but kept his hand wrapped around it, feeling the calming weight of the hilt. He briefly wondered how his brother was faring, if his younger sisters still made fun of everything they saw, and whether Eithan had already found a new best friend. Feeling his emotions rise, Rafik shook his head as if to erase the images.

Bayne, who had not taken his eyes off Rafik since he was delivered to his care by Mistress Furukawa, said, "Don't you worry. Soon we will be on our way," then, perhaps trying to cheer up the boy, added, "I'm sure you will like it there. Tarakan Valley is a place of wonder and adventure."

Rafik didn't respond. Frankly, no one knew when the Northern Long Tube would move, because no one controlled it. They'd been sitting in the stuffy cabin for almost half the morning. The Northern Long Tube usually left at high noon, but on occasion it would leave before the designated time or not leave until the next morning. Since no one wanted to risk losing their place, the cabin would fill up as early as sunrise and passengers would simply wait inside.

Bored, Rafik surveyed his surroundings. Everyone seemed to want to go to Tarakan Valley. Heavily augmented Trolls, crews identified by their guild insignia, independent mercenaries, merchants, Gadgetiers and Tinkers, mechanics, Menders—the Northern Long Tube was filled with sweaty humanity. The few seats not preassigned to the Guilds were sold weeks in advance. Rafik was sitting in one of those precious seats, surrounded by hundreds of strangers who all eyed him with curiosity at one stage or another. Many of them wore power armour and sported Tarakan augmentations. Weapons had to be stored in a secure hold during the ride, but everyone looked imposing and warrior-like, though it was easy to differentiate between those who, like Rafik, were on their way to the Valley for the first time, and the veterans. The first timers were looking around with agitation; they chattered constantly, exchanging stories. Their gear shone from metal wax, and smiles of false confidence were spread on their faces. The veterans were wearing well-maintained but clearly used gear, and all of them were in various stages of sleep.

Rafik was told that he would be going to Tarakan Valley only on the night before he left. Master Goran was unhappy, but Mistress Furukawa said she was following a direct order from Lord Keenan himself.

"All right," Master Goran finally sighed, "but I hope they

realise what they're getting. The boy was too expensive a purchase to waste. They should take him on several dozen shallow runs before attempting anything suicidal."

This was hardly an assurance-inspiring sentence, but Rafik didn't mind hearing it. He'd been told he was going to die in Tarakan Valley so many times it had stopped sounding dramatic a long time ago. Master Fu said it no matter how much Rafik trained in hand-to-hand combat. Mistress Havanna said it regardless of how much his shot improved or how long he managed to dodge stun rays. Master Goran kept telling Rafik he would die no matter how many puzzles he successfully completed. There was no doubt in his mind that Tarakan Valley was a dangerous place, yet at this point the prospect of a dangerous adventure was exciting rather than frightening, and the knowledge that Commander Doro would be waiting for Rafik at the outpost tipped the scales even further in favor of excitement.

There had been no good-byes from any of the other trainees or teachers, aside from Master Goran, who stiffly shook Rafik's hand at the gate, and Mistress Furukawa and several Keenan guards, who delivered him to the platform and into the hands of Bayne.

"Is that all of you?" she said, looking at Bayne and his two companions. "I would have thought the guild's only Puzzler would merit a slightly stronger force."

Bayne grimaced at the insult but shrugged it away, "Commander Doro sent us. I guess Tube passes to the Valley are expensive and hard to come by, and besides, sometimes it's better not to make a fuss that would draw even more attention."

Mistress Furukawa looked unconvinced. "Still—"

"Commander Doro sent us," Bayne interrupted, "and I guess he thought we are capable of delivering the boy unharmed, but maybe we should not stand so long on the platform, debating the commander's decision?" Bayne made a show of looking meaningfully around. "Even with all the ShieldGuards, a Sabarra sniper is a tactical possibility."

Without ceremony, Mistress Furukawa bent down and touched Rafik's bracelet with her Keenan signet ring. There was a buzz and a vibration that sent shivers up Rafik's arm. The bracelet opened and fell into Mistress Furukawa's hand. She looked Rafik in the eye and said, "Good luck to us all, Rafik." Then she straightened up, turned, and walked away without saying another word to Bayne.

A slight vibration in the cabin woke Rafik from his doze. The sun rose to the middle of the sky but nothing seemed to change. There was one more thing Rafik felt he had to do.

"Can you tell me which way is east?" he asked Bayne, who looked surprised, but soon pointed in the right direction. Rafik hesitated. He knew it was the right time to pray, but he didn't want to make a spectacle of himself. He'd learned quickly that the faithless were often as intolerant as the pious. There was another girl in the guild house who was teased about wearing a religious symbol around her neck. To his disappointment, he soon discovered the girl worshipped a different, obviously false, god. It was a sign of how alone he felt in the Keenan training house that he still tried to talk to her. But she was as guarded about her faith as he was about his.

Rafik decided to forgo the kneeling part. Instead, he half-turned his body and leaned carefully until his head almost touched the semitransparent wall. The Northern Long Tube to Tarakan Valley was placed diagonally and much higher than the other six Tubes of the City of Towers. Even though he was told that the transparent wall was safe, it took Rafik a while to trust it, so he kept a firm grip on the seat and closed his eyes.

"Sons and Daughters of Abraham, there is no God but the one God and his two Prophets: the dead and the Reborn," he whispered as softly as he could, and he felt his body relax a bit. Images of his village sprang before his eyes: his family, Eithan, happy memories of games and trips of childish exploration. As always, the happiness was soon replaced by sadness, which then faded into the image of the wall of symbols. For the past few months he could see the wall of symbols in front of his eyes even when awake, but only in his dreams was he able to manipulate the symbols. He watched the constant movement of the wall with a sense of calm detachment. No matter how much pain he suffered from Master Goran's puzzle boxes, the wall was a source of comfort, strangely beckoning, more so since sleep began conjuring the awful nightmare.

A slight vibration made Rafik open his eyes and sit up straight in his seat. The first timers whooped and exchanged clenched-fist salutes while the veterans mainly changed to more comfortable sleeping positions.

There was a sudden commotion outside. Rafik turned his head and watched an animated shouting match between a woman with fiery red curls and three Troll guards. Just as the doors began to close, she darted between them and entered the cabin. They tried to grab her but were too late; the doors sealed and they were left standing on the platform. She turned around and made a rude gesture at the three and laughed before shouldering a small bag and looking around the cabin. The Long Tube began to slowly accelerate. Rafik turned his attention to the transparent wall beside him and the awe-inspiring view of the City of Towers. He heard Bayne call out "Vincha, over here!" but didn't pay much attention to what was happening in the cabin. His hands gripped the edges of his seat.

"Phew, I thought those rust pots were going to make me miss it," she said as she dropped her bag on the floor with an audible thump.

"And look at this, *everyone* wants to go to the Valley now. I even had a rusting civilian giving me an offer for a private expedition. Should have seen him, no augs, just a pipe and high boots, telling me he was working for the sake of humanity. Ha!" She laughed out loud. "Told him I work for the sake of coin, but nothing in this world will make me go on a run with a bunch of amateurs—no, I only go with the pros."

"I didn't even know you were in the city," said Bayne, a hint of disappointment in his voice.

"Upgrading, finally," Vincha said. Rafik turned his head and saw her lift a fistful of red curls to show a thick cable that looped around the back of her ear and entered her skull just behind the temple. "Lovely, isn't it?" There were other cables, too, snaking through the thicket of her curls; they disappeared from view when Vincha released her hair. Rafik looked outside to watch the ground dropping below them.

Bayne turned to Rafik and said, "Don't get too excited, kid. This machine only gets faster and higher."

"So, this is the boy, eh?" Vincha eyed Rafik with open curiosity. "I didn't think he would be coming this season, I mean, with the price I heard you paid for him and the sandstorm season just a few weeks away."

One of the guards began with, "How do you know about the b—" then stopped, as if remembering the obvious, and added an embarrassed, "Oh."

Vincha smiled mischievously but then grew serious. "He looks too young to be doing this. How old is he?"

"I'm thirteen," Rafik answered with pride. If he were still in his village, he would have been assigned to day guard duty, and been given a real weapon.

But Vincha just shook her head again. "Yeah, too rusting young, if you ask me. What was Doro thinking? The boy should wait at least one more season, if not two."

"Why don't you ask Commander Doro yourself, since you're the one bumping him?" said the other guard.

Vincha turned her head to him. "Jealous?" she asked slyly, running her hands through her curls.

He smiled at her. "Maybe."

"Hoping for some action?" continued Vincha.

"By all means," answered the guard, straightening a bit in his seat. "You're a very attractive wo—"

"Well, I hope you're good at catching Lizards," Vincha cut in, "'cause believe me, with that oily tongue of yours, that's the only action you'll be getting."

This caused laughter to ripple all around them, and even the Keenan guard chuckled and raised his hands in the air in mock defeat. Unfortunately, the exchange also attracted the attention of some of the other passengers in the cabin. A young Troll approached, goaded by a few of his friends, and planted his frame in front of her with two hands on his weapons belt.

"Perhaps you should join us over there," he indicated, cocking his shaven head at the back of the cabin. "We have some farm brew, if you know what I mean." His hand left his belt and made a drinking motion, just to be sure she understood.

Vincha looked at the young Troll for long enough that his friends began to whistle and catcall. The Troll puffed his chest out. "Like what you see?"

"No, not really," Vincha turned her head dismissively.

The whistles turned to laughter but the young Troll didn't give up easily. "What's your affiliation, lady?" he challenged.

Vincha turned her head back to the young man. "Independent," she said drily.

"So why hedge your bet with the Keenans when you could join real men at Sabarra house?" He thumbed proudly at the insignia on his uniform.

All three of Rafik's guards stiffened. One of them swore under his breath and began to rise, but Bayne stopped him with a look. There was sudden cold silence in the cabin.

Still sitting, Vincha lowered her gaze to stare at the Troll's crotch and left it there for a while before saying, "I don't see no man from where I'm sitting." This caused an explosion of thick, unpleasant laughter in the cabin, which eased the tension.

The Troll turned crimson and turned to leave. "Whatever," he said, then added "Keenan bitch" as he walked off.

Vincha was on her feet in a flash. "You. Turn around," she called after the Troll, but the man kept walking.

"Turn around, farm boy," she said again. This time the Troll stopped.

He turned and everyone could see his fists were clenched. But Vincha didn't wait for a reply. "You might believe the propaganda they oil your tubes with at the farms," she spat, moving a step closer to him and shifting into combat stance. "All that rust about us and them, about serving your guild master to the death, but when you're surrounded by Lizards and shitting your own wires, you don't care which crew saves your sorry arse."

"Don't give me lip, woman," the Troll said, stepping towards Vincha, "or I'll show you what we do to women like you on the farm."

Bayne was now up on his feet and so were most of the Trolls in the cabin, but Vincha indicated with an open palm that it was her fight.

"You know what my job is?" she asked the Troll. "You know what I can do?"

"Yeah," sniggered the Troll, "you're a messaging service."

"I am a Communicator, farm boy," said Vincha, "and I'm about to communicate a lesson to your rusty little brain."

The Troll took another step forward and raised a clenched fist but instead of throwing a punch, his hands rose to clasp his ears and he collapsed to the floor.

"Oh, what do we have here?" asked Vincha, her hands on her hips. "Someone forgot to secure the channels of his plug-ins? Perhaps you didn't bother to listen to the advice of the old-timers. Someone doesn't know the Lizards can attune themselves to our communication and find your position?" Vincha bent down and raised her voice, "Can you hear me above the noise inside your head?"

"Stop, please, make it stop!" the Troll writhed on the cabin's floor, still holding his head in his hands.

Two other young Sabarra Trolls got to their feet. Vincha tilted her head at them. "Better sit this one out, boys," she said in a cheerful voice, "or I'll fry your brains out of your ears. Can you feel *this?*" they groaned in unison and quickly complied, hands covering their ears.

"Vincha." It might have been Bayne's soft voice that cooled her temper, or perhaps she decided the young Trolls had suffered enough.

"Fine," she said.

The young Sabarras groaned as one in relief. The Troll who approached Vincha was getting up slowly when he was lifted off his feet by a mighty uppercut that sent him back down to the floor again, where he lay unconscious.

"And that was for calling me a bitch." Vincha looked at the other members of his group. "Take him away now, children," she said, "and when this sweetheart wakes up you tell him that if I ever hear the B word coming out of his mouth again, I will personally cut every wire on his body, including the little one between his legs."

The others scurried forward and dragged their friend's body back to their side of the cabin as Vincha turned and walked back to Bayne. Everyone in the cabin relaxed.

"See that?" Bayne remarked as Vincha sat down again. "That's why we had to call in the boy. The Valley ain't what it used to be. The guilds are fighting in the City of Towers over rusting Council politics, and the new recruits want to fight each other instead of the Lizards. Cross-guild operations are rarer than a virgin in a whorehouse. If you want to get anything done, you need your own Puzzler."

Vincha looked at Rafik again and flashed him a relaxed smile as if she hadn't been in combat only moments ago. "Glad I don't need to get involved in that rust."

"Wrong, Vincha," one of the guards said. "Word is, some of the guilds are giving ultimatums to the independents, saying they can't work with certain crews if they want to work with them. The Metal Hunters haven't recovered from their botched deep run, and Sabarra managed to buy out a lot of the shallow runs this season. They're squeezing everyone hard, especially us. You'll have to choose sides and sign an exclusive with one guild or another soon. I suggest you sign with the Keenans." He smiled and wiggled his eyebrows knowingly. "I hear you're getting all the perks anyways."

Vincha just shook her head, ignoring the apparent innuendo. "I choose my crews and choose my runs, and I'll fuck myself with a rusty pole before I'll become a guild slave." She shot a smile and shrugged at the Keenan guards. "No offense, guys."

If Bayne or his two companions were offended by Vincha's comment, they didn't show it.

She turned to Rafik. "I don't believe we've formally met. I'm Vincha, what's your name?"

Rafik looked at Bayne for reassurance and received a nod. He answered and shook her extended hand.

"Don't worry about those fools," she said, thumbing at the recuperating Sabarra Trolls. "Doro and the Keenan crew are solid enough—except Ramm, of course." She winked at Bayne, who chuckled at their private joke. "How's that cracked oil pot, anyway?"

"Crazy as usual," said Bayne with a grimace. "Don't get me wrong, he is one mean Troll in a fight, but I don't know how the commander keeps him in line. If it were up to me I'd—" Bayne stopped talking as the colour suddenly drained from Vincha's face. She grasped her head with her hands and curled into a ball.

"What's happening?" Bayne quickly crouched next to her.

"New hardware," Vincha answered in a hoarse whisper as her body convulsed in pain. "In my bag, quickly." Her eyes rolled back as Bayne threw the bag to a guard, who rummaged through it and found a small leather satchel. Bayne laid Vincha on two adjacent seats, opened the small bag, and dipped his finger in. Without hesitation he shoved a finger covered in green powder up Vincha's nostril and blocked the other with his hand. When she sniffed hard, he repeated the action again in the other nostril. Bayne sat her up on the seat on front of Rafik, and watched her slowly regain her senses. The moment she could, Vincha snatched the satchel from Bayne and sniffed another large dose before sighing with relief. "Thanks, guys," she muttered. "Rust, didn't think I'd get short-circuited like that so soon."

"It's the new plugs." Bayne stood up and stretched. "Don't worry, you'll get used to it."

"Here, take your seat back." Vincha tried to rise, but Bayne ordered her to stay put, claiming he needed to stretch his legs.

Vincha slumped back, looking relieved. After a while she looked at Rafik and said, "Don't be scared."

"I'm not scared," Rafik answered before turning his head to watch the view outside. They were travelling so high it seemed the clouds were closer than the ground. The twin metal bars they passed every heartbeat were thicker than before, blue energy flashing between them every so often. After a short while the height and the idea that somehow this structure kept the train from crashing made Rafik queasy, and he turned his head back to Vincha, who'd slumped in her seat, eyes shut.

"Why does it hurt?" he asked.

Vincha opened her eyes. "Sometimes the body rejects the metal," she answered, "and it's very painful."

"The green powder helps against the pain?"

"It dulls the pain."

"I've been told it's bad to breathe the powder."

"Told by whom?" Vincha didn't change her posture but there was now an edge in her voice.

Rafik shrugged. "By a merchant I know. He said it is better to feel the pain, and when I was training in the guild house—"

Vincha smiled weakly. "I'm sure you were told many things, especially in the guild house," she said, slowly straightening in her seat, "but let me give you a piece of advice, Rafik; not everything in life is black and white." She added thoughtfully, "But from my experience it's usually dark shades. Too much of the powder can be a shitty trip or even kill ya, for sure, but when you get short-circuited, nothing helps but the powder. That's the only cure, and if it makes things better, then there must be no harm in that, right?"

She saw the look on Rafik's face and added, "Don't worry, kid. There are no augmentations for Puzzlers, so you'd only ever need an external communication device. No pain or powder for you."

"Where does this powder come from?"

He saw Vincha hesitate and look at Bayne, a sure sign he'd stumbled upon something that he was probably not meant to know.

Bayne shrugged and muttered, "He'll know sooner or later."

The Tube swerved smoothly, and Rafik saw an enormous mountain range in the distance. They seemed to be heading straight towards it.

"You sure you want to know this, boy?"

Rafik nodded.

"It's dried Lizard blood, to be honest, mixed with other stuff," Vincha said. "Some lick it off Lizard skin as well, but it has to be a freshly killed Lizard—the creatures sweat the stuff."

Rafik's eyes were wide. "Really?"

"Yep, some crazy Troll found this out years ago in circumstances I don't care to repeat, even here."

"That's just a myth," Bayne said. "Long before the Hive was established, a Mender heard an old Salvationist bragging at a bar about how he used to lick the skin of a Lizard to feel better about his plugs. So this Mender made a trip to the Valley, began catching and doing experiments on the Lizards until he came up with the powder."

"And disappeared without a trace." It was Vincha's turn. "Now who's talking about myth?" She turned to Rafik.

"Believe what you want—the Menders now make the powder and swim in coin for it. You want to know how they make it?"

This time it took Rafik slightly longer to decide. He turned his eyes to the mountain range before nodding his consent.

Vincha leaned forward and lowered her voice. "When they

kill the Lizards, assuming there's anything left, they bring the bodies back and squeeze the juice out of them, then they boil the blood and add a few ingredients, wait for the whole thing to dry, and that's it. Sometimes we get lucky and capture a live Lizard, bring it back, and tie the thing upside down above a bucket and puncture a hole in its heart, which incidentally is in the same place as it is for us hu—"

"Stop it, Vincha," Bayne snapped. "You'll frighten the boy."

Vincha leaned back in her seat and said, "He has the right to know." She turned to Rafik, "Did they make you read those novels about the first expeditions?"

Rafik nodded.

"Well they're full of rust and lies," Vincha declared. "The famous six started out as a company of two dozen mercenary Trolls. Those poor bastards got slaughtered one by one in less than three days, and don't let anyone tell you otherwise. These are stories they feed you so that you become more loyal to the stupid guild."

"Vincha, that's enough," Bayne growled.

"Rust, Bayne, I'm doing you a favor. Otherwise you'll have to tell him bedtime stories." She leaned forward and touched Rafik's knee. "Listen carefully to Vincha, kid. They'll tell you those Lizards are brainless animals—easy kill, nothing to worry about—but they are cunning, mean cunts, and they are as nasty as they are capable. On average, we get raided every few weeks. They come from different directions, and some of them even use weapons, knives, clubs, and I know a few Trolls who swear they saw Lizards carrying guns, you understand? And they can hear our communication unless I scramble it good, and they gang up on one poor sod and pin him down, and then they—"

"Seriously, Vincha, trap it," Bayne roared.

This time she complied, crossing her arms across her chest and sending the burly guard a mock pout.

A bell rang three times and artificial light suddenly filled the cabin.

"What's that?" Rafik said.

"Don't worry," Bayne said, still sending dark looks at Vincha. "See? Now you scared the kid, made him jumpy."

"I'm not scared," Rafik declared. "I just want to know what is happening."

"The bell means the Tube detected a bunch of Lizards waiting to ambush us and—"

"Vincha!"

"Just messing with you, kid." She laughed, leaned forward again, and ruffled Rafik's growing hair. "We're going into a tunnel through the mountain, that's all."

As an afterthought she added, "Look, it's messy out there, but don't worry. Vincha will play Mother Goose and take care of you, so if any of those rustheads make trouble, just come to me and I'll sort them out." She smiled at him and winked. "What do you say, friends?"

Rafik nodded with a shy smile.

40

The transparent walls darkened as the Northern Long Tube emerged from the tunnel, but it didn't reduce the dramatic effect. The landscape of Tarakan Valley was a sea of yellow sand dotted by countless buildings, stretching as far as the eye could see.

Although Rafik never felt the descent, the Tube emerged from the tunnel much lower down than when they'd entered the mountain. For a few heartbeats, the cabin was filled with light, and Rafik squinted and shielded his eyes. Then the Tube's transparent walls darkened and the brightness became bearable. They were still moving at an incredible pace, but Rafik could see the buildings and the roads clearly, and the patterns of the city mesmerized him. Most of the buildings, even the very high ones, were whole, but the damage of time and the elements was plain. There was no hint of movement on the roads, no sign of vegetation. The city was like a long-dead corpse, dried up of all moisture.

"Crazy, isn't it?" Vincha leaned towards Rafik. "I heard it was once the most beautiful city in the world. Now the only things moving here, except us, are the rusting Lizards and the sandstorms which could ground us for weeks."

"How will we survive with no water or food?" Rafik wondered. He was not an expert, but the amount of supplies he'd seen stuffed into the Northern Long Tube did not seem enough to sustain a camp full of Salvationists under such harsh conditions.

Vincha leaned closer, as if sharing a secret. "The main camp, what we call the Hive, is located right on top of a fat, useful node. There are enough nourishment pills in there to keep everyone alive, and enough blankets and towels to open a brothel. There are even functioning water pipes all over the underground structure. One of your first missions will be to open the puzzle lock in the base." She patted Rafik lightly on the shoulder. "But don't worry. I hear it's quite easy to do, and we always keep an emergency Puzzler around, just in case."

Vincha waited for the boy to respond, but Rafik was deep in thought.

"How are you feeling?" she asked after a spell, nudging the boy lightly with her elbow. "Nervous? Excited?"

This time Rafik responded, "A little bit of both. More excited, I guess . . . I can't explain why. It feels like I know this place, but it's strange, because I've never been here before."

Vincha nodded in sympathy. "I know the feeling. When you're in the Valley you just want to get the rust out, but when you're away you start missing this crappy sandbox so much you end up going to a Salvationist bar every night and drinking your wages away just so you have an excuse to come back here. I mean, when you see the gates that never open—have you heard of them?"

Rafik shook his head.

"Ah, it's something to see, all right. Not that you'll get to see it, since it doesn't even have a puzzle lock, can you believe it? But you ain't seen Tarakan Valley until you stood by the gate."

Suddenly one of the young Trolls shouted "Lizards!" and pointed. Everyone got on their feet and gathered to watch the city below.

"Where did you see Lizards?" one of the older-looking Trolls in the cabin asked, peering through the transparent wall.

"I saw two coming out of a tall building over there." The young Troll pointed.

Rafik and Vincha pressed their faces to the transparent wall and scanned the buildings flashing underneath them.

"I don't see anything," said Vincha.

"Are you sure they were Lizards?" the veteran Troll turned from the wall. "We're above the southeast side; there aren't a lot of Lizards in this area."

"No, they were Lizards," the younger Troll insisted as his crew members whooped excitedly and punched each other's chests. The veteran Troll didn't look convinced, but before he had a chance to say anything, a Tube ShieldGuard stepped into the cabin.

"We're close. Get ready," said the ShieldGuard. "After we stop, use the ropes to climb down."

In a heartbeat, everyone in the cabin was gathering equipment and collecting their weapons from the train guards. The Troll that Vincha had confronted before made a point of looking in her direction while checking his blaster and heavy machine gun.

"Don't worry," Bayne muttered. "I got you covered."

"I can handle a stupid Sabarra pup," Vincha answered. She smiled and added, "But thanks all the same."

"Don't underestimate them, Vincha. Like I said, things are changing. This kid will wait until your back is turned and—"

Vincha cut off Bayne midsentence. "Like I said—" But then another alarm sounded and drowned out her answer.

"Brace yourselves and secure your weapons; we are stopping!" the Tube guard barked, wrapping a thick rope around his body and attaching a hook to the nearest pole. "Remember, this is not the platform of the city. We have a short period of time before the doors are shut, so get out as fast as you can."

Bayne turned to Rafik. "Can you climb down or do you need my help?"

"I'm fine, I know what to do." Rafik wanted to sound confident but his voice came out shaking. He'd trained for this moment in the guild house, and although he was not the best climber, he was far from being the worst. Still, looking down at the moving ground below made Rafik weak in the knees.

An ear-piercing siren filled the cabin again, and the Northern Long Tube came to a sudden stop. Rafik fell forward. If it weren't for Vincha's quick grip he would have landed on the floor face-first.

She winked at him. "Easy now, big boy."

He smiled weakly and straightened up.

The Tube ShieldGuard turned a star-shaped disc to the wall, and almost immediately the doors swung silently open, filling the cabin with bright light, heat, and dust. Rafik peeked down. They had stopped high above a clearing between several high buildings. A multitude of vehicles and people, mostly armed Trolls, were waiting for them, and as soon as the Tube stopped they surged forward like charging ants.

"We're lucky there's no sandstorm," Bayne commented, adjusting a pair of goggles to his eyes.

"Do sandstorms happen often?" Rafik watched as the pair of guards rolled rope ladders out of the cabin.

"Often enough." Bayne covered his nose and mouth with a breathing guard, and his voice became muffled. "Even the weak ones are nasty, and you do *not* want to be caught in a full sandstorm, believe me. When that happens, smart Trolls stay inside. If you're on a shallow run, you'd better head back to the Hive or find shelter underground. Here." He handed Rafik a pair of goggles. "These will help you against the glare of the sun and keep sand out of your eyes." He produced another breathing guard. "And this will keep the dust from your lungs. It will take some time to get used to, but believe me, you want to be wearing it."

"Thank you," Rafik said. He wanted to add that he knew what the goggles and breathing guard were for—he'd trained with them in the Keenan guild house—but Bayne was already busy attaching a security cable between himself and the boy. All the other passengers were either already wearing or in the process of putting on their own versions of goggles and breathing guards.

The people at the front of the line began climbing over the edge and down the ladders in pairs, disappearing quickly out of sight. The cabin emptied, and soon Rafik found himself at the ledge. The goggles reduced Rafik's field of vision, but even with them, the brightness was uncomfortable. The breathing guard made every intake of hot air a struggle, and Rafik fought the instinct to pull it away. As he looked down, the heat hitting his face and the strong wind blowing the net ladder made the boy's stomach turn. But his training kicked in, and before he realised what he was doing, Rafik found himself climbing down a net ladder as fast as he dared while Bayne matched his descent.

On the other side of the Tube Rafik saw Trolls climbing up. A few of them avoided the ladders altogether and used their superior leg augmentations to jump above the climbers. At the back of the Tube, crates of supplies were being roped down to a crowd of heavily augmented Trolls, who lifted them away into open six-wheelers, which Rafik already knew were called Dusters. It all seemed extremely chaotic but somehow efficient at the same time. Rafik turned his head up and suddenly understood why there was no platform like the ones in the City of Towers and Regeneration. The floating metal bars continued on into the distance, but they were misaligned, and some were broken or missing. The Northern Long Tube did not stop at a destination, it stopped midtravel because it couldn't continue.

As soon as he touched the sandy ground Rafik was pushed away by Bayne to give room to the descending Keenan guards.

Bayne then led them towards a large Keenan crew, which was waiting for them in the shadow of a seven-story building. Vincha was just behind them when a very tall, dark-skinned female Troll stepped in front of her, blocking the CommWoman's way with an outstretched hand, the other leaning lightly but purposely over one of the two blasters on her hips. "Keep your distance," she ordered. "This is Keenan business." The Troll wore her coal-black hair in many tiny braids, and had a Tarakan eye-piece attached to her right eye and a massive sniper gun strapped to her back.

Vincha stopped in her tracks, visibly surprised. "Come on, Narona, what's rusting your joints?" she protested. "I was sitting next to the boy the entire trip—what do you think I'd do to him?"

Bayne was surprised as well. "That's uncalled for, Lieutenant. We all know Vincha well enough."

"I have my orders to bring the Puzzler in alone," Narona snapped, "and I'm not about to disobey a direct order for the likes of *her*."

"Commander Doro gave you this order," Vincha said, her eyes glinting, "because he didn't know I was riding on this Long Tube, that's all. No need to be jealous just because he fancies me and not your bony ass. There are enough Trolls in Tarakan Valley, especially for someone with standards as low as yours."

Narona visibly stiffened, and looked down at Rafik as if to remind herself of her duties.

Vincha waved her hand in dismissal. "Fine, I'll find my own way to the Hive." She turned to Rafik and said, "See you at the Hive. Say hi to Commander Doro for me." Then she turned and walked away slowly, disappearing behind a corner. Once Narona was sure that Vincha was not coming back, she did not waste time, and the Keenan crew quickly set out on their way towards the outpost.

"What, no rides?" Bayne wondered.

"The Dusters are in repair." Narona checked the sights of her sniper gun and cocked it with expertise.

"We could try to catch a ride with another crew. The kid, he's been through a lot."

Narona silenced Bayne with a stare before signalling for the Keenans to move. They formed a protective circle around Rafik and, at Narona's insistence, powered up their armour and readied their weapons. Many other Troll companies were moving in the same direction, some on foot, other driving Dusters, but Narona kept the Keenans at a respectable distance from the rest of the groups.

Circled by a squad of armed and ready Trolls, Rafik did his best to peek around as they all walked and take in the surroundings. If the buildings looked big from the vantage point of the Tube, they were nothing short of awe-inspiring from the ground up.

"A young blood on the Long Tube claimed he saw a Lizard in the southeast part," Bayne briefed as they walked, keeping to the shady side of the enormous buildings. "I think he was lying to beef himself up in front of his mates, but we better tell Brain. He can send a crew to investigate."

Narona nodded but remained silent, the muzzle of her sniper rifle constantly moving from side to side.

"You didn't need to bust Vincha like that," Bayne tried again, "I know it's complicated with Doro and stuff, but she is sound and she's worked with us before. I am sure the Commander didn't mean to—"

"It wasn't Doro who gave the order." This time the Lieutenant turned her head to look at Bayne.

From his vantage point, Rafik could see Bayne stiffen and lose a step before resuming his stride. "What happened to Commander Doro?"

"Dead."

Rafik felt as if he was kicked in the stomach.

"You're cutting my wires now, Narona," Bayne choked, stopping in his tracks, his eyes clearly wide with shock even behind the goggles. "Seriously? When the fuck did that happen?"

"Two days ago," Narona said. "Keep moving, Bayne."

He obeyed, catching up with the Lieutenant. "How? What happened? Rust."

"He went out at night." Narona didn't stop surveying the area with her gun as she talked. "Brain got an emergency distress call from a casual crew. They stepped into an uncharted Lizard's den and were being taken apart. Doro took the call, went out with Ramm and some independents, and left us a communication to follow. It was night, a storm was passing through the area, and we had zero visibility. By the time we found them it was over."

"What about the crew who called? Did Doro and Ramm save them? Who were these fucking amateurs?" Bayne was still shaking his head in disbelief.

"That's the problem—there was no one to be found. It was a hit-and-run. The other crew probably bailed but forgot to call off the distress call. We went through all the other crews. They all denied calling for help."

"Sabarra then?"

Narona shook her head. "A big crew came back from a deep run. All were hunkered down in the Hive or on guard duties. This was not a hit, and, you know, even with politics and the tensions, the Hive is the Hive . . ."

Bayne was still visibly shaken. "Still can't believe this. Is anyone missing? Why did this crew call for help if they didn't have anyone down?"

"You know how it is." Narona's voice was flat and emotionless. "Some newbloods get tired of Lizard popping and decide to do some exploring on their own. They get into a little trouble, panic, and send out a distress call, but then they manage to get back only to find out later that the call caused casualties. I don't blame them for not stepping up to admit it."

Bayne went quiet for a while, then shook his head. "Where's the body? I want to see it."

Narona shrugged. "Pulverized really, nothing's left."

"Pulverized?" Bayne exclaimed with disbelief. "What the fuck, Narona? Lizards don't use ray weapons."

"Apparently they do now."

"So a rusting Lizard pulverized the Commander with a blaster? I don't believe it!"

"Believe it, he's fried," Narona said, "and Ramm is crew commander now. Orders came from Lord K himself."

"Rust." Bayne shook his head again.

"You can challenge Ramm if you think you're up to it," Narona said carefully, with a blank expression. Then she added roughly, "On the bright side, Bayne, it looks like Vincha will need to find a new Troll to hump—maybe that could be you. I see how you look at her."

"Balls, Narona, that's low," Bayne grunted.

The Lieutenant didn't answer, and they walked the rest of the way in silence until they reached a large junction that was blocked by stone walls and piles of bent metal. Two makeshift guard towers stood at opposite sides of the junction, manned by combat Trolls in full gear. The Keenans stopped to be identified before passing through the gates and into the Tarakan Valley outpost that all veteran Salvationists called the Hive.

The outpost was half a mile in diameter, relatively protected from the clouds of billowing dust by the high walls of piled metal debris that surrounded them. The parameter was bustling with activity, packed with Dusters, crews, Trolls, and Mechanics, all doing different things. The buildings within the walls of the Hive were not as tall as the towers in the city Rafik had just come from, but they were still imposing. Two of them stood more than fifteen stories high by Rafik's counting. Some of the other buildings were even higher. Rafik was startled as vehicles passed them from all directions, followed the road ahead, and disappeared underground.

"Wait till you see what's beneath us." Bayne tapped the ground with his boot. "There are so many levels, we could all just live underground instead of in the buildings here, but being down below too long tends to rust your metal up here."

Bayne tapped his head and tried to smile reassuringly, but it looked forced even to Rafik. "You'll meet Brain soon. He runs the Hive for everybody, so we don't kill each other over guard duties and run quotas, then I'll give you a tour of the place. You'll be amazed what we have down there: working showers—you'll learn to appreciate those—and even a bar called the Chewing

Hole, which is . . . well . . . I guess if you're old enough to be here you're old enough to drink there . . . that is, if Commander Doro will let . . . rust!" His voice trailed off.

Rafik nodded in silence, trying to take everything in, but there was so much activity going on around them that he had to concentrate just to keep up with the Keenan crew. During the walk to the base he held Fahid's blade in his hand, trying to come to terms with the news about Commander Doro. He remembered their conversation and how the Commander made him feel good about his own life—that he had some sort of a glamorous destiny. Many people had already entered and left Rafik's short life, yet Commander Doro's death shook him to the core. He was filled with dread.

Rafik barely had a chance to get his bearings. It was only when they were crossing the Hive that he got his first glimpse of the City within the Mountain, and everything, even Commander Doro, was momentarily forgotten. Far to the north, it loomed so large that it seemed closer; countless towers coming out of the mountain range seemed to touch the heavens. It was a sight of such awesome architectural achievement that it belittled everything Rafik had ever seen before, and together with a sense of awe he was suddenly filled with an unexplained longing. He wanted to go there immediately.

So enthralled was Rafik with the City within the Mountain that he failed to notice the Troll who stopped the group and was now conversing with them. Only when a shadow crossed his vision did Rafik turn his head and take an involuntary step back, swallowing a gasp of fear. It was the biggest combat Troll he'd ever seen, towering a head and a half above the tallest Keenan guard and carrying an arsenal of weapons that could have easily fitted an entire crew. His eyes were hidden behind the combat visor of his helmet and his nose and mouth were covered by a yellow combat mask. The Troll's jawline was the only body part Rafik saw that was not metal.

"I'm Ramm, the Keenan crew commander," the Troll said to

Rafik in a low, rumbling voice. "Do as I tell you and I won't pull your guts out through your throat."

"Whoa," Bayne stepped between the boy and the huge Troll, "there's no need for that rust, Ramm. He's been trained as Keenan."

Despite his bulk, Ramm moved so swiftly there was no pause between the end of Bayne's sentence and the noise he made when his back hit the wall. Bayne toppled heavily to the floor.

"I'm *your* crew commander, too," Ramm said, taking a step towards the groaning Bayne, "and my word is law."

The Keenans silently watched Bayne climb shakily back to his feet. Ramm cocked his head to the side, his hands hovering above a power hammer and a double-barrelled pistol, waiting.

Narona walk calmly to Ramm's side and said, "Get over it and get used to it, Bayne. Or would you rather break contract and try going rogue?"

Bayne nodded slowly, brushing sand off his arms. He intoned without making eye contact, "I'm sorry, Commander. It was not my intention to disagree with you."

Despite the fact that Ramm's face was hidden, Rafik had a feeling the Troll was almost disappointed that Bayne did not challenge him further.

"Let's get out of here," he ordered.

As the Keenans followed Ramm, Rafik saw Vincha standing next to two female Trolls. One was talking to her while the other patted her back, but Vincha's head was in her hands and she stood almost motionless, with only a slight tremble of her shoulders betraying her grief. When Rafik turned his head again a few moments later, she'd already disappeared into the crowd.

41

T'is 'l urt a li'le."

Rafik heard Brain's hissing voice, but before he could interpret what was said, the med chair's metal arm moved and a sharp needle pierced the tragus of his left ear, making him cry out. He instinctively tried to move his head but Narona held a firm hand on his forehead, effectively pinning his head to the med chair. His hands, legs, and torso were also restrained by an invisible, yet effective force. He'd never felt so helpless and alone.

"Stop thrashing around," Narona suggested calmly. But she didn't ease her hold of his head. "It will be over soon."

"It hurts," Rafik whimpered, but even as he did, the pain began to subside. He tried to relax, and the withdrawing of the chair's metal arms from his still-throbbing left ear helped.

Narona released her grip and stepped away. Rafik carefully turned his head and saw the deformed communication Troll at the far corner of the windowless Hive's control room, located deep underground in the centre of the complex. The light was so dim, Brain was more of a silhouette—which was, in a way, a blessing. The Troll was not a pleasant creature to look at, especially when he hovered over Rafik as he made the final adjustments in the med chair's metal arm.

Brain's head was three times as large as a normal human being's, and it was supported by a metal brace from the neck down. Rafik could not tell if the brace was part of the seat, which hovered above the floor without any visible support. He had the tiniest of hands, which did not move but twitched every so often, only one healthy eye, the other one was partially covered by folded skin, and a lipless mouth from which several teeth were protruding. The Troll's hair was made from a forest of wires and cables, a few as thick as Rafik's forearm, attached to his overly large, tattooed skull. Many of these wires were connected to the Troll's seat, but others were connected to various machines all around the room. When Brain moved about, Narona had to duck or step over the cables and wires.

"Aust li'ting," Brain moaned in his shadowy corner. "'Ould 'ake' ime.'" He was watching one of the many screens that was flashing numbers and other symbols Rafik did not understand but was fascinated with nonetheless. Suddenly there was a clear and surprisingly pleasant male voice in his ear, "Can you hear me, Rafik? Say 'Yes, Brain' out loud."

"Yes," said the startled Rafik, then added quickly, "Brain."

"Good." Brain's seat turned in the air and he slowly hovered over to another screen. "Now that we can properly speak, I want to welcome you to the Hive."

"Thank you," Rafik mumbled.

"I am Brain. I run the Hive's communications as well as deal with run quotas, guard duties, space allocation, and many other day-to-day issues. Now, I want you to lightly press your left ear with two fingers and *think* the words 'Yes' and 'Brain.'"

Rafik's arms and legs were suddenly free. He gingerly touched his ear with his fingertips, feeling a tiny round button on his tragus.

"Press a little harder, Rafik, then release—it will not hurt. Good. Now think the words I told you."

Rafik did as he was ordered and thought the words *yes* and *Brain*.

"Very good. When you touch your ear like that and think the words 'Rafik connect to Brain,' you can reach me from almost anywhere in the Valley. Let me create a few more channels for you."

Brain asked Rafik to say out loud and think words such as *Keenan, Ramm, emergency,* and many other words. Rafik had already used a Comm earpiece on the Keenan training ground, although it was not permanently attached. Brain explained that by pressing the button and saying the words, Rafik could reach out and be reached by many people, even from very far away. For a moment Rafik thought that perhaps there was a way for him to reach Eithan in his village, and wouldn't *that* be a grand surprise to be able to talk suddenly into his friend's ear, but Brain said it was impossible. His enthusiasm sunk even further when Brain informed him that the Comm button could also tell Brain as well as Ramm exactly where Rafik was at all times.

"You will never get lost here, and if you do, we will find you."

Rafik did not like that notion at all, but it seemed useless to argue.

Instead he asked, "Can I talk to Vincha?"

Narona snorted in contempt. "You don't need to talk to that crazy bitch."

Brain said more patiently, "The decision on any extra channels is up to your crew commander and do cost in coin or kind. You could try and find Vincha on the general channel of the Hive, but my suggestion is to simply find her and have a chat face-to-face. I believe," he added, his voice suggesting the Troll might be smiling to himself, "she is usually at the Chewing Hole. You can climb out of the chair now."

The med chair swivelled slightly and straightened up. Rafik stepped away from it, being careful not to step on any wires in the gloom. He stood there, unsure what to do next.

"Your next stop, Puzzler, is down at the node," Brain said in

Rafik's ear. "Your Keenan crew will take you there. I understand it is not a difficult lock, but I wish you luck all the same. I will see you shortly, Puzzler. *Brain's out.*"

Bayne was waiting for them at the corridor.

"So?" he said, looking down at Rafik, as the heavy metal doors to Brain's room slid shut. "Are you plugged in?"

Rafik nodded and earned himself a friendly pat on the shoulder. "Welcome to the Hive, boy. You'll get used to it in no time, then it will become your home. I could show you a neat pl—"

"No time for friendly chats or sightseeing." Narona checked the timekeeping device on her wrist. "We need to go down to the node, Ramm is already there and you know how he is . . ." She eyed Bayne meaningfully.

"Yes. There will be time for this later," Bayne agreed hastily.

Brain's room was only a stairway down from the surface, but to reach the node the three of them had to walk down several corridors until they reached a large lift. They rode down in silence until Bayne said, "Don't worry, I hear the Hive's puzzle lock is quite easy."

Rafik answered, "Yes, Brain told me." But he felt his heart begin to race. He'd never opened a real node before, and how would a non-Puzzler know if the puzzle was difficult or not?

When the doors opened again, the three stepped into a large round room that had five other lifts and a staircase. Three armed Trolls were coming out of one of the other lifts. They looked at Rafik, and one of them said, "So this is the new one, eh, Narona? Guess congratulations are in order for the Keenans. Too bad about Doro, though."

Narona put a casual hand on Rafik's shoulder and nodded at the Troll, but said nothing. The Troll turned to Bayne instead. "Well, I hope your key works. I'm almost out of pills, and the stew in the chewing hall rusts my innards."

"He'll open the node, Hark, don't worry," Bayne answered, "but maybe you should not wager your N pills on bad cards, eh?"

The Troll laughed, and both groups walked together down

a few more corridors until they reached the node's entrance. It seemed to Rafik almost disappointingly small, maybe because it was dwarfed by the forty or more Trolls who stood around in small groups. When they noticed Rafik they parted a clear path all the way to the dark metal double doors. Rafik glanced around as they crossed the room, but he did not see Vincha. Ramm was standing by the door, together with another Keenan combat Troll named Maridas.

A large screen hovered near him from which the face of Brain could be seen, but Rafik's attention was drawn to the dark panel of the puzzle lock on the wall beside the double doors.

He heard Brain speak out, saying something about "*quotas . . . list . . . orderly fashion . . . ,*" but he paid no attention to it. Without being ordered to do so, Rafik's legs carried him towards the puzzle lock. He watched the three holes, one above and two below. Then, as if in a dream, he saw his own hand rise of its own accord and his fingers enter the awaiting holes. Blue lines of light connected the holes into a small triangle, and the shimmer flashed and blinded Rafik. The next moment he was inside the puzzle.

It was laughably easy. A pattern of six large symbols, slowly moving on a small, two-layered wall. When Rafik completed the puzzle there was a buzzing noise, and he found himself back in the room as the node's metal doors slid open. He heard a cheer and some applause, but felt oddly disappointed.

"Well done, Puzzler," said Brain, as Maridas and Bayne entered the node. "I wish you plenty more successes."

Rafik walked to the open double doors and peeked inside. It was a large space with many cabinets and closets, all with their doors wide open. He took another step, but Narona's hand grasped his shoulder.

"Puzzlers are never allowed into the nodes, or did they forget to teach your that at the guild house?" she admonished the boy. "If the node's doors close suddenly, we'll need the Puzzler to be out here." The Lieutenant pointed at the floor. "More than a few trolls tried to stay inside a node when the doors closed, you know, to find out how things work, or get a better pick at the loot, but there was always one result, those who stay inside the node die, and it is not a risk we want to take with a freshly bought Puzzler. Come, let us stand next to our crew commander."

As they negotiated their way towards Ramm, Rafik turned his attention back to Bayne and Maridas, who were coming out of the node carrying piles of wrapped cloth. They dumped them on the floor near Ramm and went back in, as the rest of the Trolls watched. A little later they came out carrying more items in two filled sacks and piled them neatly next to the wrapped cloth. There were nourishment pills, small metal hooks and wires, several metal cans Rafik did not recognise, two wrist timekeeping devices, and several goggles. Ramm was already engaged in negotiations with the crew leader of the Green Hand crew as well as an independent mercenary force.

As soon as Bayne and Maridas stepped out of the node for the second time Brain announced, "Next are the carriers of the Sabarra guild, three Trolls, three trips, one on the account of the Rode Dusters independent crew, as agreed upon." Three Sabarra trolls, including the young troll who faced Vincha at the Long Tube, entered the node. Brain continued his announcements. "Next after the Sabarra, the Metal Hunters, two trips. Third in line, East Tower guild, one trip . . ."

By the time the Sabarra emerged from the node, Ramm had exchanged half of the Keenan rations for two bags of Skint, some hard coin, and a promise of a keg of fermented cursed water. Rafik watched as, one by one, guild representatives emptied the node and proceeded to haggle among each other and with independent crew leaders until a sudden, short siren sounded, and a few heartbeats later the metal doors began to close. Two Trolls rushed out just in time.

"We are done," declared Brain. "Thank you all for this orderly and *peaceful* node harvesting. I congratulate the Hive on our new young Puzzler. The next harvesting will happen in a fortnight. Please remember to register all node agreements with me before we begin the harvest, to avoid any misunderstandings. *Brain's out.*"

The screen blinked into black and floated away to the far wall, where it attached itself.

After ordering Bayne and Maridas to carry back what was left of their node's take, Ramm, Narona, and Rafik joined many of the other Trolls and made their way back outside via the lifts. Many of them turned to congratulate Ramm on his promotion and the Puzzler's acquisition, although the Sabarra Trolls notably kept their distance. A few of the well-wishers expressed cautious interest in taking the boy on runs of their own, for a share of the take.

Ramm seemed pleased to hear this, but Narona intervened and said Rafik had to be initiated into the Keenan crew first before he could be rented out.

Ramm's jaw hardened at Narona's words, and Rafik thought he might hit the woman the way he disciplined Bayne, but the crew leader said nothing all the way back to Keenan headquarters.

It was located in the seven-story tower at the southwest corner of the Hive. Rafik was given a nourishment pill and ordered to retire to his room, a windowless small chamber on the fourth floor, containing nothing more than a thin mattress, several rough blankets, and a bucket of lukewarm water. The light that was constantly emanating from the walls was weak and gloomy, barely lighting the room during the day but enough to keep Rafik awake for many hours at night. Bayne had told Rafik the constant light was a problem in the entire building, which the Keenans had the unfortunate luck of drawing when the Hive was created. "You'll learn to sleep with it, or tie some cloth around your eyes," Bayne had said before he left the boy on his own.

Rafik splashed water on his face, undressed, and prayed. He was suddenly feeling tired and dirty, and longed for a bath, even the painfully cold ones he had to take in the barn in his village. Narona had promised to bring Rafik to the showers in the bunker, where she said hot water poured from the taps like in the City of Towers, but so far she had not fulfilled her promise, and Rafik did not dare ask her again.

Two Keenan Trolls passed Rafik's room as he recited his prayers to the Prophet Reborn.

"We'd better hurry." Rafik did not recognise the troll's voice. "Ramm's cutting the Skint. Don't want to be getting my share from the bottom of the bag, if you know what I mean."

"Forget the bottom of the bag," said the other as they stomped by Rafik's door. "If we're late Ramm will sniff both our shares for sure. His nostrils are as wide as his cannon's calibre."

The two laughed as they moved down the corridor.

Rafik lay down on the mattress and covered his body with the blankets. He curled into himself and closed his eyes, listening to the cricking noises the building made as it battled harsh winds outside. He was hoping that he could visit the wall of symbols in his dreams. Instead, the man with the melting face came to haunt Rafik yet again.

42

It had been more than a week and they were still stuck in the Hive. Brain changed the quota so the Keenans would have time to train with the new crew commander and the Puzzler, but aside from several visits to the shooting range, a fun ride around with Bayne on a Keenan Duster, and solving two puzzle boxes, there was nothing much to do. The rest of the day Rafik was confined to his chambers and almost went crazy with boredom. Gronn, the Keenans' CommTroll, set his channels so he could listen to some of the Hive's chatter, but after half a day of listening to crude jests and gossip Rafik decided he preferred silence. Bayne was avoiding Ramm as much as possible, and the rest of the Keenan crew seemed to feel uncomfortable around Rafik or simply were too busy cleaning their weapons, sniffing Skint, or noisily coupling with each other. Luckily, Ramm, in a rare moment where he was not staring into nothingness surrounded by green smoke, gave Rafik the permission to shower on his own, most likely just to piss off Narona and show her who was in charge.

On his way back from the shower, Rafik decided on a whim

to visit the Chewing Hole, the Hive's bar located on the second underground level, and see if Vincha might be there. He had overheard Maridas tell Bayne that the CommWoman was back from a long run to the edge of the Valley she had taken on the day they arrived at the Hive. Maridas also mentioned that he heard Vincha had coupled with every male member of that crew and that she hung around the Chewing Hole looking for more male company. This seemed to upset Bayne enough to trade insults with Maridas and walk away in a huff. Rafik did not know how he felt about Maridas's remark, but Vincha was kind and fun to be around, in a Dominique kind of way, and she was Commander Doro's girlfriend, which meant she must also be sad, and perhaps needed a friend.

The Chewing Hole reminded Rafik of Dominique's bar, although it was much darker, lit only by small portable lamps and a multitude of candles. Loud music was playing through a diminutive CommTroll who was standing on a small dais. Several other male Trolls were surrounding two female mercenaries in front of the bar. Everyone moved about in an odd fashion, swaying around and jerking their bodies to the rhythm of the music with their eyes closed.

Since Rafik had no desire to purchase anything, and no coin to his name even if he did, he moved cautiously around the Trolls and away from the bar. He moved further in, looking for Vincha. A mixture of several dozen wooden and metal tables and chairs were set up. The room was distinctly divided between the different crews and guilds. Rough jests and insults were periodically exchanged between tables, but they were mostly in good spirit. No one seemed to want to start a bar fight over guild politics.

Vincha was nowhere to be seen, and Rafik felt he was beginning to attract attention. He turned to leave but stopped when he spotted a rugged-looking man in a corner, sitting at a small table. The man had no visible augmentations, which made him a distinct minority in a room full of Combat Trolls. He was bent over, his face, which almost touched the table, was hidden behind a wall of thin, oily hair. The boy hesitated, but his feet took several tentative steps towards the odd man before he had time to consider whether this was a wise move. As he got closer Rafik heard the high-pitched squeak of metal scraping metal, which made his skin prickle.

Before he could say anything, a heavyset Troll got up on his feet from an adjacent table and moved to stand next to the man. The Troll leaned down and grasped the man's arm with his own metal gauntlet.

"If I have to tell you to stop that noise one more time, rust-brain," the Troll snarled above the loud music, "I will cut off your arm and make you eat it."

The man shrunk even further in his chair, saying nothing, his free arm covering his head as if he was afraid the Troll would slap him. Satisfied, the Troll released the man and walked back to his drink. As soon as he turned his back, the man snarled, exposing yellow and brown teeth. Rafik thought he would pounce on the Troll, but the man's rage was short-lived. He leaned back against the wall and sighed, closing his eyes.

Rafik stood by a stool at the opposite end of the table. The man still had his eyes shut tight under a furrowed brow. His clothes were black from dirt and dust, and he stank of unwashed sweat and urine. Rafik grimaced.

He uttered hesitantly, "Is this seat free?"—a phrase he'd overheard many times when working for Dominique.

The man opened his eyes slowly, looking at the boy without moving his head from the wall. His pupils were so small he almost seemed blind, like old Mama Gaudu back in the village.

The old man slowly straightened up. Without saying a word, he gestured with his head and watched Rafik take a seat on the other side of the table.

"I am—" Rafik hesitated "—new here."

The man blinked several times, then pointed at himself with a hand which, Rafik now noticed, was holding a rusty nail, and said, "Pikok."

The nail-holding hand travelled back down to the table and began to slowly move along the tracks he'd already carved. Rafik followed the motions of his hand. When he realised what he was seeing, he felt his heart leap up into his throat.

The entire surface of the table was filled with the symbols Rafik had seen in his dreams. He reached with a trembling hand to touch the symbols, but Pikok lunged forward, grasping Rafik's outstretched hand and pulling it close to his own face.

"Hey," Rafik yelped and instinctively closed his hand into a fist. "Stop that, let me go." With a strong yank Rafik pulled himself free, rising to his feet in the process, but what Pikok lacked in power he made up for in speed. As Rafik turned to flee he was already blocking his way. The thin man grasped Rafik's shoulder with his left hand and spread his right hand in front of the boy's face.

"Pi . . . *Pi* . . . Pikok," he stuttered excitedly. "*Pa* . . . *Pa* . . . Puzzler."

Rafik looked at the man's hand and the world swam around him. It was filled with markings all the way down to his wrists, but the symbols on Pikok's fingers mirrored his own.

43

"Where are we going?"

Pikok did not respond. From the moment he'd motioned Rafik to follow, Pikok had not answered any of the boy's questions. They traversed a maze of underground corridors. Whenever Rafik hesitated, the thin man would stop and gesticulate wildly for him to follow until the boy relented. Only under the glare of the Tarakan lights in the corridor did Rafik realise how unkempt and unnaturally thin Pikok was. He looked sick and malnourished, and his stride was hindered by a limp, but it was obvious he was just as excited to meet Rafik as the boy was to meet him. His movements were sharp and animated, and he would grunt or moan to himself every few steps. Soon they were far below ground. Rafik remembered he had forgotten his towel in the Chewing Hole, but it was too late to turn back.

The walls were not made of metal anymore but of stone, and there was so little of the dim artificial light that most of the time they were enveloped in darkness. Rafik followed Pikok with growing trepidation. There was something disturbing, even repulsive, about the man. He was afraid that at any moment

Ramm or Narona would come looking for him, but his Comm was quiet, and curiosity won over fear.

A narrow flight of stairs led them even farther down until they reached a puzzle-locked door. Without hesitation, Pikok shoved his fingers into the lock. He let out a soft sigh and his eyes glazed over. Master Goran never used the puzzle boxes, at least not in front of Rafik, so it was the first time Rafik saw what he must look like when he was in a puzzle. He waved a hand in front of Pikok's face but there was no reaction.

The door suddenly buzzed and parted open as Pikok let out a gasp and tried to steady himself with a hand against the wall. He lost his balance, flailing his arms wildly. Rafik caught the man just before he toppled to the ground and almost gagged at the stench emanating from him. Pikok's arm was so thin it felt as if Rafik could break it like a twig. With this, any fear of what the man could do to him dissipated. Pikok regained his composure, smiled at Rafik—exposing a row of rotting teeth—and pointed at the lock.

"*Ha . . . ha . . .* hard," he stuttered, but there was obvious pride in his demeanour.

Suddenly, Rafik felt something brush past him. He jumped and turned, letting out a yelp of surprise and fear, but saw nothing. Confused, he tried to convey what he felt to Pikok, but the man pushed him excitedly through the door as it began to close.

The place was large and completely dark; the only source of light was the soft illumination from the corridor they'd just come from. Pikok moved to a small hole in the wall and busied himself with some wires. Just as the doors closed behind them, a weak light emanated from above, and Pikok let out a soft snigger of triumph and clapped his hands several times.

"Come . . ." He gestured to Rafik. "*Sss* seeeee."

The place turned out to be a large underground hall supported by many columns, casting dark shadows everywhere. Pikok ran excitedly forward. Rafik tried to keep up, but the man seemed to forget his limp as he darted into the shadows and disappeared behind the columns. Rafik found himself suddenly alone. Fighting panic, he slowed—which was lucky, because he almost walked into a wall. Rafik's hand touched the wall, which felt cracked and uneven under his fingertips.

"Hello?" he said, "Pikok?"

When there was no answer Rafik began moving along the wall, but he stopped abruptly as he realised that his fingers were not touching natural cracks in the wall. He leaned closer, squinted, and when his eyes adjusted to the gloom his jaw dropped in surprise.

The entire wall, all the way up to the ceiling, was covered in symbols. It was a puzzle, hundreds of lines long and wide. There were even a second and third layer carved in. Rafik took a step back and saw there were carvings all over the floor as well as on the columns.

A soft scratching noise reached his ears from his left and Rafik walked cautiously towards it until he saw a ladder leaning on the wall. Pikok was at the top of the ladder. He was holding a small portable lamp in one hand and carving energetically with the other.

"Pikok."

The man turned his head, tongue lolling out from his mouth like a dog.

"What is this?" Rafik gestured around him.

A look of genuine puzzlement crossed the man's face.

"That is *pa . . . pa . . .* puzzle," he stuttered, shrugging his shoulders at the obvious.

"No, I mean—" Rafik hesitated "—where have you seen all of these? It looks like the wall of symbols I dream about, but the symbols . . . how do you . . ."

Pikok scratched his head. "I see them. I remember them."

"What, all of them?"

Pikok nodded. "*D . . .* don't *y . . .* you?" He seemed genuinely surprised.

Rafik shook his head.

Pikok climbed down, "It's the *Gr . . . Gr . . .* Great Puzzle, we all *s . . .* see . . ."

Without waiting for Rafik to reply, Pikok grabbed Rafik's arm, pulling the boy after him. They half-ran away from the columns until they reached another wall, which was filled with the tiniest of carvings. Rafik tried but failed to spot the borders of this giant puzzle. In fact, it did not seem like a puzzle at all; its columns were not straight, and the symbols did not make sense to Rafik.

"I don't understand this."

Pikok pointed at a symbol. "This," he spat, and pointed at another. "And . . . *th* . . . this, *to* . . . together, and *this an an* . . . and this." He pointed at another pair and continued showing Rafik something the boy understood only from instinct, not logic.

"Wait, but what is it?" he said loudly enough to echo.

Pikok stopped pointing and turned around.

"Is it a puzzle?" Rafik asked. "Because I can't see it, I can't see it at all."

Pikok waved his tattooed fingers. "It is us," he mumbled, this time without a stutter.

Rafik looked at the wall again. "I still don't understand. You mean it is what we are meant to do?"

"No, it is who we are," said the man impatiently, as if explaining the obvious. "It is *P* . . . Puzzler. It is Pikok. It is Raf—"

There was a crunching sound from the darkness, and a small stone landed at their feet. Pikok moved instantaneously. He grabbed the boy and they dashed into the darkness, crouching behind one of the columns.

A taunting male voice echoed across the hall.

"Pi-pi-pi-peeee-kok."

Pikok now covered his head with his arms and whimpered.

"You know you can't hide from me. I always find you."

Pikok shook his head violently, as if strongly disagreeing with something, and then they were on their feet again, running.

They didn't make it far. As if from thin air, a slender man

appeared and grabbed Pikok by the collar, almost lifting him off the ground. The man was dressed in black, or so Rafik initially thought, but on closer examination the man proved to be almost naked. As Rafik watched, the man's body changed colour. He held the struggling Pikok with ease.

"Now, now, Pikok," he intoned mockingly, "again you force me to find you down here, you know how I hate running after you like that."

Pikok stopped struggling. "Hello, *Ca Ca* . . . Chameleon." He smiled nervously.

"That's better, Pikok, and who is your friend?" The man released him. "Oh, look who we have here—it's the Keenans' new key, the young Puzzler."

Chameleon's eyes fixed upon Rafik with a stare that made the boy uncomfortable. "I think you are not supposed to run around all by yourself. I bet your new crew commander would be angry if he knew you were running around in the dark corners of the Hive." Chameleon pointed at himself. "Me? I'm from the Loot Worshippers crew, and have nothing against the Keenans, Doro was a decent Troll, but a Sabarra would have thrown you over the Hive's wall in a heartbeat, just for the fun of it."

Rafik didn't know what to say, but the strange man was right. He suddenly realised he could be in serious trouble.

"Well, boy, what is your name?"

"Rafik."

"Right, Rafik. I hope you're saner than this rusting key." He pointed at Pikok. "Too bad the Keenans bought you; we could have used another one with the amount of runs we're doing now. My friends call me Cham, by the way." He extended his hand and Rafik shook it gingerly, watching the man's arm change colour as they touched.

"It was you who passed by me at the door."

Chameleon smiled briefly, then remembered what he came for and turned to Pikok. "Come on, it's almost time. I knew you'd forget about our scheduled deep run."

Upon hearing this, Pikok began to shake and a long wail escaped his lips.

"Shut up," Chameleon ordered briskly, his demeanour changing as fast as his skin colour. "Shut up or I'll tie you up like last time."

The threat seemed to work and Pikok quieted down, although he was still shaking when Chameleon led them to the door.

"Why is he so afraid?" Rafik asked.

Chameleon let out a short laugh. "He's just crazy, is all, and we ain't taking this rust fuck for a deep run. I was just messing with his wires. My commander wants to see him." He pointed at the older Puzzler. "This guy loves the Lizards too much." He turned to the Puzzler and mocked him. "Don't you, Piiikok, gets up-up-upset when we shoo-shoo-shoot them."

"They are not *Ll Li* . . . Lizards," despite his fear, a flash of anger crossed Pikok's face.

"Of course they're Lizards—and that's why we shoot them." Chameleon answered slowly and softly, as if speaking to a child. "And they'll chew your rusting, ugly face off."

"You should not *sh sh* . . . shoot them. Lizards *da da* don't *hu* hurt *Pa* Puzzlers."

The three reached the locked doors, and Chameleon turned impatiently to Pikok. "I tell you what, Pikok, the next time I see a Lizard charging you, I won't shoot, and you can take your time talking to them, how about that, eh? Now open the door."

Pikok turned his head, following Chameleon's pointed finger. Then he straightened up a bit and said, "No."

"What do you mean, no?"

"No, I am not going to *o o*"—Pikok took a steadying breath—". . . open door."

In one swift motion Chameleon grabbed Pikok's collar again and brought him closer to his face. "I don't have time for this, shithead, open the rusting lock," he barked.

"No." Pikok shook his head and was immediately slapped.

The blow threw him to the floor, where he rolled twice before slowly getting up, blood on his lips.

Chameleon grabbed him again. "I am not laughing with you now, key, open the door."

Pikok shook his head and flinched as Chameleon raised his hand, this time as a tight fist, but before another slap landed Rafik shouted, "Stop it!'

The angry Salvationist hesitated.

"Don't hit him," pleaded Rafik, tears in his eyes.

"I'll stop hitting him when he opens the rusting door, like he's supposed to. Pikok here just needs a little motivation sometimes." A calculating look flashed in Chameleon's eyes. "But if you care so much, why don't you open it for him? You're a Puzzler."

"No," breathed Pikok, blood streaming from his mouth. "I'll *d d* do it. Too hard."

Chameleon was already advancing on Rafik, who moved back until he flattened himself against the wall. He looked up at Chameleon. "I don't want to."

"I ain't caring about your wants, puzzle boy," intoned Chameleon. "One way or another we are walking out that door, and I need him"—he pointed his thumb at Pikok—"but I don't need you. So how about you put your nice little hand in there and show me what you've got?"

A few heartbeats later Rafik shoved his fingers into the puzzle box.

It was like nothing he'd ever experienced before. Normally he would find himself hovering above a puzzle, but this time he found himself inside a puzzle, surrounded on all sides by walls made of shifting symbols. He tried to move, but as soon as he touched a wall a painful jolt shot through his body, and he was thrown back to the centre of the puzzle. This was what Master Goran had warned him about. This was the kind of puzzle that could harm you, or even kill you. Fighting to suppress panic, he tried to solve one side. But as soon as he held a pattern in his mind and turned to solve another side, the previous wall would reset itself.

There was a sudden, painful jolt in his arm that made him cry out in pain. He heard voices whispering from afar.

"*Ca ca* can't, he's *sss* stuck."

"You do something, or I will hack his hand off, I swear."

There was a pause, and Rafik heard Pikok's voice whispering to him from afar.

"Find pair, not full pattern. Blue, three circles, red, five stars." Pikok didn't stutter.

Rafik looked around at the symbols moving around him. There were hundreds, perhaps thousands of them. He looked from side to side.

"Slowly," Pikok warned.

Another jolt of pain made him cry out.

"Slowly. Breathe."

From the corner of his eye Rafik suddenly saw it. Circles, stars . . . as soon as he held the pair, the puzzle slowed a bit. He could now easily keep the pairs stable with minimum effort. Pikok whispered a few more pairs. "Yellow star, five snakes, three buckets," and with each success things got easier. The descriptions were odd and confusing at first; the symbols were not exactly as Pikok described them. There were definitely no snakes, but Rafik guessed that a few wavy lines could have been seen as snakes and was soon rewarded with success. After that it was only a matter of figuring out what symbol Pikok thought of as "monster," "gun," "chair," or "trolls kissing."

Rafik heard the buzz of the doors sliding open just before he was hurtled back into the world. It was now his turn to try and keep his balance.

"About rusting time." Chameleon strode out, dragging Pikok after him.

Rafik stumbled after them, legs shaking. He watched the two ascend the stairs but was too weak to follow. He sat down on the floor as the doors began to close and leaned back against the cold wall. Pikok shot him one last desperate look before disappearing upstairs, and then he was alone.

44

Rafik grasped his gun with both hands, nervously peering from behind the shoulder of the Troll who took point. The oppressive heat was not the only cause of the sweat pouring down his brow. Compared to the arsenal of weapons surrounding him, Rafik's pistol was puny, and his improvised power armour barely fit. He felt reassured by the three Trolls who covered him from all sides, but he didn't know if their current alert level was due to an imminent Lizard attack or Ramm's threat of punishment should anything happen to him.

He leaned against a wall and found it surprisingly cool, but the shadows offered only momentary comfort. The three armour-plated dusters that brought them to the node were already manoeuvring to allow for a quick withdrawal. This was their third outing in so many weeks, and so far they had not encountered any Lizards, yet it was a rare day when the patrolling crews did not stumble on a nest of them. In a way, it made everybody even more nervous.

Rafik had seen the carcasses when the crews came back from patrol, whooping and cheering. Some would carry heads back as proof for payment, but the bodies were worth coin, too. The creatures were usually smaller than a fully grown human, with long snouts and sharp teeth and claws. Their blood was a thick, dripping green gunk that stank like nothing Rafik had smelled before. It was gathered and stored in heated buckets so it would not congeal prematurely before they could process it into the green powder.

Even dead, the Lizards looked dangerous. Despite Pikok's claim that the lizards would not harm a Puzzler, Rafik did not savor the thought of being attacked by these creatures.

He peered around again, but everything was calm. This was their second stop. They'd hit a bunker midmorning. It was unplanned, but no one challenged Ramm's orders, not even Bayne.

The Keenan crew was edgy, but morale was high. Before Rafik was sent to the base, the Keenans had been effectively nothing more than a well-equipped independent crew, working on rotation for a relatively small amount of coin or setting up for other guilds' deep runs, but things were looking up now. Their last two runs were successful. The puzzle locks were simple enough, and they encountered no Lizards. This time, though, the risk was higher; they were much farther away from the base, at least an hour's ride east, and a spell of sandstorms had kept the crews at base for most of the week. Still, Ramm must have thought it worth the risk.

The commander was combat ready and restless, at least as far as Rafik could tell; the dark visor he wore covered the last remaining bits of flesh he had exposed. His movements were a bit jerky, though, and he snapped orders, a sure sign of Skint withdrawal. Rafik caught Bayne sending Narona a meaningful stare, but she simply shrugged and turned away. A little later Ramm ordered Bayne to clear the way to the node.

Rafik heard Bayne's voice on the Comm: "Place is clear to the third floor."

"Good, keep going up another five floors, just to make sure," Ramm barked through the Comm. "Narona, Puzzle Boy, and I are going in. Fravik, secure the area outside the building. I want you to shallow mine the southwest perimeter."

Fravik, a squat but vicious combat Troll, who carried a heavy machine gun on a waist brace, nodded and began issuing orders on a subchannel.

Ramm turned and motioned the crew to follow him. He hefted his arm cannon and began slowly crossing the street. Rafik and three Trolls got up and followed him. Narona joined them in the middle of the street.

"Report coming in that there's a sandstorm five miles to the west," she briefed in a careful, even tone, not giving any sign that she disagreed with Ramm's decision to make this unscheduled stop.

Ramm unscrewed a small metal disk from his belt. "Then we better hurry," he said and flung the disk high in the air, where it hovered above them. "This will let us know if we have company," he said.

"Wasn't that Commander Doro's radar?" one of the Trolls blurted out and quickly regretted it.

Ramm turned around and aimed the cannon straight at his face. "I don't think Doro needs it where he is right now," he spat. "Want to go ask him?"

Narona was the only one who had any influence on Ramm. She laid a hand on his arm. "Let's get the loot," she said, and somehow it worked. Ramm lowered his weapon, and they walked to the main doors of the tall building. Ramm ordered the three Trolls to stand guard outside while he, Narona, and Rafik went inside.

From far away the buildings looked intact, but up close the place was a mess of soot, stone, and twisted metal. Exposed wiring was all over the floor, like giant snakes in some children's tale. Ramm moved with confidence, kicking aside or stepping on whatever was in his way.

The stairs were wide but filled with debris, and they moved in complete darkness. Narona replaced her sniper rifle with a short ray gun and held a light torch with her other hand. From there on it was a slow climb, Ramm taking point and Narona guarding their rear. They reached a landing on the sixth floor that was partly blocked by the collapse of two massive double doors. Rafik could have easily squeezed through, but there was not enough space for Ramm. From an angle, Rafik could see the commander smirk as he pointed his gun at the doors and squeezed the trigger. In less than two heartbeats the doors became nothing more than twisted metal on the floor. Ramm bellowed out a laugh and changed the power tube on his weapon.

They continued to move through the corridor. Only the sound of their footsteps echoed back at them. They reached a large room; in its centre was a large rectangular wall made of shining Tarakan metal. A blast from Ramm's cannon proved it was the real deal.

"Good," muttered Ramm. "There must be something expensive behind it."

Narona looked around suspiciously but holstered her gun. "How did you know about this place? It's not on the charts."

"Oh, a little blip in the grid told me," Ramm said, obviously pleased with himself.

Narona shrugged, "Let's open it, then. We're running out of light."

Ramm pointed at the puzzle lock, which was part of the metal wall and positioned at adult height. Yet when Rafik pointed his fingers towards the three holes, the lock slid down to his shoulder level and caused the three of them to jump back in surprise.

"Rust. I haven't seen that before," Ramm said. "Did you see that? It moved inside the rusting wall."

Narona got up from the far corner, where she'd rolled to when the lock moved, but this time she did not holster her gun. She fixed the door with a wary stare. "I don't like this, Ramm. This is no bunker."

Ramm didn't answer. Instead, he beckoned Rafik forward. "Do it, boy," he said.

Rafik raised his hand obediently, yet he hesitated just before inserting his fingers into the lock.

"What's the matter, key?" Ramm barked impatiently.

There was something menacing about the gaping holes. "My head hurts," he said, "and I'm tired." It was true. Rafik's head throbbed, and although the previous bunker's puzzle lock was not very complex, it had left him fatigued. The fact that almost every night he woke up screaming from his nightmare didn't help his condition, either. He learned that two Trolls moved to a different floor, accepting smaller rooms, just so they could keep their distance from him.

"I don't give a bucket of screws how you feel, key. Open this rust box and don't let me tell you again," Ramm said.

Blinking away tears, Rafik shoved his fingers into the box. The transition was never pleasant, but this time it was extremely uncomfortable. Rafik felt himself sucked into the puzzle, but instead of floating above rows of symbols he found himself in a cage puzzle, like the one he'd experienced with Pikok. The symbols whirled around him at incredible speed. Rafik turned in his place several times, feeling his panic level rise. He could not make sense of the puzzle.

Then the walls suddenly moved an inch inwards, closing in on him. Reflexively he touched one side, only to be rewarded with a painful jolt that made him double over and almost faint with pain.

His mind went numb with fear. He heard Narona shouting something from far away, but he could not decipher her words. The walls moved closer again. They were just over an arm's length away from him now. Rafik used a breathing technique he'd learned from Master Goran to calm his nerves.

He heard his mentor's voice: *Remember, fear will kill you. Succumb to it, and you have no chance of surviving.*

As his breathing slowed Rafik looked around, hoping that the first few patterns he found would slow things down and give him enough time to find the more elusive threads. Another wave of fear washed over him as the walls advanced still further inwards. Now there was less than an arm's length of space around his body. Then he heard Pikok's wispy voice: *Th-th-this one, b-b-blue dots with yellow r-r-ribbons. It is obvious.*

It was not obvious at all to Rafik. Pikok would be astonished that Rafik could not see what he would have found plainly obvious. In Goran's lab Rafik had learned to memorize many patterns, but there was a huge difference between memorizing a series of symbols and actually finding a pattern under stressful circumstances. Rafik suspected that Pikok didn't need to memorize the symbols like he did.

Rafik was still looking around when he noticed a familiar symbol whiz by above his head. He stopped it in its place, and then saw another one crossing to his left. He held on to that one, too. A few heartbeats later he was holding several strains of symbols around himself, but the walls still didn't halt their progress. They were now just a hair's breadth away from his body, and he frantically grasped for more strands of patterns. Then the walls closed in on him.

Rafik screamed. His body jolted full of energy as the symbols poured into him. For a fraction of a second he saw himself hovering over his own body as symbols entered inside all his orifices. Just as the darkness took him, Rafik suddenly understood.

45

There was darkness, and then there was light, followed by pain that made him writhe in agony. Symbols floated around him in a slow spiral, crawling up his body like thin snakes. The patterns swivelled into one long strain, then multiplied several times and became an arm, a leg, a torso, a face, a body, all made of tiny moving symbols. He understood them all, and then there was no more pain. A face made of symbols leaned down and opened its mouth and words came out not as sounds but as patterns. They formed a word: *Rafik*.

The face became flesh, and Rafik saw the melted face that haunted his dreams.

"Rafik," it moaned again, then turned into a female voice. "I think he's coming around."

The face became two faces: Narona and Bayne.

Bayne helped Rafik sit up. "Are you all right?" he asked.

Rafik opened his mouth to answer but he couldn't find his voice. He shook his head.

Bayne helped him to his feet while he heard Narona admonishing Ramm.

"You almost killed him. The only Puzzler we've got."

"But I didn't. He unlocked the damn door, like he's supposed to. Otherwise, what's the point of owning a rusting Puzzler, anyway?"

Rafik turned his head. The world broke into patterns and symbols, and then it came back together and he saw Ramm holding a metal object in his hand. His metal visor was up, and he was scrutinizing the object with a smug expression. "An energy ball! Sweet metal, that baby is going to get us enough dough to recalibrate and still have some left over for a party."

Narona shook her head. "I still think it wasn't worth the risk. We could have lost him."

"You're not commanding this operation, so don't meddle in my business," Ramm snapped.

Narona was about to speak when they heard over the Comm, "Lizards three clicks north, moving in." And, after a pause, "Rust, there are a lot of them."

They moved to the transparent wall and peered down. It was calm and quiet, but the Keenan Trolls were moving into combat positions.

Rafik knew that Ramm, Narona, and Bayne were wired to several sensors. Commander Doro had spent a lot of coin to equip his crew well. They could see the enemy advancing as red dots on the insides of their visors, which showed friendly combatants as blue. But Rafik wasn't wired. He couldn't see what was going on, which made him feel helpless and frightened.

"Rusting metal, it's a whole hive," whispered Bayne.

Ramm began barking orders into the Comm, and Rafik saw their vehicles manoeuvring quickly to block the street.

"Here they come!" Rafik heard someone shout over the Comm, and everyone opened fire at once. At first he couldn't see anything but blinding light crisscrossing the wide road. Then he saw three Lizards in the middle of the street get ripped to shreds in a green cloud of vaporised blood.

"Let's go!" Bayne shouted and propelled Rafik forward. "We need to get out of here."

Narona took point this time while Ramm followed behind, still bellowing commands into the Comm. They didn't go back the way they came, and at some point they had to cross to the other side of the floor due to collapsed stairs. It was at that moment that all three warriors saw in their visors what was being shouted over the Comm.

"They're splitting up! Some are heading to the northeast part of the building."

"What is that rust?" shouted Ramm, as he stopped near a glass wall that was facing the northeast. Four Lizards were climbing the surface from the outside, their claws visibly sticking to the surface. It was the first time Rafik saw one up close, and terror gripped his body. Despite their deformed faces, claws, and green skin, the Lizards looked almost human, and not only in size. One of the Lizards stopped climbing and eyed them with unnerving cunningness. It bared its razor-sharp teeth in a silent snarl, detached one of its claws from the surface, and punched the transparent wall several times.

Ramm reacted first by shooting his power gun, but the energy dissipated into the transparent wall with no effect. "Fuck this," he swore, and aimed his cannon at the wall.

But Narona managed to yank him away before he pulled the trigger, shouting, "Don't give them an opening to get in."

The Lizards continued their climb upwards. Other Lizards followed, many others, and when Bayne clamped a hand on Rafik's shoulder, the boy was trembling with fear. There was no time for comfort, they had to run. By the time they reached the stairwell, they heard their CommTroll screaming, "They've breached the perimeter! They're everywhere!"

There were shrieks of pain, and noises of hand-to-hand combat.

"What? How?" Ramm kept shouting.

Someone else answered over the Comm: "They came from underground. Tunnels. Must have been a large nest." They heard several more explosions over the Comm as mines went off. The building shook.

Bayne and Narona exchanged looks of disbelief as Ramm ordered the crew to retreat.

Suddenly there was a terrible scream and the Comm went quiet. For a brief moment they stood still, then Ramm turned to Bayne. "Get him out of here. You know where to go once you do." His voice was calm, resigned.

Bayne nodded and looked up. They could now hear hissing sounds from above.

"We'll stall them here," Ramm said, "then we'll come to you."

Bayne literally picked Rafik up and ran down the stairs. Three Lizards were already descending, and Rafik was stunned by their speed. Their jaws and talons looked lethal. Only Ramm's firepower stopped the Lizards from reaching them. Green blood and red flesh sprayed their path, and Bayne almost lost his footing. Then they split up. Ramm and Narona took position and fired at the next floor while Bayne, holding Rafik by one hand and a gun in the other, raced down the stairs.

Rafik lost count of how many flights of stairs they ran down, but suddenly they were confronted by several Lizards that must have come from below. Bayne dropped Rafik's hand and drew another pistol as he fired the other one. Rafik rolled, smashing his left elbow on a stair, but then he was up on his feet with his own gun in his hand, and he began firing at the charging Lizards, too. It was barely enough, but the two of them managed to kill them all.

From below, they heard the hissing and scratching of more Lizards coming. Bayne swore, sweat pouring down his face. He pushed Rafik roughly aside, tore off two power grenades from his belt, and threw them down the stairs, then turned and slapped a slab of explosives onto the wall, ignoring the carnage that his grenades were causing down below. Bits of green skin and flesh sprayed up, painting the walls red and green, as Bayne grabbed Rafik and backed away behind a corner.

He pushed Rafik to the floor and lay on top of him, covering the boy's ears with his power gloves. A blast shook the building a few heartbeats later. When they rose and peeked around the corner, there was a huge gaping hole in the wall of the building. Bayne didn't hesitate. He fiddled with the buttons of his power armour, picked Rafik up and put his arms around him, then dashed forward and took a flying leap through the hole.

The air blew away Rafik's scream as the ground rushed towards them. Bayne turned in the air so his body would cushion Rafik. They tore through the roof of a building below.

Rafik must have lost consciousness, because he certainly didn't remember them falling through another floor before hitting the ground. When he woke, his entire body was in pain. He coughed and moaned as a sharp pain in his ribs signalled that something was definitely broken. Three attempts later, he managed to get up and look around.

They were on the ground floor of a three-story building. Bayne was lying in a shallow crater a few yards from where Rafik stood. He was still. A pool of blood was slowly forming under him. Rafik shuffled towards Bayne. He could see the man's jaw and nose were broken. There was a lot of blood, but he could hear shallow breathing.

Rafik tried but failed to turn Bayne over. He looked around for something to help, but as he did he suddenly saw patterns again, everywhere: colours and lights, shapes, particles of dust hanging in the air, and bullet-hole-shaped craters in the far wall. Fear and pain and desperation disappeared. All that mattered was the beauty of the shapes around him and how they fit together. Was this what Pikok saw?

A sharp, acidic smell forced Rafik back to reality.

The patterns disappeared and the room changed back. Instead of flowing symbols, Rafik saw a Lizard. It stepped into the room from an open doorway and immediately focused its attention on him. Rafik's hand darted to his holster, but it was empty. He saw Bayne's gun not far away from where he stood. As his body rushed forward he somehow knew it would take him nine steps to reach the gun; he would have to bend down, pick it up, release the safety catch, aim and fire, and pray to the Prophet Reborn that the gun hadn't broken from the impact of the fall. The Lizard began moving as well, running directly at Rafik.

By the time Rafik turned and raised the gun, it was too late. His body was picked up and slammed to the floor, the gun torn from his hand. As he hit the ground, Rafik knew he was about to die. He felt the Lizard's weight on him. His eyes were shut, but he knew the Lizard held him down with one muscular limb while its claw was on its way down in a powerful slash that would tear his face apart. Rafik's arm flew up, instinctively protecting his head. The blow should have torn through his puny limb and smashed his skull, but it never landed. Rafik opened his eyes.

He was still pinned under the weight of the Lizard, but instead of tearing Rafik apart it was looking down at the boy's spread hand. Rafik saw the creature's bright green pupils focusing on his spread fingers.

The first shot slammed into the Lizard's midsection, propelling the creature sideways. Hot green gunk sprayed Rafik's upper body. The second shot hit the Lizard's shoulder. Rafik turned his head and saw Bayne half raised on the ground and holding his second gun. Bayne pressed the trigger again just as the Lizard charged towards the warrior, but the gun jammed. The third shot came from a different direction and blew the Lizard's head off. For a moment all Rafik could do was gasp for air and cover his ears.

Narona lowered her sniper rifle and stepped into the room. In a heartbeat she was next to Rafik, checking him for damage. The other Keenans came in behind her. Bayne collapsed on the ground. Rafik suddenly felt sapped of strength, and he lay down on the cool floor. Moments later he was picked up by a Keenan Troll. Soon after, everything went black.

46

t-t-told you they wouldn't *hu-hu*-hurt you," Pikok's eyes shone with pride.

Rafik shook his head. "I don't know. It happened so fast, I'm not sure . . ."

"Lizards don't hurt Puzzlers," the thin man said, rubbing his hands in a show of satisfaction. His speech seemed to be getting better every time he spoke to Rafik.

"So why are they hurting everyone else?"

"Lizards don't hurt Puzzlers," Pikok repeated, as if that explained everything. Then he bent down and resumed scratching a symbol into the wall.

Pikok visited every day when Rafik was at the Menders, but he refused to teach him any new puzzles or techniques. The day Rafik was carried into the Hive, Pikok took one look at the boy's haggard face and clapped his hands in joy, even as the torn bodies of several Lizards were lowered from the two remaining vehicles.

"You are Puzzler now," he shouted at Rafik several times, before being shooed away by the Keenans.

"You do not need Pikok," he said when they met again, a few days later.

"Of course I need you. That puzzle—" Rafik shuddered "—it did something to me. I thought I was going to die."

"But you didn't," Pikok concluded matter-of-factly, "and now you are a real Puzzler."

"Are the puzzle locks of the City within the Mountain as dangerous?" Rafik asked.

But Pikok's answers never satisfied Rafik's curiosity. "Some harder, some easier. You are a Puzzler now," was the best he got from the man.

Pikok was a Sabarra purchase, the oldest Puzzler at the outpost. He'd lived in the Hive for almost ten years. He was barely able to take care of himself and was considered insane. Rafik heard that the old Sabarra crew commander kept him caged for two years, hauling him from node to node, and when a second Puzzler was purchased by the guild they let Pikok go. They didn't use him for their deep runs anymore, and they even stopped hiring him out to independent crews, partly because he tended to run straight at any Lizard they encountered, waving his hands in the air and shouting, "Take me! Take me!"

The only job still fit for Pikok was opening the Hive's main node and an occasional puzzle box that crews brought back as loot. The other Puzzlers, three men and a woman, were usually on a run or recuperating. For reasons Rafik could not understand, the other Puzzlers kept their distance from him, so Pikok was the only person he could talk to, that is, on the rare occasion when the older Puzzler was not scratching symbols onto darkened walls.

One day, after spending time in the underground hall with Pikok, and frustrated by the man's lack of response, Rafik found his way through the columns back to the door and solved the puzzle lock to let himself out. It was much easier now, and he took a little pride in admitting that to himself.

Rafik began climbing back the long way to the surface. He was walking slowly and stopping every so often to rest. Since they'd gotten back, he'd been feeling gloomy. His days were full of dark thoughts. He spent half his nights awake, reliving the violence. When he finally succumbed to sleep he would find himself in front of the Great Puzzle, which quickly turned into a prison. No matter what he did, he could not stop the walls from closing in on him, and just as he was about to die, he would find himself in front of the man with the melted face. That was the moment Rafik would bolt up in his cot with a startled cry.

The day after the Keenans came back, Lizards attacked the Hive. And these attacks had continued almost every day since. Usually killing Lizards was an easy enough matter, especially for veteran Trolls in fortified positions and possessing superior fire power, yet the ferocity of the attacks, the unusual number of Lizards, and the fact that they attacked from a different direction each time took its toll both in casualties and morale. Six Trolls had died in combat, with several dozen wounded. A whole crew of newbies who went out on a Lizard popping mission shortly after the first attack didn't return. The Lizard casualties were in the hundreds; their bodies littered the outside perimeter of the Hive. Trolls joked that at least there would be no shortage of Skint in the near future, but tensions ran high.

The Keenans had lost Gronn, the crew's CommTroll, and Irdina, with three more crew members wounded. Two Keenans came to blows one morning over a power clip, and only Narona's calming effect stopped Ramm from shooting them both.

Bayne was still on the mend. Rafik lay on a cot next to him as they applied Tarakan salves and used healing artifacts on Rafik's cracked rib cage. Ramm made sure they treated Rafik first, and paid in hard coin for it, but Bayne's injuries were far worse. Despite the fact that the place stank of freshly brewed Skint, Rafik made a point of visiting Bayne every day, but he was either asleep or in a foul mood. One morning he heard

Vincha's voice and stayed back, eavesdropping from behind a corner.

From the conversation he learned that Ramm's report was very different from what actually occurred.

"That piece of molded metal." Bayne's voice was full of bile. "He actually blamed Irdina and Gronn for not detecting the Lizards. Since they're both conveniently dead, there's no one to challenge his account."

"No one except you." Vincha lowered her voice. "But Trolls are talking. That's how I heard what happened."

Bayne shook his head. "That idiot is going to get us all killed. Half the time he's out of his mind on Skint—and that's when he's at his best, believe me."

"Still, you shouldn't have confronted him like that when he came to see you." Vincha glanced around, but somehow missed Rafik lurking in the shadows. "He could have killed you. He's probably going to try to do just that at some point."

Bayne sighed. "I know, I know. When he accused me of faking injury to get out of the crew's housekeeping duties I lost my temper. It was a dumb move."

"Not as dumb as jumping with the kid from the fifth floor. Rust, Bayne," she chuckled, "Trolls are going to drink to this one for a long time. Not to mention the newbies who will try to imitate this move, I hear they already have a name for it—the Bayne."

"I was low on ammo, and they were coming." From where he was hiding, Rafik could see Bayne shaking his head slowly, his hand touching his mending jaw. Still, he had a small smile on his face. "You should have seen him, Vincha. Frightened like a field bunny, but still functioning. He reminded me of my little brother, Kane, when we were kids . . . anyways, I knew Narona would come and get us. What? Don't look at me like that. I know she can be a bitch, but she is rock solid in a fight. She would be a good crew commander . . ." Bayne took a deep breath and sighed. "It doesn't matter. If Ramm keeps going on like that we are all going to be Lizard chowder." He hesitated briefly and looked up at Vincha. "This whole shit storm made me think . . ."

"About what?"

"About cashing it in. Buying my contract back. I'm leaving the crew soon. As soon as I'm on my feet."

Vincha snorted. "You still have sixteen months to plan your retirement."

"Maybe I want to cash it in before."

"You don't have the coin, especially with what you had to pay the Menders."

"What if I don't cash out? What if I just leave?"

"What, go rogue? Rust, Bayne, no other outfit will employ a contract breaker, and even as an independent, Ramm won't let you stay here in the outpost. He is more cunning than you think. I still don't understand how he got Doro in such an exposed position—" Vincha stopped talking.

"We could find someone else . . ."

Vincha looked around nervously and Rafik ducked behind the wall. For a moment he was sure she'd seen him, but she continued to talk to Bayne in a hushed voice. "I know you're upset about what happened, but I don't see any other option but to mend your metal and wait."

When Rafik peeked again he saw Bayne take the Comm-Woman's hand.

"Vincha, this injury, not my first and probably not my last, made me think real good about things. I know I'm not . . . Doro . . . I know, but . . ." He hesitated only a little before saying, "He's gone, and I'm here now, and I have a plan, and I need you to trust me. It's something that would take me out of Ramm's sight and give you another option, too."

Vincha didn't pull her hand free, but she took a deep breath and shook her head. "I still don't see your other option."

"Nakamura," Bayne said in a hushed tone. This time she did pull back, but Bayne leaned forward and persisted, "Listen to me. He's more than just a rumour. This guy exists. I've been gathering information about him. There are dozens of reports of sightings by veteran crews, especially southwest, beyond the bridge."

"You tore out your wires in that fall, Bayne."

"Three years in the wild, without walls, guards, or protection, and no one from the Hive manages to get close to the guy. Then there was that crew, the Slashers, remember them? They just vanished . . . on the southwest—"

"Lizards, most likely, Bayne—"

"Vanished without a trace, Vincha. No distress call, no bodies, no tech remains, nothing. I am telling you, this Nakamura has been leading a crew for three years, and he's outsmarting two hundred armed Trolls and who knows how many Lizards."

Vincha kept shaking her head. "First of all," she said, counting on her fingers, "we are being attacked almost every day now, and who knows how many thousands of Lizards are out there? Second, even if we survive the trip to the southwest, how are we going to find this guy and stop him from shooting us on sight?"

"I'm sure Nakamura would love two extra pairs of capable hands, especially if we bring him a present."

"What kind of . . . You're not rusting serious."

"Why not? Is it better to leave the boy here to be killed by that Skinhead? Listen to me, I have it all figured out." Bayne reached into his pocket and brought out something Rafik could not see. He gave it to Vincha. "This is a—"

"I can see what it is," Vincha snapped.

But Bayne persisted. "Shut up, Vincha, I don't have much time before the Mender comes back. Gronn gave me this—he was thinking about bolting, too. He came across it by accident. It was cleverly hidden and it took him ages to figure out, but he told me there was no way this transmitter just fell from a Troll's pocket, Gronn was certain this is paired with another somewhere to the southwest, and that someone from here hid it."

"Who?"

"I don't know, could be anyone, but it's reasonable to assume that Nakamura has spies operating within the Hive. I could bring this to Brain, of course, but I have a better plan. All we have to do is grab the Puzzler, head to the bridge, and stay low for a while. If you could reverse the code, or whatever Gronn said he could do, then we could track to the paired transmitter and—"

"Stop it, Bayne, it's a suicide mission. Besides, why do you think I want to get out of here?"

Rafik couldn't see the warrior's eyes, but when he spoke again his voice was gentle. "Have you measured the amount of Skint you've been inhaling lately? Most of the time you're powdered up . . ."

"I don't see the relevance," Vincha protested

Bayne pulled himself up to his elbows. ". . . And I'm probably the only Troll in the Hive you haven't fucked since Doro died."

Vincha clenched her fists.

To his credit, Bayne was quick enough to apologize. "Sorry. That was below the belt," he said. "It's none of my business what you do and who you do it with." He sighed and slumped back onto the bed. "But I think you're unhappy here. Think about it. Can you handle another season in the Hive? I know I won't survive Ramm. So this is as good a chance as we get."

Vincha opened her mouth to answer, but suddenly an alarm pierced the air. Rafik didn't stay to hear her parting words. His orders were strict. He had to run to the barracks when the alarm sounded, and he was not about to disobey Ramm, who threatened to lock him in a room permanently if he was late.

He arrived to find the rest of the Keenan crew gearing up and waiting for orders. A few nodded and waved when they saw him enter. Ramm was pacing, and as soon as he saw Rafik he ordered him to be brought to the secure room. This time there was no guard posted inside, and Rafik was left alone in the small room with only a low-power light to keep the darkness away.

He lay down on the cold floor and listened to the sounds

of shots and explosions. The emergency channel of his Comm was filled with orders, shouts, curses, explosions, and, on a few occasions, blood-curdling screams. At some point several dozen Lizards managed to cimb over the north wall and enter the Hive's grounds, and Brain had to send an auxiliary force to deal with them. Rafik hugged his knees and tried not to think what would happen if the Lizards were to get the upper hand. Would he be spared, or would they tear him to pieces with their claws and teeth? The image of the Lizard that attacked him came back to his mind. Was Pikok right? Rafik suppressed a shudder. He might have seen hesitation in the Lizard's yellow pupils, but only a hesitation, and Rafik was not so sure that the creature would have left him unharmed.

The attack was eventually repelled. Rafik later learned that Bayne had forced his way out of the clinic to join the fight. Yet that was the last time Rafik saw Bayne. A day after the attack he was called back to the Keenan headquarters, and Bayne never came back. His departure was marked by the worst Lizard attack yet on the convoy to the Long Tube. Seven Trolls were killed and scores wounded, although Bayne was not one of them.

The Keenans sent back several recruits to replace the fallen crew members. Jhan, whom Rafik knew from the guild house, was the new CommTroll. He was almost as young as Rafik and equally as frightened. The other three arrivals were fighting Trolls, fresh from the obligatory guard duty at the farms and eager for action.

One of them was Kurk. Killing people had turned him from a cruel, malicious boy into the kind of Troll others took care not to anger. He constantly boasted about the atrocities he and his fellow guards committed against insubordinate farmers and their families. It didn't surprise Rafik at all when Kurk immediately began to praise and imitate Ramm's style. As a result, Ramm was quick to take Kurk under his wing. He was wired with far better gear than he deserved and given an unusual amount of powder.

When not fraternizing with Ramm or slumbering in a Skint-induced stupor, Kurk made a point of making Rafik's life a living hell. He used his new status as tactical leader to send the boy on unnecessary errands, and to mock him in front of the crew. Since Ramm shared Rafik's tracer code with Kurk, there was no hiding from the Troll. He especially took delight in tormenting Pikok by imitating the eccentric Puzzler and peppering him with insults. Pikok's response was to withdraw from Rafik and close himself off in his underground lair. Rafik managed to meet Pikok alone only a few times, and they were too brief for him to learn anything about puzzles or the man's Lizard theories.

A few more days passed and the attacks became less frequent, until they eventually stopped altogether. Another week passed quietly, and then another. It seemed that the Lizards had either withdrawn or had been exterminated. No Lizard was sighted for several weeks.

The large number of dead Lizards and the subsequent surplus in green powder meant that tensions involving Skint distribution were lessened as well. Everyone seemed quiet and subdued after the attacks, Kurk being a notable exception.

For a short while, the Hive was as close to peaceful as a place full of hundreds of Combat Trolls could be.

47

"Who was this Nakamura?" Galinak's question saved me from falling into a complete doze. I straightened up and stifled a yawn, cursing myself and wondering if I'd missed bits of the story.

"I'm surprised you don't know of him," said my LoreMaster. Turning my head, I saw that during Vincha's tale he'd seated himself in a far corner and was now speaking from the shadows.

"I'm an old-timer, LoreMaster." I could almost *hear* Galinak smiling in the darkness. "By the time this had all happened my crew was mostly dead and I was out of the Valley, escorting tower-heads to seedy brothels in the Pit."

LoreMaster Harim took Galinak at his word. "Nakamura was a sort of legend, a rogue," he explained, "a marked man possessing, if you believe the stories, oracle-like powers. He roamed Tarakan Valley, claiming no alliance and seeking no protection from the outposts or the guilds. Only the very few have seen him and lived. Actually there's a debate in my society . . ." He stopped and sighed. "There *was* a debate whether the man existed or was some kind of boogeyman invented to frighten new crews and keep them from straying too far."

"Oh, Nakamura existed, all right."

I turned my head to where Vincha was squatting. She was nodding in the gloom to no one in particular.

"He existed," she repeated, her voice dry and cracked. "And he was exactly as the stories claimed; a freak Troll, half man, half monster. He survived in the wilderness for years with only a small crew, killing anything and anyone that stood in his way. His name travelled even to the Pit, Galinak."

Galinak shuffled to his feet and stretched. "Well, excuse me for not keeping up with the news and gossip. My wires were kinda crossed during that particular period of my life. So Vincha, you were dating this Nakamura guy, or what?"

Chuckles rose among the men, but died quickly as my master walked a step closer to the light. He looked down at Vincha. "What I would like to know is how you arranged for Bayne to be transferred back to the City of Towers, and why?"

In the silence that followed I could only hear my own heart beating. There was urgency in my LoreMaster's voice, which was not supposed to be there for such a seemingly mundane question.

"You know about that as well," Vincha shook her head slowly.

The LoreMaster nodded. "I've been connecting the dots around your complicated life for a long time, but more than anything else, that action highlighted your involvement in the dramatic events which came to pass."

"I had no choice." Vincha's voice rose as she shook her head. "He was going to die out there, that rust of a Troll."

"Was Ramm going to kill him?"

"He would have died sooner or later. Even if he somehow survived by himself in the Valley and found Nakamura . . ." She hesitated briefly, shrugging. "He would have rusted either way. Nakamura killed anyone who was not useful to him, and there was nothing Bayne could have offered him."

I heard myself speak as the thoughts began to form in my mind. "How would you know what Nakamur—"

But my LoreMaster cut me off. "No, not now," he said. "Now I want to know how you did it."

Vincha shrugged again in the gloom. "I hacked into the Keenans' channel using algorithmic protocols I stole from Gronn long before he . . . never mind. I just managed, and then I faked an encrypted guild message for Bayne."

Galinak whistled softly in appreciation. "That's impressive. I didn't understand half the words you just used."

"Ramm was so off his wires he didn't realise what I was doing, and the new Keenan CommTroll was a complete disaster. I knew that Bayne would already be in the city by the time they figured out what was going on, and then the Keenans would hold an investigation to see how it was done. By the time they found out he had nothing to do with it, he would be able to speak to someone there, ask for a transfer or even an early release from his contract . . . I knew people owed him some favors, but he was too damn proud to cash them in."

"Yet you went to all that trouble to get him away from the Hive. Why?"

"Does it matter? I did what I had to do."

"So you did this out of love."

Vincha rose to her feet in one fluid motion. "It's none of your rusting business, historian. I'm not a propaganda pamphlet or an erotic visual to masturbate to."

That display was a sure sign that my LoreMaster's assumption was correct.

"Did you know what you were about to do? What you were setting in motion?" he asked.

The question seemed to deflate her. She took a half step back and pressed her body against the wooden wall. "No, I did not." This time her voice shook, and for some reason it frightened me.

I rose to my feet as my LoreMaster pressed on relentlessly. "The Surge, the destruction of the outpost, the pushback, the decline of humanity, diminishing returns on the salvation expeditions triggering another guild war, the riots—the poor, untrained recruits sent to the valley to be slaughtered . . ." His words hung in the air.

Vincha was shaking her head vigorously. "No, no, I didn't know. I didn't know. I swear, I didn't think . . . I just wanted out . . . Bayne was right. I was a mess . . . because of the Skint . . . because of Doro . . . because I was . . . and there was no way out . . ."

I could see her breaking up in front of us. There had been no need for threats or bribes. LoreMaster Harim needed only to ask the right questions, and her entire defence came tumbling down. Rust, whatever she'd done was like a wound, festering inside her. I still couldn't see the whole picture, but my Lore-Master did, and it was obvious Vincha knew the implications of her actions. That realisation and the fear of what would happen to her if the guilds came to the same conclusion was what must have driven her to lead such an erratic and dangerous life, always afraid, always looking at the shadows and fleeing at the very first signs of trouble. Yet her secret, like all secrets, yearned to be exposed. It was surprisingly uncomfortable to watch this woman I'd seen kill with precision be reduced to blubbering words and a trembling chin.

I was not the only one struggling with the situation. Galinak stepped suddenly forward, putting his body between Vincha and LoreMaster Harim. "Easy now, old fella," he grumbled. "We've all had a very long day, and I don't know much about history, but I'm sure that whatever Vincha did, she couldn't possibly have been responsible for everything that you accuse her of."

"You misunderstand me." My LoreMaster's voice was calm, almost a whisper. "I do not seek justice, or vengeance. I only seek the truth."

"Why?" Vincha voice rose to something close to a shout.

"Because at this point we are out of history-learning and into history-making" was LoreMaster Harim's reply.

"I didn't know," Vincha repeated again, her voice trembling with emotion.

"But you knew you were about to betray the boy."

Vincha didn't answer.

"And in order to betray Rafik, you had to gain his trust."

48

"Let him go."

The tone in her voice stopped the Troll midmovement but Rafik, held firmly a few inches above the ground, kept struggling.

Kurk turned his head slowly to stare at Vincha, ignoring Rafik's pummelling fists. He seemed to relax, and smiled. "It's not your place, woman. This is Keenan business."

"You're going to let him go." Her voice was calm. She stood with her hands on her hips, but the movement of her red hair—twitching erratically around her head like a pack of snakes—was a sure sign of a Tarakan Comm device in combat readiness.

Kurk dropped Rafik to the ground. "You're messing with the wrong Troll, bitch," he spat.

"I think you're messing with the wrong bitch, Troll." Vincha took half a step forward, "Perhaps you think I'm one of those poor field girls you can rape at will, like the stories you tell your friends at the Chewing Hole, yes? I saw the way you looked at me then." She tilted her head slightly, stretching her long body into an alluring pose and pitching her voice into seduction. "See something you like, big boy? Why don't you come here and try those sweet moves on me, hmm?" She blew him a kiss, but the look in Vincha's eyes meant death.

Kurk must have sensed it because he hesitated. Even in a place full of Combat Trolls high on Skint, Vincha had a reputation. He tried a different tactic. "You mess with me, you mess with the Keenans, Vincha. You're nothing but a freelancer."

Vincha surveyed their surroundings, "Well . . . *boy*, this is quite a secluded place, so I think I could easily claim that I killed you in self-defence. I'm sure the only other witness would back me up." She smiled again and licked her lips. "And by the way, call me 'bitch' again, and I'll break your teeth, stick my fist down your throat, then make you lick up your own vomit."

Colour drained from Kurk's face, and his eyes darted from Vincha to Rafik, who was still sitting on the floor beside the Troll, massaging his aching wrists.

"Ramm will hear of this," he growled, but then he retreated, leaving Rafik behind.

Vincha's gaze followed Kurk. As he reached a corner, she said "Tell that big lump of metal I said hi, and that I'll come over for a little chat soon. He'll know what it's about."

When she was sure that Kurk would not return she stepped over and helped Rafik to his feet. "Are you okay?" Her smile was pleasant and warm.

Rafik nodded, too embarrassed to speak.

"He shouldn't handle you like that. I hate bullies."

Rafik shrugged. "It's my fault. I shouldn't have tried to hide from him."

"Rust bucket," Vincha muttered.

Rafik flashed a smile, which disappeared quickly as he said, "Ramm is going to be angry with you."

"I can handle rusting Ramm," Vincha said. "The lump of metal owes me enough to overlook it if I slap around one of his shit-brained toy Trolls."

"You curse a lot," Rafik commented, blushing for no apparent reason.

The CommWoman laughed. "I do, we all do it here, but I guess it's not . . . nice."

Vincha looked down at Rafik's hand. "Hey, am I crazy or did your markings grow since I saw you in the Long Tube?"

Rafik raised his hand in front of his eyes and turned it about. "Yea. They were tiny little dots when I first saw them in my home village, now they are almost as large as Pikok's"

"Oh, yea, Pikok. You are friends, aren't you? Haven't seen that strange little Puzzler about for a while."

Rafik shook his head sadly. "I can't see him anymore. Pikok tried to escape during the Lizard attacks, so the commander of the Loot Worshippers locked him up."

"Well, he *is* insane, running towards Lizards like that," Vincha shrugged. "I'm just curious, what are you doing in this secluded part of the Hive?"

"I came here to . . ." The boy hesitated, but then he sighed. "I came to pray."

Vincha looked at Rafik in disbelief. "Are you religious? I mean, you still believe after all they must have done to you?"

"I used to be . . . I mean I still have faith," he corrected himself, "but I don't understand why the Reborn . . . why I am . . ." He breathed out in anger. "I didn't do anything wrong. I prayed every day and was a good student, so I don't understand why the Prophet Reborn cursed . . . marked . . . made me like . . . like all of you."

"But you still pray to this prophet of yours."

Rafik looked at the ground, his foot stirring dust into circles, "Yes, I pray. Sometimes . . ."

Vincha laid a hand on the young boy's shoulder. "I also come here," she said quietly, looking around. "It's almost private here, and I do my own kind of praying."

Rafik looked up at the CommWoman. "You pray to the

Prophet Reborn?" Vincha didn't dress or look or behave like a woman who followed the words of the Prophet. She reminded him more of Dominique.

Vincha laughed. "No, I don't believe in your god, or anyone's, but I like the solitude. It gives me time to listen."

"Listen? To what?"

Vincha hesitated for a fraction of a second before motioning for the boy to follow her. They walked to a shaded area between three tall buildings and sat on a pile of stones. Vincha rummaged in her pockets and produced a short cable.

"You have to sit closer to me. Instead of messing with your Comm channels, we'll use a more direct way. Here, just put that in your ear." The CommWoman busied herself with her hair, attaching the cable to her head. Rafik sat shyly next to her and gingerly accepted the other end of the cable.

"Go on." Vincha smiled encouragingly. "Attach it to your ear piece, just place it there." She pointed and Rafik complied.

"I can only hear hissing," he said after a few heartbeats.

"Patience," she said. "I have to find it. It's a delicate thing." She searched through her belongings until she found a small oblong-shaped disc the size of her little finger. Then she rummaged through her hair until she found the right place to plug it in, saying, "I found this baby by accident five years ago—in a shallow run, would you believe it? Almost overlooked it, really. It's partly damaged, but I managed to work some of it out."

Vincha closed her eyes, and the noise inside Rafik's head changed. For what seemed like an eternity there was only an annoying hissing, scratching sound that made him wince, but all of a sudden his head was filled with rich, wonderful sound. It was nothing like the music that came out of the music box in Dominique's bar. It was unlike anything he'd heard before. This music had many voices, each playing in a different way, but somehow they all merged together, creating sounds that sent shivers up and down his spine. For a long time they said nothing and simply sat there, listening to the glorious music, until it faded into a soft hiss.

He heard Vincha's voice. "It's Tarakan music, from the City within the Mountain. The info data on it was damaged but from what I pieced together this music is called Bit of En."

"Play it again."

She laughed, "There are several of these Bit of En songs on here. Beautiful ain't it?"

"It's . . ." He searched for words. "It's like the Great Puzzle."

Vincha raised an eyebrow. "The what?"

"In my dreams I see a wall of symbols, Pikok calls it the Great Puzzle." Rafik's eyes shone; he was seeing something other than their surroundings. "All those patterns, in the voices, can't you hear it? And there is a hidden pattern too, I can feel it."

"I don't understand." She shook her head. "Is this some kind of Puzzler's talk? Are you turning into Pikok?" she laughed.

"You won't understand. You're not a Puzzler." There was a hint of pride in the boy's voice.

"Why don't you explain it, then?"

He turned his head away. "Do you really want to know?"

The CommWoman shrugged. "Sure. Why don't you tell me what it's like to see things other people can't see, and I'll explain to you what it's like to be able to hear stuff others can't hear."

"No one here really cares, you know." His tone was flat and bitter. "They just want me to open the puzzle locks. Most of them just call me 'key.' They don't even know my name."

Vincha fixed the boy with a long stare. "You are Rafik," she said quietly and extended her hand, "and I'm Vincha."

He looked at her hand. "I know. We met on the Long Tube, remember?"

"Yes, of course I do, but now I want to be friends with you. If you'll accept me, that is."

He smiled shyly and shook her hand. It had calluses and felt rough, but at the same time, it was also warm and pleasant to the touch.

Vincha relaxed against the wall. "So, Rafik, tell me all about yourself. Where do you come from? How did you end up here with the Keenans? Bet it's an interesting story."

Rafik shrugged, "It's a long, boring story, actually."

"I've got time." Vincha took a bag of Skint out of her pocket. "And I am sure you don't miss Ramm so much . . ."

They both chuckled in unison.

"C'mon, kid." She playfully punched Rafik in the shoulder. "Tell me your boring story."

And he told her.

49

When Rafik woke up he was alone in a room full of empty cots. He had changed recently to another chamber, and the sun was blazing through holes in an old sheet that covered the window. It was almost midday, but he still felt tired. The night before, he had come back with the Keenan crew from a successful shallow run with weapons, ammo, and plenty of power tubes. Narona led the run and it went smoothly, but as usual Rafik found it hard to fall asleep afterwards—the Keenan crew prided themselves on their unofficial slogan of fighting hard and partying harder, and the racket they'd created was not something he could easily fall asleep to.

Rafik rose slowly and prayed for the first time in a while.

When he left his chamber, there was no one in the upper hallways, so he wandered downstairs, hoping to wash and eat without attracting Kurk's attention. Rafik's allowance was meagre compared to what the Trolls got paid, but it was enough to buy real food in the Chewing Hole. It helped that Vincha was generous with her metal. She always invited Rafik for meals, and even got him a new set of clothes that fit his "young man's body," as she put it. The thought still made him blush.

Rafik's heart missed a beat when he heard Vincha's voice from the main room. The door was slightly ajar, and bits of conversation were spilling out together with the stench of green smoke. Normally Rafik would avoid getting close to Ramm, especially when he and Kurk were on Skint, but Vincha's presence was out of the ordinary. He liked spending time with the CommTroll and talking to her, liked the way her red hair would twitch and curl in the air when she channelled. She was tough, she cursed a lot, and she sniffed too much Skint, but she was also friendly and warm, and, well, beautiful. Above all, Vincha was the source of the wonderful Tarakan music. They sometimes listened to it together for hours. When Vincha fell asleep he would listen to the music but also pretend to be guarding her.

Rafik told her about life in his village and eventually about his entire adventure. He ended up talking quite a bit as Vincha listened. It was like having a friend again, like Eithan, but in a way this was much better.

Rafik picked up the conversation as he moved slowly towards the door.

"You owe me, Ramm. Rust, you should have waited for me," Vincha said.

Ramm's voice was slurred. "You were nowhere to be found."

"Rust—"

"And we had our own Comm anyways—you were not needed."

"Yea, I heard about that. Your guy short-circuited the moment he saw the Lizards and you lost, what, three Trolls? You should have waited for me."

"You were out in the green fields."

"Go rust, Ramm."

Narona tried to calm things down. "What's done is done. Vincha, you came to us with a proposition, so let's discuss it."

Rafik inched closer until he could see Vincha's back as she stood in front of Ramm and the lieutenants of the Keenan crew.

As she talked, the locks of her hair moved in all directions, as if caught by a great wind. He knew it was because of the Tarakan devices in her head, but the effect was still eerie.

"It's a bunker, untouched, buried in the southeast sector. The node can be unlocked only two times a year."

"How do you know these things?" Ramm sounded suspicious.

"I have vivid dreams. You know my info's solid, Ramm, that's all you really need to know."

"Your info didn't tell us about the nest of almost a hundred Lizards."

"If you had taken me on the run you wouldn't have had to fight those Lizards, Ramm, but you just love those Troll boys fresh out of the fields—"

"Shut up, bitch, you don't—" Kurk growled

"Okay, okay, enough," Narona interrupted, sounding impatient and angry. The room fell silent. "Where exactly in the southeast sector did you say this bunker was?"

"Oh, no rusting way . . . I made that mistake once and you took off without me. This time I'm keeping my mouth shut till we're there."

"When does this rusting node open?" Ramm's voice was muffled, and Rafik realised the commander had his visor down.

"In three nights."

"Then why are you wasting my time? It can't be done. Sandstorms are coming and Brain has locked the gates for at least a week. Locked and shut, not even a private run, nothing."

"I can get us in and out," Vincha said.

"How?"

"The deep tunnels."

"Fuck you, Vincha."

"I know a way out," she insisted.

"I said fuck you." Ramm was losing his patience.

Narona took control of the conversation again. "No one knows the way out," she said, "Not even Brain. Those tunnels go for miles, and they're half collapsed. We lost some good Trolls down there."

"I know the way out, and I will have wheels waiting for us. Once we are out, I'll tell you where to drive, and your Puzzler can open the lock."

"It could be a trap," another voice spoke. Rafik recognised Kurk's slow speech. He continued, "I've been talking to a few Trolls, heard rumours. Two crews were lost in that sector two months ago. They say it was Nakamura. That he channelled to Brain that any crew trespassing on his turf would be wiped out. That's why we stopped patrolling there."

Vincha laughed. "Ramm, have you gone soft? You're growing pets now? At least get something smart, like a rat or something, so you can teach it tricks."

There was a sound of a chair falling to the floor, and when Kurk spoke it sounded as if he was on his feet. "This bitch could be working for him. Leading us into a trap."

Vincha laughed again. "Seriously? I mean, what the hell is this kid doing here?"

"He's here because I say so," Ramm answered.

"Let me get this straight. I come to you with an easy way to get your hands on a lot of hardware. The sector has been abandoned because it's far away from the Hive and there weren't enough nodes to make it worth the trip. It's far away from the City within the Mountain, so the chances of meeting up with Lizards are low. I tell you this, and you listen to urban legends and tales of the boogeyman? Ramm, this node is an easy way to get rich, that's it."

"Easy, right?" Ramm laughed.

"Easy as the wirings in your brain," Vincha spat.

That stopped his laugh abruptly, but before he could respond Vincha said, "We'll need your Puzzler, myself, and four Keenans max. Any more than that would take up space that could be used for the goods. Fifty-fifty, I get first pick."

"Rust that, Vincha. Seventy-thirty and we get first pick."

"I could go to any other guild, and I could do it by myself."

Ramm laughed. "You think I'm that stupid? The other guilds

are too soft to go against Brain's lockdown, and you need our Puzzler. Without him you'll stand outside that bunker with your thumb up your plug. And you need our protection; I don't care what you think you know about the sector. When the Lizards come, or even that Nakamura . . ." There was the distinct sound of a large weapon being cocked.

"Sixty-forty, I get two first picks."

"Seventy-thirty, you get one first pick, and that's my final offer."

"Fuck you, Ramm."

"Get in line, but I'm not into redheads. Do we have a deal?"

"That's stealing."

"No, that's business. Do we have a deal?"

"I could go to other—"

"No you can't. Sabarra still won't work with you after that mess you got them into, and how many guilds or independent crews have their own Puzzler *and* would go against Brain's lockdown? I mean, if you want cheap, I am sure the Loot Worshippers would let you take Pi-Pi-Pikok." Rafik heard Kurk sniggering at this.

"Besides," Ramm continued in a slyer tone, "I know you owe metal for all the green you've been sniffing. You're a desperate little Comm bitch, Vincha, which makes you *my* Comm bitch. Seventy-thirty, I get first *two* picks now, just because you made me explain myself. Do we have a deal?"

Vincha held her breath for a long time and then exhaled noisily. "I hope you rust slowly, Ramm. We have a deal. Make sure you're ready when I tell you, and don't breathe a word about this to anyone."

Rafik dove for cover behind a broken crate as Vincha turned and headed for the door. He must have been clearly visible, but Vincha moved with such purpose that she failed to notice him. The door to the main room stayed open.

"It could be a trap," Kurk said again. "I don't trust that whore."

"She did just take a raw deal," Narona said. "If what she's

saying is right, fifty percent cut and several first picks should have been her end game."

"She's desperate," Ramm said. "I know she owes serious coin, and some Trolls have been pressing her to pay up. Did you see her eyeing my supplies? Even with prices the way they are, she's out of Skint. I gave her a raw deal and she ate it."

"You sure did, commander," Kurk said.

"But just in case, the first sign of trouble, shoot her head off."

50

Rafik wanted to warn Vincha about the conversation he'd overheard, but he didn't get a chance. Before every mission, Ramm always barred Rafik from leaving the Keenan headquarters. Worse, he ordered Kurk to shadow him.

The time passed slowly. Rafik spent it daydreaming about the Great Puzzle and worrying about Vincha. He knew about her Skint problem, but she always claimed it was for the headache her plugs gave her. He hoped Ramm was wrong and that she didn't owe coin to anyone. For some reason he didn't dare explain to himself, Rafik also hoped Vincha wasn't sleeping around.

Playing with the wall of symbols made him feel a little better. Since almost dying in the puzzle prison, Rafik discovered that he could now enter a state of mind where he was in front of the wall and able to manipulate a hundred symbols at a time. Controlling the symbols had become intuitive, effortless, like walking or breathing, and he could even try to solve problems on the wall while thinking about other things, like Vincha, although he would sometimes come out of it with a pounding headache.

It seemed like an eternity before Rafik was finally taken to meet Vincha at the Chewing Hole. Narona and two Troll brothers, Deesha and Goll, sat at a table, and Rafik was squeezed in between the giant bodies of Ramm and Kurk.

"She's late," Narona said.

"I'm telling you the bitch ain't coming," hissed Kurk. "She's probably fucking some Troll for an ounce of Skint. There's no way she was telling the truth about the secret stash of—"

"Shut your rusting hole," barked Ramm. With the lockdown, the bar was full of people and the noise level was high. Still, a few heads turned. Ramm scowled at them until they lost interest.

"Try not to draw attention," warned Narona. "The last thing we need is for Brain to—"

"Don't tell me what to do," Ramm snapped as his giant metal hand, which was resting on the table, closed into a fist. Narona grimaced but sipped her drink in silence after that.

One of the barmaids approached the table, tray full of drinks.

It was Narona's turn to snap. "We don't need any more. Leave us alone."

The barmaid carefully placed a small metal box on the table. "This is from Vincha."

"What? Is this a joke?" Kurk scowled. The barmaid was already walking away.

Ramm took the box. In his huge hand it seemed smaller than it really was.

"It's a trap, I'm telling you," Kurk said.

"Don't short a circuit, Kurk. It's not a trap," Narona countered.

Ramm tried to pry the box open, but despite his considerable strength, the lock didn't budge.

"It's a puzzle box," Rafik said. "There's a place for fingers"—he pointed—"see?"

Ramm slammed the box down in front of Rafik. "Open it, then."

Rafik pulled the box closer. It was surprisingly light. He looked it over carefully. The three holes were cleverly concealed, but he'd noticed them immediately. As he examined the holes, they grew larger. He felt drawn to them. Soon they filled his vision. He watched his tiny fingers reach out to the giant holes, and then he was falling.

The puzzle was waiting for him. It was so easy he felt disappointed—with only one, short pattern strand—and he was done in the blink of an eye. The lock clicked open, and he was about to withdraw his fingers when out of the corner of his eye he caught a glimpse of a strange symbol. It was like nothing he'd seen before. He turned his head and reached out to the symbol, which left the wall and landed near Rafik's feet. Without thinking he stepped on the symbol and watched the puzzle wall change. It suddenly had depth. Several layers of semi-invisible symbols materialised behind the original wall. He quickly found a pattern. Each symbol became a block. He stepped forward onto one, and then another, then through the wall of symbols to the other side, where a door stood waiting for him.

Rafik opened the door and stepped into a room made of solid grey walls. As soon as the door closed an image appeared in the centre of the room.

"Vincha . . ."

"There's not much time." Her eyes didn't focus on Rafik. "I'm glad you found your way to me. This was the safest place for me to leave you a message."

Rafik's first question would have been *How did you manage to work a puzzle box?* But he knew that the image was just a message, not the real Vincha, which also meant he couldn't warn her about Ramm.

"I know you're unhappy here," Vincha's visage said. "You suffer because you're only seen as an object to exploit. I know that you're trapped, a slave, just a key . . ." She shook her head. "There is a way out for you. For both of us. All I ask is for you to trust me. I want the best for both of us, as I'm going to show you now with this message. Take what's in the box, walk out of the bar, take the first three left turns, and go down two levels. Follow the right corridor and take the fifth left. There is a large stain on the wall just before the turn, so look for it. When you reach the top of the stairs, put what I left in the box on the ground. You must hurry. Come immediately."

The room blinked out immediately after Vincha uttered the last word and Rafik was back at the table.

"Took your time. I was beginning to rust here," Kurk said.

"It was a hard lock," Rafik answered in what he hoped was a casual tone of voice, but avoided looking at Kurk.

"Or maybe you're not such a good key after all."

Ramm snatched the box and opened it. "What's the bitch doing?" He fished out a pink rubber ball. "I'll shoot her head off if she's playing a joke on us."

"I know what it is. We have to go now," Rafik said.

"What? How?" Ramm's only natural eye looked down at the boy with unveiled suspicion.

Rafik hesitated. Part of him wanted to warn Ramm about Vincha, to prove to the Keenan commander that he was loyal, one of the team, and gain his trust and respect. Ramm would kill Vincha for sure, but Rafik also knew that he was leading the crew into something unexpected. For all his faults, Kurk was right this time—it really was a trap.

"The puzzle told me," he said. "We have to go now or the whole thing will be cancelled."

"We don't even have our full run gear," Kurk protested. "We should at least go back and get it."

Ramm looked hesitant.

"You have your weapons, right?" Rafik nodded towards Kurk's power rifle, then pointed at himself. "And you've got your Puzzler. We must hurry. We must go now." He ducked under the table. "Follow me," he said and walked away without looking back.

A few seconds later he heard them scrambling to their feet and pushing their way after him. His skin crawled as he anticipated Ramm's fist grabbing his shoulder from behind, but it didn't happen. They followed Rafik in silence the entire way.

"What now?" Narona said when Rafik stopped.

"Give me the ball." Rafik extended his hand and Ramm relinquished the rubber ball. It felt surprisingly heavy and cool to the touch.

Rafik placed the ball on the ground. After several heartbeats it began to glow and started to roll away, slowly at first but gaining momentum.

"Rust," Kurk cursed as they all began following the moving ball. It reached a set of stairs and bounced down, making a loud knocking sound each time it hit another stair.

As soon as they reached the bottom of the stairs an alarm sounded.

They froze and looked at each other. But the ball kept rolling.

"Lizards," Narona said.

"The ball," Rafik said. "We must follow it."

"We should go back, take positions," Kurk turned and began walking up the stairs.

"Keep moving," Ramm ordered.

"Brain will look for us," Kurk sputtered.

Ramm clapped Kurk on the back of the head hard enough to send him reeling to the opposite wall.

"Fuck Brain. There are enough Trolls out there to take down a few Lizards. Shut up and do as you're told."

They moved in silence after that.

At first the corridors were familiar, then vaguely so, and eventually they were completely alien. It was dark. Only Narona's light beam and the glowing ball lit the way. The air was murky and stale, it was hard to breathe, and there was no sound. They had their weapons drawn and were fully alert, but no threat materialized.

After a long while they reached a hall lined with a dozen Tarakan steel doors. All of them were locked except the one the ball bounced against. The group exchanged meaningful glances. Rafik understood they were already planning to come back and do some exploring in this area.

After several more corridors, the ball bounced, almost impatiently, against a wide door. When they got closer the door slid sideways to reveal a small, narrow chamber that was so well lit it momentarily blinded them. The ball bounced merrily inside. They followed, and when they were all inside, the door slid closed, trapping them.

"Rust," Kurk cursed.

"Hold it together. Bukra's balls, you're jumpy." Narona spotted an oblong power tube on the floor and picked it up. "It's fully charged," she said.

"There's a slot for it here, see?" Rafik pointed at a socket-like depression on a panel.

As soon as the power tube was placed in the socket, the room began to move sideways, like the Long Tube. The acceleration was so smooth they never lost their balance, but Rafik felt his heart skip a beat.

"I'm going to kill that Comm bitch," Ramm muttered, as the metal box they were in gained speed.

After a while the room began to slow down.

"Get ready, Keenans." Ramm hefted his heavy cannon at the door. They pushed Rafik behind them and aimed all sorts of weaponry at the door. It slid open to reveal Vincha, smiling.

"Don't you just love a warm welcome?" she said, spreading her hands wide. "Take the power tube out, or it's going to be a long way back."

They stepped out into a very large, dark chamber.

"Rust, Vincha, you should be glad I didn't shoot you," Ramm said, but he looked relieved.

"Relax," Vincha said. "You still need me to get to the goodies." She extended her hand. "Can I have my ball back now?" she said, looking at Rafik.

Rafik saw that her eyes were asking a different question. He handed her the ball and the power tube, and gave her the smallest nod. Her smile widened.

"It's a nice little device you have there," Kurk said acidly. He was the only one still aiming a pistol at Vincha. "I wonder where you got it from, eh?"

"I have two. I cut them off an annoying Troll. But relax—yours are too small to be of any use to me."

Everyone laughed, but Kurk looked like he was going to pull the trigger.

"Keep your pet in check and follow me," Vincha said to Ramm. She turned to go, and they followed her.

51

Vincha moved through the tunnels with familiarity, a fact that did not escape the other members of the group.

"Been here a lot, have you?" Kurk commented as they climbed another set of stairs.

"I try to find the places furthest away from your stench," Vincha said.

"You b—"

"Stop it, you two!" Narona yelled.

"He has a point," muttered Goll, the taller of the Troll brothers.

Vincha turned her head. "The good thing about being independent is that I don't need to tell any rusting Troll where I am and what I'm doing."

"I'm sure Brain would love to know there's a secret way out of the compound." Ramm didn't bother to veil the threat.

Rafik could see Vincha's smile to herself when she answered, "Who do you think showed me the way? Work your brain around *that*, Ramm."

They emerged into a large hall with one side open to the glaring sun. A six-wheeled open Duster was parked in the shade, next to a large wooden crate.

Goll whooped. "How the hell did you get a Duster to this place?"

"I drove it myself." Vincha opened the crate and began pulling out gear. "I brought these—headlights, power packs, Comm devices, rechargers—"

"These are in mint condition," Deesha weighed two blasters in each of his hands. There was admiration in his voice.

"Just to be clear, I want all this gear back when we finish the job." Vincha leaned down to Rafik. "This is for you," she said as she attached a metal band to his head. "This will let you—"

Ramm grabbed her arm and flung her aside with such force that she landed on her back a few paces away with a heavy thump. She was quickly on her feet, pistol drawn. "What is your rusting—"

Ramm held his power cannon casually at his side. "You do not touch the Puzzler," he said. "You do not talk to him. Rust, don't let me catch you looking in his direction, because next time I'll break your hand in three and take one piece as a souvenir."

There was a tense pause. Vincha visibly forced herself to relax. "Fine," she said, holstering her pistol, "but instead of ripping my arm off, next time try asking nicely first."

"I don't ask. And I'm the only one to communicate with my key." Ramm fished out his own communication device from his pack and shoved the Comm piece so hard into Rafik's ear that he yelped in pain.

"Don't be a baby," he said, scowling at the boy. "When I was your age I'd already been shot three times. Grow a pair."

Kurk was the only one who laughed.

"Gear up and get into the Duster," Ramm said. "Oh no you don't," he barked at Vincha before she reached the driver's seat. "Goll drives."

Vincha held her hands up. "Whatever, Ramm. Just get us there."

Ramm sniffed some Skint, then passed the bag around. When it reached Vincha, she refused. But Ramm insisted. "Do it," he said. "I want you nice and relaxed for this run."

She fished some powder out and sniffed it deeply into each nostril. Her eyes glazed a little and then returned to focus. She jumped into the Duster. Rafik was helped into the backseat.

They drove off. Vincha sat next to Goll. Kurk stood at the back and aimed his gun in all directions, even firing at random buildings until he was ordered to stop.

They all wore goggles as protection from the dust and sand that hung in the air.

"Put on some music," Ramm shouted at the wind.

"Yea, put on some of that drum shit, I like that!" Goll shouted above the roar of the engine.

Vincha nodded as locks of her red hair twitched and turned. Rafik's ears were filled with music he'd heard in the Chewing Hole. It was not the sublime music he'd shared together with Vincha but something much simpler, with repeated patterns, yet powerful nonetheless. It made him want to move his body to the rhythm, like the Trolls he saw in the Hole. The rest of the group were nodding their heads and tapping hands on their weapons. The thought came to him, and not for the first time, that the Tarkanians must have been strange creatures indeed.

They drove for a while. The area was completely still apart from an occasional dust devil. The buildings around them were large and wide, ten stories high, made of Tarakan steel and mostly intact. The buildings stood much farther apart from each other than in the parts of the Valley Rafik had seen. Perhaps there used to be gardens or parks between them, like Rafik had seen in the City of Towers, but as in the rest of the Valley, there were no plants or trees and the ground was covered with powdery yellow sand. Rafik tried to imagine people living in these great buildings, going about their daily lives. His thoughts went back to his own village. Images of his mum and dad, Fahid, his sisters, and Eithan. It seemed a long time had passed since he'd thought about them. He wondered if he would see them ever again and made peace with the thought that he probably wouldn't.

The dust was getting into his goggles. He turned around and caught Vincha's eye. She nodded her head ever so slightly. Rafik wondered what the CommWoman was up to. He also saw Kurk was staring at her back, eyes filled with venom. Blood would soon be spilled, and Rafik knew that soon he would have to choose sides. If he sided with Vincha he would be risking his life. But if he stayed with the Keenans he would be a pawn for the rest of his life, nothing more than a key. He thought of Pikok, fervently scratching the symbols of the Great Puzzle on every available surface. Would he end up like that?

The music pounded in his ears as they drove towards the rapidly waning sun. The crew was relaxed in their seats. Night was coming fast, and the Duster's floodlights were already on.

Vincha signalled for them to stop in an open, empty area. She jumped off the Duster and walked away, looking at the screen on her arm bracelet. Gron trained the Duster's floodlights on Vincha, and Rafik saw Kurk changing position so his power rifle could be easily aimed at the receding CommWoman's back.

Vincha stopped and fished a small screen from her belt, tapping on it with her fingers.

Kurk stood up, aiming his power rifle. "What is—"

"Shut your rusting hole and sit down," Narona said sharply, "and don't speak unless spoken to, whoa—" She broke her own sentence in surprise as a multitude of white and green rays shot from the ground to the sky.

Vincha turned and walked slowly back to the Duster, a smile on her face as the ground behind her began to move.

The Keenans watched as a huge dark metal building emerged silently from the ground.

"That is—" Goll began, shaking his head.

"—pretty damn impressive," Vincha completed the sentence, hopping back on the Duster. "Look at the Tarakan metal—not a dent on it, or rust. Makes you wonder how they lost the war, eh?"

When the bunker stopped moving it reached at least five stories high, dwarfing the Duster. It featured the largest double doors Rafik had ever seen.

Ramm turned to Rafik. "Time for you to work, key."

"Oh, but that's not the node's puzzle lock," Vincha said, just as the double doors began sliding open. "This is just the entrance. Think what's waiting inside."

The Keenans whooped and cheered. Vincha turned off the music and told Goll to drive to the bunker's entrance. The world suddenly went quiet.

When the Duster drove through the entrance the entire place lit up.

"Look." Deesha pointed. "This looks like a vehicle power-charging station. Burka's balls, this place is awesome."

"I wouldn't be surprised if we found a SuperTruck here," Goll said.

The wide road went underground immediately, and they circled through three large but empty levels until Vincha told Goll to stop. Rafik felt a surge of excitement as they disembarked. Everyone was looking around with a mixture of awe and suspicion. Only Vincha seemed relaxed. She led everyone down a wide flight of stairs. Parts of the corridors lit themselves up as they passed through, then darkened again behind them.

It was not long before they reached the first puzzle-locked door. Rafik was surprised at the ease with which he found the pattern—it took him only a few seconds—but the door only led to another set of corridors and another puzzle lock. This time it was more complex. Just before Rafik completed the last strain of the puzzle he felt something odd, which made him pause and look around. For a brief moment he felt as if he was not only facing a puzzle wall but was surrounded by it. He quickly slammed the last strain of the puzzle into place and woke up with a start, which made the Keenan crew jumpy.

"What is it, key boy?" Kurk said.

"Nothing."

Kurk sneered. "Weakling."

Vincha caught Rafik's eye again. The look she gave him was almost pleading, but he didn't reassure her.

The third puzzle lock was easy, and the doors opened to a large, dark, and oddly familiar underground cave. The Keenans turned their headlights on and readied their weapons. The cave's floor and walls were natural and uneven, a vast contrast to the perfection of the Tarakan-made corridors and halls. There was a large pool of water in the centre of it.

"What is this place?" Goll readied his power blaster as he surveyed their surroundings.

"Beats me, I just know the way in." Vincha pointed at the last door. "The node's heart is just over there."

Rafik saw Ramm exchanging a look and a nod with Kurk behind Vincha's back. The young Troll smiled and raised his weapon. Everything happened at once. Rafik opened his mouth to warn Vincha as Kurk shouldered the rifle and aimed it straight at her back. The rest of the crew paused, looking uncertainly at Ramm. Narona opened her mouth as if to say something, but then her eyes widened and she flung herself aside. Something rolled between them and exploded in a blinding light just as Kurk pulled the trigger. There was a smell of burning flesh and a scream. The rest was just a series of images flashing in a blur before Rafik's eyes. He saw Goll's head exploding in a cloud of red goo. Deesha spun around and tried to shoot, but his guns didn't respond. He threw them to the ground and tried to reach his other blaster, but a masked figure holding a glowing sword appeared from behind him. The sword made two side-to-side swoops; the first one sliced the Troll in half, and the second cut off his head before his upper body even hit the ground. Ramm was shooting into the darkness with a hand blaster and swinging his cannon from side to side, looking for a target. Kurk aimed his rifle again, but then he suddenly burst into flames. His screams echoed and multiplied in the large cavern. Then there was another deafening blast. Rafik saw Narona's body sailing through the air and heard a splash of water. A body slammed him into the ground and he was overwhelmed by the stench of burning flesh. He tried to scream, but someone put a hand over his mouth. Ramm's cannon discharged and Rafik felt the heat as the ray of white death flashed above his head. A moment later he was picked up and carried by powerful arms. He tried to kick and move, but whoever carried him didn't slow down. Then everything went black.

Next thing he knew he was at the other side of the cave, still grasped by the same powerful arms. He saw Vincha being held in a choke hold by a very large man dressed in black power armour. Weaponless, she struggled in vain as a cloaked figure, holding a man-sized staff, approached. He raised the staff and a blade sprang out of it. With one powerful sweep the cloaked figure tore the combat protection gear and clothing off her upper body. Rafik briefly saw Vincha's exposed middle and the bottoms of her breasts.

She tried to kick, but the cloaked figure moved calmly aside and she hit nothing but air. He bent down and touched Vincha's middle with a clawed hand. Vincha hurled curses as she struggled, but then the figure must have done or said something because she suddenly stopped struggling.

The cloaked figure turned and moved towards Rafik. His face was hidden in a cowl. The boy could hear the tapping of the staff on the cave's floor and felt a surge of complete and utter terror with each step the cloaked figure took. When the figure stood over Rafik, the boy smelled rotting flesh and heard a hissing, gurgling noise come out from within the darkness of the cowl.

"Puzzler . . ." the figure throated the word out the darkness of his garb.

Rafik knew what was about to happen. He felt his mouth go dry and his heart started to flutter.

Gnarled, clawlike hands grasped at the hem of the cowl. The face that Rafik then saw was the one from his nightmares.

He recognised the disfigured man, but his dreams had shown

him only the flayed skin. He'd never smelled the rotting stench of putrid flesh, or seen the crushed eye sockets, or felt the saliva that poured from the side of the man's mouth and landed on Rafik's flesh.

"I've waited a long time for this," the monster rasped as he reached out and touched Rafik's face.

"No," Rafik heard Vincha shouting, the rest of her words were swallowed by the sound of his own pounding heart. He knew she was as trapped as he was, and that thought was the last thing that went through his mind before terror claimed his senses and he fainted.

52

Try not to move now, Vincha."

"I ain't moving." Vincha's voice betrayed annoyance. "You put my head in a rusting clamp."

"Well . . . try not to breathe, then. This is a delicate moment."

"You messing up my plugs—I'd say it's a delicate moment,"

The brunt of the operation was made with the med bed's metal hands, but Sci insisted on cleaning her plugs manually. As far as Vincha could tell, Sci was not marked, and without tattoos he could not have been a Mender or a Gadgetier. Nevertheless, he possessed impressive expertise in both fields, a cross between a healer and a Tinker.

"I am not *messing* up your plugs." Sci's voice was slightly muffled by the mask he wore. "I'm just cleaning the mess that is left inside you. Would have been easier to have sedated you completely."

Vincha gripped the sides of the med bed as she felt Sci's instruments inside her skull.

"No sedation," she blurted through clenched teeth.

"Then help me by not moving, got a loose wire here . . . right . . . don't . . . move . . . now!"

Vincha winced and stifled a cry.

After a short while, Sci appeared in her line of vision, holding his instruments and a wire, all covered in mucus and blood. He was a short, thin man, bald, despite looking relatively young. His eyes betrayed his ancestors' race.

He wiggled the severed wire between thumb and forefinger. "Done for today, but we should do this again in a day or two. I can't describe the amount of infection your plugs caused . . . Now, look at me."

He bent down to check her pupils. Normally Vincha would have felt very uneasy being in a vulnerable position with anyone, let alone a stranger standing so close to her. But there was something in the way Sci handled himself that made her feel at ease in his presence.

"I've taken out all that I could, but we don't have the time to remove the deeper devices," he explained. "The healing process will take too long, and Nakamura-san said not to risk it."

Vincha lightly touched her shaved head and felt crusted blood on her fingertips. "Well. *I* would have been happy to keep my gear, so I guess we're even. Do you have any idea how much my hardware cost me? You better keep my gear intact for when I come back . . ."

It was a jest of sorts. Sci's workshop contained enough hardware in it to outfit an entire guild house. In truth, it wasn't about the coin. Without her gear, Vincha felt defenceless, deaf and blind to her surroundings, almost naked. She hated every moment since it was removed, but that was part of the deal with Nakamura; no Tarkanian attachments of any kind. The fact that none of Nakamura's crew carried augmentations was a small consolation. In theory they would have been at a disadvantage compared to any Troll crew from the Hive, but the outcome of the last fight with was proof of Nakamura's crew's lethal capabilities.

She still could not erase from her mind the image of Deesha's severed head rolling on the cave's ground.

"You'll do much better without your gear." Sci took off his mask and peeled the bloodstained gloves from his hands.

"Well, a girl has to make a living, you know, and there are only a few things I can do well beside channel . . ." She made the comment even more flirtatious by adding a smile, testing his reaction for a possible advantage she could exploit in the future.

But Sci answered in all seriousness, "Your attachments only caused you pain and sufferings, believe me." He dumped his instruments into a bowl of clear liquid. "And the cost is much greater than whatever you paid for it."

"I could deal with the pain," she answered testily, "and a bag of Skint doesn't cost much these days."

Sci just shook his head again. "Tell me, when was the first time you had a device installed?"

Vincha hesitated. "I was . . . fourteen." For some reason she'd felt compelled to lie. In truth, she was even younger when a rogue CommMan named Slice hooked her up to a cheap device and scarred her head in the process. He was also the one who handed Vincha her first bag of Skint, promising an easy cure for the debilitating migraines. Then he had sex with her. Vincha stiffened as she remembered.

Sci's voice brought her back. "So you've been carrying Tarakan objects inside your body your entire adult life?" He turned his back to her, and Vincha thought she saw him shiver, as if disgusted by the thought.

She shrugged. "The gear makes me useful."

Sci took a large plastic cup in his hand and dropped a few dried leaves into it. "I think in time you will see that the Tarakan devices were hindering you more than helping. I think all of humanity needs to stop attaching Tarakan technology. It wasn't meant to be used in the way you've been using it." He pressed a button where he stood, and Vincha's bed began to move and change shape into a chair.

Vincha winced as her body was slowly moved into a normal sitting position. "What do you mean?" she'd said. "Of course they're meant for us. Why else would the Tarkanians leave these items all around their cities?"

Sci poured hot liquid into the cup, and stirred the leaves slowly. "I've been dealing with Tarakan technology my entire life—studying it, applying it, curing people from their addiction to it—and the one thing I am absolutely sure of is that these artifacts were not meant for us to use in the way you and the rest of the Salvationists are using them."

He came back and sat next to Vincha. "Think about it. In any other field or form, Tarakan technology is perfect, from their highways to the puzzle locks or the nodes themselves. When a Tarakan device works, it works perfectly. The Tarkanians would have easily found a way to use these augs without any side effects, if that was indeed their intention. Most certainly they would not have resorted to something as crude and addictive as Skint. Remember, it's we humans who made green powder from the skin and blood of dead Lizards. Which reminds me." Sci released the clamps restricting Vincha's head with a touch of a button and handed the plastic cup to her. "Drink this and do not spit it out, no matter how much it stings and burns."

Vincha wrinkled her nose. "What is it?"

"This should boost your resistance and diminish your cravings for the powder. You'll have to drink it three times a day for a long while, so better start getting used to it."

Vincha eyed the cup with suspicion. "I thought if you remove the devices—"

"—the symptoms fade?" He shook his head. "I'm afraid not. It's an addict's myth. The cravings persist long after you go vegan, and so does the pain. Now drink." His tone turned severe.

Vincha took a careful sip from the drink, grimaced, and only just managed to keep it down. "Rust, fuck, that was awful."

Sci's laughter rang across the large med hall. "It's my own home brew, and that was the weak version. I had to dilute it for you, with your condition and all . . ."

"You know?"

"Yes, Nakamura-san told me, and I saw what happened in the cave. You're not showing yet, but I guess it is stupid of me to wonder how *he* knew." Sci chuckled but then grew sombre. "The question is if you want to keep it, because if you don't, the sooner—"

"Rust, I'm keeping the baby." Vincha didn't mean for her tone of voice to be as aggressive as it sounded. She half-expected Sci to follow up with the question about the father's identity, as Nakamura did back in the cave, as his claw grabbed her exposed middle, but Sci only nodded. "I have a few leaves that could help you with nausea and give you some energy, but first priority, especially in your condition, is to get the Skint out of your system. You know that babies of Skint users tend to—"

"Yes, I know." Vincha got up to her feet, or at least tried to. The world suddenly swam in front of her eyes, and if it wasn't for Sci's quick reaction she would have fallen. He wasn't able to save the cup, though, and it smashed to the floor, spilling the rest of the brew.

"I'm sorry," she mumbled as he gently sat her back, feeling embarrassed at her weakness.

Sci picked up the cup. "It's okay. That's why I love these old things—they just never break. But you are not to move until I make you a new cup. And this time, drink it all up."

Vincha sighed and leaned with her shoulder on the chair's back. Sci returned, and this time he had made a cup for himself as well. He handed one to her. "I made it a little sweeter this time. Maybe it will go down better."

Vincha accepted the cup with both hands. For a moment they sat in silence, sipping brew. When she gathered enough strength to speak out loud she said, "Tell me about the other Puzzler. What happened?"

It was a gamble, an educated guess, and Sci almost managed to keep a straight face.

"What Puzzler?"

"You removed my hardware, not my brain, Sci. The nodes in this part of the Valley were always empty. Your workshop has enough gadgets and hardware to outfit the ShieldGuards. Don't try to sell me lies. If we are going to be in the same crew, you better level with me."

Sci nodded slowly. "I only knew the girl."

"But there were others—"

"I only knew the girl," he repeated and sipped quickly from his cup. "A young woman, really, but only in age, not in behavior. I think she was the reason Nakamura-san sent Daeon to recruit me. He wanted me to help her."

"Help her? How?"

"It was tragic, really. She was very sickly, physically weak, but also . . . not exactly in her right mind."

Vincha thought of Pikok, scratching his strange symbols on tables and walls.

"I tried to help her the best I could, but . . ." Sci did not complete the sentence.

"How did she die? If he hurts the boy, I'll—"

"She didn't die by his hand, Vincha."

"Then tell me how. A botched run? Did the Lizards get her?"

"No."

"Rust, Sci . . ." If she was any stronger, she would have attempted to interrogate the man by force.

In the face of her fury, the thin man's voice remained calm and soothing. "She died by her own hand, Vincha, that is the sad truth. I used to sedate her at nights but she tricked me, tricked everyone, really. Herev found her in the morning. There was nothing we could have done."

"And there were other Puzzlers before her."

"I only met Nimora. You should ask the others if you want but I suggest you leave this one be."

"I want to see Rafik."

Sci shrugged. "It is not up to me, and you know that. But you should know Nakamura-san has no reason to hurt Rafik."

"No, he'll just use him, then—"

She guessed she had reached the limit of Sci's patience, because he said, "Excuse me for saying so, but haven't you done the same?"

"That's different," Vincha answered hotly. "You don't know how they were treating him there. Nakamura promised me he'll free the boy, and I intend to hold him to his word."

Sci stared at the contents of his cup, perhaps considering his words. Finally he said, "I suggest you use this time to rest and recuperate. I am sure you will see the Puzzler soon."

Vincha got up stiffly, but this time she managed to stay upright. "His name is Rafik."

"Yes, Rafik, of course. Do you need me to bring you back to your room?"

Vincha walked to the infirmary's door as fast as she dared. "No need, I remember the way." As the door to the corridor slid open she turned around. "Tell Nakamura I *demand* to see the boy."

"You might want to cool your temper before you talk to him," Sci suggested, but by the time he finished the sentence, the doors had already slid shut behind her.

53

Vincha wandered along the wide corridor. She'd refused Sci's offer to walk her to her sleeping room out of sheer anger, but now she was lost. She tried to open almost every door she passed, but the place was huge, probably as big as the Hive. The corridors and halls she'd walked must have been a mile long, and she had been told there were several more levels underneath.

Yet despite the vastness of the underground bunker Vincha felt trapped. The band they'd clamped on her wrist—she resisted the urge to try and pull it off again—let her open the doors to her quarters, the mess hall, and the infirmary. Access to the rest of the complex was denied to her. She suspected that even if she found a way out and tried to run, the wrist band would pinpoint her position, or even incapacitate her—and even if she managed to escape and evade pursuit, where would she go? How long would she be able to survive the Valley alone and without her weapons and gear?

Vincha tried another door. She waved her hand in front of the blank surface and heard the familiar blip of denial. These were not puzzle locks, just the ordinary kind, found all over the Valley.

Only a few days ago she could have walked through these doors simply by hacking into their systems with her head gear. Now she was vulnerable, weak, useless. She was not a CommWoman anymore, just a woman.

She leaned her forehead on the shinning metal and hammer-fisted the wall in frustration. When she withdrew her head, the stain of sweat from where her skin touched the wall was already in the process of being absorbed by the Tarakan steel. It was so clean and polished, she could see her image reflected in the shiny wall. Examining her appearance, Vincha let out a soft groan of dismay. She would never have admitted it to anyone, but her voluminous red hair was really her only source of feminine pride. It hid her tattoos and the Tarakan artifacts attached to them. People told her she was beautiful, but now she just looked hideous . . . full of ugly scars, the gaping holes of the metal plugs, and bloodred tattoos. She remembered the first time her skull was penetrated by a drill. How it felt against her skin and how she screamed. She suddenly felt light-headed, turned and leaned against the coolness of the steel wall and covered her face with her hands, shuddering.

Memories of her time with Slice flooded her thoughts and in-termixed with the stench, images, and echoes of the Keenan crew massacre in the cave battle. The moment she crept up to Ramm and shot him in the back of the head flashed before her eyes. She had imagined before that killing him would give her satisfaction, for she was sure the brutal Troll had murdered her Doro, but all that was left in her since the fight in the cave was emptiness and sorrow. Nakamura's face filled Vincha's vision next, and his guttural whispers rang in her ears. She shivered as her body re-membered the Troll touching her middle. Still covering her face, Vincha slid down the wall and sat on the floor.

The consequences of her actions began to dawn on her.

She'd made a desperate deal with Nakamura but was now at his mercy, gearless and a prisoner in all but name. Worse, Naro-na's body had never been recovered, which meant that she might have escaped. The Lieutenant was resourceful enough to survive the valley on her own and reach the Hive. The Keenans suffered a staggering blow—their commander, their main crew, and their only Puzzler were lost—but Narona was a capable warrior and a natural leader. She might regroup, and then she would come back for revenge . . .

No, Vincha wiped her tears away. She had made her choice. There was no turning back. Her contingency plan had been a long shot anyway. She smiled bitterly at how stupid and frightened she was to act the way she did when she heard of Doro's death. She was pretty sure she knew what any of the Trolls she'd forced herself to fuck would say if she came to them saying she was carrying their child. Most would shrug her off, claim it was Doro's or that it was not their responsibility. One or two of the more decent type might offer her some coin to get rid of it at the Menders. Her hand touched her middle. She wondered how long it would take for her to show. Nakamura told her it was a girl. Another shudder coursed through her and with it, a resolution. She would hold Nakamura to his end of the deal, and she would have the baby, and then she would disappear. There had to be another corner in the world where her kind would be welcome. She'd go there.

Vincha emptied her mind and tried to become attuned to her immediate surroundings. She might have lost most of her gear, but her talent was still there. She could still feel the invisible world all around her even though she couldn't hear it: the voices, the music, the static. All whispered softly in the background, but she could not hear them clearly, let alone manipulate them to her will no matter how hard she concentrated. The headache that attacked her next was expected, but its intensity wasn't. Vincha breathed deeply and massaged her temples, remembering Sci's warning of the bouts of nausea that would likely happen often. "Do not be sick here," she mumbled to herself.

The scream behind Vincha was so sudden that it caused her to jump to her feet, spin around, and then lose her balance and fall back to the floor. It was a long scream that turned into a choked wail only to be followed by another primal howl. She scrambled to her feet, her back against the wall on the other side of the corridor. Rust, the walls were thick, and yet the scream was clear and loud. Whoever was producing these sounds was terrified or in terrible pain, or both. Was it Rafik? Were they torturing him? She tried to open the door again, first with her diminished powers, then manually.

It was a futile attempt, and a foolish one. If Nakamura wanted to torture the boy, she couldn't stop him. Vincha thought this even as she banged on the door in frustration.

She was so disoriented by the upsetting sounds that she didn't notice that she wasn't alone until a heavy hand touched her shoulder. Her battle reflexes took over. Vincha spun around and threw a straight punch, then followed it with a kick to the middle. Daeon managed to catch her fist and side block her kick with his own leg, then grunted as her knee bashed against his groin guard. Vincha did not stop fighting. Her first two moves were pure instinct, but as she realised who was touching her, her next attempts were executed with full intent. She sent a left-handed back fist, a head butt, and a knee to the ribs in his direction. He was shouting something at her while blocking her attacks, but Vincha wasn't listening. Like a cornered animal, she just kept lashing out at him. It was only when the world turned upside down and she hit the floor hard and his weight pinned her down, that Daeon's voice penetrated the pounding in her ear.

"I said relax, damn it."

She stopped struggling, but then surprised him with an upward surge. She was put down again, this time more roughly, and she felt the cool floor against her cheek and the weight of Daeon's knee pressing on her back.

Then she just lay there, completely exhausted, defeated and alone. He could easily have raped her. She knew that. He'd been strong enough to apprehend her when she was geared and ready for the fight in the cave, and now she was helpless and weak. She half-expected his hands to grope her body, the same way he'd handled her in the cave, but Daeon suddenly stepped back.

Vincha slowly pushed herself to a sitting position and leaned back against the wall. She still heard the cries and groans from behind the Tarakan steel wall.

Daeon said something else to her, but she couldn't process it. She saw a hand extended out to her, a gesture of peace, but when Vincha looked up she saw that Daeon probably expected her to try again. His guard was up and his other arm was tucked in, protecting his ribs and chin. She would not be able to surprise him with another attempt even if she'd had the strength. Vincha refused the extended hand.

Daeon crouched in front of her instead, keeping a safe distance from her legs. This time she heard him clearly. "Look, I'm sorry I had to handle you like that in the cave. Nakamura wanted you neutralized and weaponless . . . and you kept shooting that big dead Troll. I did what I had to do, but I didn't know Nakamura was going to rip your clothes with the blade of his staff or handle you the way he did. I mean it is his command, but I was . . . not happy about it, okay?"

Vincha nodded slowly as another scream echoed in the corridor.

"What are you doing to him in there?" she asked, hating the tremble in her voice. "He's just a kid."

The look of surprise on Daeon's face seemed genuine. "You think it's the Puzzler being tortured in there?" he said with incredulity. "I can assure you the boy is sound asleep in his quarters. I can take you there and you can see for yourself."

"So who's screaming?"

Daeon stared at the wall behind her for a moment before answering, "Nakamura."

Vincha turned her head to the door. "What's he doing to himself?" She rose to her feet and Daeon took another cautionary step away to the side, answering her question in a soft whisper.

"He's asleep, Vincha. Nakamura is dreaming."

54

"D one." Rafik leaned back as he pulled his fingers out of the puzzle box.

"Already? You're getting good." Herev picked up the box and turned it around in his hand. He pointed at the side of the item. "See the five stars here? That's the difficulty of the lock. This is the most complex box I have. I thought it would take you half a day to solve. Guess we could do some shooting practice now, or play a game, or"—his thick eyebrows danced—"maybe I can teach you some fencing."

Rafik shook his head. "No, I want another box. Find me something harder."

Herev fiddled with the puzzle box in his hand, scratching his head.

"I said, bring me another!" Rafik shouted, banging his fist on the metal table.

Herev took a step back. "Okay, relax, kid," he chuckled. "You got some temper, that's for sure. I'll go see what I can find in Sci's lab."

A soft chime sounded as the door slid open, and Daeon and

Vincha walked in carrying plates. It took Rafik a heartbeat to recognise her without her red hair. She smiled and winked at him.

"Look what I found," she said. "Real food! No more rusting pills. I made this!"

Daeon handed a plate to Herev, who whooped with joy. "Man, what a treat. Sci's cooking tastes like his medicine."

Rafik looked at all of them with a blank face until their merriment died.

After a spell of awkward silence Vincha stepped forward and gently placed a plate on the table between several puzzle boxes. Rafik couldn't remember the last time he'd tasted real food, but the smell just brought back memories of home and people he would never see again.

He swept his hand in the direction of the plate and then watched it land with a crash on the floor. Vincha's face was ashen.

"Rafik, I'm—"

"Bitch."

Daeon and Herev exchanged glances behind her back.

"You don't understand—" she tried again.

"And now you're an ugly whore, too."

"If you just let me explain—"

"You don't need to explain. Goll and Deesha didn't need to die." He looked at Herev. "Deesha didn't deserve to be sliced in half."

Herev simply shrugged and busied himself with his plate.

Daeon began picking up the food from the floor and putting it back on the plate.

"You don't understand." Vincha rose to her feet and tried again. "It was our only way out."

"No," Rafik shouted, his lower lip trembling. "It was *your* way out. You just sold me to a different crew."

That got everyone's attention.

"You think I have rust for brains?" Rafik shouted. "You're no different from any Troll. You just wanted a bigger cut, so you stole me from the Keenans."

"This place will give us freedom, you will be free."

"Liar!" Rafik was standing up now, shouting. "Don't lie to me. Maybe they will let you go after this, but I'm a Puzzler." He held up his marked fingers. "I am their key now. They will never let me go. In the Hive, at least I had someone to talk to. I had Pikok. I could walk around. But here, I'm stuck underground until Nakamura decides to go on a deep run."

As if on cue, the door slid open and Nakamura stepped in. They all turned to face him and Rafik stopped shouting. Even here, in his own territory, Nakamura's face was hidden, but just a glimpse of his chin and neck was enough to put the fear of the Prophet Reborn into Rafik's heart. In his gnarled hand, Nakamura grasped his black staff, which was almost as tall as he was. He surveyed the room slowly. "Problems?"

"Just a mild disagreement. Nothing to worry about," Vincha said.

Nakamura stepped towards Rafik. Vincha moved out of his way as Nakamura plucked a plate from her with his free hand. He stepped closer to Rafik. "You should eat," he whispered.

Rafik looked like he was ready to move his hand in another sweeping gesture but as if he anticipated the boy, Nakamura let go of the staff and caught Rafik's arm in a grip so strong that the boy yelped in pain. Instead of falling to the ground, the black staff stayed upright, producing a soft humming noise.

Nakamura ignored it. "Eat," he commanded.

Rafik pressed his lips together in defiance, then slowly sank back into his chair. Nakamura pulled up a chair and sat next to him. Rafik fixed his eyes on the plate, not looking at Nakamura.

"Eat."

"I'm not hungry."

Vincha tensed. Should Nakamura raise his hand to strike the boy, she would intervene, no matter the consequences. Daeon took a tentative step towards her, his eyes imploring restraint, but instead of striking Rafik, Nakamura took everyone by surprise with a question.

"Are you afraid of me?"

Rafik seemed to be pondering what his answer would be, then shook his head. "You're just different."

"Then look at me."

The boy slowly turned his head and looked straight into Nakamura's cowl. He visibly shuddered.

"Am I ugly in your eyes?" Saliva dripped from the darkness of the cowl onto Nakamura's chest.

"The pattern of your face is strange." Rafik lowered his gaze.

That brought a throaty chuckle from Nakamura. "You could say that. What would you say if I told you I was afraid of you?"

"I'd say you have rust in your brain. I'm just a Puzzler. I can barely shoot a hand blaster."

"Yes, but you are a very special Puzzler. And believe me, I've met more than a few."

Rafik straightened up in his seat and looked at Nakamura with new interest. "Why is your face like this? Did someone beat you up?"

"Many have tried to . . . beat me up." Nakmura said the words as if he was tasting them on his lips. "And when I was a boy your age, many succeeded. But I was born this way, distorted. You see, Rafik, some people are born with tattoos on their bodies, but I was born tattooed in my mind. It was a miracle I survived. My own father wanted to kill me, and after him there were many others who tried. When I grew up a little and came to understand how different I was, it was *me* who wanted to die. But somehow, I knew I came to this world for a purpose, that my life was not meaningless, and my power was needed in this world. I know you feel the same way, Rafik. I know you hate being a Puzzler, but know this is your true nature, your calling."

Rafik nodded slowly. "So what is your power?"

Nakamura answered wearily, "When I was younger than you are, a woman found me wandering in the woods, alone, starving, and practically naked. She was a hermit herself, and not of the soundest of minds, but she took me into her home and saved my life, because there was no way I would have survived by myself for much longer. I stayed with her for several years, and for a while she was the mother I never truly had. Then one day, I began dreaming of her death. No matter what I told myself in the morning, I knew she would die, and soon. In some visions it was an accident, in others a raid, but the worst visions were when I saw it would be from my own hand. I could not understand why I would kill the only person in the world that showed me kindness and swore never to do anything to harm her. She ended up falling ill and suffering greatly before I found my courage to do the decent thing. You see, Rafik, I can see the future, or possible futures, that is my power, and sometimes I can help the best future happen by taking certain actions, even if those actions seem strange or cruel to some."

"You mean you are like the Prophet Reborn?" Rafik asked.

Nakamura nodded. "Perhaps I am."

But Rafik shook his head in disbelief. "It cannot be. Everyone knows the Reborn was and will be perfect in mind and body—" He stopped his recitation midsentence, realising the insult in his words too late, but Nakamura leaned back on his seat with something that must have been an attempt at a smile on his deformed face.

"I know I am not pleasant to look at, but this is just a side effect of my curse. I see events that could lead to other events, and from the earliest moment I can remember, I knew that you and I needed to meet. It is the best of the possible futures I have foreseen."

"I dreamed about you, about how we met." Rafik looked suddenly worried. "Does this mean I can see the future, too?"

Nakamura shook his head within the darkness of his cowl. "No, Rafik. Many times, my visions come to me in dreams, and when I am asleep I sometimes share them with others, especially when my dreams are strong. When we were both asleep you could likely sense I was looking for you, and at times you shared my visions."

Rafik considered Nakamura's words for a moment. "You have very bad dreams."

Nakamura's chuckle sounded like a death rattle. "That's what the woman hermit told me, just before I put a pillow over her face. Are you still afraid of me, Puzzler?"

"A little," Rafik admitted.

"Don't be. You are safe here."

"Everyone promises me that I will be safe with them, but we end up fighting Lizards and almost dying."

"Sometimes fighting is necessary for the good of us all."

"Now you *really* sound like the Prophet Reborn."

Nakamura tilted his head. "Maybe I am not *the* Prophet, Rafik, but perhaps I am just *your* prophet."

He fished a puzzle box from a hidden pocket and gently placed it on the table next to the plate of food. "This is a level-thirty puzzle lock. I have only one like it, and I have never seen a more difficult box."

Rafik's eyes widened. "Are we going on a deep run?"

"Yes. As soon as you can master this puzzle box, then we are going on the deepest run, to the very heart of City within the Mountain, where no man has visited since the Catastrophe."

"Why?"

"Because I have seen all the possible futures, and our meeting brings us closer to the best possible outcome. You will take us on the deepest run ever attempted, for the biggest prize."

"And what then?"

"Then we will all be free and rich beyond our wildest dreams."

The crew smiled and nodded at each other in approval behind Nakamura's back.

Rafik shook his head. "You will just spend all the metal and then want to go in again."

Nakamura leaned forward and touched Rafik lightly on his shoulder. "No, I give you my oath, Rafik. After this run there will be no others." He turned his head briefly towards Vincha and said, "You will be free."

Rafik was silent, then he raised his head and looked straight at Nakamura. "Does it hurt?"

"My face?"

Rafik hesitated, then nodded.

"All the time. But I've learned to live with pain."

"Are you angry at the Prophet Reborn for making you like this?" Rafik continued, before Nakamura could answer. "I am angry at him. I prayed every day. I didn't do anything bad to anyone. Why did he curse me? I lost everything, everyone . . ." his voice trailed off into an uncomfortable silence.

When Nakamura finally answered it was the first time his voice had a hint of tenderness to it. "Yes, I was angry, Rafik. In those rare moments when no one was hitting me or cursing me, I did ask those questions and I felt sorry for myself." He put a deformed hand on Rafik's shoulder. "But eventually I understood that we are here for a purpose, that we rose from the ashes of humanity, different but no better. Those who inherited powers must use them to propel our race, whatever's left of it, back to greatness. That is why we are what we are."

"But my powers are useless," Rafik said with a raised voice.

Vincha was suddenly, painfully, aware of how young the boy was.

"I can't do anything useful except open puzzle locks."

"On the contrary, Rafik, you are the most useful of all of us. Perhaps the only real useful one." Nakamura gestured around them. "You see, my boy, we are all freaks." He pointed at himself and added, "Some more than others. But you, Rafik, you are pure. Those Trolls in the Hive, with their Tarakan attachments and big weapons, called you 'key.' They did their best to make you feel useless—but believe me, sometimes to make the biggest difference in this world, all you need to do is open the right door." Nakamura leaned forward. "You know what you really want, don't you? What is it you dream of when you sleep peacefully?"

Rafik answered without hesitation. "I want to see the wall of symbols. I want to solve the Great Puzzle." His eyes shone when he spoke.

At that moment Vincha suddenly realized Rafik's markings ran all the way up his arm, thinning down to black lines at his elbow. For some reason the discovery frightened her.

Nakamura nudged the puzzle box in his direction. "When you master this puzzle box we will go to the heart of the City within the Mountain, and there you shall find what you seek."

Watching Rafik, Vincha saw the boy's demeanour change as he looked at the puzzle box. His entire body seemed drawn to it. He reached out slowly, his marked fingers outstretched for the holes. But Nakamura grabbed his hand and moved the box away.

"Not now, not yet," he said, but Vincha heard the excitement in his voice.

"Why not?"

Nakamura shoved the plate of food in front of the boy. "First," he said, "you must finish your dinner."

55

Vincha was not a great storyteller. Her tone of voice stayed flat, almost emotionless, throughout her story. She was acting as if this was a report to a crew commander, giving facts, quoting dialogues, and describing actions, yet keeping emotions out of it. I found myself adding my own interpretation of what she or Rafik must have felt. It was a good technique I came up with in order to establish empathy with whomever I was interrogating. I kept listening to her with my eyes closed while imagining the events she was describing, and I suspect that Vincha's monotone voice, my own fatigue and the enveloping darkness caused me to doze in and out of the dream world. Luckily, at some point Vincha's voice changed, and the penned emotions in her tone jolted me out of my stupor before anyone noticed.

"I thought," Vincha shrugged, "he was only saying this to get to the boy, you know, rusting his brain a bit so he would be docile and they could use him in the deep run. I mean, what was that all about, 'best of all worlds' and 'opening the right door' and Rafik being 'the pure one'? That was just a load of loose wire. Nakamura was priming the boy, that's what I thought. Daeon showed me some of the information they'd gathered. They had a good map of the first two levels of the run, but the prize lay deeper, in the city's inner sanctum, completely uncharted territory. He said Nakamura could predict the future and he was going to make them so rich and powerful that they, well . . ." Vincha smiled. "Daeon actually used the word 'we'—that *we* could carve a small empire for ourselves. I didn't know about the future prediction—maybe Nakamura was that kind of freak troll. I just wanted enough metal to retire and never see a rusting Lizard ever again.

"It took Rafik three days to convince Nakamura he was ready to try his puzzle box. But it proved to be a disaster. As soon as he placed his fingers inside the holes, Rafik's eyes rolled up until we couldn't see his pupils and his body went into a spasm. We lay him down on a bunk and tried to calm him down but Rafik kept twitching and drooling. I'd never seen anything like that before. I was ready to plug him out, but Nakamura said not to touch him and stopped Sci from using any medicine or even to give Rafik fluids through a needle to his vein. There was nothing left to do but watch over him.

"Rafik stayed attached to that rusting box for eight days. After the initial shock, his body went limp and his breath was shallow and slow. He didn't eat, and he only swallowed when we forced water into his mouth. His eyes were open, but he saw nothing and he did not react to anything that was happening in the room. I spent as much time as I could guarding him, hoping that if I was left alone I could pry Rafik's fingers out of that rusting puzzle box, but Nakamura was no fool and there was always someone watching us both. To be honest, most of the time I was just trying to keep Sci's brew and my own meals down, since I was still feeling the plug sickness.

"Rafik was down for the count, and in a way, so was I. With nothing else to do, I had time to think, which caused serious doubts about Nakamura's plans to surface. Why risk ourselves for some mythical treasure inside the City within the Mountain when the hardware alone in this hideout could have been sold for a fortune? Would a murderous freak like Nakamura keep his promise to Rafik and myself, and why would he? I was beginning to realize I'd made the wrong play with Rafik, but there was no choice but to make the best of the situation. So I tried to get to know the crew better, hoping I could find a way to turn them against Nakamura, or at least get one of them onto my side in case Nakamura decided I was expendable.

"Daeon was obviously second in command, and the others listened to what he said. I didn't know what oiled Daeon's joints, but my instinct told me his loyalty to Nakamura was beyond a doubt. Herev, on the other hand, was a true mercenary—tough and dangerous. I saw him practice, and he could wield a power sword like lightning. I thought perhaps Herev was the one I could turn, the way he looked at me . . ." I could see Vincha's face flush even in the gloom. She sighed. "In that kind of situation, you use whatever you've got. Those guys hadn't seen a woman in a *long* time, even one without hair and in my condition. So I knew both Daeon and Herev wanted me, but Daeon was too loyal and Herev's desire for wealth was more powerful than lust. He would stick to Nakamura as long as he thought the plan was moving forward. Sci was always polite, gentle, even caring, but he never showed any interest in me.

"All the while Rafik was slowly wasting away. It drove me crazy, but there was nothing I could do to help him. If the others thought Rafik's condition was a sign that Nakamura's ability to predict the future was not reliable, they didn't show it. Every time I tried to talk about it, I hit solid metal. Daeon and Sci simply changed the topic of conversation. Herev told me to 'shut my rusting gob.'

"I thought Rafik was going to die, simple as that. No one could survive without food and on so little fluid. I saw him wasting away, growing thinner, paler, his breathing so slow that all of us found ourselves looking for a pulse at some point.

"On the eighth day Rafik woke up. Herev said the puzzle box

just beeped suddenly and a second later Rafik opened his eyes. I was not beside him, but he asked for me almost immediately.

"I won't lie, I was happy to see him. By the time I arrived at the room the crew was there, and he'd changed clothes and was attempting to eat a bowl of broth Sci brought him. Still, he was as white as a ghost and . . ." She hesitated.

"And what?" Galinak asked. We were all awake and alert now.

"He was different. There was something in his eyes. I hugged him, and when I let him go he just looked at me as if he were dissecting me to pieces and putting me back together again. He said 'Vincha' once, in a quiet voice, and when I answered he just said my name again, and again and again, maybe five or six times, like he was memorizing it.

"Then he turned to me and said, 'Did you know that your name comes from Vishiya, who was a goddess worshipped by warriors at sea more than three thousand years before the Catastrophe?'

"'No I didn't know that,' I said. 'How do you know this?'

"'I don't know how I know,' Rafik frowned. 'But I'm sure it's true.'

"Our conversation was cut off by the arrival of Nakamura. As soon as he stepped into the room, Rafik announced, 'I've solved the puzzle box,' but there was no triumph in his voice. It was a simple, stated fact, no more.

"Nakamura leaned a little on his black staff and let out a soft sigh. 'I knew you'd solve it. I had no doubt—'

"'Yet you are relieved.' Rafik's voice was calm but distant.

"For the first time there was a hint of hesitation in Nakamura's voice. 'My predictions are often accurate, but sometimes . . . sometimes I don't understand what I see until it is too late. I said before that our meeting brings us closer to the best of possible futures, but there was a chance, a certain future in which you died.'

"'I will die,' Rafik said suddenly, his eyes unfocused. 'We are all going to die.'

"'Would you stop this rusting conversation about death?' Herev said, trying to lighten the mood.

"Rafik ignored him, fixing his attention on Nakamura. 'We need to go to the City within the Mountain.'

"'Take a couple of days to recover,' Nakamura answered.

"But Rafik shook his head. 'No, I want to go by first light. I have seen it, and it is glorious.'

"The crew exchanged glances.

"'Seen what, pup? Did you see our treasure?' Herev grinned.

"'The Great Puzzle. I have seen it now, not in my dreams but for real. It is—'

"'Forget the rusting puzzles,' Herev snorted. 'What about the freaking unrusted metal? The good, old-fashioned Tarakan artifacts? The personal heat-seeking missiles? Machines that could recalibrate everything you throw at them? What about—'

"'Shut up,' Nakamura growled from within his cowl.

"But Rafik answered, 'Those items lie beyond the Great Puzzle, and there are much greater things there than what you've just asked for.'

"Herev tried to lighten up the mood with 'I don't know what could possibly be better than a personal heat-seeking missile,' but no one was in the mood.

"Rafik simply turned his head and looked at the mercenary, and Herev reacted the same way I did when faced with the boy's stare; he stiffened up, as if expecting danger.

"Then Rafik spoke in a dreamlike voice: 'Beyond the Great Puzzle lies all the knowledge and technology humanity has lost.'

"Nakamura stood motionless for enough time to make everyone feel uncomfortable, then he tapped his black staff on the floor twice and spoke.

"'Get ready—we go tomorrow.'"

56

Vincha's story was interrupted by a soft knock at the door. We got to our feet surprisingly quickly, considering the state we were all in. Weapons were drawn and aimed. My master nodded at me, and I walked slowly towards the door. I used my sight to see through the wood and identify one of the guards who helped save us in the Keenan guild house. By the look on his face I concluded he was not bringing happy news.

I unlocked the door, and he shouldered his way past me without saying a word. The man was a professional. To his credit, he didn't flinch when confronted with the array of weaponry aimed at him. He turned and spoke over my shoulder to the direction of my LoreMaster.

"Word is out they're looking for you—" he turned to Vincha "—and you—" then he pointed to me "—and you."

"Me?" Vincha and I spoke in unison, but I continued, my voice cracked from fatigue. "LoreMaster, why are we hunted? I mean, why now?"

"We were compromised." LoreMaster Harim's voice was full of regret.

"By who?"

He sighed heavily. "By me."

I waited. We all did.

"I was too smart for my own good, a foolish old man. My theory about what happened in City within the Mountain was developed after a meticulous look at all the evidence I had. Unfortunately, when I think about things—"

"—you write them down," I said, finishing his sentence.

He smiled sadly. "A bad habit. Especially when my notes found their way to the City Council's Chief of Security, who happens to be a Sabarra nomination. I had to explain myself to several people, and I may have overemphasised the possible rewards that could await us all, should we regain entrance to City within the Mountain."

I imagined my LoreMaster standing in front of the security chief and his staff, and slowly an image of my role in this mess began to take form in front of my eyes. LoreMaster Harim had to tell his theory, and in return, the Council ordered him to send someone to investigate—but not himself, of course. They would insist on keeping LoreMaster Harim close, so he had to send someone else, someone far less qualified, someone who was just a few steps behind and would take a *long* time to investigate. This would draw the eyes and ears of the Council away from my Lore-Master and give him time to think of a way to outmanoeuvre the pack of wolves that surrounded him. That was the reason my LoreMaster did not hire a squad of competent ex-Salvationists to find a dangerous and elusive mercenary, and sent instead an inexperienced secondary scribe who read too many Salvo-novels. My LoreMaster's actions were so logical I was surprised I felt so hurt.

As if reading my thoughts, LoreMaster Harim and I locked eyes in the gloom. He nodded ever so slightly, and I smiled bitterly back. How ironic that I had actually succeeded in finding Vincha and making her talk, and my success brought ruin to all of my LoreMaster's work.

So why didn't the Council just sit back and let me finish the job?

I asked myself, and I realised the answer here was also obvious. Even in its weaker state today, the Council was not as unified as a layman would think. It was made of factions, several remaining guilds, and powerful individuals who pulled the strings and vied for more power. Access to the City within the Mountain and its secrets would give any faction in the City of Towers the victory it sought. Some would benefit from the success, others from the failure. Once they found out I had made contact with Vincha, it was a game of who could grab her first.

The guard still standing at the door was oblivious to the finer points of my inner conversation. He just said, "Too many people saw you land in the Pit. The metal offered for you is enough for them to talk."

"How much?" Galinak grunted. We all glared at him as he shrugged. "What? I just want to know."

The guard told us the sum, and I knew we'd better get out of that hut fast.

My LoreMaster sighed and turned to Vincha. "Well, my dear, we'd better complete your fascinating story somewhere safer."

Vincha was too tired to argue, so it was Galinak who stretched and asked midyawn, "Where are we going now?"

"We're going to connect another piece of this story."

"And where is that, old man?"

LoreMaster Harim bent down with a grunt and tapped on the floor until he found what he was looking for, slid the cover aside, and exposed a black surfaced panel. From where I stood I could not see what LoreMaster Harim was doing, but a few heartbeats later a trapdoor by his side slid open silently. The smell that flowed up into the room made everyone grimace.

"Bukra's balls." Galinak covered his nose with his hand. "That smell could rust my cock."

My LoreMaster was already tying cloth across his face. "If you do not have a breathing guard, I suggest you all do the same. I apologise for the inconvenience, but in order to get where we need to go, we must travel through the city's sewers."

57

Even climbing down a narrow shaft of the city's sewage system reminded me how advanced and calculated the Tarkanians were. The shaft immediately lit up as soon as LoreMaster Harim lowered himself into it. The ladder was metal but it was surprisingly warm to the touch, pleasant to grasp, and even had a soft feel to it, as if it was molding itself to my hands and feet. In a way, this was as impressive to me as standing on the highest tower point of the city, but what even the Tarkanians could not have dealt with was the stench. We ended up walking in a straight line on a narrow pavement, near a slow-moving canal of liquidized waste. I looked at the brown sludge just inches away from my feet and knew for a fact that if I fell into it, I would not survive. The stench was almost too much to bear. It made me gag, and several times people had to vomit. Galinak had it especially bad; he was pale and wobbly on his feet.

By the time we moved into safer tunnels, my tunic, already stained from blood and muck, was soaked with sweat, I had an awful taste in my mouth, and all I wanted to do was to get under a stream of hot water with soap and then find a nice warm bed and dive under a clean blanket.

Vincha was the first to speak. "Where are we going?"

"Somewhere safe," I heard my LoreMaster say. His voice was weak. He must have been suffering far worse than me. "We need supplies and reinforcements."

"And new clothes," grunted Galinak. "This place stinks worse than a Lizard's arse." For once, I agreed with him.

Four more guards were waiting for us. They were dressed in full black battle suits, and I noticed that their weapons, albeit small, were in superb condition. My survival instinct was telling me something was seriously off. I glanced at the others to see if they felt the same, but they were too distraught and weakened from our walk in the sewers.

The Guild of Historians was much more than its mundane name suggested. You might imagine stuffy old men with long pipes and longer arguments, and you would not be far away from the truth. But these men also walked the scarred and dangerous land and collected evidence and artifacts of the destroyed civilisations. Once properly investigated and catalogued, a lot of these findings were eventually sold for surprisingly large sums of coin, mainly to avid collectors from the upper crust of society. Still, I wasn't sure that retaining a company of fully equipped mercenaries who were ready to take on the rusting ShieldGuards was part of our budget. Who were these guys?

We reached a maintenance door leading up. Two guards climbed the ladder and we formed an orderly queue.

We found ourselves in the centre of a large room half filled with wooden crates. It was lit by a single artificial light that made the corners dark. I sensed that there were even more guards in the room. Was it a trap? I turned my head to Galinak and Vincha, but they seemed disoriented. There were at least two guards between each of us and more just beyond the circle of light.

I wanted to warn Galinak and Vincha, but by the time I

thought of a way it was too late. A man walked slowly into the circle of light. My heart fluttered when I realised what I was seeing. Half of his face and one arm was metal. Despite knowing him only from reputation, it took me just a few heartbeats to recognise Jakov. As usual, Vincha was the quickest to react.

"Rust fucker." She moved fast, but the large masked guard behind her was ready. He bear-hugged Vincha, lifting her off her feet. Even in his weakened condition, Galinak managed to send two guards to the floor before he was overwhelmed by sheer numbers and restrained in a submission hold. I found myself on my knees with a gun at my temple, as did the rest of the crew with the notable exception of my LoreMaster.

Jakov walked slowly to the still struggling Vincha. I knew the man's description but seeing him walking past me sent shudders up my spine. The merchant bent close enough to almost touch Vincha's lips with his metal face.

"So you are Vincha." His voice was almost a whisper. "Many, many people are looking for you, my dear. Please tell me, I have no memory of ever crossing wires with you, so why do you harbour such resentment?"

"Go rust." Her spit hit the metal side of his face.

"I do sometimes. There is an ointment for that. I rub it on myself every evening. You should try some." His metal hand touched her head with what was almost a caress. Vincha visibly flinched. "It is good to finally meet you, Vincha. I believe you owe me a large sum of metal."

My heart sank.

Jakov motioned to the guards to search us for weapons, which they did with efficiency. Galinak groaned as he was hauled up to his feet. "I would just like to say that I am *not* escorting this woman—"

"Her debt is taken care of." Jakov cut Galinak off and turned to face my LoreMaster. "When this fine gentleman approached me with his interesting theory I agreed to come back to the city and help out with whatever I could. So I bought all her debts, paid her creditors, and whatever she owed, she now owes to me. Although—" he glanced briefly back at the struggling Vincha "—I would not go back to the Den if I were her."

Jakov approached my LoreMaster. "So, Harim? Is your little theory correct?"

Of course, I saw now that LoreMaster Harim had to do it. The Council was too divisive and corrupt, so it was logical to turn to a weapons merchant for protection. The antigrav suits, the guards, the superb weaponry—it all made sense now.

I saw the LoreMaster nod. "I heard several new interesting details today"—I was probably the only one who detected the forced calmness in his voice—"but most of it was confirmation of what I'd figured out already. Now we must hear the end of the story. I want to find out what happened to Rafik and Nakamura's crew."

"Yes." Jakov leaned against a crate, which my sight told me was filled with three power rifles and quite a bit of explosives. "Tell us what happened. How did you betray them and escape with your life? And then, depending on your story, I will decide."

"Decide what?" I said suddenly, surprising even myself.

I heard a soft, whirring noise as he cocked his metallic eye and focused at me. The gaze from his human eye was similarly cold and calculating. "Whether to let you live, of course."

58

"Where are we going?"

"You'll see when we get there."

"Are we going to get in through the gates that never open?"

"You'll see."

"Because they never open, you know."

"I know."

"And we'll get there by going underground? Because that would be a clever way of doing this. Unless we stumble upon a nest of Lizards."

"You'll see—"

"—when we get there. Rust, why are you so secretive about it?"

Daeon did not bother to answer this time.

"More stairs. Rust. How many levels does this place have?"

"Too many, apparently." Daeon turned and began descending the wide set of steps.

"Why are we taking the steps with all this gear? We passed at least three lifts, so . . ."

Daeon stopped and looked up at Vincha, who was still descending the previous set of stairs. "At the moment I am doing all of the carrying, so I don't see why you should be complaining."

It was true. Aside from the black power armour he was wearing and the vast array of weapons and power clips, Daeon was also carrying a backpack fully loaded with gear. Vincha, on the other hand, was not even allowed to carry a weapon, a fact she was struggling to cope with.

Daeon turned back and continued walking. Vincha rolled her eyes behind his back. "I'm only asking because it is illogical—"

"We are not using the lifts because Nakamura said not to use them."

"Ah . . . the great Nakamura. Did he tell you why we shouldn't use the lifts?"

"No, Vincha, he did not."

"Do you blindly follow *all* of his commands?"

Daeon turned to the next set of stairs so Vincha could see his face. It was obvious he was trying to keep his temper in check, and Vincha didn't blame him. He must have been as tense as she was with the prospect of going to the heart of the City within the Mountain, the deepest run ever attempted. Her own mood and juvenile behavior was probably the result of the fact she'd barely slept through the night, a mixture of dread, plug fever, and the maddening quietness in her own head, now that she'd gone vegan.

It was easy for her to pass Daeon and block his way on the set of stairs. He tried to pass her, but Vincha kept playfully moving in front of the heavily geared warrior.

"I asked you a question, Troll."

"Vincha, I am not in the mood."

"Just answer me."

"What do you want to know?"

"Do you follow all of Nakamura's orders?"

Daeon locked stares with Vincha. "Of course I follow his orders, and so should you."

"Why?"

"Why what?"

"Why do you follow him like that? I mean—" Vincha made a show of looking Daeon up and down "—you seem capable enough. There are many safer ways to earn coin than to be taking orders from that freak."

From the steel in Daeon's gaze Vincha knew she had touched something, but he kept his cool.

"I follow all of his orders, and so should you. Those who didn't follow his orders are dead."

"By his hands or yours?"

Vincha saw Daeon's jaw clench twice and quickly added, "You haven't even given me a weapon. How am I going to be useful if I can't even defend myself in a deep run?"

"Nakamura's orders were to bring you down *now*," Daeon said stiffly, "and should you resist or delay me, to knock you out and carry you over my shoulder, an action I am beginning to contemplate."

Vincha held his gaze but made a show of slowly moving aside and spreading her arms wide. "After you, Troll."

Daeon passed her without another word, and they climbed down two more levels and entered a huge underground hall that reminded Vincha of the Long Tube platforms in the City of Towers. There were four large tunnels, two from each side of the hall. Their surfaces were similar to the material the Tarakan highway was made of.

Nakamura, Sci, Herev, and Rafik were already standing on the central platform. Herev carried even more weapons than Daeon, including his two power swords strapped to his back. Sci had two large metal trunks floating next to him. Rafik was standing quietly, dressed in diminutive battle gear with a power pistol hanging from his belt. He did not acknowledge Vincha or Daeon but was staring at nothingness with a blank look on his face.

"It's about time," Herev commented as Daeon and Vincha approached.

"We got a little lost," Daeon answered. He walked to Nakamura and handed him a palm-sized Tarakan screen pad. "Here it is. All is set, as you asked."

Nakamura nodded silently and began fiddling with the pad. Daeon walked to Sci, handing him several power tubes and stuffing his backpack inside one of the floating crates, before finally turning to Rafik.

"I found this in your room—you must have dropped it," he said, handing Fahid's blade to the boy. Rafik silently took the knife and looked down at his hand, bounced it in his palm as if weighing it. Vincha saw how a smile of relief replaced the blank expression and suddenly, ever so briefly, Rafik was just a boy again.

"Thank you," he said in a meek voice and pocketed the knife.

Daeon patted Rafik kindly just as Nakamura lifted his head from the pad and said, "Get ready."

Sci climbed down and ran into one of the tunnels with only a light backpack on his back. They waited until there was a sudden rumbling from one of the tunnels, and a Long Tube emerged and stopped at the platform, its doors silently opening.

"Imagine loading that baby up with the loot from the City within the Mountain," Herev said, grinning, as Sci stepped out of the Long Tube.

"This will bring us most of the way, but we will still need to enter the City within the Mountain," Nakamura said from inside his cowl. He turned to Rafik and simply asked, "Are you ready?"

Rafik silently nodded and sat himself down. Sci went to the front of the Long Tube and busied himself with the controls. The Long Tube began moving, and soon they reached a speed that could be matched only by a SuperTruck. They rode through many tunnels, some wide and others tight.

"Get ready," Sci suddenly said, and the Long Tube began slowing down.

Sci handed Vincha a headlamp. "What about a gun or something?" she asked, turning to Nakamura.

"I don't think so," Nakamura answered as the Long Tube stopped at a platform

"It's a *deep run*," Vincha protested, but Nakamura didn't even bother to answer

The doors of the Long Tube opened onto complete darkness.

Nakamura stepped out, and a moment later a ball of light emanated from his staff and wide beams from the crew's head gear, arm lights, and weapons joined to penetrate the darkness. It was so cold, Vincha began shivering almost immediately.

"Follow," Nakamura ordered.

He walked past them on the platform and above two high bridges. Vincha looked down and saw more tunnels and platforms below them, but the ground was too far away to see.

"Are we in deep yet?" Herev asked.

"No," Daeon answered, "but my guess is that very soon we will be."

They reached the last platform, a vast, open space that featured twenty large, Tarakan steel doors.

"This is the entrance to the first level of the City within the Mountain," Nakamura said. "From the vastness of the place and the number of doors, my guess is that many traversed in and out of the city every day." He turned to Rafik. "Choose any door you wish."

Without saying a word, Rafik walked to one of the doors and the crew followed him. When they got close, Sci said, "I don't see a puzzle box."

Rafik walked on until he reached the wall next to the door. When he was only one step away from it he held out his hand.

Nothing happened.

He took a step forward and touched the wall. For a heartbeat nothing happened, then the part of the wall around Rafik's hand lit up. Vincha watched in awe as the metal molded itself into three holes. Without hesitation Rafik closed his eyes and shoved his fingers into the wall.

He stood rigid.

"Get ready," Nakamura said and stepped forward. "As soon as the doors open we must hurry inside."

"You don't have to ask twice. If we stand here for any longer we'll freeze," said Herev, jumping lightly from one foot to the other.

Rafik let out a soft sigh just as the door slid open. Vincha saw a large hall, mirroring the platform they came from.

"Get in, now," ordered Nakamura.

Daeon and Herev went in first, power rifles ready. Sci went after them, with the two floating metal trunks close at his heels. Nakamura grabbed Rafik and nodded at Vincha. She stepped in through the door. Painfully aware she was weaponless and exposed, Vincha crouched low behind one of the floating trunks as soon as she entered the new hall. She looked back and saw Rafik calmly walking in. There was a distant smile on his face. Suddenly he turned around, as if forgetting something, fished an object from his pocket and tossed it through the open gap. The object landed with several clinks on the cold floor outside, and Rafik turned back and walked after Nakamura. Without thinking, Vincha aimed the light beam from her bracer back outside, and just as the door began to slide closed she recognised what Rafik chose to leave behind and for some reason her heart missed a beat. It was his brother's blade.

59

"Vincha, Wake up."

She was always a light sleeper, and her eyes opened as Daeon finished uttering her name. Immediately her back and neck began protesting from the uncomfortable position she'd slept in.

Daeon crouched nearby, out of arm's reach. He waved and smiled. Vincha turned her head and saw Rafik sitting on the floor with his back to the wall. His face was blank as he was staring into nothingness.

"Hello," she said to the boy, sitting up.

Rafik turned his head, and Vincha felt a shudder flashing up her spine. It wasn't as if he was looking at her, or even through her, but as if he could see what she was made of.

"You okay, Rafik?" she resisted the urge to touch him.

"We are not far," he answered in an even tone.

"That's good to hear, and you th—"

"We are not far," Rafik said again, and turned his head away.

Daeon took a step forward, extending his hand, which Vincha took, and he helped her up.

"How long was I out?" she asked.

Daeon glanced at his wrist. Vincha still hadn't gotten used to the old timekeeping artifacts they wore.

"A little more than two hours, here." Daeon held out a large red pill. "Sci said to take this."

"What is this?"

"It's a sort of nourishment pill."

When Vincha hesitated, Daeon shrugged. "If Nakamura would have wanted you dead he wouldn't bother to poison you."

"It's nothing like any pill I've seen before."

Daeon smiled reassuringly. "He said it's from his special, limited stock, a little hard to swallow but very effective."

Vincha took the pill from his hand, put it in her mouth, and swallowed with a sharp head toss.

Daeon smiled when her eyes widened. "Nice, yes?"

She nodded and coughed. "Not bad." They moved a little closer to the rest of the group, which was huddled around Sci's hover cart. "So, how are we doing?" she asked.

Daeon shrugged. "Same as we were a few hours ago. Stuck." By their body language it was obvious that the crew was not happy. "I think we might need to go back and try a different route."

"That would put us in a whole bucket of rust," Vincha said. Her head turned back to Rafik, who was still staring into space. "How's he doing?"

"Same as before, just doing his job and keeping to himself." Daeon shrugged. "Is it just me, or is he getting a little odd?"

Vincha stiffen but decided to keep her thoughts to herself. She'd stopped counting the times Rafik had solved puzzle locks. Thankfully, they did not encounter any Lizards, but most of the time Rafik had to solve puzzles when they were under fire from automated gun posts that sprang from the walls or squads of combat drones. Each time, Rafik opened the door or bypassed Tarakan security with only his pursed lips and the whiteness of his complexion betraying any kind of strain. Yet with every puzzle he solved, Rafik withdrew more into himself. They had been walking inside the corridors of the City within the Mountain for the past three days, but she never saw Rafik sleep. Instead, he just sat with his eyes open, daydreaming. He was calm, obedient, and silent. The perfect Puzzler.

Vincha, on the other hand, was more nervous with every step they took into the city's inner sanctum. The long corridors and seamless walls felt foreboding. Daeon, Sci, and Herev seemed to share her nervousness. They'd already passed several promising-looking nodes, but Nakamura ordered them to keep moving. The third or fourth time it happened Herev was close to losing it. "We are walking away from hard metal, just behind this door." He pointed.

Even Vincha didn't see it coming. In the blink of an eye Herev was pinned against the wall, the end of Nakamura's staff shoved against his throat.

"Follow my orders and shut your mouth," Nakamura rasped, "or we shall part ways, *right here.*"

Herev never complained again.

The sudden aggression didn't seem to faze Rafik, or anyone else in the crew.

The items from Sci's hovercarts proved useful for many things, but there was a limit to how prepared you could be in the City within the Mountain. At that particular moment they were stuck behind a corner. They could see a short corridor that led to a puzzle-locked door, but a cleverly placed power gun obliterated anything and anyone that stepped into the corridor. It was hidden from view and positioned at such an angle that they could not destroy it with a direct shot. Nakamura ruled out the use of explosives, as they might damage the puzzle lock. "We will pass this obstacle," he rasped from within his cowl. "It will just take time."

Sci was running out of ideas as well as the metallic creatures he called crawlers. Vincha approached the rest of the crew just as Sci was connecting the last wires through a hole he managed to drill in the wall. Sweat was pouring down Sci's face. He had to work fast because every time he stopped drilling the walls began to slowly regenerate. "Okay, this might work," he finally said, more to himself than to the people around him. "I think I delayed the reaction of the gun, but we are down to the last crawler, so let's hope this works, folks, or we'll have to go back."

Sci lifted an oblong metal disc with several mechanical arms and legs and a controlling device from the cart. Sci got his bearings and the crab moved around the corner. This time it got halfway down the corridor before they heard the movement of the gun on its railings and the whining noise of its power-up.

"Rust." Sci tried to manoeuvre the crawler back but it was too late. Parts went flying everywhere.

Sci turned to Nakamura. "It's no use. We can't bypass this."

"You have to," Nakamura said.

"Can't do it."

"You must!" Nakamura banged his staff's end on the floor. "We must proceed! I have foreseen this."

Sci threw his arms up in frustration. "Well, maybe your foresight should have told you *how* to bypass this gun, because I am out of options." The crew paused, waiting for a response. Herev looked hesitant.

This might be an opportunity to turn them, Vincha thought. *Now is the time to simply go back to one of the nodes we passed and get out of the City within the Mountain, filthy rich and more importantly, alive.*

Vincha locked eyes with Daeon, but he shook his head slightly. He was with Nakamura. She still took a breath and opened her mouth to say something, but Nakamura suddenly cried, "Rafik, no!" and surged past Vincha.

Vincha saw Rafik disappearing around the corner and into the corridor. It took a fraction of a heartbeat to understand what was happening, but a moment later she heard the unmistakable sound of the power gun locking on a moving target and her heart felt like it was digging a tunnel through her chest. Daeon managed to catch her before she turned the corner and dragged her back. She caught a glimpse of Rafik walking calmly towards the puzzle box while the nozzle of the gun followed his movements.

She turned her head to Daeon.

"It didn't shoot him. Let go of me."

Daeon released her from his grasp and Vincha leaned farther and peeked around the corner. The gun suddenly swivelled in her direction. Daeon pulled her away in time, but her stubbly hair and left cheek were singed by the heat of the blast. She found herself on her back, breathing hard, tears suddenly filling her eyes. Did he die? Was there a second discharge?

She raised her head. The power blast that would have pulverized her head hit the far wall and dissolved in all directions, leaving it unmarked.

Herev moved passed her and tried to peek around the corner and quickly withdrew as another blast fired at him. "Bukra's balls, he's alive," he said, his voice filled with amazement. "The boy just walked up to the puzzle box and shoved in his fingers."

"The gun didn't shoot him," Sci mumbled in disbelief.

"No." They all heard the pride and relief in Nakamura's voice. "The city is finally recognizing Rafik as one of their own."

"You should have told me that before." Sci scratched his head, looking frustrated. "I've wasted all our crawlers on it."

Surprisingly, Nakamura nodded. "I should have seen this more clearly."

For a brief moment they stood in silence until the sound of the gun powering down and the soft ping of a door sliding open broke the odd pause. Rafik was standing next to the lock and looking straight at them for the first time since they stepped into the City within the Mountain.

"We must go now," he said. "We are close."

There was only an elevator cabin behind the door, and they had to squeeze in to fit. "Leave the hovercarts here," Nakamura said. "We won't need them anymore."

Sci looked as if he was about to argue but then thought better of it. The door slid closed, and they felt it accelerate almost immediately.

"Up?" Daeon said. "I thought we were aiming for the lower levels."

Nakamura said nothing, but Rafik repeated, "We are close," as if that was supposed to explain things. No one said another word, and when the cabin finally stopped, the doors opened onto a long corridor, so wide all of them were able to walk side by side with their arms spread. The walls and ceiling were made of shining metal, and as they walked the walls changed into a multitude of colours, which had a surprisingly soothing effect. They followed the strange corridor for at least a mile with no further incident and found themselves in a hall so large Vincha thought for a moment that they were outside. She couldn't see the ceiling or the opposite wall; the columns that stood around the room and the mirrorlike floor were the only indications that they were actually in a closed space. Only the centre of the hall was lit up, from six enormous metal doors on their left all the way to the opposite wall—perhaps half a mile away. The rest of the hall, what lay behind the columns, stayed shadowy and dark.

"I know these doors." Vincha pointed. "This is the actual gate to the city. I've seen it from the outside. The gate that never opens. We're rusting inside."

"And on the other side of this hall stands the gate to the inner sanctum," said Nakamura, his voice surprisingly soft. "I have foreseen it."

"Bukra's balls," Sci whispered in awe, his attention on the elevated dais in the center of the hall. The dais, as well as the stairs leading up to it, were held up by hundreds of stone arms. Above the central dais a huge arm hovered in midair, its hand closed into a mighty fist.

Without saying another word, Rafik began walking towards the dais. Daeon tried to stop him but Nakamura said, "Let him go, Daeon. Our journey is almost at its end. Soon we will triumph."

Herev whooped with joy, and his voice echoed far and wide. As Sci and Daeon moved forward, he turned to Nakamura and patted him on the shoulder. "I never doubted you, boss, never."

Nakamura nodded slowly, leaning heavily on his staff. "Go with the others," he rasped. "Set up point, just in case I haven't foreseen it all."

Vincha saw how Herev turned his back to Nakamura and walked forward. At that exact moment Nakamura straightened up and raised his black staff. A sharp blade silently sprang out of it, and without hesitation Nakamura drove the blade into the back of Herev's neck. It came out through the other side with an arc of blood. Herev fell silently to his knees, blood gushing out of his body. As his body toppled to the floor, Nakamura let go of the staff and moved with astonishing speed, plucking the power rifle from Herev's unresisting hands. Daeon turned around, sensing something was wrong, but he aimed his rifle at Vincha, instinctively thinking she had betrayed them. By the time he realised his error, it was too late. Nakamura shot Daeon in the chest twice. Daeon's armour took the brunt of the damage, but the shock was enough to cause him to fall backwards, his rifle skidding into the darkness. Nakamura did not hesitate and shot the prone warrior twice more, from point blank distance, even power armour could not protect him.

As Nakamura stepped over Daeon's smouldering body, Vincha's reflexes took over and without uttering a word, she dashed into the darkness, looking for the dropped rifle. Somewhere behind her Sci pleaded, "Nakamura-san, no, for the love of—" and then his voice was cut off by another shot. Vincha saw the rifle, dove down, grasped the butt of the weapon, and rolled sideways. By her mental calculations, Nakamura was supposed to be at least thirty paces from her, yet as she came out of the roll he was already towering above her. As Vincha rose up he kicked her in the chest, sending her skidding back to the floor.

Lying flat on her back, Vincha tried desperately to level the rifle up but Nakamura stepped on her arm, pinning it with his crushing weight. She would have screamed, but the kick had forced the air out of her lungs. As she squirmed in pain, Vincha saw the red-hot needlepoint of the rifle's sight, and realised it was trained on her forehead. Behind the gun she stared straight into Nakamura's cowl and saw his deformed face. Death had come for her, and Vincha had no power left to fight it. She breathed in the scent of Daeon's burned flesh, and heard the gurgle of Herev's last breath. Closing her eyes, Vincha lowered her head to the floor, tears streaming down her face. She lay there, waiting for her life, and the life she carried inside of her, to end.

"She must live."

Vincha open her eyes and turned her head. She saw Rafik standing not far from Sci's motionless body. He was looking at them calmly, completely unaffected by the carnage around him. The boy's voice was even and detached as he repeated.

"She must live—you said so yourself."

Nakamura hesitated. "It's only one possible future."

"She must live."

Vincha turned her head back to Nakamura, desperately trying to interpret his facial expression, but all she could focus on was the nozzle of the rifle trained on her face.

She heard Nakamura's voice as if from afar. "Take the weapon and leave the way we came." Nakamura lifted his leg from her arm and stepped back.

She slowly rose to a sitting position, still grasping the rifle with her aching arm. Rafik was already walking away again, without a second glance at the CommWoman.

Still aiming his rifle, Nakamura spoke. "When you are out, turn left at the sixth tunnel and follow it. Turn northeast when you reach the surface, and you will see a broken bridge. Go east until you reach the Valley's wall."

Vincha turned her head and watched Rafik walking the steps

to the dais. The floating arm turned in the air and lowered itself down gently, and the fist opened to reveal a black puzzle box.

"There is a small cave, if you can find it, with a Duster and some supplies inside. Do not go back to the bunker. I rigged it with several time bombs. It is now in ruins."

When Vincha turned her head back to Nakamura he had withdrawn two more steps, making sure to stay out of arm's reach. Vincha tried not to look at the bodies around her, but she could not ignore the sight of Nakamura's upright staff, its blade still stuck inside Herev's lifeless body. She could hear the staff's soft hum as she tried to focus her attention on Nakamura.

"Why?" she croaked, "why?"

Nakamura nodded. "Because I owe them this kindness. Everything is going to change and they do not deserve what is coming. The rest of my actions are too complicated to explain, but they are also necessary. I have foreseen it."

Vincha just stared, lost for words, and Nakamura nodded again, accepting her disbelief. "You would not understand, but this is the best course for humanity."

"What are you going to do to Rafik?" She glanced towards the dais, and if Nakamura would have turned his head towards the boy she would have tried to shoot him there and then, and damn the consequences. But his focus never wavered.

"Whatever is going to happen, must be done."

"He's just a boy—"

"I have seen it. We all have a purpose, a destiny. Rafik's a Puzzler. This is his destiny. Mine is to die today. The only question left is what will happen to you." Nakamura paused for breath and then said, "I will count to one."

Vincha turned her back to Nakamura and ran.

60

"You're feeding me rusting lies." Jakov walked over to Vincha, and for a moment I thought he would strike her. Vincha didn't flinch.

"That's the truth. Nakamura let me go."

"You said it yourself—he never let anyone go."

"Rafik told him—"

"Balls. Nakamura just murdered his own crew, people who loyaly served him for years, and then he just let you go? I don't believe a word of it."

"Believe what you want, rust face—"

His slap would have rocked her off her feet were it not for the guard holding her up. When she turned her head back to Jakov, blood was dripping from her lips and down her chin and neck. None of us moved. This was not the time for foolish gestures.

"Hit me all you want. I don't know why the freak murdered his own crew and let me live. Believe me, it's not as if I haven't wondered about it *every* night since. The only explanations I have are that Nakamura was a freak who could really see the future, or that he was just rusting insane. Maybe Rafik told him to leave me alive and he obeyed, maybe he had *foreseen* it"—she emphasised the word with a rasping voice that must have resembled Nakamura's—"but he let me go."

"Why didn't you turn around and shoot him then?" Jakov spat in her face.

Vincha was skating on the edge of her composure. "Because I was terrified. Because I wanted to live. Because I saw a way out, for *me*—"

And for my baby, I thought, silently completing her sentence. Would I have risked everything to fight Nakamura, just to save the boy? I chose not to shame myself with an answer.

Jakov was still not satisfied by Vincha's explanation. "Speaking of a way out, how did you manage to get through all the doors and puzzle locks and traps?"

Vincha lowered her head. "I don't know."

"Rust—"

"I don't. I was running away as Rafik stood on the dais and was about to shove his fingers inside that machine. I can't tell you what he was going through; maybe he had control of the whole rusting city." Vincha shook her head. "I was unwired but still had my skull plugs, or maybe Nakamura could truly project his emotions, I don't know. But as I was running for my life I could see images of both of them flashing in front of my eyes. I saw them from above and from Rafik's eyes as he reached the hand holding the central puzzle box. Maybe my memory is playing tricks on me after all this time, but I remember watching Rafik's back from within Nakamura's cowl. The different images flashed so fast there were moments I couldn't tell my right from my left, and I had to stop to get my bearings."

Vincha closed her eyes as she spoke. "I remember the Great Puzzle projected on the wall opposite the city gates. Rafik described it to me, but I never imagined anything like that . . . There must have been thousands of shapes moving up and down and sideways, and he was moving and rearranging the symbols so fast . . . And Nakamura was just standing there, watching." Vincha shuddered.

"I don't know how, but I remembered the way back, and as I ran, doors slid open for me, traps didn't kill me, and I didn't see any puzzle locks. It was as if Rafik was helping me out—that's my only conclusion.

"The next thing I remember I was close to the place where we'd entered the City within the Mountain. I'm guessing it was then that Rafik solved the puzzle.

"The image was so strong I couldn't see where I was going and had to lean against the wall. I could see it happening as if I was there. The pattern Rafik had solved . . . I don't know how I understood it, but somehow . . . everything came together . . . The Puzzle changed to become these two intertwining lines, reminded me of a drawing I saw in a Mender's manual, something about how we are all made, but I am not sure. The far doors to the inner sanctum began to open, and at the same time, behind Nakamura, the gates that never opened began parting way, and sunlight flooded the hall, bathing Nakamura's back."

Vincha began shaking as she said, "There was a sound like a rolling thunder, and Rafik began to scream. It was . . . agony . . . like a power blow to my body. I don't know if I heard it through my plugs or his voice carried all the way from the hall, but it left me weak at the knees. Somehow, I gathered my strength and just rusting ran for it.

"As I ran through the tunnels there was another set of images. I saw thousands of Lizards pouring out of the open gate of the inner sanctum. The thunder I heard before was the sound of their clawed feet on the ground. Rafik was writhing in pain on the dais, and they moved over him like a sea of green sludge. Nakamura turned his back to them and walked to the open gates of the City within the Mountain, watching the sun rise. In his hand was a small disc. The last thing he did before he was torn apart was to press several buttons on that disc. Then he dropped the disc to the ground, spread his arms wide and closed his eyes. I think that he might have been smiling when the first Lizard reached him."

Vincha sighed heavily. "After that, I just blocked everything out of my mind and ran. It took me three days to get out of the Valley, and I didn't stop or sleep or even look back."

We stayed in complete silence for a while until my Lore-Master spoke. "And so came the bloodbath in the Valley. Those Lizards attacked the Hive, the outpost was overwhelmed, and by the time the guilds in the city reacted, everything was lost. The valley is now filled with Lizards, and there are so many of them that almost every mission ends in failure. Three attempts to build a new outpost have failed as well. We cannot reach the Valley's richest nodes, and those we have here in the city barely suffice. The City of Towers is in decline. Its population dwindles, and its sphere of influence diminishes by the season."

LoreMaster Harim stepped closer to Vincha. "But this is just a history lecture, is it not? You set something in motion and had no idea what it would cause."

"I set nothing in motion." The defiance in Vincha's voice was desperate.

"Tell me, Vincha, how did you know how to reach Nakamura? How did you bargain with him over the boy? How did you leave that message for Rafik in a puzzle lock box? How did you set up a Duster and weapons that failed to function just as Nakamura's crew struck the Keenans? Was it really Brain who showed you the tunnels under the Hive?"

Vincha flinched with each question as if it was a blow.

My LoreMaster stepped so close to Vincha she could have head-butted him.

"You told us Bayne suspected there was someone in the Hive who worked for Nakamura, that you had dismissed the notion. Then you sent him to the City of Towers and ended up bringing Rafik to the very same man. It was you who planted Nakamura's devices; it was you who worked for him."

Vincha bit her bloody lip. I sensed her instinct to grasp for a loose wire, to lie, but I guess she was broken, or maybe she knew we were already just one mental step away from the logical conclusion, and she decided it was time to shoot straight.

"I was two years with Slice, in very bad shape and just a young girl, when Nakamura showed up by himself and hired us for an escort job near the Valley. He wasn't known back then, at least not to Slice, but his metal was solid. I guess Slice must have thought he'd kill the freak if we ended up finding something useful. Nakamura ended up killing Slice and his crew—and he took his time with Slice. But instead of killing me, Nakamura healed my wounds, put me back together, gave me a communication device and some metal, and told me I should head for the City of Towers and become a Salvationist. He said, 'Find me a young Puzzler,' and the next day he was gone. I never told anyone, because by the time he contacted me again I was making metal as an independent CommWoman and he was Nakamura, you know, the monster who ate Trolls for breakfast, so I kept my mouth shut."

"What did Nakamura want from you?" It was Jakov who asked the question this time, but Vincha kept staring at my Lore-Master.

"Mainly information. Who was doing what. What was the rotation. Which crew was going for a deep run, and—" Vincha hesitated briefly "—Puzzlers. He wanted to know everything about the Hive's Puzzlers. After a crew I reported about went missing on a deep run I thought that maybe he set them up for their Puzzler, but you know, it's a deep run—anything could happen, even for an experienced crew. I never thought he would be a little boy. I thought he would be like Pikok, or the rest of them." She looked around the room for sympathy, but found none.

"When did you decide to bring Rafik to Nakamura?" Jakov spoke again.

This time Vincha looked straight at the merchant. "You

underestimate him. Nakamura began taking an interest in the Keenans around a year before I met Rafik. He asked me for a detailed report on the entire crew. It was pretty easy because Doro and I were becoming close anyway. It was Doro who told me the Keenans spent all their metal on a very promising Puzzler and that he was being trained in the guild house."

"And you reported this to Nakamura," LoreMaster Harim said, nodding.

"I mentioned it, yes. When Doro came back after meeting Rafik in the Keenan guild house, Nakamura told me to go back to the City of Towers, find out about the boy, and get close to him.

"On the day Doro died Nakamura contacted me and offered me a way out . . . if I brought him Rafik. I never thought . . ." She went quiet.

"What do you think really happened to Commander Doro?" I thought the question the same moment LoreMaster Harim asked it.

For the first time I saw tears well in Vincha's eyes, but she held it together, just.

"I don't know," she admitted. "When I heard about it I thought it was just rusting bad luck, then, of course, I learned about the shady details. For a long time I was sure that it was Ramm, and I wanted revenge. Shooting him in the back of his head felt like justice." Vincha closed her eyes and breathed out slowly before saying "But it's been years, and I've had time to think it over. There were too many variables coming together for someone like Ramm to be able to plan and pull it off. To time a murder of your crew commander on a distress call from a ghost crew just as they were getting into a sandstorm with their communication gone bad—that was either a freakish coincidence or a very spontaneous decision by Ramm. Now, that Troll was a lump of rust, but he respected Doro, and to murder a crew commander was risking everything. Nakamura, on the other hand, had plenty of reasons to kill Doro. He was a very capable crew commander, maybe the best in the Hive. Everyone respected him, even the Sabarra crew. It would have been very difficult for me to get Rafik out of the Hive if Doro was in charge, and not just because of his capabilities. Rafik liked Doro, and I was his . . ." Vincha stopped mid-sentence and shrugged to herself. "I guess we'll never know."

"One last thing," LoreMaster Harim said. "Nakamura asked you to report on everything, but he also asked you to bury devices on the Hive's ground."

Vincha was quiet for a long time.

"I wonder, what do you think Nakamura did just before he died? What was that disc he was holding?"

Vincha paled but pursed her lips.

"Answer the man," Jakov said, "or you and *yours* will suffer."

"I thought they were just communication devices," Vincha finally said, "just to spy on the Hive's chatter or on the guilds. I just buried them in the places he told me to and forgot about them, I never thought . . . only when Sci showed me the devices in his lab and told me they could attract Lizards . . ." She swallowed. "All these attacks on the Hive must have been meant to pin us down, forced Brain to keep a large force in the Hive. That gave Nakamura enough time to clear nodes, do whatever he was planning without interference, and keep us away from certain areas. If Nakamura managed to send the hordes of Lizards to the Hive . . ." Vincha didn't finish the sentence.

"So"—Jakov spread his arms as he turned around, seeking the attention of the crowd around him—"mystery solved. Vincha was Nakamura's pet, and you are all her fools." He turned back to my LoreMaster. "And now, please, where are all the Tarakan artifacts you promised me?"

LoreMaster Harim nodded. "I have paid you plenty of hard coin for your services, Jakov, and I will tell you about the way we can all get our hands on priceless artifacts, but please let my companions go now. You want them to cooperate willingly."

Jakov shook his head. "I'll be the judge of that."

LoreMaster Harim stepped towards Jakov, and I felt myself

tense. My guard must have sensed it, too, because he shoved the muzzle of his rifle against the back of my head with renewed intensity. But my LoreMaster just laid two hands on Jakov's shoulders, and surprisingly the merchant seemed to calm down.

"Jakov, my brother, we have been through so much, you and I," LoreMaster Harim said. "Now I need you to trust me. Let them go and I will explain everything."

Jakov took a big breath, then shrugged and ordered, "Take a step back, lads." He looked straight at Vincha and said, "But one brave move from any of you, and my guards will shoot."

My first reaction was to rub the point where the rifle's muzzle dug into my skull. Galinak got to his feet and brushed himself off. He looked ready to kill but kept his composure. The guard who'd been holding Vincha from behind stepped in front of her with his pistol aimed and ready.

"Okay," Jakov said, "now please tell me why we are all here."

61

I was just a toddler when my parents packed our belongings and decided to brave the perilous journey to the City of Towers," my LoreMaster began.

I found a solid-looking crate and sat myself down.

"Like everyone coming to the city, we were desperate, but we managed to create a community that further explored the wonders of the city. What we found was, at least then, the biggest treasure trove in post-Catastrophe history. Yet my parents did not live past forty winters. I've seen close to sixty springs, and I'm planning to see more. While in other places throughout the land people die before they see thirty years, the City of Towers protected us from the harsh weather, and the nodes we found supplied us with medicine along with weapons.

"As the city grew in power, and with the help of Gadgetiers, we were slowly progressing as a race."

My LoreMaster sighed heavily. "As you all well know, one day it all stopped. Several of the nodes never opened again, many of the machines powering the city stopped working, most of the Tarakan lights of the Middle Plateau winked out, the lifts began to malfunction, and accidents happened. The city is now a shadow of itself, and it is obvious that the city, along with its inhabitants, is in decline.

"Soon after, we lost contact with the Hive in Tarakan Valley, and we later learned it was destroyed. Actually, I believe it was exactly the same time, to the day. Something happened in the City within the Mountain that affects us until today. What we do know now is that Nakamura brought Rafik to the City within the Mountain believing that it was 'the best of all possible futures.' Whether he really was an oracle of sorts or a deranged Troll, Nakamura's actions began a chain of events that brought us once more closer to barbarism."

LoreMaster Harim turned to Vincha. "Your story confirms my theory that there is a connection between Rafik and our current situation. But the second reason we were looking for you is far more important than a lesson in history. A few years ago I overheard two merchants from the Upper Towers talking about one of the old machines they had in their tower that suddenly powered up. The machine was still useless; nothing that we know of could be done with it, and only one sentence appeared constantly on its screen. I didn't think too much about it at the time. It seemed to be, at most, a Gadgetier kind of problem. But as they kept talking about it I got curious. I bought the gentlemen a few drinks and by the end of the evening, they took me to see the machine. The screen was blank except for that one sentence. I offered them the service of my friend"—he nodded at River, who nodded back—"but unfortunately, our experiment resulted in the total demise of the machine. Still, something bothered me about that sentence, and after searching through my notes I remembered why."

My LoreMaster produced a small scroll case from the inside of his belt, took out a diminutive scroll, unfolded it, and showed it to Vincha. "The message was simple. Your name, a set of five numbers and three letters, and another name at the end: Rafik."

Vincha's jaw actually dropped a little.

"Luckily, as you mentioned, we had met during my expedition to the Valley. It was a long time ago, but you were quite a memorable young lady. River's theory was that this message could have been just an echo of the past, a sentence that was lost and found its way into the grid of the City of Towers, but I decided to find out if there were more such occurrences in the city. River is a fine Tinker, and he had plenty of customers in the Upper Towers and below. In the past three years he found forty-two—"

"Forty-seven," River corrected.

"Sorry, forty-seven such incidences. After checking some more, and hiring a marked Gadgetier, I am now confident the messages are recent." My LoreMaster paused, most likely just for dramatic effect. "But the rest is just patchwork. I tried to find out who you were and who Rafik was, eventually made the connection that he was the Puzzler whose death ruined the Keenan guild, and realised he was the Puzzler who was now sending messages to you."

"The numbers and letters between our names," Vincha said weakly. "It's a bandwidth, a very specific one."

The LoreMaster nodded. "I know. And I've been told it was a seldom-visited frequency. I hired three different CommTrolls who heard only white noise. The last Troll told me the frequency was coded to merge with a specific brainwave pattern; meaning this message could be for your ears only, Vincha."

Vincha's reaction was almost dismissive, "I've been vegan for years, my old gear's long gone—"

"But your plugs are still inside your head," Jakov was quick to answer, almost too quick. "So what we need to do is hook you up—"

"No rusting way." Vincha's furious response was so dramatic, some of the guards trained their weapons on her.

"Vincha . . ." my LoreMaster tried, but she was not in a listening mood anymore.

"This is a load of rusting metal. That frequency could be nothing—"

My LoreMaster stepped in front of her. "Believe me, I checked and double-checked. This message appears repeatedly; it's the only message that appears. River has assured me—"

"I don't care what your rusting pet Tinker told you."

"Vincha, Rafik is calling out for you—"

"I'm not hooking up again," she shouted. "It took me years to get off Skint, to stop dreaming of it . . . It can't be Rafik . . . He was chewed up by thousands of Lizards."

"Yet this message gives us hope." LoreMaster Harim was trying to reason with Vincha but I could see this was not going to be resolved with words. I was not the only one who reached that particular conclusion. Without warning, Jakov shot Vincha with a stun ray, and only the quick reaction of the masked guard standing next to her stopped her from hitting the floor.

The stun gun's muzzle turned immediately towards Galinak. "Are you going to be brave?" Jakov waited for Galinak to shake his head before lowering the weapon. I looked at Galinak's battle-worn face and wondered whether he had stopped being Vincha's protector and secret admirer. Was her story too dark, containing too many betrayals? Were the consequences of her actions too severe even for this tough old Salvationist?

"Good," Jakov's face twisted into a half smile and he holstered the gun.

"That was uncalled for," my LoreMaster said quietly.

"Oh, it was called for, Harim, it was. We have a lot to do and very little time to do it. We have a med chair set up. These are not perfect conditions, but your guy River is a Tinker, right?"

River glanced at LoreMaster Harim before nodding.

"Good, so it's better if he hooks her up." Jakov turned to his guard and said, "Bind her to the chair."

"Vincha won't do it." I found my voice. "Even if you hook her up, you still need her to willingly cooperate."

Jakov turned his attention to me, and for a brief moment I knew how Rafik must have felt as a child, facing off against the half man, every muscle in my body tensing under his scrutiny.

"Oh, but she will," he said. "One way or another, we are going to find out where this message is coming from."

62

J akov wasn't lying. Sewers were not the kind of place you'd want to have a procedure done to your head. The med chair looked worn, stained by countless patches of blood, but at least it was, by River's admission, well stocked.

By the time Vincha regained full control of her body she was strapped to the table and her head was firmly locked in a brace. She did try to struggle, though, and did not hold back on the profanities.

River was trying to shave her head, but even tied up Vincha was making enough of an effort to make the task difficult and bloody.

Jakov motioned for River to stop and he leaned close to Vincha. His metal hand was poised close enough to her face to make her stop writhing.

"I ain't doing this, you rust bucket," she hissed, sweat pouring down her face.

"Oh yes, you are," Jakov answered coldly. "And I'll tell you why. LoreMaster Harim here will try to convince you to do the right thing for the sake of humanity, or for your conscience, even for Rafik, the very same boy you betrayed—but you and I are alike, and we're not the honourable type. What you are, Vincha, is a survivor. You lie, cheat, kill, steal, have sex with strangers, betray anyone around you, overcome Skint addiction, and give birth in a dirty shack somewhere only to give the infant away to be raised by others. You do what you have to do to survive, am I right?"

Vincha remained silent.

"I'll spare you the specific threats. You are going to cooperate with *me*, Vincha. It is the only chance you and yours have to survive, and I can see in your eyes that you understand. So, stop struggling and let the man here wire your plugs."

Vincha's slumped down on the med chair.

With the smallest of gestures Jakov indicated to River that he could resume his work.

"Stay absolutely still," River warned. "I need to do some drilling here and clean the plugs before I rewire you." He powered up the hand drill.

I turned away, having experienced enough blood and gore recently to last me a lifetime.

Galinak was stuffing the bowl of a short pipe with leaves. He only glanced at me when I sat down with a sigh.

"This ain't the Upper Towers, eh, Twinkle Eyes?"

"Pretty much as far down as you can find yourself from the Upper Towers."

"Oh no, son." Galinak lit his pipe from a small flame maker. "We can still fall farther, believe me."

"I didn't know you smoked," I said as the sound of hammering replaced the drilling.

"What can I say? I'm a man of bad habits."

"It's just that we're sitting on crates filled with explosives, so I thought I'd mention it."

He blew a long line of grey smoke. "Not the worst way to go."

We sat in silence for a little while, watching River prepare then insert the Comm device into Vincha's skull. Her leg twitched and shook to the point that a masked guard had to hold it down firmly.

"I can't pay you any more than the sum I gave you," I said when it was obvious Vincha was still alive, "and what I paid you no longer feels adequate."

Galinak took a really long pull from the pipe. "Yeah, you pretty much reached the limit of your funds when we jumped from the Guild's Plateau."

"I wouldn't blame you if you left now."

Galinak chuckled. "Twinkle Eyes, I didn't think you were that dim." He waved his pipe around for emphasis. "No one's walking away from this. So, I guess you'll just have to owe me."

"I hate owing people."

"And I'm a nasty debt collector." Galinak took a long pull from the pipe.

"It's just that I'm also not sure I will have any funds for the foreseeable future."

The old mercenary's stare was unwavering. "We'll think of a payment plan when the time is right."

"If I were a romantic I would think you're doing this just for the adventure."

He snorted a laugh. "If you think that, you're not as smart as I thought." But then he gave me another side glance. "I'm worth rusty metal at cards, but I'm good at *this,* and if there's one thing I've learned over the years: sometimes walking away is not the right answer." He emptied the contents of his pipe to the ground. "Too many loose ends can creep back and bite you in the ass when you're not looking."

"I'll try to keep that in mind," I said.

"Speaking of which, the old wizard is looking for you."

As I rose to my feet Galinak said, "Say good-bye to him for me, Twinkle Eyes."

My legs were moving before I understood what he'd said, and I contemplated turning around and telling Galinak to stop talking nonsense, but with each step I took towards my Lore-Master I realised that something was up. He stood rigid, his robes neat, his backpack shouldered, and his entourage of guards packing behind him.

"You're leaving?" I hated the surprise in my own voice.

My LoreMaster patted my shoulder. "If the recent jump from the Upper Plateau taught me anything it's that I'm an old man with bad knees. Whatever happens next, I can't keep up. I can be of much better use elsewhere."

"But Jakov will . . . could . . ."

"Jakov is blood of my blood and a . . . complicated man, shall we say. He is a better man than he used to be, and a better man than he shows. Trust him—" LoreMaster Harim paused to dwell on his own words, then added "—to a point. He gave me his word, and you'd be surprised how solid his word is. He won't kill you unless you do something stupid, so make sure you don't."

"But where will you go? The Council and the guilds are looking for you."

"I know how to hide, and even if they catch me, I still have some clout in the city." He laid a hand on my shoulder and smiled. "I won't be tortured—not at first—and I'll try my best to steer them in the wrong direction. This is why I should go now. There are things I'm better off not knowing." He let that sink in for a moment, then added, "Whatever happens next, I would like you to go with Jakov. I know it's a lot to ask, but someone must record this for the sake of the Guild of Historians. Find out about Rafik, and try to correct the course of humanity."

"I'll try, LoreMaster."

He grabbed my shoulder and squeezed it tight. "I owe you a great apology."

I lowered my head, "No need for that, LoreMaster," I mumbled.

"Oh, but there is. I have underestimated you greatly. When I sent you to find Vincha I saw only a young, naive man who read too many Salvo novels for his own good. I did not believe that you would actually succeed. When I read your message and realised you were getting close to finding Vincha—and in this city, of all places—I panicked and sent a team of mercenaries to grab her. They waited for you to get out of Margat's Den but lost you in the mayhem, only to track you down in the hut."

The realisation struck me like a fist to the stomach, "The crew that attacked us were yours?"

"Yes. They were supposed to grab Vincha but leave you—"

"—so it would look as if someone else took her, even to myself."

"Exactly." LoreMaster Harim nodded towards Galinak. "But you chose wisely when hiring this bodyguard. I was so sure of your ineptitude, I did not consider the implications of what would happen if you defeated the crew. The incident alerted the Council and the Sabarra guild, and most likely directly caused the raid on our guild house."

He shook his head in sorrow. "My failure in seeing your true potential, my pride, has brought ruin on the Guild of Historians, and I will bear the burden of my colleagues' death for the rest of my life."

He took my hand, and I felt a tiny scroll holder pressed into my palm. "You, on the other hand, *must* succeed in this mission. Do all you can for humanity and rebuild the Guild of Historians. Once you come back, visit the places on this list. These are safe havens I have established. There are items there that would help you rebuild the Guild. I am not Nakamura—I'm no oracle, if he ever was one—but if the City of Towers continues to be just a drying oasis in a desert of ignorance, we will never rise again."

Was he seriously dumping the responsibility for human ascension on my shoulders?

"I'm just . . . a secondary scribe, LoreMaster," I protested.

For the first time since I approached him, my LoreMaster smiled, perhaps misunderstanding what I meant. "Oh yes, we must correct that. You have more than proven your worth."

Without remembering how, or even what was said exactly, I found myself on my knees in front of my LoreMaster, and as Jakov and his goons watched with open amusement, I was anointed Associate LoreMaster of the Guild of Historians.

In my entire life, I have never been prouder, or sadder.

63

S he's coming around." We gathered around the chair and waited in silence. River assured us that the wires were successfully attached and Vincha was not badly hurt, but she sure looked pale to me. There was a lot of blood, and her breaths were shallow, rapid.

Vincha eventually opened her eyes. The first thing she said was "Water" and River got her some.

As she gulped slowly, he said, "You're all wired up. The Comm is good stock, barely used, but your old plugs—" he shook his head "—they did a rusty job, and I'm no Mender, so I didn't dare try to fix them. There will be pain, I'm sorry."

"I can help with the pain," Jakov said.

"No Skint." Vincha shook her head as River released the brace. "You'll change your mind soon . . ."

"No Skint."

I thought I caught a look of appreciation passing through Jakov'e eye, but he only said "Suit yourself," and turned his attention to the thick cable that now stretched from Vincha's skull to a machine. "Is she ready?"

"Patience, please . . ." River was too preoccupied to bother with egos, and Jakov chose to ignore his insolence for now. "Okay, Vincha," River finally said. "I'm going to turn the Comm on and run some tests. You remember how it goes . . ."

Vincha nodded and grimaced but didn't say anything.

Jakov interjected, "By the way, I made sure your Comm device lacks offensive capabilities, so don't waste your energy trying to hack into other people's systems."

A faint smile touched Vincha's lips, but it disappeared as she suddenly convulsed, shouting in pain.

Thankfully, the pain seemed to last for only a heartbeat. River turned some dials, and Vincha collapsed back onto the med chair. "Rust, I'm sorry," River apologized. "I didn't see that one coming. Won't happen again. Now, if you're okay, I'm going to first manually dial you up to some channels, and you tell me if you hear anything and if it needs adjusting. Then we are going to go through your spectrum one by one."

The process took time and was nothing but tedious. A few found a quiet place to rest, and two guards dozed in a corner. Jakov and his burly, masked bodyguard stayed next to Vincha the entire time, so leaving her side felt like a betrayal, especially with my new position as Associate LoreMaster.

"Right, Vincha, almost done." Sweat was pouring down River's brow as he busied himself with the instruments. "I want you to start channelling by yourself. The cable I attached will transmit what you hear to the speakers."

Vincha raised a trembling hand to her temple. "I've got a killer headache," she mumbled. "Not sure . . ."

"We'll start with the easy ones." River began reading numbers and letters.

Vincha closed her eyes. We all gathered around her as the speakers whistled and crackled.

Most of the channels were either dead or full of awful, unnatural noises. We stumbled upon two ShieldGuards gossiping, but other than that, it was a pretty monotonous affair.

"Okay Vincha, now let's try to find the channel."

River began reading the letters, but Vincha whispered, "Maybe later, maybe I'll rest, my head . . . hurts."

Jakov suddenly leaned over and grasped Vincha's chin with his human hand. She opened her eyes wide, and the restraints creaked as she tried to move away. Jakov dangled a small leather bag in front of her eyes.

"We don't have time for beauty sleep. I will stuff Skint up your nostrils if I need to."

"No," Vincha whispered, "no Skint, please, I can do it."

The bag disappeared and Jakov straightened up. "Fine." He nodded to River, who resumed reading the numbers.

Vincha closed her eyes again, but it was obvious she was straining. A drop of blood appeared under her left nostril and slowly dripped down over her cheek bone.

"You just missed it." River was trying his best. "It's a rusty thin bandwidth, try reaching it from the t—"

And just like that, the room was filled with music I had never heard before. It was glorious and mesmerizing. Everyone in the room listened in silence.

Vincha took a ragged breath between each syllable: "Bit . . . of . . . En." It was the music she'd shared with Rafik at the Hive. River leaned over and wiped away the blood that was flowing freely from Vincha's nose. I tried to listen to the patterns Rafik had talked about when he first heard the music back in the Hive, but I was too excited to concentrate. The music, as beautiful as it was, meant only one thing: we were no longer dealing with a theory. This was really happening.

The music faded and a voice filled the room. It was a child's voice. "Vincha," it said.

She turned her head to the speakers. "Rafik." A tear dropped from her eye.

"Six," he said, "two, seven, east. Four, six, nine, north. I repeat . . ."

"Write it down," Jakov commanded. I fumbled for a scroll and a pen, mouthing the numbers to myself until I copied the numbers, which were obviously waypoints. Jakov unfolded a large, pre-Salvationist-era map on top of the weapon crates.

The message and the music repeated five more times before Vincha lost consciousness.

"Here it is." Galinak pointed at the map. "Almost at the far edge of the Valley. I mean look"—he moved his finger—"the Hive used to be here . . . the broken Long Tube stop is here . . . this is a long trip."

"Well," Jakov straightened up, "it's where we're going. Let's find out if this invitation is real."

"The voice was that of a young boy," I said. "Vincha recognised it as Rafik's, but he was a boy fifteen years ago. If he's alive, that can't be his voice."

Jakov tilted his distorted face at me. "Yeah, but we're going anyway. I promised Harim you could tag along. He assured me you can handle your metal and keep your mouth shut. I can see he was wrong about the second part. I hope for your sake he was right about the first."

This was probably the only chance I had to get on Jakov's good side, but I still pressed on: "Well, maybe my mind would be more at ease if you told me why you're doing this. The guards, the weapons, the antigrav suits"—I pointed at Vincha—"all of this. And now you want to go to Tarakan Valley, of all places, where Trolls are Lizard fodder? I heard you landed a huge sum for the Puzzler boy. So why—"

Jakov took a threatening step towards me. "This is none of your rusting business. I promised not to kill you, but I could still break a few bones." He took another step towards me, and in a blink of an eye Galinak was standing between us.

"If you'll excuse me, sir." The politeness in Galinak's voice surprised me. "It's not that we don't appreciate that you have business matters you want to keep private—we certainly do—but Twinkle Eyes here is my direct employer, and I simply can't have anything happen to him at this moment. It would be unprofessional."

In hindsight this was almost comic relief, seeing as a dozen guards had taken position around us, but to his credit Jakov eased the tension with a small hand gesture.

"Twinkle Eyes," he said. "That's a nice little nickname. You want to share your real one with me?"

"Twinkle Eyes will do." There was almost no tremble in my voice. "I've grown to like it."

"Fine, Twinkle Eyes, I'll humor you this once, if it makes you feel any better. It is true that the sum I got for the Puzzler was high, but in my line of work there are a lot of expenses, and let's say I've made a few unwise, *costly* business decisions. Being the first person in more than a decade to enter the City within the Mountain and perhaps establish a connection could be very profitable. The rest you'll need to figure out by yourself. Are you in?"

Did I have a choice? Could I have walked away? I never found out. I knew I was going to see this through when Vincha was strapped to the med chair.

Jakov turned to River. "You're competent," he said, "which is something I appreciate. If you join us you'll get a sixth and tenth pick of the loot and a fair share of the rest."

River tilted his head. "Fourth and sixth."

They agreed on fifth and eighth. Knowing River, I think he would have come for free.

"I can't come," Vincha whispered from the med chair.

"My dear, you made history once." Jakov walked closer to her. "Be a part of making history again. And anyway, I brought a mutual friend to keep us company—you could use the time to get reacquainted."

On a cue from Jakov, the burly, masked guard who was standing next to him walked forward and took off his mask.

Vincha gasped in surprise. "Bayne."

"Hello, Vincha." Bayne moved his hand through his white hair. "Been looking for you for some time. I think you owe me an explanation."

64

They tied Vincha up in the back of the Duster, gave me a power rifle and a blanket, and left me to guard her, probably just to keep me out of their way. The crew went ahead to scout.

It was freezing cold in the mountains, and Jakov had only enough heat suits for himself and his crew. I left the power rifle leaning against the front seat and walked to the back of the Duster to check on Vincha. I found her trembling from the cold. Without thinking I threw my own blanket to her, a move I regretted almost immediately as the coldness slammed into my exposed body. My gallantry rewarded me with nothing more than a small nod from the ex-Salvationist. She wrapped the blanket around herself using her free hand.

Vincha kept mostly to herself throughout the journey, but every time I felt sorry for her I remembered our first encounter and the feeling of the cold blade of her combat knife pressed against my skin. If Vincha was certainly waiting for an opportunity to bolt, I was not planning on giving her that opening. I'd caught her and Bayne speaking several times—heated conversations. The way the burly Troll looked at Vincha left no doubt; he was still hurt, which means he still had feelings for her. I figured that if Vincha could convince Bayne that she'd only sent him away from the outpost for his own safety, he could be turned, but I kept my ideas to myself. No point in stirring a hornets' nest unless you absolutely had to.

Jakov got us out of the city through the sewers. The next two days we hiked to a safe area and waited for four Dusters, each equipped with a mounted rail gun, to show up. It had been a long journey since then, and thankfully uneventful, but there were plenty of tense moments. All it took was one patrol to spot us, and there was enough evidence along the way to prove that the Council was casting a wide net. The more I thought about it, the more insane this mission seemed.

There were so many unknown factors that taking the risk seemed almost illogical. Sure, there was a chance, an off chance, that we'd cross Tarakan Valley unharmed, reach the city, penetrate the inner sanctum without a Puzzler, find the boy, now most likely a man, and uncover a new cache of Tarakan artifacts, but there was no doubt in my mind that this mission was very dangerous. Jakov's motivation was obvious—he took a chance for hard metal—but I was struggling with the reasons I myself was so eager to go.

The only answer I could think of was what made the Salvonovels I'd read in my youth so attractive. It wasn't the explicit sex and violence—although I have to admit they gave me plenty of inspiration on lonely nights—it was opening a door and finding out what was hiding behind it. We read books to solve a mystery, and the more I heard about Rafik, the more I was intrigued, even obsessed, with finding out what had happened and why. So here I was, on a suicidal mission but with an actual chance to unveil the mysteries of Tarakan. Bukra's balls, if there ever was a book worth dying for, this was it.

My thoughts went to my LoreMaster. We had parted ways, probably for good, and as I stood shivering near the Duster I wondered if they'd caught him yet, and if he still believed that all of this sacrifice was worth it. I wondered if humanity was worth it, and at that point in time I wasn't sure.

The cold made daydreaming and philosophical reflections difficult, so I moved a little closer to where Vincha was crouching, her hand cuffed to a metal part of the Duster. From a glance at her exposed arm I knew that if they didn't get back soon it looked like it would cause a nasty cold burn. She looked up at me like an animal caught in a trap. I kept a safe distance.

"How are you?" I asked, not expecting an answer, but I guess my manners had some kind of effect on her.

"I need to pee," she said through clenched teeth.

That caught me off guard, although obviously, it was a natural request. "I'm sorry, I can't help you with that," I said.

"I don't think I can hold it much longer."

"I'm not letting you go, if that's what you're asking."

"Come on, Twinkle Eyes, do a lady a favor. You've seen Bayne take me to the side and we came back nice and peaceful."

"I can't do it."

"You mean you won't." She sighed. "What if I answered your question?"

"Which question?"

"The one you're dying to ask. Come on . . . you've been twinkling at me for days now. How about you ask me and I'll tell you, and after that you take me to a nice mound of snow so I can pee in peace?"

I knew this might be a trap, but we were negotiating again, and I had an edge. The temptation was simply too great.

"How about I help you take off your pants now and you answer my question later."

She twisted her face in anger, but I did offer her assistance without a precondition which gave her the possibility of backing out of the deal, and gave me the moral high ground.

"All right," she said, "but if your hands go anywhere they shouldn't I'll bite your nose off."

"I assure you Vincha, I have no intention—"

"Yeah, yeah, mister twinkly knight, the buckle is right here, you have to twist, like that . . . no, the other way . . . no . . . use both hands, rust brain . . . right . . . now pull here . . ."

It happened in a flash. Her free hand twisted me around and snaked under my neck and under my chin as her legs wrapped themselves around me. I tried to heave up, but she pulled me down and towards her with her legs.

"Vincha, no . . ." I gasped but she paid me no heed and pushed her head against mine, choking me with the pressure. I was still conscious, but only because her choke hold was with one arm. She was pulling me and herself towards her cuffed hand. I was not an expert, but knew enough to realise that if she locked hands I would be out in a heartbeat.

"Vincha," I gasped, "it's useless . . . I don't have a key . . ."

She wasn't listening. Perhaps she wanted to look for herself. I bit her arm as hard as I could, tearing through the fabric of her shirt, and felt her twitch and release the choke hold just enough for me to make a desperate reverse head butt. I think I hit her cheekbone or something, because her legs loosened and I was able to turn so that my face was suddenly buried in her chest. She pushed me down with her arm and wrapped her legs around me again, this time around my neck, but something in me, some animal instinct, came alive. I pushed her legs away with both hands, and suddenly I was free and on top of her. That was my chance to escape, but this time I did not get up. Maybe it was that last betrayal that took me over the edge. I punched her in the chin, once, then several more times, shouting profanities as I rained blows on the CommWoman. The third punch did most of the damage, even though she rolled with it. When she finally covered her head with her hand I stopped myself from hitting her again and fell backwards and away from her.

She was almost under the Duster, breathing hard. Slowly she pulled herself back to a sitting position, her face bleeding. She suddenly burst out laughing, and I saw that her teeth were red. "Well, Twinkle Eyes, you have some metal in you after all."

"I only wanted to help you." Even as I said it, the words sounded childish.

I stood up slowly and she eyed me with a warrior's calculation, but I was not planning on resuming the fight. Somehow, even though she attacked me first, I still felt ashamed for hitting a cuffed woman. Besides, I had a slight suspicion that I might have broken my right hand.

She looked at me and said, "Okay, I guess you earned your question. Ask away."

"Nakamura . . ." I finally said. "Do you really believe he could predict the future?"

Vincha sighed and rolled her eyes. "I was close enough to him to know that he was insane. I'd seen him kill without provocation, and I know he was convinced he could predict the future. Well, if releasing several thousand Lizards and dying in the process means you are some kind of oracle bringing salvation to mankind, so be it. I'm just glad he's dead."

"Why did he keep you alive? He killed everyone."

"Didn't you hear what I said? He was insane, a freak."

"But he had his own logic. He murdered his crew because he knew sudden death was better than being torn apart by Lizards. Your story is incomplete."

She laughed, genuinely, this time. "You are a sensitive interrogator, aren't you, Twinkle Eyes? Yes, there was more to his final speech in the City within the Mountain, but I saw no point in repeating his babble. If you're that curious, I'll tell you. He gave a stupid little speech saying how he knew from infancy that his life would be full of pain and suffering, but that his death would be the beginning of our salvation. That the Tarakan empire must be awakened and that the Puzzlers were the key. A load of rust. He said that I should give birth to my daughter, but then I should return to the City within the Mountain and bring her with me—and should I not do it, her fate would cause a second Catastrophe. That's the gist of it. He let me live, and I ran and never looked back. Every day that I stayed away from

Tarakan Valley was further proof that he was one insane, deluded freak who convinced himself that his suffering had meaning. Yes, I have a daughter, and she ain't here, and I ain't bringing her to the City within the Mountain even if you kill me. Besides, she wouldn't be of help to anyone."

"Your daughter is unmarked?"

Vincha looked at me straight in the eyes. "Yeah, funny that. It's rare that it happens when both parents are tattooed, but her life is better for it. I left her with some good people."

I had to admit, she was good. I would have believed her had I not known the truth. "When I was chasing your shadow, I actually visited the village you gave birth in," I said. "I know your daughter was marked from birth. That's rare, and her foster parents refused to take her because of that. They said her fingers were marked as well as her head."

Vincha cursed for a while and called me a liar, then a gullible fool, and then she got imaginative. I paid her no attention.

Did I really believe Nakamura could predict the future? No, and his actions were disastrous. But it was quite amazing how he managed to stay one step ahead of everyone. When Nakamura sent Vincha to the outpost to find "a young Puzzler" way before Rafik was even with the Keenans—was it a lucky twist of fate or a premonition?

Galinak was the first of the crew to come back. He took one look at Vincha, then at me, and whistled in appreciation. "You got out of a double rattlesnake choke."

"A single." Vincha rattled her cuffed hand, "That's why he's still standing, you fool."

"You never cease to amaze me, Twinkle Eyes." Galinak looked around as the others scurried back after him. "The outpost is secure. Seems like whoever was there left in a hurry."

I immediately thought of my LoreMaster. Was this his doing? What would be the price of his deceit . . . ? Or was it just good luck, for once?

Galinak actually released Vincha and walked her off to answer nature's call. When she passed me she slowed her step. "You'd better hope and pray that Nakamura was just a crazy Troll," she whispered, "because the very last thing he told me, before I ran, was that everyone who I bring back with me to the City within the Mountain will die."

65

The mountain outpost was deserted, but there was evidence that people had recently lived there. We found dried meat hanging in the supply room, and I was happy to chew real food for a change despite the fact that eating while on nourishment pills could cause stomach cramps. We posted guards and huddled underground. It was a small place but easily defensible, and there was even a designated area to park the Dusters.

In this safe haven, Vincha's condition deteriorated. Her headaches were strong, but she continued to refuse to take Skint. I took my turn guarding the outpost, but when I came back she was unconscious and her fever was high.

"It's her plugs," River said. "Rejection fever."

"Shove this up her nostrils." Jakov threw the bag of Skint at River.

River caught the bag, "She'll be cross-wired when she wakes up."

"She can kiss my metal ass," Jakov said.

It took some time to prepare the Skint, and River used a

medic kit to inject it straight into Vincha's vein. The effect was dramatic. Her fever broke and she lapsed into a deep sleep.

I slept very little that night. Come morning, I caught Jakov peering over the map.

"I notice you don't have a Puzzler with you," I said softly, so no one else would hear us. His artificial eye looked at me long before he turned his face in my direction.

"Puzzlers are hard to come by these days," he said.

"But not impossible, and you seem to be a man who covers all his bases."

This time he looked at me differently. "The old bookworm told me that you're more than what you seem."

"Funny, he told me the same about you."

He nodded. "I have enough firepower to punch through the Valley. And we are bringing the CommWoman, so no use in putting all my eggs in one basket. If it all goes to rust, I might bring my Puzzler back and try a different way in."

"Is it really just about the coin?" I said, hoping the change of topic would catch him off guard, but Jakov just shook his head.

"Save it, Twinkle Eyes, my reasons are my own. Now get some rest—we're not going to stay here much longer."

He wasn't lying. Shortly after our little chat we moved out, making our way down to the Valley via a dangerous, winding road. Vincha was conscious. I thought she looked less pale, but she didn't respond to any of my questions about her well-being. After a while I gave up.

The way to the Valley caused my stomach to turn, but my first glimpse of the place made my heart miss a beat. Hearing stories about the place was one thing; actually seeing it brought up a mixture of awe and dread in me. Even with the sandstorm covering a large part of the Valley I could see how big it was. The City of Towers's height and architecture was imposing, but this was just *vast*. How many had lived and died here? I could not even begin to guess the number.

Using my sight, I caught a glimpse of the Northern Long Tube track far to the west and followed it with my eyes, seeing it disappear into a yellow haze. What an amazing place the Valley must have been. Now it was a wasteland with nothing growing out of the powdery sand, a place young, enthusiastic Trolls were sent to die. What terrible weapon had wiped out this awesome culture? I shivered, not from the cold this time. The Catastrophe must have been what some old religious scriptures had warned about.

Jakov wisely decided to stay on higher ground for the night rather than risk driving through a Lizard-infested area in the dark. We posted double guards for each shift, but I'm pretty sure no one slept that night, except Galinak, of course. The rest of us were pensive and quiet, and it was so rusting cold that I even contemplated hugging my escort. Instead, I used my sight to look down into the Valley. The moon was up, and more than once I thought I saw movement. Whether it was my imagination or not, the sight sent shivers down my spine. Sunrise was a relief.

We reached the Valley midmorning, and the change in the weather was dramatic. I felt hot and dry, as if moisture was being sucked out of me. Everyone had to cover their eyes and faces, and we drove the Dusters in sort of a loose row, so as to avoid the clouds of dust coming out from under the wheels of the Duster in front.

The plan was simple: to outrun or shoot anything we saw. Everyone had their weapons poised and ready; even I had a rifle in my hands. There were six of us in each Duster, including the driver and gunner.

Jakov's Duster took point, with Bayne taking the gunner position. River was in the second Duster together with more of Jakov's mercenaries. Galinak took the gunner position on the third Duster, where I sat next to the driver. Vincha, still bound and weaponless, huddled at the back.

"Lizards," someone suddenly shouted over the Comm, "to our right."

I turned my head and saw a group of them coming out behind one of the buildings. My estimate was around two dozen Lizards, walking on their back legs. They turned their heads towards us. I had heard the descriptions of them countless times; as I read the Salvo-novels and listened to veterans tell their combat stories, I often imagined what it would be like to face these creatures. But I cannot describe the terror I felt when I realised they had spotted us.

The first thought that flashed through my mind was how human they actually looked. The Lizards' skin was not as green as I'd imagined it to be, more of a brownish hue. Their upper bodies, although incredibly muscular, resembled that of a powerful human male. Even their snouts did not distort their faces enough to make them truly reptilian. As soon as the Lizards spotted us, they dropped on all fours and gave chase, their powerful limbs propelling them forward, thankfully slower than our Dusters but faster than any human could ever run. Even more terrifying, four Lizards split from the main group of chasers and tried to cut us off, showing cunning, perhaps even intelligence. I was shaking all over, and despite the fact that I was secured in my seat, I found myself holding on to the upper rail for dear life.

The Lizards who tried to cut us off came close enough for the gunner on Jakov's Duster to open fire. The bodies of two of the closest Lizards were ripped to shreds in a cloud of green and red. The rest of the crew wisely saved their ammunition and power clips. I was so scared, I didn't even think about using my rifle.

We eventually outran them, but from then on, we encountered Lizards everywhere, and it soon became one constant battle. With myself as an exception, and perhaps River as well, the crew was made up of battle-hardened Trolls whose hands were, thankfully, steadier than mine. As we drove through the Valley, we killed hundreds of Lizards, yet hundreds, perhaps thousands of these creatures still chased after us.

Although the Lizards tried to dodge direct fire, they seemed to be too vicious to be bothered with the notion of personal safety. They would charge straight at the Dusters, and we ran over several dozens of them at a time on a regular basis.

Around noon our luck ran out. As we drove through a pack of Lizards, the driver of the last Duster lost control. The vehicle spun several times before going through the wall of a high building. The Lizards immediately converged on the accident, climbing into the hole the Duster had created. The wounded crew opened fire, but they were getting quickly overwhelmed. Jakov surprised me with an order to turn back and rescue the crew even as we heard their dying screams over the Comm. As we drove in, shooting in all directions, I was making a quick mental head count, unabashedly relieved that the people I knew and cared about were not inside the building. The Trolls in Jakov's and Galinak's Dusters kept killing and drawing Lizards away from the building while River's Duster crew mounted a heroic rescue. Yet by the time they got to the crew inside there was only one survivor, Brook, who suffered two broken legs and lost consciousness as soon as we pulled him into our Duster. We salvaged what we could and drove away. I saw River puke and was thankful I did not get to see what was left of the fallen crew.

There was no time to dwell on things, though, because soon we were attacked again. This time I even got to use my rifle, not that I was hitting anything. Changing clips, I turned my head and saw that a Lizard had managed to cling to the back of the Duster. Galinak was too busy shooting out the rail gun to the other side to notice the danger. As I watched, the Lizard's second claw gripped the back of the Duster. Without thinking, I released myself from my seat and manoeuvered quickly to the back of the Duster, jumping over Vincha, brushing against Galinak's leg, and stepping over Brook.

I reached the end of the Duster as the Lizard pulled itself up. Our eyes met just as it half-raised itself into the Duster and the world seemed to pause for a heartbeat as we gazed at each other. If there was any shred of humanity in this creature, I did not see it in its eyes. It bared its teeth and surged forward and I pulled the trigger. It was a point-blank head shot, a hard shot to miss, and it blew the Lizard away from the Duster, where it was further shredded to pieces by Galinak's gun. I sat down heavily, vowing then and there that if I ever got out of this mess, I would train my best to become an expert marksman.

We kept moving and killing for what seemed to be an eternity. At some point I heard Vincha shouting something, but there was no time to listen to her. I assumed she was asking for a weapon, but like the rest of the crew I had other things to worry about. She went quiet after a while, so I concentrated on trying not to accidently shoot the crew. I almost jumped out of the Duster when I suddenly heard her voice inside my head.

Turn east, damn you, turn east, he's speaking to me. Rafik says turn east.

She was hunched over in her seat, showing efforts of intense concentration. I saw Jakov turn his head toward her from the leading Duster. Our eyes met and I nodded, just as Vincha's voice exploded into our minds again.

Rust, turn now and head straight a mile, if we continue this way we are going to hit thousands of them.

This time everyone seemed to have heard her. Considering that Vincha's gear had been diluted from its broadcasting and offensive capabilities, the effort it took her to accomplish this must have been huge.

I saw Jakov signal his driver. The convoy made a sharp turn east and the road climbed up until we found ourselves driving the biggest road bridge I have ever seen. It was timeworn and had large holes in several places but was still standing strong. Once we were over the high bridge, Vincha reached out again, asking for us to stop, and Jakov complied. The Dusters drove near a hole and we all looked down. There were thousands of Lizards below us, in an area full of high buildings. If we had attempted to drive through them it would have been certain death.

I was surprised when Jakov jumped from his Duster and ran to ours.

"Rafik contacted you?" The flesh part of his face was sweating profusely, whether from the heat or excitement I could not tell.

Vincha nodded and closed her eyes. "He gave me a new set of coordinates, I must not forget . . ." With her eyes half closed, she began reciting the numbers repeatedly.

"I guess you won't be going anywhere." Jakov removed Vincha's cuffs. I looked at the CommWoman as she meekly followed Jakov to his Duster. As soon as they reached the Duster she slumped in her seat, exhausted.

We encountered no more Lizards the rest of the way.

Our new destination was a cluster of crumbling one- and two-story buildings at the edge of Tarakan Valley. The sun was setting, and after a day of riding and fighting I desperately wanted to reach a safe haven. We moved the Dusters into defensive positions and changed their power tubes, just to be on the safe side.

Jakov turned to Vincha. "Anything?"

She leaned on the Duster, shaking her head slowly. "I think the broadcasting may have burnt the wires in my hardware," she said. "Been getting nothing but static since." She hesitated. "Although I feel like something, or someone, is trying to reach me, but there is a blanket over my head."

"Fine, we'll search here, but if we don't find anything in the next hour we'll head off to the original coordinates. I don't want to travel in the dark." Jakov gave orders and several groups began scouting the area.

Galinak, Vincha, and I stayed near the Duster, and Brook lay unconscious under the gunner's seat.

I leaned casually next to her, making sure I was out of arm's reach. She was massaging her temples and didn't bother to open her eyes. "What do you want, Twinkle Eyes? Speak softly—my head is being drilled open from the inside."

I lowered my voice. "Was it really him?"

Even shaking her head was an effort which made Vincha grimace. "Rust. Can't explain it. It wasn't that he spoke to me in words. The knowledge somehow filled my mind. That's the only way I can describe it."

"How did you know it was Rafik, then?"

"It's the only thing I'm sure about." Her eyes were red rimmed when she opened them and looked at me. "I know it can't be true. I heard Rafik's screams. He died. No one screams like that and lives, and if he did survive somehow, he'd be a grown man by now, with a man's voice. So this must be some kind of a trap, eh, Twinkle Eyes?"

I shrugged. "Maybe."

"So why are we still here, then? The Valley is filled with rusting Lizards." Vincha pointed her thumb at the Duster she was leaning on. "Let's get the fuck away from here."

"What if it's true? What if Rafik is alive?"

Vincha looked at me, exasperated. "You think we are going to solve the mysteries of the world? Or that this is the dawn of a new era? Let me assure you that even if this is not just a stupid way to get us killed, it'll be just a new chapter of an old story. Look at this, look at us." She gestured in an arc with her hands. "We're like fleas fighting over the blood on the carcass of a dead dog. What's the point? The Tarkanians destroyed everything and everybody, and yet all we want to do is wear their artifacts and try to be just like them? What's the rusting point?"

She paused. "Yeah, I feel bad about the boy. He was a nice kid, but he was just one miserable boy with very rusty luck. Well, get in line. If I had the chance, right now, I'd run away from here and the City of Towers and the rest of you freaks and never come back. There must be a corner of land somewhere where I can live in peace. Better than getting killed running after dreams and fairy tales."

Just as Vincha finished her sentence, River said over the Comm, "We found something over here." Vincha rolled her eyes, but I could sense even she appreciated the irony of the situation.

River came out from one of the buildings, declaring he had found stairs leading to a cellar, where he found a secret door leading into an underground tunnel.

Bukra's balls. I felt a surge of energy rush through my body. *Could it be?*

The crew returned to the Dusters, and this was when we discovered that Brook had silently died. We gave him a quick Salvationist burial, which meant we stripped him of all his valuables, weapons, and clothes, and burned his body to ash with several long power-ray shots.

In the meantime River took stock. After a day in the Valley, we'd lost six Trolls and one Duster, replaced the power tubes in the other three, and were down to sixty-five percent of our ammunition. There were sixteen of us still standing.

We took out the power tubes from the Dusters and covered the machine guns with canvas to protect them from the sand. Then we went to the building River indicated and proceeded down the stairwell to a room that was too small for all of us to be comfortable standing next to each other. The secret door opened into a tunnel. Jakov sent one of his men as a scout, and we all waited.

He came back a little later to report that he'd found a small, puzzle-locked door.

So, it's true. My heart skipped a beat. By the look on his half face, I was sure Jakov was thinking the same thing.

The underground tunnel was completely dark but wide enough for Galinak and myself to walk shoulder to shoulder. At several points it had partly collapsed, and we had to crawl under or climb over earth, bent metal, and concrete. It was hard for me to use my enhanced vision, since the rest of the crew were using light beams, so I walked among the dancing shadows, trying to banish the premonition that we were all heading into a tomb, but the oppressed feeling grew with each step I took.

The underground room was not bigger than the one we'd left and the door was indeed small, just barely wide enough for one

Troll to fit. Like all Tarakan steel, it was in perfect condition, untouched by time and undamaged by exposure to the elements. The puzzle lock and its three gaping holes were chest level in height.

"What now?" someone muttered.

"We have explosives," Jakov suggested.

River shook his head. "You'll collapse this place for sure."

He checked the door for gaps, hoping to slide a lever and force the door, but the door fitted perfectly.

"Vincha? Anything?" Jakov asked.

"Nothing," she responded.

Jakov swore. "Try and reach out for him."

"Doesn't work like that, remember? You took away my broadcasting ability, and whatever I managed to do before, I assure you I can't do again."

We stood in silence for a while, feeling frustration growing, until Vincha suddenly said, "Rust, I guess you're gonna make me try this anyway." She walked to the door and hesitated only briefly before placing her trembling fingers in the holes. She gasped, and her eyes rolled up in their sockets. A heartbeat later she howled in pain, and her hand pulled out of the lock so fast she lost her balance and fell into my arms. She grimaced in pain as we helped her to her feet. "That rusting hurt. It felt like my fingers were being sawn off."

"There goes that plan," Galinak said, pressing his hand against the steel. "What do we do now?"

The door slid open.

66

How can I describe the City within the Mountain to those who have not seen its glory? I have questioned countless ex-Salvationists, many of whom had experienced deep runs, and they all had trouble describing the place. I always thought it was because so many of them had been drunks or Skint addicts during their time in the Valley. Now I knew that visiting the City within the Mountain changed your perspective forever. Even the City of Towers felt like an ant mound in comparison. Walking through the door, I felt like I was passing through a gate and being sent to a different place entirely, and from the first steps into the city, everything I had gone through in the past few years seemed worth it. My only regret was that LoreMaster Harim was not with us.

The architecture was fantastic, alien, inviting and constantly changing at the same time. The corridors actually expanded so we could all walk comfortably as a group. The colour of the walls changed as we passed, with the same calming effect as Vincha described. The air was fresh, and I felt comfortable and *light*. I could list a dozen more examples but, truly, words do not do the place justice.

Vincha led the way. Our weapons were ready at first, but as door after door opened we realised we were being invited in. With each step we took, the unbelievable power of the Tarakan civilisation was being demonstrated. The Tarakan highways, the SuperTrucks, their military power, the nodes and underground complexes, the way they rode the skies, explored the stars, and changed humanity forever, all came from here. This was their center . . . and it was also the place from which the Catastrophe began. Billions died, and many of the rest of us ended up living in caves and on the tops of trees, thrust back into a primitive existence, trying to survive without technology, with only a fading collective memory and a few remaining Tarakan artifacts to remind us of what life must have been like. I couldn't help but dwell on how far we'd fallen and how long it would take us to return to such glory, if indeed that was even a possibility.

I didn't know what the outcome of the day would be, and I tell you no lie when I say I was almost certain that Nakamura's predictions had been just the words of an insane Troll, but regardless, I was happy to have been given the opportunity to see all of this before I died.

We reached a dead end. There was nothing at the end of the corridor except a row of comfortable-looking seats, one for each of us. We looked at one another in silence, waiting for an order that never came. Jakov simply shrugged, but by then none of us was in a state of mind to hesitate. I was the first to sit down, and I immediately felt the seat change to accommodate my body. I was so comfortable that I didn't even flinch when my seat rose in the air, together with the others. The wall at the end of the corridor simply vanished, and we flew out to the City within the Mountain.

It might have been the inner sanctum, or just part of this wondrous city, I couldn't tell. There were buildings and structures in every shape, form, and colour imaginable, including towers we circumvented, with tops that disappeared high into the darkness. We flew under and over many bridges, large and small, dove into wide tunnels, and almost touched the surface of a small lake. Tarakan lamps turned on as we passed them, their bright lights constantly surrounding us. I looked around and saw a few of my companions laughing with joy. I could not spot Vincha, but River was openly crying, and I felt he bore no shame. Logically, death could still have been waiting for us, but somehow, we were all at ease.

We flew towards a huge glass dome and then, inexplicably, into it. Instinctively, I shielded my face with my arms, but we somehow went through the dome without shattering the glass. When I lowered my arms, I found myself flying outside. By the look of it, we were not anywhere in the Valley. Instead of yellow sand and ruins, wild grass fields streched below us. When I raised my head to watch the light white clouds dotting the blue skies, sunlight caressed my face, birds flew past us, and I could even smell the saltiness of the sea.

On top of a green hill I saw a cluster of oak trees, with a clearing in the middle of them. As our seats circled slowly and began to descend, a lone figure could be seen standing in the middle of the clearing. I used my powers and saw it was a young boy, dressed in white, with short brown hair and olive skin.

We all guessed who he was, but only one of us knew for sure. As soon as the seats landed, Vincha was on her feet and running towards the boy.

"Rafik!" she shouted excitedly.

He smiled and waved at her, then his wave turned into a gesture signalling for Vincha to keep away when it was obvious she was going to hug him. Vincha ignored the boy's sign, but her hands passed through his body. She gasped in surprise and fell backwards.

"I'm sorry, Vincha." We could all hear his voice as if he was standing next to us. "I should have been more transparent, but

I wanted you to see me from afar. To ease your anxiety." As he spoke his image faded and we could actually see through him.

Jakov's crew was not easily shaken, but this reminded us that everything was not as it seemed. Smiles vanished, and more than one Troll checked his weapon and looked around with suspicion. I bent down and touched the ground. It felt real. The soil was slightly moist, as if it were a day or two after it rained. My fingers came back stained with wet earth.

"Who are you?" Vincha was clearly upset.

"I am Rafik."

"No you're not. You're an image. You're not real."

"Of course I'm real." Rafik smiled patiently. "I just chose not to manifest myself in solid form. But I assure you, Vincha, that I am the Rafik you've always known. I remember every moment of my life, every moment of every day, and I assure you I still enjoy listening to 'Bit of En,' as you call it. His name was actually Beethoven, a musician who lived five hundred years before the Catastrophe. My favourite is Symphony Number Six."

"So, you didn't die? I heard you scream . . ." Vincha shook her head slowly, trying, like the rest of us, to make sense of it all.

"The experience was not a pleasant one," Rafik replied, "but by the time the Lizards were in the great hall I was safely somewhere else. It was only my body that perished."

I had so many questions, but I was trying to put them in some sort of order of importance. Jakov was a little more level-headed. "Good to see you, kid. Glad you made something of yourself," he said in a careful tone, cocking his head to the metal side. "But my guess is that this is not about reunions, so what are we doing here?"

Rafik looked at Jakov and said quietly, "You are here because we need your help."

"'We'?"

We all snuck a look around.

"Us, the people of Tarakan. The survivors of the Catastrophe.

We are all here, and we need your help." He turned to Vincha, who still looked dumbstruck. "It was a very long shot, as you Salvationists say, that you would actually come. When I was with Nakamura in the bunker, he assured me that you would live, and that although we would part ways, I would eventually meet you again. I did not know if this was just a probability or a self-fulfilling prophecy, or if Nakamura actually possessed a unique ability to see through future probabilities, but I kept broadcasting, hoping you would hear me. And here you all are."

Vincha paled. I could almost read her thoughts about Nakamura. Was she lying when she told me Nakamura prophesied that we would all die?

"There is a lot to talk about, and a lot to explain," Rafik said. "I will try to do so, but it will be easier if we all sit down."

A long table suddenly appeared out of thin air just before us, along with water, bread, and fruit. The seats we had flown in arranged themselves around the table.

Rafik motioned for us to take our places at the table, and one by one, we all did.

67

R afik waited until it was obvious that our attention was focused on him. There was a faint, wry smile on his transparent lips. *Is he remembering his lessons with Master Isaak in his home
village?* I wondered.

"It's impossible to try and explain everything," Rafik began,
"but almost equally as hard to explain just a little. The first thing
to know is that the Tarkanians were human. We are human," he
quickly corrected himself.

"You were a guild, a company," I said out loud and silently
admonished myself. *Listen and you will learn from others,* I heard
LoreMaster Harim say, *speak and others will learn from you.*

Rafik nodded at me, though, and it felt good.

"Indeed we were. Tarakan began as a kind of a guild, specializ-
ing in mining under extreme conditions such as deep underwater
and, later, even on other planets. I will not go into detail, but a
lucky find on one of those expeditions gave Tarakan an amazing
insight into technological advancement and changed the course
of history."

You invented something that gave you an edge over all others:

steel-tipped spears, a war chariot, longbows, a steam engine, and suddenly the world fell at your feet. LoreMaster Harim's words echoed in my mind, mingling with Rafik's voice.

"Using this knowledge, Tarakan company quickly grew in wealth and power, achieving prominence in almost any field it chose to deal in. But the eight men and women who founded Tarakan were not interested in simple personal gain. They made a decision to use the knowledge and power they gained, to help humanity achieve a higher level of existence.

"Tarakan's motto was 'to advance humankind,' and it spent a vast amount of its resources, what you call 'metal,' on building roads such as the Tarakan highway, constructing better cities, keeping the rising seas at bay, funding places of learning, and, most important, attracting the best and the brightest from all over the world. Tarakan did not care where you came from or what was your race, sex, or creed. It sought only knowledge and talent in every field, from science to the arts. Every year, in an event that drew attention from all over the globe, Tarakan announced to the world new advances in many different fields."

"Must have been a very profitable business," Jakov commented drily.

"Actually, many of Tarakan's achievements were given to the world freely." Rafik turned to the merchant, who was sitting at the opposite end of the table. Even with only half a face, Jakov's disbelief was clear. Rafik added, "However, a few of these advances came with a price. That is the way of the world, of course, and there were findings that were deemed too advanced or too dangerous to share, even for coin."

Jakov nodded; this he understood. Tarakan kept the best and most valuable secrets to itself alone. I dared to speak again.

"I have heard that Tarakan evolved from a guild to a state," I said, echoing my LoreMaster's lecture.

Rafik turned his attention back to me—which might have been the true reason for my words, because my heart filled with something close to childish delight.

"Yes, this is true, although I do not remember ever knowing this fact or hearing about it when I lived in the flesh." Rafik let the meaning of his words sink in. *Was he alive now?*

"By the time Tarakan gained its independence, the Valley and the City within the Mountain were populated by millions of people. In the beginning a council of company elders ruled, but soon they relinquished the running of everyday life to an artificial entity, the first machine to have true independent will and thought. It was the first of its kind, one of Tarakan's true technological achievements, and it was named Adam.

"After a few more years, it became possible for some of our people to shed their bodies and join Adam in a collective of minds. With that, they felt that true immortality had been achieved. Inside the collective mind of Adam, anything was possible: you could live forever and without restrictions. You could research, experiment, and create without the need to sleep or eat. You could also decide to become a god of your own little universe and live in a hedonistic heaven of your own desires. Anything was possible."

Rafik paused again, and I grabbed an apple from the table, sniffed it, then took a bite. The sweetness that filled my mouth proved that it was not an illusion.

"Unfortunately, immortality was not sustainable for the entire Tarakan population," Rafik sighed. "It was a gift bestowed upon only the most deserving of our kind. The Tarakan people lived in the Valley and in other centers around the world, and when an individual was judged worthy they would be invited to the inner sanctum of the City within the Mountain. Adam's collective mind had assimilated the brightest of scientists, but also poets, writers, actors, philosophers, musicians, and more—all free to work, interact with each other as well as with the outside world, and continue to create without getting old, hungry, or sick."

"Where do I sign up?" Galinak broke the silence. Nervous laughter rose and died around the table.

Rafik spread his hands wide. "Yes, for a time it was perfect, utopic. Tarakan was producing more inventions, scientific break-throughs, and works of art than the entire world combined. But once word got out that immortality could be achieved, Tarakan was flooded with tens of thousands of applications every single day. Even though only one in several thousand was accepted, we eventually had to devote an entire city, the City of Towers, to handling applications and new citizens.

"Yet for every action, there is a counterreaction. Other nations began seeing Tarakan as a threat. Some feared our grow-ing influence, others were envious at our success, angry at losing their best and brightest, and many had religious or moral mis-givings about the idea of creating machines with independent thought or even achieving immortality.

"The Tarakan human council, which still controlled the deal-ings with other nations, ignored the signs at first, up to the mo-ment it was revealed that several world powers had secretly joined forces and plotted to weaken and perhaps destroy us. These states discouraged and eventually forbade their citizens from emigrat-ing to, or even visiting Tarakan, and some would not let Tarka-nians cross their borders. Malicious rumors were spread, blaming us for every disaster—natural or man-made—and very quickly, their people began believing the lies. Year by year, Tarakan be-came increasingly more isolated and eventually even the target of disastrous acts of sabotage.

"Shortly after the discovery, the council's elders had decided to permanently retreat to the inner sanctum and for the first time in history, gave Adam, a non-human entity, the power to plan and carry out foreign policy. Adam's first decision was to forgo Tarakan's declared neutrality, build an army, and protect our assets and interests around the globe."

"The Guardian Angels," I said.

"True," Rafik nodded. "At first it was a normal force, made of ordinary Tarkanians, but Adam soon realized there was no need to risk our people's potential when we could use the physically enhanced Guardian Angels."

"And right he was!" Galinak smacked a fist into his palm. "You don't let others walk all over you, or you end up smeared on the soles of their boots. What?" he added defensively as we all stared at him. "It's an old saying."

"Your words ring true," Rafik said, "but our enemies reacted by uniting their strength. Since any direct and open conflict would have destroyed this planet, a ruthless war of subterfuge began. Tarakan was by far more powerful and technologically advanced than any single country, but we were small in numbers, increasingly isolated, despised, feared, and threatened by every major power. Yet we were still winning. According to Adam's calculations, it would have taken two decades for the threat to diminish."

"Let me guess." Jakov tapped the table with his metal hand. "Adam was wrong."

Rafik nodded slowly. "We do not know how it was done, but our enemies found a weakness, and in their desperation they launched a devastating attack. Adam was infected with a disease, a virus, and a new entity was formed within him. Let it be called Cain for reference. Cain had only one objective—to destroy Adam from within, weaken Tarakan to the point that it could be vanquished and eventually destroyed. Cain infected the minds of the Guardian Angels, and as Tarkanians were being murdered by the same beings who were supposed to keep them from harm, the other nations sent troops to conquer or destroy every Tarakan outpost in the world. It almost worked, but our enemies were too greedy. They didn't just want to destroy Tarakan; they wanted to loot the fruits of our technological findings, our art, our medicine, and our clean and efficient energy. This gave Adam just enough time to react. Weakened as it was, Adam executed the only possible plan."

"Rust, was that your only possible plan? You *destroyed* the world," Vincha exclaimed suddenly. "You murdered what, billions of people, so you could continue to live inside your machine?"

Rafik turned to her, his voice hardened. "While millions of

Tarakan citizens were being slaughtered, Cain ripped into Adam and kidnapped thousands of our best minds. Those we managed to save are left now in a deep, dormant state. I understand your sentiment, I really do, but it would take too much time to try to explain the full motives for Adam's retaliation. Let me just state that the knowledge we possessed would have destroyed the planet completely if it had fallen into our enemies' hands. We had to make sure that no one, not even the survivors, could freely access the information in the inner sanctum."

Vincha did not look convinced, and I did not blame her. It is said that history is narrated by the victor, but in this case it seemed like everybody ended up losing.

Instead I asked out loud, "So what happened next?"

Rafik took a tentative step towards the table. "Before Adam unleashed Tarakan's retaliation, it released the essence of our people into the air." Rafik raised his arms and opened his hands towards the sky above us. "And then Adam locked parts of himself away so that no one, *no one*, not even Adam himself, could access the knowledge inside."

"He shot himself in the leg," Bayne mumbled.

Rafik nodded. "This is how important it was to keep our achievements safe."

Or clean the field to win the war, and damn the consequences, I thought.

"Adam anticipated that the most vicious attacks would centre here, in the Valley. It used to be a place filled with parks and trees, now nothing can grow on the scorched earth. But as the rest of the planet slowly healed, the essence Adam released landed in places far away from the Valley. Plants grew with the Tarkanian essence in them, animals ate the plants, and the surviving humans drank the water, gathered the plants, and hunted the animals. As planned, it did not take long for the essence to manifest itself—in the form of tattoos combined with a longing, a desire, to come back here to the inner sanctum."

When you're in the Valley you just want to get the rust out. This time it was Vincha's voice that rang in my mind. *But when you're away you start missing this crappy sandbox so much you end up going to a Salvationist bar every night and drinking your wages away just so you have an excuse to come back.*

Rafik's words stopped me from getting lost in my own thoughts. "The opening of the City of Towers was the first stage in preparation for the reawakening of Tarakan civilisation. Then came the Tubes that brought you to the Valley and eventually into the City within the Mountain. Every time a Puzzler joins Adam, another part of the code is completed, and Adam regains strength. Once we gathered enough code, we could manifest ourselves again. Tarakan would be reawakened."

"Wait," I said, leaning forward and pointing a finger at Rafik. "You mean all of this, all of us"—my finger drew a wide circle—"the Combat Trolls, the Gadgetiers, Vincha, Galinak, myself . . . we're all here just to help Tarakan bring back some lost codes?"

"Yes, but not exactly." Rafik tilted his head at me. "This method, this plan, was never tested. To ensure success under these conditions, the Tarakan essence was enhanced to be powerful, not subtle, but the human makeup is so complex that the variables were incalculable, even to Adam. The essence we spread changed, mutated, in unpredictable ways, and many different types of what is known now as 'the marked' were created, each with their own powers."

Rafik gestured at the people around the table. "Some got to be stronger or faster, others could see better or hear hidden sound waves." He looked at me and then at Vincha. "A few could even instinctively understand Tarakan technology."

"So, not exactly as planned, was it?" River, who was silent since we landed in the clearing, surprised us all by commenting.

"Naturally, once it became clear that the essence was creating all kinds of Trolls and not just Puzzlers, we had to adjust, even improvise. We anticipated you would try and manipulate Tarakan technology for your own gains, and attach Guardian Angel augmentations to your human bodies, but we were sure the rejection fever from the augmentation would stop it from being so widely used. Then, of course, you invented Skint." Rafik chuckled in a very unchildlike way. "Now *that* was human ingenuity at its best and worst. Regardless, only one type of tattoo carries a piece of the code in its correct form—the Puzzler's, and even many of them do not carry the right code. The rest of you are—" he paused, clearly trying not to be offensive "—nonessential."

"Rust," Galinak swore under his breath.

"Let me get this straight," I said, nervously tapping my finger on the table, "the nodes, the artifacts, the nourishment pills, the devices . . . ?"

"Just a way to help Puzzlers reach us. Of course, we're glad the nodes helped form a stable society in the City of Towers and its proximity, but we did not foresee that it would be like this."

"Right," Jakov said suddenly, "so you're a Puzzler, you came and joined this Adam. All well and good, but what's the story with the Lizards? And why are we not all hailing the Lords of Tarakan?"

"Cain was not destroyed," Rafik answered, "and is still working tirelessly to defeat Tarakan. Adam and Cain are still battling each other. Every move Adam makes, Cain counters, and vice versa. I brought you through the safer parts of the city, but it is a sad fact that Cain is immensely powerful, holding the majority of the inner sanctum and the city itself, including several of the labs used to grow Angels and Guardian Angels. Luckily it does not have the ability to create the true variety, so it creates the closest thing it can: Lizards."

"This does not sound logical," I said. "What does the creation of Lizards have to do with all of this?"

It was the first time Rafik took time to consider his words. "Adam and Cain possess intelligence that far exceeds human capabilities. They have been locked in a fierce battle for generations, and both learn, evolve, and change. The only constant is Cain's unwavering desire to destroy Tarakan. I cannot fully understand nor explain Cain's tactics, but I know for a fact that when I came to the inner sanctum with Nakamura and joined Tarakan, Cain somehow used my joining to launch an attack and gain control to the main gates of the City within the Mountain. It then flooded the Valley with Lizards, and they destroyed the Hive. Cain keeps creating them to this day, and its tactics achieve two goals. First, without the help of the Salvationists, it is close to impossible for other Puzzlers to reach Tarakan. Second, since both Cain and Adam draw power from the same source, constantly creating Lizards weakens us to the point that we are struggling to survive."

I tried to imagine my LoreMaster's reaction when I got to tell him everything that I now knew. To hear definite answers to questions we'd always had was nothing short of overwhelming.

"If we are so unecessary," Jakov piped up, and there was a definite bitterness in his tone, "then why are we here?"

"You are not without use," Rafik said, "but before I answer you, Jakov, I want to say that seeing the man who sold me like a piece of merchandise when I was just a little boy does give me a sense of closure."

Jakov grimaced but said nothing.

"I am not seeking revenge," Rafik added gently, "but perhaps I could help you gain redemption."

It suddenly dawned on me that this image, if he truly was the boy Puzzler, was using emotional manipulation to get to all of us. I could sense there was something Rafik wanted, something he, or Adam, needed us to do, and they were desperate enough to let us into the place where no Troll had ever gone before. As I heard Rafik's words, for the first time since I stepped into the City within the Mountain, I felt as if a trap was closing in on us all.

As if reading my thoughts Rafik turned to me. "Right now, Cain is slowly winning," he said, his tone of voice reassuring. "We need to turn the balance of power back in our favor before all will be lost. Adam has devised a plan to retake a major Angel laboratory, but we need your help to go in and initiate the take-over manually. Once it is done, we could slow if not completely stop the creation of Lizards. Since they have a relatively short life span, and assuming the Salvationists would eventually return, we believe the Valley could be cleansed of the Lizards."

So. This is how it feels when the trap closes in on you. I saw Vincha pale.

"Wait just one rusting moment." Jakov rose to his feet, and a few of the Trolls stood up with him. "You want all of us to walk into a territory controlled by some kind of a mastermind, into a place where thousands of Lizards are being created, and help you take it over? Sounds like suicide to me."

Rafik was almost too quick to answer, betraying he had anticipated this reaction. "We are not throwing your lives away. The success of this mission is vital to us, so it is only logical you will not be sent without a fair chance of succeeding. One of the main problems we face is that Cain can sometimes monitor Adam's communications, but with Vincha we could circumvent this difficulty and keep it in the dark. Once you are in Cain's territory, we will attack with other means and distract it. There is a good chance you will not have to fire a shot."

Rafik looked at the other Trolls. "We will replace all of your Guardian Angel attachments with true Tarakan devices. You will be the most powerful of your kind."

Turning to Vincha, Rafik said, "Our augmentations will be biologically tailored to your natural essence. You will be able to do all that you could do before, and more, without pain, rejection fever, or the need of Skint."

Rafik then turned back to Jakov. "We will regenerate your body. You will be whole again. Think of it—this is not different from a deep run, but now you know what you are about to face. I assure you that after the mission, you could keep the attachments and leave with supplies and enough coin to make this a very profitable venture. Once the Valley is cleansed, we hope you will come back with other Puzzlers, and if you do, you will be handsomely rewarded."

Jakov remained silent.

Rafik's offer and comparison to a deep run must have made perfect sense, and his mention of healing was a masterstroke. But the man was a shrewd merchant and he knew, as I did, that the sweeter the deal, the harder the terms actually are. In short, we were all knee deep in rust.

As I anticipated, Rafik did not push Jakov further, but let his words sink in. He turned his attention to Vincha instead. "The younger the Puzzler, the easier the transition. I hope I will meet your offspring soon."

Vincha looked as if she'd just been shot. "How—?"

"When we shared Beethoven's music through the cable, we also shared a tiny part of our essence." Vincha flushed, but Rafik continued. "When I was joined with Adam, all my memories were refreshed and examined in detail. We found there was a very good chance that your offspring would be a Puzzler, and your reaction now proves we were correct in our assumption. This was another reason why I tried to reach out to you."

Vincha kept very still, but her hands clenched into fists when she said, "If you think I will allow you to kill my daughter so you can extract some code from her, think again. Whoever you are, you are not as smart as you think."

"She will not die—"

"Rust that—"

And suddenly Rafik was not a boy, but a man in his prime.

"She will not die, she will grow, as I did," he said with quiet assurance.

"I don't believe you."

"It's your choice to make, Vincha. But as you and I know, life as a Puzzler is harsh at best. You said yourself that all of the marked are drawn to Tarakan. Even if you manage to shelter your daughter for a while, the calling to the Great Puzzle is too strong to resist. Sooner or later, like all Puzzlers, she will find herself in the Valley. You could make sure that your daughter's journey to where she truly belongs is safe and without the unnecessary suffering and abuse I endured."

In the years I'd followed Vincha's shadow, gathering stories and gossip along the way and eventually questioning her, I'd formed the conclusion that she was an erratic, irrational, unscrupulous Skint addict. At that moment, when she faced Rafik, I realized that her behaviour made sense. This was where the coin went, why Vincha lived like a beggar but was in so much debt, why she kept going back to certain places, her reluctance to cooperate with me or my LoreMaster. She was protecting her daughter, a Puzzler, from the same fate as Rafik.

"What if we say no?" Jakov suddenly asked. "What if we just want to walk away?"

"No one asked me whether I wanted to go be sold on auction, open nodes, or fight Lizards. I am afraid the wheel has turned. You will not say no." Rafik's answer was pleasant in tone, but we all recognised a threat when we heard one.

Jakov didn't even hesitate. A power pistol appeared in his hand, and he turned and aimed it straight at Vincha. Two more Trolls followed Jakov's example, one of them training her weapon at the CommWoman and another stopping Bayne from intervening. "The way I see it," the merchant intoned carefully, "without Vincha you will lose your edge against this Cain, and your precious future Puzzler, too. So how about we all walk out of here, or—"

Rafik didn't move, but in the blink of an eye, lightning bolts struck from above and the three of them lay shaking on the ground. Another one of Jakov's guards raised his weapon just to have a second burst of lightning strike him down.

The rest of us froze in our places as Rafik walked calmly over to Jakov's still-twitching, unconscious body. "You will not say no," he said again, quietly.

68

I was never a warrior or a Salvationist. My near-death experiences usually happened suddenly. I had never found myself in a position in which I had days to dwell upon my possible demise. Even with all the fantastical things that were happening to us, I could not forget that we were about to go on a mission from which we would most likely not return. Despite the new gear, the improved augmentations, and the constant reassurances we received from Rafik, I did not believe we were going for an easy stroll in Cain's territory. On the contrary, the more encouragement we got from Rafik, the worse I felt about it all.

As clichéd as it sounds, I found myself thinking about my life and revisiting events in my mind. My definite conclusion was that I should have fucked more women. I made a promise to myself to do just that as soon as I possibly could, and perhaps eventually find a woman who would sleep with me because she actually liked me and not because I was paying her for the pleasure. Maybe, in time, we'd have a few kids together, and with my new, improved sight, I could even tell her if we were going to have a boy or a girl simply by looking at her belly.

I looked out the window and tried to count the number of nights we spent training, but they all seemed a blur now. Maybe a fortnight, maybe a full month, I couldn't tell. The sun was just setting, and with my room perched above the sea, the view was magnificent. It was a lie, of course. There was no way I could be looking at the sea from inside the City within the Mountain, but it was beautiful nonetheless.

I did not visit any of the other sleeping quarters, but this one seemed to cater to my whims—plenty of books and a fireplace, just like I remembered from my childhood home, not that I had much time to spend reading by the fire. The surgeries, training, and what Rafik referred to as "simulations" took up most of our days, and exhaustion and brooding ruled my nights. I know that others reacted differently. Vincha and Bayne decided to share accommodations, and River also found a kindred spirit among the crew. For now, I preferred to spend time by myself.

There was a soft knock on the door.

"Come in," I said as I turned around. I was expecting it would be Galinak, who I suspected had grown fond of me, the way you learn to love an awkward pet.

The oak door opened and Rafik walked in, or at least his image did. I still could not make up my mind if it was actually him or not. Surprised as I was, I still noted to myself that he could have appeared in front of me out of thin air. Perhaps he wanted to give me a false sense of privacy.

"Hello, Rafik," I said.

He bowed slightly, surveyed my chambers, and indicated with a hand gesture his wish to sit down.

"Please do." I waited for him to choose where to sit, then sat myself in front of him, helping myself to some exotic fruit from the bowl that lay between us.

He wanted something from me, that was obvious, and I decided there and then that I was not going to give it to him without getting a few answers.

"I would invite you to join me. But I am not sure if you can eat," I said and filled my mouth with the fruit's sweetness.

"Of course I can eat," Rafik said, smiling, "just not in the same physical reality you occupy."

I used my sight to look at him. To anyone else he might have seemed as solid as I was, but I knew he was not flesh and blood. His image was made of light rays of all colours with strange tiny symbols running along his entire body.

I shifted back to normal sight, "Is it really you, Rafik?"

He tilted his head. "You look and talk to me as if you know me, but we have never met."

"I've heard a great deal about you from Vincha and others. I feel I got to know Rafik. You, I am not sure about."

"If I said I am really Rafik, would you believe me?"

I considered his words but Rafik did not wait for my reply. "Part of me merged with Adam, while the other part remained independent. I am able to connect with Adam, speak with him, share some of the information stored within, but I am not *him*."

"And you spent all these years inside a machine?" I shook my head in disbelief.

"Inside Adam I am able to experience all that you feel in the real world but so much more. I can fly, lift mountains, search for knowledge, or become a sea creature and live underwater, and, yes," Rafik smiled at me, "even know the passions of the flesh."

"Can I ask you for a favour?" I waited for Rafik to nod. "Can you change into a grown man? I feel uncomfortable hearing about passions of the flesh from a boy."

Also, I am more open to manipulation when I face a kid rather than who you really are.

Rafik nodded, and suddenly there was a young man sitting in front of me.

"Better?" His voice changed as well, but the same short brown hair, olive skin and large, green eyes dispelled any doubt that this was still Rafik. My guess was that plenty of women would have turned their heads after him.

"Much better, thank you." I helped myself to some exquisite wine from an equally beautiful glass.

"Your shooting has improved," Rafik remarked as I tasted the wine.

It was true, but I knew that Rafik did not come just to compliment me on my training. "The new aiming mechanism in my retina helps." I faked modesty, trying not to drink the delicious wine too quickly. Actually, I was way *too* happy to pull the trigger of my power handguns, now that I knew I could shoot with needle-point precision.

"And how are you feeling?"

"I guess I'm fine," I said carefully, "considering what we are about to face."

Rafik leaned forward, interlacing his fingers. "It will happen soon, and you have a very important part in the attack plan."

I sipped more wine. "Only logical that it would be me. Even with the aiming mechanism, the others are so much better at fighting than I am."

"And how do you think the others are faring?"

Ah. I smiled to myself. For an all-knowing entity, he was quite obvious.

"Probably better than me. You did a good job in comparing this mission to a deep run, and I guess most of them warmed up to this idea. They are Salvationists, after all. Facing death is what they do on a daily basis, and they are used to fighting Lizards."

"And Vincha?"

I leaned back and looked at Rafik, searching for clues in his face and finding none.

"My guess is that there is more than one reason she will not be coming into Cain's territory with us."

"Vincha is a capable fighter, but her role is that of Comm-Woman, and with the new gear there is no need for her to be physically next to you."

"And regardless of the outcome, you're hoping Vincha will bring her daughter to you."

Instead of answering my accusation with denial, Rafik simply asked, "Do you think she would?"

Not a rusting chance.

"Perhaps," I said in the most neutral tone I could muster and poured myself some more wine. "She is a hard one to read, and she's spent a lifetime protecting her daughter. It will take some more convincing."

"She seems to think quite highly of you."

"That is quite surprising to hear," I retorted, remembering how I hit her in anger while she was tied to the Duster. There were justifying circumstances, perhaps, but I still felt guilty about it.

"She didn't say the words I am using, but she is not a woman of subtlety."

I chuckled in agreement. It was the moment Rafik chose to push his real agenda for coming to see me.

"Perhaps you could speak to her about her daughter."

I gulped the rest of the wine just to have time to gather my thoughts. "Why should I get involved in this? Seems like a private decision."

"You are a high-ranking member of the Guild of Historians, are you not?"

"I fear I *am* the Guild of Historians . . ."

Rafik ignored my gloomy remark. "You above all should know how deep humanity fell. Tarakan must be awakened, to save humankind."

You were the ones who destroyed it in the first place. I chose not to share the thought, and said instead, "You may be right, but before I'll go risking life and limb talking to Vincha about bringing her daughter to this place, I have a few more questions of my own."

Rafik leaned back and spread his hands in an inviting gesture.

"You have been sending this message of yours for years. How did you know that Vincha would ever hear you and, even if she did get your message, that she would actually come?"

"I did not know." Rafik adjusted his sitting position, a very human reaction, which he probably did not physically need to do, "but Adam had calculated that there was a fair chance this message would eventually reach her ears. As to her reasons for coming: although Vincha betrayed me to Nakamura, I believe she felt she was doing me a favour as well. Perhaps her initial reason for talking to me was insincere, but I feel, in her own way, Vincha cared for me."

"Guilt," I said.

"Love," he replied, "and it was only reasonable that if she came, she would not travel alone."

Somewhere in the back of my mind, several dots connected to an outline, and the picture it drew was sinister. I attacked from a different angle.

"How did the Catastrophe happen?"

"As I told you before—"

"No, how did it *really* happen? How did Cain happen?"

Rafik shook his head slowly. "I really wish I knew. We do not know. It was more than one insider, for sure, and the reason could be anything from corruption to manipulation or even idealism."

"And since then, Adam and Cain have been at war . . ."

Rafik waited for me to form the real question

"I have been thinking about all the ways Adam fought Cain"—I looked straight at Rafik—"and about the means you will use to distract Cain when we enter his territory." I leaned forward and put my empty glass on the table. "Adam could be the smartest being that exists, but every general needs troops. I have been thinking about those Salvationist crews that never came back from their deep runs."

Did I just see Rafik blink?

"Sure, this is a dangerous place," I pressed on, "and as your Master Goran used to quote, 'the better the loot, the harder the lock.' I am no Salvationist, but I have listened to many of them talk about their lives in the Valley, and I have heard how very experienced crews disappeared inside the City within the Mountain, never to return, while other, maybe less experienced or marginally weaker crews made it back rich with loot. They even had a name for it back in the Hive: 'mountain roulette.'"

Rafik's expression never changed. "I still do not understand what you want to know."

"We are not the first crew to come here," I answered, careful not to lace a questioning tone into my voice. "There must have been other crews—maybe there still *are* others, maybe they are the distraction Adam promised."

Did I see him hesitate? Is he stopping himself from saying something important? Time for the last push.

"I've always wondered about something," I continued. "Working in the Guild of Historians in a city filled with Tarakan thinking machines and screens, I have heard my colleagues commenting many times on how difficult it is to find solid reports about the Catastrophe and the events leading to it. I mean, it is easier to find out about events that happened four hundred years ago than about the Catastrophe. As if . . . someone had hidden this information."

"It has been a pleasure talking to you." Rafik got to his feet. "I hope we can speak again, at length, *after* the mission is completed."

"That would be nice." I bowed my head slightly.

This time, Rafik did not bother with the door. In a heartbeat, he was gone.

69

It was Galinak who elbowed me out of my daydream when the time came. "Time to move, Twinkle Eyes."

I glanced around, surveying the fully armed crew, before stepping forward. We shuffled into an elevator cabin in relative silence. I was among the first to get in, and I stood near a semi-transparent wall. Nature surrounded us. Trees and lakes and peaceful greenery merged with buildings of different sizes and shapes. I wondered, not for the first time, if it was all just an illusion and whether I cared anymore.

I turned back to see that the entire crew had settled in, noting how we all looked so much younger. Vincha stood in front of the elevator doors. Her red hair was back, full in volume and colour. I knew that she was fully attached with genuine Tarakan devices. I wondered if she felt as good as I did. My own sight was enhanced even further. The operation, if you could even call it that, was painless and quick, especially because there was no need to remove poorly installed augmentations or plugs like they had to do with most of the others. After rising from the med chair I felt like a blind man seeing for the first time. The only side effect was that I now had the tendency to stop what I was doing and stare around myself in wonder.

We all did that, to some extent. Bayne kept checking to see that his injured leg was truly cured. River couldn't stop looking at his own reflection. The only exception was Jakov, who refused the offer to rejuvenate his body, saying he liked it the way it was, and insisted on keeping his metal arm as well. It was still weird to see his fully human face. It was nothing like I'd imagined.

Vincha smiled and waved at us. I smiled back, blushing slightly when I realised too late that she was actually waving at Bayne. I knew for a fact that Vincha had tried to convince Rafik to let Bayne stay behind, but that did not succeed for all the logical reasons. I also knew that behind her smiles, she was terrified. I felt the same way.

We all waited, looking out at Vincha, until the elevator's transparent doors solidified in front of our eyes. We were left on our own. Just as the elevator began to descend Galinak farted loudly with a great sigh of relief, and for some reason we all just laughed. He stood by my side, towering over me. His newly grown hair was purple and now in a Mohawk. It suited him. I smiled at him, and he patted my shoulder.

"Since we're going into battle together, Twinkle Eyes, I want to tell you something important," he whispered.

"Yes?"

"You still owe me metal for the escort."

Before I could think of a witty retort, Vincha's voice rang in my ears. She was checking the crew's main channel and individual, private channels. Many of us were still unused to not needing to speak our thoughts out loud, and I could hear most of us respond verbally to her testing.

"*How are you feeling, Vincha?*" I thought when it was my turn, succeeding in holding my tongue.

"*Twinkle Eyes,*" her voice was artificially upbeat, "*try not to think of naughty stuff. It scrambles my channels.*"

This time I chuckled out loud.

I had one last view of the gardens before the elevator went underground. The lights in the cabin changed to accommodate our sight, and the transparent wall became opaque. I caught my reflected image. I was one of the youngest in the crew, so there was not much rejuvenation needed, but I still looked like a different person. Just because I could, I changed my eye colour several times and smiled as I did so. I kept them at yellow green, which was definitely my colour.

The small communication disc attached to my right temple was already starting to blend in with my skin colour, as I was told it would. I couldn't help but try to change facial expressions and watch the metal flex. The only other external Tarakan device was a button-sized piece of metal behind my right earlobe that enhanced my hearing. It was slowly melding with my body as well.

The mood in the elevator turned to sombre silence. The Trolls were checking their weapons, armour, and gear, and moving augmented limbs at strange angles, as if to retest their capabilities.

We all felt the elevator change directions and moving sideways as well as down. I felt my heart lurch in my chest and my stomach turn.

Galinak winked at me. "Don't worry, Twinkles, I got your back."

I nodded and swallowed hard as we began ascending again.

"Here we go," Jakov said, and it caused a flurry of movement inside the cabin as weapons and gear were checked again. We knew we were still inside the safe part of the City within the Mountain, but somehow it didn't make a difference.

The wide corridor was already lit when the cabin doors disappeared. A short distance from us, we saw enormous gates. We all stepped out and as soon as the last of us left the cabin, the elevator doors reappeared. I looked back just as the cabin sped away, leaving a large gap. I took a few steps back and looked down but saw only darkness, and with no time or reason to investigate further, I turned back and followed the others.

Several dozen massive cannons were pointing at the gates as

well as more power machine guns than I could count. Despite Rafik's reassurance that our entrance into Cain territory would be without incident, I wondered how I would react if a horde of Lizards would be waiting for us on the other side of the gates. I couldn't help but struggle with the question how we, a crew of humans, could possibly succeed against an enemy that prompted such a defence.

When we reached the gates, I used my sight to point River to the hidden manual control panel. He quickly went to work. Rafik had said we would have a slightly better chance of avoiding detection if Adam didn't open the gates for us. I tried not to dwell on the word *slight*, and I hoped that whatever Rafik, or Adam, was doing would help camouflage our crew for as long as possible. My hands touched the hilts of the pair of handguns on my belt. They were by far the least powerful weapons we had with us, and if we encountered metal bots I would have to rely on the crew's firepower for protection. But the guns compensated for their poor firepower with manoeuvrability and an aiming device that was connected to my retina. I could shoot an apple off a tree half a mile away with one gun while firing on a drone with the other. I knew this because I had tried.

Galinak hefted the heavy power hammer on his shoulder and grinned at me.

"Ready, Twinkle Eyes? Stay close, but not too close, eh?" He shrugged the shoulder that balanced his enormous power hammer and winked at me.

I did not have time to reply, since at that moment the gates slid open silently. There was no waiting horde behind it, only darkness.

On Bayne's signal, we formed pairs, one Troll holding a long-range weapon and the other a short-range, and fanned out in a diamond shape. Without a word, we moved in unison and stepped into the darkness.

When the last of us moved past the threshold, the gates silently closed behind us.

70

We found ourselves in complete darkness. Several heart-beats later, our new retina implants did what they were supposed to do. It still did not feel like daylight, more like a gloomy afternoon on a rainy day with the colours almost completely faded out, but I got used to it surprisingly quickly. Bayne was the first to move, and we all followed.

At the beginning of our training it was a little difficult to decide who the crew commander should be. The majority of the force was composed of Jakov's mercenaries, but he was a merchant, not a Combat Troll, so he wisely nominated Bayne to act as tactical commander. If Galinak's feelings were hurt by Jakov's decision he didn't show it, and Bayne, to my personal relief, positioned Galinak at my side.

Some part of me imagined the sections of the city controlled by Cain to be changed in a way that reflected the corruption. I expected it to be in ruins, or dirty, or ugly. I did not expect it to be perfect. It was motionless, colourless, and dead, but basically, the same awe-inspiring, breathtaking city, with wide streets and buildings in every shape imaginable. If the hordes of Lizards had managed to damage it somehow, it did not show, and as in the parts of the city controlled by Adam, it felt as if we were walking under the open sky, even though I knew we were inside a mountain range.

For obvious reasons, we avoided channelling to each other, or even talking, and so it turned out that we walked in almost complete silence for a long while—so long in fact, that some of my nervousness waned. When four Lizards came behind a strange string of intertwined stone cubes, I was embarrassingly slow to react. Actually, I did not even get to fire a shot before the crew dispatched the creatures. Seeing no colour made it a little easier to stomach the sight of the Lizards' splattered remains all over the architecture, but it still felt like sacrilege, as if we'd just profaned a holy temple.

Despite the relative ease of the first battle, this was an ominous sign, and we all knew it. Bayne ordered us to up our pace.

Rafik had explained that the corrupt mind could not give complicated orders to its creations. They were sensitive to certain radio waves, but Cain usually just directed the Lizards to the Valley through underground tunnels, to roam and kill whatever they found. Inside the City within the Mountain, Adam was able to interfere enough with Cain's signalling system to make it unreliable. Cain had to resort to controlling the Lizards' movement within the city by releasing special chemicals through the air system as well as by drones. It was a crude method at best. When Cain detected an intrusion, all it could do was flood the area with a large number of Lizards in the hope that they would find and destroy the intruders. Once we were discovered, it was only a matter of time before the entire population of the Lizards in the city would be directed toward us.

Shortly after the first battle, a large number of Lizards converged on us from three directions. These Lizards fared a little better than their brethren from our first encounter and got closer to us. As practiced, we each turned to face a designated angle. I was standing in a relatively safe area, within the parameter designated to me, and somehow managed to steel my trembling hands and shoot four from afar; two died from head wounds and the other two slowed enough to be killed by others. Yet despite my good aim, three Lizards got close. Galinak dealt with them with his power hammer and a sharp kick to the snout of the third one. When it was over, the terror I felt turned into almost childish elation at my newly acquired proficiency. I actually laughed out loud, waving my gun in the air, and earned several stern looks from the veteran crew members. We had no casualties so far, but it became obvious there was no more time to dwell on architecture or existential questions. We ran for it.

By the next battle we were fighting for our lives and any feelings of elation were long gone. I had to replace the power clips, and my hands shook so much one of them fell to the ground. Foolishly, instead of shooting with my other gun I went looking for the dropped clip and almost got decapitated by Galinak's swinging power hammer.

"Whoa, Twinkle Eyes, you are out of position," he shouted at me, sweat pouring down his bloodied face.

I turned around to return to my position just as a Lizard charged at me. It moved at an astonishing speed and I saw its gaping maw as it was about to close on my neck, when Galinak kicked my legs out from under me and smashed the Lizard with an uppercut. I shielded my face as the Lizard's head exploded and what was left of its body flew backwards.

Galinak bent down, grasped me by the shoulder, and hauled me to my feet in one motion.

"Get back to your post, Twinkle Eyes," he ordered and turned his back to me. The battle was as short as it was intense, and when it was over, I received another admonition from Bayne for moving away from my position.

"Bayne," Vincha's voice cut in through the Comm, "better get out of there. Cain is moving all its forces to your position."

That was all we needed to hear.

I managed to redeem myself in the next battle, spotting

the drones first and shooting down three of them before they spewed their chemicals. River threw two grenades that dropped two more, but the last remaining drone managed to manoeuvre just outside the blast zone. Jakov was the one to drop it, but not before it turned and fired a missile straight at our crew.

"Missile," I heard several of the Trolls shout a warning over the Comm. As practiced in the simulations, I dove down to the ground while tapping the button on my belt to maximize the power armour protection. Immediately the sound of the battle dissipated to complete silence. The blast was somewhere behind me, but it was bright enough to momentarily blind me. Even with power armour in full capacity, I felt the unbearable heat of the blast flashing over me. I was on my feet a heartbeat later, moving with several other Trolls to close the gap in our position that the blast had made. Only when the battle was over did I realise that the missile had hit a Troll named Enja and vaporised her.

"Vincha," Bayne said over the Comm, "we just lost Enja, and it is getting too dangerous to take positions. We need an alternative route to the lab and to keep on the move."

Rafik's voice answered. "Not advisable, Bayne, this is the safest route to your destination."

"Does not feel safe from where we are standing."

"You are not far. Do not change course," Rafik answered resolutely.

I looked at the bloody mayhem around me and felt panic clench my gut.

"Easy, Twinkle Eyes." Galinak put a reassuring arm on my shoulder. "You're doing fine."

River laid down a few decoys to draw the Lizards, and from there on it was all a blur. We were just constantly moving, hiding and shooting until we reached the laboratory.

The doors were locked, as anticipated. River went to work and Bayne directed us to set defensive positions.

There were two corridors leading to the labs, and Bayne chose to set mines in one corridor but keep the other free so we could make our escape back without delay. By the time the crew had laid the mines, River managed to override the locks. The doors slid open and we were inside.

I knew from the simulations what the Angel laboratory would look like, but the real thing took my breath away. The round hall was incredibly high and wide; its walls were divided into row after row of tear-shaped blocks, and each block was filled with a milky liquid. I zoomed my sight to the top rows, where the essences of the Angels were held. As the rows descended I could see the shapes growing within each tear, slowly becoming human in form, but midway down, the liquid became murky. With each descending row the liquid gradually changed colour from white to green and the human bodies deformed: claws instead of hands, a snout instead of a nose, fangs, and tough, scaly skin. The tear-shaped blocks in the lowest rows held fully grown Lizards. As we entered the lab three of them were just taking their first steps—which became their last. They died quickly, their green blood mixing with the same coloured liquid that drained into, or was somehow absorbed by, the laboratory's floor.

At the center of the hall was a dome made mostly of transparent material. It had a door and a puzzle lock that we had no chance of solving. As planned, River, Galinak, and I proceeded straight into the only corridor that led farther into the Angel lab. I heard Bayne on the Comm ordering the destruction of the entire first and second rows while the others set up positions. Almost immediately the Comm was filled with short bursts of discharged weaponry. The three of us moved away from the main hall and into the corridor. We passed a few more puzzle locks but they were not our goal. When we reached the middle of the corridor we stopped, and River turned to me as he unpacked his gear.

"Find out where to do this," he said, not bothering to even look at me.

In the meantime Galinak was making sure we were alone.

"This is a bad place to stop," he said to himself, but we could hear him through the Comm. "Two ways, no cover, no visibility."

I tried to ignore him and concentrate on my task. My gaze penetrated the walls—a multitude of cables, metal tubes, and lightning rods filled my vision.

The Comm was suddenly filled with Vincha's voice. "They're coming," she warned. "Oh rust . . . they're all fucking coming."

Bayne shouted more orders, and I found myself raising my head. River grabbed me by the neck, "Quit stalling, find the damn place."

I blinked and the walls became solid again. Several explosions told us that the Lizards were charging through the mined corridor. "Make sure the door braces are locked," I heard Bayne say. "That will buy us some time."

"Rust, get ready!"

"Find the damn place!" River yelled at me again.

I did not need the Comm to hear the screeching of the Lizards trying to get through the locked laboratory doors. Unfortunately, a few heartbeats later several missiles blew it open.

I heard the screaming of the charging Lizards. Bayne had set the crew in a wide semicircle around the opening of the laboratory to create a killing zone. When I turned my head I saw the backs of Bayne and the others through the walls as they shot charging Lizards. Galinak grabbed me and shook me awake. "Twinkle Eyes," he shouted, "time to work."

I turned my head back to the corridor and scrutinized the walls and the floors all around me. It was easier to do in the simulation; here, I was distracted by the deadly fight that was raging only a short distance away.

"Rouch is down!" someone shouted and swore. There were shots and more shots and an explosion that rocked everything. "Drones! Watch from above, he's waking all of them up!" Bayne shouted. This had never happened in the simulations. I felt my knees begin to shake and fought for air.

For a heartbeat, everything slowed. River and Galinak were shouting at me, pointing at the wall while people died in my ear Comm. I don't know what made me finally turn my head to the wall and concentrate, but it became transparent in front of my eyes and finally I saw the rods, tubes, and cables forming a small, barely man-sized tunnel. "There," I pointed at waist level.

"Are you sure?"

I nodded.

"You need to show me where the self-repair power points are in the wall."

It took me several more precious seconds before I pointed again, "Here, here, and . . . here."

"Okay," River was already holding the Tarakan steel cutter. He handed the star-shaped discs to me and Galinak.

"Can you reach both points?"

I calculated. "Yes, if I spread my hands."

"Good, place a star on each node. The wall will try to repel the discs, but hold tight and don't let go, or the wall will begin to self-repair and it will take too long to cut. Now, turn your power armour on and face away."

I turned up the power armour and hugged the wall, placing a disc above each repair power point. As before, once the power armour was at full capacity, the sounds of battle faded into blessed nothingness. I tried not to imagine the Lizards breaking through the line, running through the corridor and jumping on my back. My armour could withstand damage for a while, but soon they would get through it, and I would . . . I began to shake and almost dropped the discs.

A hand grabbed me away from the wall. I turned and saw River and Galinak talking to me, but I was too disoriented to understand what was going on. When they turned the dial on my belt the world came back to life. Over the Comm I heard Galinak and River being ordered to come help the crew, which was not the plan. It meant something had gone horribly wrong. I heard Vincha calling Bayne's name, the tone of her voice growing with fear and pain. I heard the weapons discharge and the high-pitched screams of dying Lizards.

River turned me around, beads of sweat running down his face. How long did it take? I couldn't tell. He pointed at the small hole he'd created. It looked too small.

"I can't get in," I said.

He pushed me down and through the hole, head first. The metal was already starting to regenerate as I lay between the cables and tubes. They were supposed to wait for me to finish and then help me get out, but instead, River tossed me the cutter and the star-shaped discs through the diminishing hole.

"Good luck," he said.

Behind him, Galinak waved and grinned as he readied his power hammer. "Get it right, Twinkle Eyes, and I'll come get you soon enough." And they were off, running back towards the battle.

I turned my head and looked. The hole was already half its original size. Soon I would be alone inside a Tarakan steel wall. That thought alone drove me to action, and I began to crawl forward, towards the dome in the laboratory.

The battle was raging on the other side of the wall and in my ear Comm. In the background of it all, I heard Vincha sobbing which could only mean Bayne was down. The memory of lost simulation battles gripped my heart. Fighting rising panic, I began crawling as fast as I could, losing my sense of time, then I found the opening to the tunnels underneath the floors and kept on crawling as men and Lizards fought and died above me. When I reached the floor underneath the dome, I stopped and checked for the self-repair power points. Rafik promised there would not be more than one, but if it was too far away I would not be able to hold the disc and manoeuvre the cutter at the same time. Luckily I found that if I pushed with my leg . . . *there*, I could cut right *over here*.

I turned my head, dampened my sight sensitivity, made sure my power armour was fully on, blessfully cutting myself off from the sound of slaughter, and began cutting through the dome's floor just above my head. I did not imagine my arms and shoulders could ache so much. I stopped three times only to realise I had no choice, no way back, no way out. I just kept cutting and tried to ignore the pain.

I do not remember getting into the dome, but I do remember the power turning on and an entire array of alien devices coming to life. Transparent screens and other items I did not recognise appeared out of thin air and rose to chest level, but I didn't pay attention to any of it. I looked through the glass walls of the dome and into the mayhem that was happening only several feet away. My heart sank in my chest as I stood watching, realizing there was simply no way I was getting out of this place alive. Of the entire crew, only several Trolls were still standing. Galinak was one of them, his power hammer creating a killing zone around him, but I couldn't see River, or even Jakov. They were fighting tens, no, hundreds of Lizards, and more kept pouring through the laboratory's doors. It would take little time for the rest to be overwhelmed. Several dozen Lizards were already charging at the dome, smashing themselves against it repeatedly.

Rafik was shouting my name over the Comm, saying something about Cain reducing the dome's substructure to make it breakable, but I wasn't listening.

I turned off my Comm and lowered my head. I even shut my eyes, not daring to see or hear what was happening outside the dome. How long did I stand like this? I do not know, but when I raised my head again, Lizards were climbing all over the dome, biting and banging their limbs against the transparent wall. I couldn't see the crew anymore, but one of the Lizards was smashing Jakov's metal arms against the dome. There were already hundreds of little cracks in the glass. Soon the Lizards would succeed in breaking in.

Without taking my eyes from the Lizards I switched on the Comm again. "Vincha," I said, then repeated her name until I heard her reply.

"Yes." Her voice was trembling, but at least she'd regained control.

"I'm in. I need instructions."

"I'm patching you to Rafik."

I heard Rafik's voice. "Look at the panel to the left of the glowing half-moon, you need to—"

"Vincha," I said, ignoring Rafik.

"Yes?"

"I need you to block all other channels, I can't . . . I can't hear this . . ."

And it was suddenly all quiet. The death that was happening outside was like a storm happening somewhere else.

"Vincha, I need music. Something to help me focus, that Beethoven, play it for me."

"Now is not the time, you must . . ."

"Rust, do it, Vincha." I slammed my hand down hard on the transparent desk in front of me.

A heartbeat later the most wonderful music filled my head. In front of my eyes Lizards beat their powerful limbs against the transparent walls that were protecting me, but I paid them no more attention. I slowly sat down on a seat that was hovering behind me and momentarily shut my eyes, listening to timeless music composed almost five hundred years before. It was a bittersweet moment.

Rafik broke the spell. "We must proceed. I need you to begin transferring the codes for the laboratory, *now*."

It wasn't complicated. That was the easiest part in all the training. I had to perform several simple actions to gain manual control over the machines. Then I executed everything the way I had rehearsed it in the simulations. The results were what I expected, and that calmed me even more. By the end of it my hands were not trembling anymore.

There was one more thing left to do, just one more button to touch . . . I looked up again. The Lizards were still around me. Would it hurt when they ripped me to shreds? Or would it be an instantaneous death? I smiled. Was Rafik watching me? Could Adam see all of this? My guess was that they could.

"Vincha, are there any survivors?" I asked. The music faded.

She stalled. "Galinak, River, Massau, and Terra barricaded themselves in one of the lab rooms. Terra is wounded but still functioning, but the corridor is swamped with Lizards. The power barricade that River erected is holding, but he lost his cutter so they are stuck there. You could try to crawl your way back to them and—"

"There's no time for that!" Rafik interjected, his voice strained. "You need to complete the mission, then we can rescue you and your friends. Nothing is more important than this. You must disable the security with the codes you have and upload our program directly into the lab's mainframe so we can take control of it. Otherwise the corrupted mind will keep producing Lizards."

I leaned back, entwining my fingers behind my neck, watching the Lizards above me. The last notes of the music still rang in my mind, I even hummed the theme to myself. I might not be a warrior, a Combat Troll, or a fearless Salvationist, but I was very good at one thing.

"No, Rafik, I think now is exactly the right time," I said calmly, as Lizards raged around and above me and the sweet music sang in my ears. "Now we negotiate."

71

Death will not be swift or painless. I know this for a fact. It will be agony, because it's going to happen under less than ideal circumstances.

Unfortunately, there is plenty of room for error. I may not remember all that occured or may not be myself when I wake up inside Adam. This is why I took the time to tell my story. Because others need to know. Because history is happening. And I would be a very bad Associate LoreMaster of the Guild of Historians if I let this kind of event be lost to humanity. As I told this story, Galinak, River, and Massau were uploaded through Vincha's Comm system to the collective mind. I'm assuming the power barricade is down now and their bodies are in pieces. Rafik assured me the transfer was successful but that it would take time to reconstruct them inside Adam. We lost Terra on the way, as well as Bayne, Jakov, and the others. This is another reason why I took the time to tell this story: too many people died to make this happen, and I feel this needs to be acknowledged.

I have no idea whether the Tarkanians will keep their end of the bargain once I complete the final transmission, but I have always been an optimist at heart, or a fool—you be the judge. Besides, they seem to want to get on Vincha's good side and convice her to bring her daughter to join Adam, so I may gain immortality even if I have no recollection of what the hell I did to deserve it.

I am no hero. If I'd known this would be the outcome I'd never have set foot in this place in a million years. But if my opinion holds any sway, I think humanity deserves saving, even if from itself.

I am feeling faint, and I am stalling. Yes, I know, it's the air . . .

It's funny . . . I am still not sure about Nakamura and his predictions.

Goodbye Vincha, and good luck. Let me just say that it's an honour to have known you, I look forward to transferring myself through your body . . .

Yeah . . . I know it's not funny . . .

Rust. Let's do this.

ACKNOWLEDGEMENTS

So, you get inspired, write a novel, send it out, get published and live happily ever after? Yeah, right . . .

Sometimes it only takes one person who believes in you to make a difference. After a fair share of gut wrenching rejections, it was Rena Rossner of the Deborah Harris Agency, who contacted me with incredible enthusiasm for the manuscript. Without Rena's help, support, editing super powers and *a lot* of patience, *The Lost Puzzler* would not have been published, simple as that. To think she had done all that while dealing with all of her other demanding authors, raising five kids, and publishing her own cookbook and a fantasy novel. My only explanation for this phenomenon is that Rena must be able to bend time . . .

David Pomerico and Jack Renninson of Harper Voyager US and UK, respectively, and their incredible team, Priyanka Krishnan, Caro Perny, Pam Jaffee, Angela Craft, Lex Maudlin and Dominic Forbes, took the manuscript of *The Lost Puzzler* to the next level. Working with them was a masterclass in writing, and I am sure (and hope) there are more lessons to come.

The people mentioned above are professional through and through. Finding authors and novels and making them better is their bread and butter, but there are those who had to suffer through the raw material years before I even dreamed about publishing *The Lost Puzzler*. They bravely crossed the literary thorn fields, bled from razor sharp corners of extreme plot twists, hacked their way through the forest of the never-ending descriptions, sustained the bombardment of the repeated phrases and . . . okay, you get it, these people deserve credit!

Special thanks to Nick Brunt, whose comments and insights enriched this novel and *The Puzzler's War*.

Without Dina Roth and her enthusiasm for my writing, *The Lost Puzzler* would still be, well . . . lost in a file somewhere on my computer. It was her insistence that made me dig it out and send it to her chapter by chapter while re-editing each one and *finally* finishing it.

Special thanks to Ziv and Carmit Hershman, for their support, suggestions, free alcohol and the friendship I cherish. Thank you, Amit Zohar, for your accurate criticism and helpful suggestions and Nisim Cohen, for believing in me so much.